STORM

D.J. MACHALE

razOr
bill

An Imprint of Penguin Group (USA)

razOr
bill

A division of Penguin Young Readers Group
Published by the Penguin Group
Penguin Group (USA) LLC
345 Hudson Street
New York, New York 10014

USA / Canada / UK / Ireland / Australia / New Zealand / India / South Africa / China
Penguin.com
A Penguin Random House Company

ISBN: 978-1-59514-667-0

Printed in the United States of America

1 3 5 7 9 10 8 6 4 2

For Mark Mitchell. My great friend for six decades.
"I hope you're reading this, Mark."

FOREWORD

I'm flying along at 39,000 feet (give or take) on the initial leg of the SYLO tour . . . the first book in The SYLO Chronicles. Touring with a book is one of the great joys of being an author. Okay, that's not entirely true. The actual traveling part isn't the greatest. There are seemingly endless flights, too much fast food, and not enough opportunity to do laundry. Very glamorous.

But those are minor inconveniences compared to the payoff. When I'm on tour, I get to meet hundreds of enthusiastic readers. There is truly nothing better for an author than having someone come up to them and say, "I loved your book." For that, I'll take off my shoes at airport x-rays and sit cramped in an airline seat for hours with nothing to eat but a tiny bag of peanuts. It's totally worth it.

Writing for young people holds its own special benefit for I am speaking to an audience that is constantly regenerating. Many readers who are now enjoying Tucker Pierce's adventure on Pemberwick Island never heard of Bobby Pendragon. On the other hand, I also meet adult readers who grew up with the Travelers. I actually met one young woman who has a "Hobey ho, let's go" tattoo! I don't recommend doing that, but I thought it was pretty awesome.

I say this to try to explain how much I love creating stories and sharing them with you. I am so fortunate that my job is to tell tales. On the career caché scale, that probably puts me somewhere below people with "real" jobs and just above clowns. (Then again, for those who have read Pendragon or watched AYAOTD?, you know how I feel about clowns, so maybe that's an unfair, biased statement. Sorry, clowns.) Thank you so much for reading my books and for allowing me to have a job that I can do in my sweats. I hope I get to meet you in person someday.

Speaking of thanks, in spite of the fact that it's my name on the book, there are many people who have helped, directly and indirectly, in getting this book to you.

The principle editor of Storm was Laura Arnold. I say "principle" because Laura has moved on to new adventures. Her talent shows in every page of this book, and for that I will always be grateful.

The new SYLO editor is Caroline Donofrio, who has taken up the reins and embraced the story. Though I had to warn her: I am now 4 for 5 with my editors (and their husbands) getting pregnant with their first child. (See the aforementioned "adventure" Laura is now on.) Caroline assures me that I will not be 5 for 6. At least not yet. I'm sure she believes that, but history says otherwise. Just sayin'. Thanks Caroline. Good luck.

I am so very grateful to all my friends at Razorbill for their support of The SYLO Chronicles. Many readers want to know why a book can't come out as soon as I finish the first draft. Well, it's not that easy. There's a process and a very long list of people who have an impact on every book that is published. Dozens of dedicated people work in marketing, sales, editing, design, production, shipping, and many other departments who work their magic to help create the book you now hold. Thanks to you all.

Of course, the booksellers who are avid supporters of reading deserve a very big thanks as well.

I am also very grateful to my personal team of Richard Curtis, Peter Nelson, and Mark Wetzstein.

Finally, my two blondes, Evangeline and Keaton, deserve thanks for being my constant source of support, love, and criticism. All are extremely valuable. Even the criticism. Usually. I love you both. I am very proud to say that my daughter, who wasn't even born when my first Pendragon book was published, has now read her first "big" book . . . and it was SYLO. Better yet, she loved it. She was also the first kid to read Storm. How cool is that? Next thing you know, she'll be giving me story notes.

That's it. Acknowledgments complete. Time to get down to the real business that has brought us back together.

When we left Tucker, Tori, Kent, and Olivia they had just escaped from Pemberwick Island and found that Portland was deserted. A few buildings were missing too. Oh yeah, and they discovered the wreckage of one of the black marauding planes that had been battling the U.S. Navy. On its wing was the logo of the U.S. Air Force. Uh . . . what?

When books end on a cliffhanger, the expectation is for the dilemma to be quickly resolved in the beginning of the next chapter. Or the next book.

Don't count on that, boys and girls.

We're just getting started.
There's a very big storm brewing.
Hobey ho, let's go.

D.J. MacHale

ONE

igh noon.

The sun floated directly above us on a warm, clear, mid-September day. The street was bathed in an intense white light that cast no shadows . . . until the world suddenly went dark. The warm, comforting rays of the sun had been blocked by what appeared to be an unscheduled lunar eclipse.

The music that came from the looming shadow told me otherwise. The dark shape had appeared from over the tops of the brick buildings of the Old Port and hovered above us like a rogue storm cloud preparing to unleash its fury.

"They found us," Kent said with a gasp.

High noon.

Showdown time.

"Back in the car!" I commanded.

The four of us scrambled to get to the Subaru we had "borrowed" after making our escape from Pemberwick Island.

Tori Sleeper was hurt. She had been shot through the shoulder and needed to lean on Kent Berringer and me in order to keep moving.

Slowing down to help her saved our lives.

The black attack plane fired, sending an invisible pulse of energy at the car that rocked it onto its side and ignited the gas tank. The wave of heat from the violent explosion knocked us back, shaken but alive.

"This way!" Olivia Kinsey shouted while running toward a row of low brick buildings.

We had been standing in the center of Commercial Street, which ran past the busy piers of Portland, Maine. The *normally* busy piers.

We hadn't seen a single living soul from the moment we hit town. Stranger still, many of the buildings in Portland had vanished. They weren't destroyed or bombed, they were just . . . gone. We knew this was the result of the attack we had seen several nights before when an enormous fleet of these flying black predators put on a light show over the city. Tori and I had witnessed the attack from her father's fishing boat as we were making our first attempt to escape from Pemberwick Island. It wasn't the only horror we saw that night. We also got a close-up view of the lethal power of these planes when three of them fired a laser-like weapon at a fishing boat that was making the escape with us. The light enveloped the defenseless craft. Seconds later it was gone . . .

. . . along with Quinn Carr.

The black planes had killed my best friend.

They had devastated Portland.

Now one of them was coming for us.

The hovering plane fired another shot that tore up the ground behind us as we sprinted for the safety of a building. It was close.

I felt a sharp sting across my back as I was hit by a wave of pulverized street.

"The alley!" Kent shouted.

With one arm around Tori's waist, I changed direction and ran toward a narrow alleyway between the old buildings.

"You okay?" I asked her breathlessly.

She nodded, but I didn't believe her. Tori had lost a lot of blood. She needed to be lying down in a hospital, not running for her life.

As we ducked into the alley, I glanced up to see if the plane was following. I expected to see it loom into view above the buildings. Searching. Hunting. These beasts could fly with the speed of a jet fighter, hover like a helicopter, and cause unfathomable damage. What seemed impossible was all too real.

Several seconds passed. No plane appeared, nor did the signature musical sound of its engines. Had it given up that easily?

The streets of the Old Port were narrow and paved with rounded stones, giving the area the feel of an old-time fishing town, which is exactly what it used to be. Now it was a tourist destination where the vintage brick buildings held restaurants, bars, and souvenir stores.

Olivia ran for one of the shops. She yanked the door open and held it so I could get Tori inside. Kent followed quickly and slammed the door shut . . . as if a closed door would keep out the boogeyman.

We found ourselves in a store packed with Maine souvenirs. Every last inch of counter and wall space was taken up with displays of model lighthouses, saltwater taffy, kitchen-magnet lobsters, scrimshaw snow globes, and anything else that would remind visitors of their trip to the Pine Tree State.

Kent hurried to the large front window and peered out with caution.

"Why are they after us?" Olivia asked anxiously. "Because we escaped from Pemberwick Island?"

I helped Tori into a chair behind the sales counter. Though she appeared slight, she was a strong girl who had spent most of her life working lobster boats with her father. But at that moment she was as weak as an old lady.

She looked at me with glazed eyes and muttered, "I need some water."

I searched the shop, hoping they stocked bottled water as well as flip-flops.

"Tucker!" Olivia cried impatiently. "I asked you a question. Why are they after us?"

"How should I know?" I replied, annoyed.

"Because you have all the answers," Kent commented with his usual dose of sarcasm.

Everyone looked at me, hoping for words of wisdom. I hated being the one who was always expected to come up with solutions.

Moments before being attacked, we had learned a frightening truth while examining the wreck of one of the black planes. The craft looked like a giant stingray, with no aerodynamic capabilities whatsoever. I thought it might have come from an alien world . . . until I saw the logo on its skin.

It was the symbol of the United States Air Force.

That morning the four of us had escaped by speedboat from

our home on Pemberwick Island and found ourselves in the middle of a sea-air battle between killer planes from the U.S. Air Force . . . and warships of the United States Navy.

"What can I say?" I answered tentatively. "It looks like the Navy and the Air Force are at war with one another."

"We were running away from SYLO," Kent said. "And SYLO is part of the Navy, so that means the Air Force are the good guys."

"How can the Air Force be good guys?" I shot back. "They just wiped out Portland."

"Yeah, and SYLO turned Pemberwick into a prison," he countered. "Oh, and they also killed Tori's father. Did you forget that?"

I didn't. I couldn't bring myself to look at Tori for a reaction.

"Maybe there *are* no good guys," Olivia said gravely.

We let that sobering thought hang in the air for a few seconds.

Tori then added in a weak voice, "Or maybe we're in the middle of the second Civil War. One side's got the Air Force, the other has the Navy and SYLO."

None of us commented. The possibility was mind-numbing.

"What are we going to do?" Olivia whined.

"Stick to the plan," I replied. "First we get to a hospital and patch Tori up. Then we head to Boston and tell the world what's been happening on Pemberwick Island. After that I don't know what—"

"Git out!" came a threatening voice from deeper in the store.

We all spun to see an elderly man standing in the doorway leading to the back room. He was a typical Mainer with a plaid flannel shirt and jeans. There was nothing unusual about him . . . except for the shotgun he had leveled at us.

"Whoa, take it easy, gramps," Kent warned.

"Don't *gramps* me," the old guy snarled. "Git outta my store."

"We will," I said, trying to defuse the situation. "But one of those planes was shooting at us and—"

"That's why I want you out," he snapped. "I've been ducking them things for days. I don't need you kids bringing 'em down on me."

"Wait," I exclaimed. "You're alive."

"Keen observation, Rook," Kent said sarcastically.

"I mean, you survived the attack," I said to the man, ignoring Kent. "What happened that night?"

"You don't know?" he asked suspiciously. "Where you from?"

"Pemberwick Island," I replied. "We saw the—"

"Pemberwick!" the guy exclaimed as if I'd said we just dropped in from Alcatraz. He held the shotgun higher but took a frightened step back and added, "You got the disease!"

"There is no disease," Tori said weakly. "The quarantine was just an excuse they used to keep us there."

"Who?" the old guy asked.

"SYLO," I answered. "You must have seen it on the news. They're part of the Navy. They took over the island and were gunning down people who tried to escape so the truth wouldn't get out."

"Truth about what?" he demanded.

"There was no virus," Tori said weakly. "We were prisoners."

"We think they were experimenting on us with this stuff called the Ruby," Kent added. "It was killing people, so we left. That pretty much sums it up."

"What about your parents?" the guy said with suspicion.

The answer would only have confused him more. Tori's father and Kent's father were dead, and my parents were part of SYLO. How could I explain that to him? I couldn't even explain it to myself.

"Look," I said, ducking the question. "Tori's hurt. Can I give her some water?"

The man's gaze jumped between us as he debated what to do. He finally looked to Tori, who sat slumped in the chair behind the counter.

"Over there," he said, jabbing the shotgun toward another counter.

There was a case of bottled waters on the floor. I grabbed one, cracked it open, and brought it to Tori.

"Thank you," she said and took a few small sips.

"Now, on your way," the guy commanded, hardening once again.

"We have to get to Maine Medical," I said. "If her wound gets infected—"

"Then go!" he barked.

"We'll never make it on foot. We're going to need a car or—"

"Look!" Olivia screamed.

The black plane was outside the window, at ground level, moving slowly along the street like a giant black shark searching for its next victim.

Nobody moved.

The lethal shadow floated by, the sound of its musical engine growing louder as it moved closer, providing eerie accompaniment while searching the streets for us. Was there a pilot? Or was it an unmanned drone being controlled from a command room miles away?

Seconds passed. The music receded. The plane moved on.

"Now go," the old man said through clenched teeth. "I didn't live through an attack on my town just to be given away by a couple of fugitives from a leper colony."

"Put the gun down," I barked. "We're not going anywhere."

The old man wasn't sure of how to react to my bold order.

"You can't shoot, or that plane will come right back here," I said boldly. "And I doubt you're a killer anyway. What's your name?"

The man blinked a few times, as if he was having trouble processing what was happening.

"Whittle," he answered tentatively.

"All right, Mr. Whittle, we'll be on our way. I promise. But first we need a car." I looked to Kent and said, "Go get one."

Kent stiffened. "*You* go get one!"

"I'm not a good driver. You've got a better chance."

Kent looked around, as if searching for an argument. He was a few years older than me, and I didn't even have my driver's license. He knew I was right.

"I'll go with you," Olivia offered. "This guy makes me nervous."

Whittle slowly lowered the shotgun, as if embarrassed.

"I'm just trying to protect myself is all," he said apologetically.

Kent stuck a finger in my face. "You are not in charge."

I shrugged. "I don't care who's in charge as long as we're smart about what we do. Right now the smart move is for you to get a car."

Kent's eyes flared. For a second I thought he might take a swing at me, but Olivia put a hand on his arm and gently pulled him away.

"C'mon," she said softly. "The sooner we get a car, the sooner we'll be out of this horrible city."

Olivia kept surprising me. I don't think many people told her no . . . especially guys. She was a spoiled rich girl with cute short blond hair who was used to getting her way. It didn't hurt that she was gorgeous. She was no dummy either. She always seemed to know the exact right thing to say to calm people down, and she was quick to help when it was needed. I guess you'd call her an enigma. Maybe that was why I liked her. That and the gorgeous part.

"We'll be back as soon as we can," she said to me, then looked to Whittle and added sweetly, "Don't go shooting anybody while we're gone now, 'kay?"

"Sure enough," Whittle replied meekly.

Olivia had worked her magic on him too.

"Be careful," Tori called out.

"Gee, you think?" Kent shot back. He looked out of the window to scan the street, then cautiously opened the door and peered outside.

"It's clear," he announced and stepped out.

Olivia gave me a small smile and followed him.

There was an awkward moment when nobody knew what to say.

"We're sorry to give you grief," I said to Whittle, hoping to get him to lighten up.

"Grief?" he said with an ironic chuckle. "You kids can't bring on any more grief than we've already got."

"Tell us what happened that night," Tori said gently.

Whittle softened.

"They came out of nowhere," he began. "No warning. No explanation. No chance to run for cover."

"Three nights ago, right?" I asked.

Whittle nodded. He spoke as if in a daze, relating a story that must have been too stunning to believe.

"It was prime time in the Old Port. Early evening. Restaurants were full, saloons were buzzing, people were out strolling, enjoying the warm night. Then the sound came. Like music. Folks stopped and stared up at the sky, pointing. It looked like a wave of bats flying in from the west. They were all perfectly spaced up there, like a pattern. It seemed like a show in the sky. But it was no show. It was a . . . a storm."

Whittle's eyes started to water. It was a painful memory.

"We were out on the ocean," Tori offered. "We saw the sky light up over the city."

"It lit up all right," Whittle said, his voice cracking. "So many people. Families. Little ones. One minute they were out enjoying the evening, and then . . . they weren't."

He looked to the ground, suddenly seeming very tired. He lifted the shotgun and for a second I was afraid he was going to turn it on himself. Instead, he placed it down on a table, pushing aside a bunch of snow globes that fell to the floor and shattered. He didn't care.

"Did they use that laser weapon?" I asked tentatively.

"Is that what it's called?" Whittle snapped. "All I saw were streaks of light coming out of the sky. The beams would join up and grow stronger, like they were coming together to build up energy. It was almost pretty, like a holiday spectacle. But there was nothing pretty about what those lights did. Whatever they hit would light up and then . . . poof. Gone. Whole buildings were there one second and gone the next. It seemed impossible, especially since it was all so silent. There were no explosions or sounds of buildings crumbling. All you could hear was the music of their engines . . . and the screams."

I knew exactly what he was describing. It was how Quinn died.

"But the buildings meant nothing compared to what happened to the people. So many of 'em were just . . . what? Disintegrated? Vaporized? Whatever you want to call it, bottom line is they're gone. Killed. Thousands of 'em."

Whittle's throat clutched. It was a tough memory to relive.

Tori said, "So sometimes buildings disappeared, and other times it was just people?"

Whittle nodded. "Being inside didn't help. It was like those evil beams could penetrate walls to grab their victims. Whole apartment buildings were left untouched, but every last person inside was wiped out. At least it was quick. They didn't suffer. Can't say the same for those who watched it happen. They knew their time was coming. Panic took hold real quick. People ran every which way, but it made no difference for most of 'em."

"How did you make it through?" I asked.

"I ducked inside here and hid down in the basement. Seems like that was the only way to protect yourself. You had to be underground. Not that I knew that beforehand. It was the only place I could think of to hide. I was just lucky, I guess. Or maybe the lucky ones are those who got gone. They don't have to live with the nightmare."

"Are there other survivors?" I asked.

"Plenty. If they were underground during the attack, they're still around. But you won't see 'em 'cause they're hiding like scared cockroaches. Those planes came back a couple of nights later for a second go at it. They're rooting out the survivors is what they're doing. Lately they've been showing up during the day. You never know when a plane might pass by. They don't use that laser-light thing during the day, though. Seems as though it only works in the dark, but what do I know? Nothing makes sense anymore. There's no TV or radio. No power. There's running water, but who knows how long that'll last? You'd think the Army would have shown up by now. I mean, we were invaded, right? Shouldn't the cavalry be riding in?"

I didn't have the heart to tell him that the cavalry was part of the problem because our own military was at war with itself.

"It's like we've been abandoned," he cried, his nerves starting to fray. "It makes me wonder if . . ." His voice trailed off.

"If what?" I pressed.

"Maybe we weren't the only ones who got attacked. What if those things hit Washington? Or New York? Or London, for that matter? If that happened then nobody's gonna care about little old Portland, Maine, because it'll mean the whole world has gone crazy."

"I hate to believe that's true," Tori said softly.

Whittle looked to her with sadness, and I could see him for what he truly was: an old man who was as scared as he had ever been in his life.

"You okay, sweetheart?" he asked warmly. "You're looking kind of fragile."

Tori shrugged. "Better than most people who get shot, I guess."

"Drink more of that water," he said with genuine concern. "You remind me of my granddaughter. She's down in Boston. I wonder if . . ."

He didn't finish the thought, but I knew what he was thinking. He was wondering if she was still alive.

"Come with us," I said. "After we hit the hospital we're going to Boston. I gotta believe we'll find answers there and—"

"Look out!" Tori shouted.

I spun to look out of the front window in time to see that the black plane had returned. I had been so focused on Whittle that I hadn't heard the musical engine. It hovered outside of the window, filling the frame. Its nose was facing us.

It knew we were there.

I dove for Tori. The second I wrapped my arms around her, the shop exploded. We fell down behind the counter as the window blew in and the world turned inside out. I felt the force of the powerful blast as the counter was knocked over on top of us. It wasn't firing the laser weapon. If Whittle was right, that only worked in the dark. Instead, it was shooting the same kind of gun it had used in the battle with the Navy. It fired an invisible pulse of energy that didn't disintegrate its target—it blew it apart. The weapon itself was absolutely silent, which meant all we could hear was the sound of the shop being torn apart.

Tori and I rolled over in a jumble of arms and legs.

"You okay?" I asked.

She nodded. "The back door."

We crawled through the rubble of plastic beach toys, twisted picture frames, and smoldering T-shirts. There was so much dust and debris in the air that it was impossible to tell which way to go. I crawled on my hands and knees and pushed aside a metal shelving unit to discover . . . Mr. Whittle. He was on his back, staring up at the ceiling with lifeless eyes. I can't say what had killed him, but as with all the other victims, it had been fast.

By his standards, he was now one of the lucky ones.

I pushed Tori away so she wouldn't see him. There was no sense in both of us having that memory. Me? I was getting used to seeing dead people.

Tori didn't hesitate and crawled toward the back of the store. I was right behind her, fearing that the dark plane would blow another shot into the store and tear the place apart . . . and us along with it.

When we passed through the doorway into the back, I felt safe enough to get to my feet. I grabbed Tori around the waist to pull her up just as the plane fired again. The floor rocked like we had been hit by an earthquake. Heavy crossbeams that had held the roof up for a hundred years came crashing down around us. We were lucky the entire building didn't come down on our heads.

"There's gotta be a back way out," I called over the sound of tearing, crashing timbers.

A heavy beam landed and rolled, slamming into my legs and nearly knocking me off my feet. Tori grabbed my hand. It kept me from falling, but she paid the price. She winced with anguish but didn't yell out. She wouldn't give in to the pain.

We had made it to the back storage room of the shop. Cardboard boxes were stacked in everywhere, creating a twisted labyrinth that I hoped would lead us to a way out. I was disoriented from having been slammed by the beam, so it fell to Tori to keep us moving. She kept hold of my hand and led me through the narrow maze of boxes as the floor shook again.

Our hunters weren't giving up. Stacks of boxes were blown apart, their contents hitting our backs and sending us sprawling. The jolt nearly knocked me senseless. I couldn't imagine how Tori felt.

"This way," she commanded.

That was my answer. Her head was clearer than mine.

When we finally reached the back door, we saw that it was a heavy, fire-safety metal rectangle with five locks to keep us from getting outside quickly. We stared at it, totally discouraged, until a massive beam crashed down behind us. That was all the encouragement we needed. Tori and I jumped forward and fumbled with the locks. In seconds we had sprung them all and pushed the door open.

We were out, but still on the run.

"We gotta find Kent," Tori said.

"First we gotta shake that plane," I corrected.

We ran down a narrow alleyway that emptied onto a wider backstreet. I pulled Tori to the left, only because it would get us farther away from the shop and the attack plane that was blowing it apart.

Running on the uneven paving stones was tricky. The rough stones may have provided a quaint New England touch for the tourists, but to us they could mean the difference between escape and death. The last thing we needed was to twist an ankle.

We reached the end of the block and turned right onto another narrow street . . .

. . . and came face-to-face with the black plane.

It had circled around and cut us off.

Tori screamed with surprise. I might have too if I hadn't gone into brain lock.

The plane hovered two feet above the ground, twenty yards in front of us. There was no time to jump back. It had us.

The stingray–shaped predator seemed to be glaring at us, as if it could think. Maybe it could. Whoever was controlling it, whether it was a pilot on board or somebody sitting safely in a command center with his hand on a joystick, we were square in its sights.

"Who are you?" Tori shouted. "Show yourself, coward!"

It was a defiant yet futile demand . . .

. . . that got a response. Two small panels opened on the front edge of each wing. They were panels I feared were retracting to uncover its deadly cannons.

Tori stood tall but reached out and grabbed my hand.

I tensed up.

The Pemberwick Run had finally come to an end.

The musical sound of the jet's engines echoed off the brick walls of the narrow street . . . and were drowned out by the sound of a car's engine and the squeal of tires on pavement. A second later, a silver SUV came screaming out of the side street next to the hovering plane and crashed into it.

The violent impact brought me back to my senses. I pulled Tori out of the street and into a recessed doorway for protection.

Whoever was in control of the dark plane never saw the car

coming. The craft actually flipped up onto its side and careened into the building, slamming its top into the wall, smashing windows and pulverizing brick. The plane seemed incredibly light, not only because it was so easily tossed but because its skin cracked and crumbled on impact.

The SUV continued forward, pinning the craft against the wall. The force of the impact inflated both airbags, though there was relatively little damage to the car. The driver's door opened and Kent tumbled out, pulling Olivia with him. They hit the pavement, fell, then scrambled to their feet and ran to us.

A sound came from the damaged plane like that of an engine revving up. It wasn't the familiar musical sound, but rather a steadily growing whine that made it seem as though power was building up inside the craft. Something was about to happen, and it wasn't going to be good.

"Run!" I shouted.

Kent and Olivia were dazed but managed to stay on their feet and stumble toward us. I jumped out from the doorway and grabbed Olivia, who was in tears. I pulled her into the doorway as Kent jumped in right behind.

Tori stood peering back around the corner, her eyes focused on the plane.

"What's happening?" she asked.

As if in answer, the plane was suddenly engulfed by a bright light that seemed to grow from within. Seconds later, it exploded.

"Whoa!" I screamed as we all pinned ourselves into the doorway for protection. A powerful fireball erupted and flashed past us. The heat was so intense I feared that our clothes would catch fire. The event lasted for only a few brief, devastating seconds. The sound of the explosion echoed through the streets of the Old Port and was soon gone.

We all looked to one another, stunned.

"Anybody hurt?" I asked.

Nobody replied. I took that as a no.

I cautiously peered around the corner to see that there was nothing left of the predator plane but the scorched brick wall it had crashed into.

The hunter had become the victim. It had incinerated.

"Did the fuel tank explode?" Tori asked, shaken.

"I guess," I replied. "But what kind of fuel would do that? I mean, the plane was obliterated."

Kent crawled to the edge of the doorway and peered back to see his handiwork.

"Woo hoo!" he screamed in victory. "I *so* nailed that bastard! Did you see? We spotted you running into the street, so I drove another block to head you off and saw the plane. There wasn't time to think, so we just went for it!"

Kent was so charged up I thought he might have taken a dose of the Ruby, but that was impossible. It was adrenaline talking.

Tori kneeled down next to a shaken Olivia.

"Are you okay?" she asked.

"No," Olivia replied. "I'm totally out of my mind."

"What do you mean?"

"I jammed my foot down on the gas over Kent's," she said, stunned, as if she couldn't believe it herself. "I don't know what made me do it. I could have killed us."

"So ramming the plane was your idea?" I asked.

"Hey, I didn't fight it," Kent announced, trying to salvage some credit. "I would have done the same thing."

Tori gave me a quick look and rolled her eyes.

"Whatever," I said. "You both saved our lives."

"Remember that, Rook," Kent said. "You owe me."

"We can't stay here," Tori said. "This is bound to bring other planes."

"We still need a car," I pointed out.

"No problem," Kent proclaimed cockily. "There's a parking lot full of them, all with keys. They must belong to tourists."

"*Used* to belong to tourists," Tori corrected.

The reality of that statement hit hard. We were in a city of the dead. The United States Air Force had wiped it out. And as horrifying as that was, we had no way of knowing the full extent of the damage. Was Portland the only city hit? Or would we find more devastation elsewhere? With all forms of communication gone, there was only one way for us to find out.

We had to travel.

TWO

Home.

It's a simple little word that means so much.

It's not just a place, it's a concept. Home is safety. It's where you are surrounded by loved ones who watch out for you. It's the one place where you will always be welcomed, no matter what craziness may be going on around you. I think for most people it's the single most important place in the world.

I know that's true because I no longer have one.

Neither do Tori, Kent, and Olivia. We may have left our homes behind when we escaped from Pemberwick Island, but we had lost them long before that. We just didn't know it at the time.

I'm not exactly sure when our homes started to slip away. Maybe it began when people on Pemberwick Island suddenly started dying. The deaths rocked the small community and were unexplainable, until we were invaded and occupied by a branch of the United States Navy called SYLO. The president of the United States himself announced that a virus had broken out, and quarantined the island for our protection and that of the people on the mainland.

It was a lie. The real reason people died was because of a substance called the Ruby that was being distributed by a mysterious stranger named Ken Feit. The Ruby gave people incredible strength and energy. I can say that with authority because I tried it. It was magical . . . unless you took too much. The human body wasn't built to perform at such a high level. It was absolutely amazing—and ultimately deadly.

Was that when our home started slipping away?

Or was it when the SYLO occupiers and their leader, Captain Granger, started pulling people off the street and throwing them into prison? Or when SYLO began killing people for attempting to escape? Maybe it was before that, when the black Air Force planes started secretly delivering the Ruby to Pemberwick. What was the point of that? If they wanted to hurt us, why didn't they just vaporize us one night like they did the people of Portland? Were we being used as guinea pigs for some hideous experiment?

I could say that I first felt my home slipping away when Quinn Carr was killed. He was such a huge part of my life until . . . he wasn't.

Or maybe I know the exact moment when I realized I no longer had a home. It was when I heard that my mother and father were working with the Navy. With SYLO. They knew SYLO was coming long before we set foot on the island when I was nine years old. They had been keeping the truth from me for a very long time. The people who were supposed to protect me and make our home a home weren't doing either. I will never forgive them for that . . . if I ever see them again.

My tragic story is only one of many that developed once SYLO came into our lives.

Tori's dad was killed while trying to fight back against the occupation.

Kent's father died when he took the Ruby to try to gain the strength to protect their home.

Olivia was visiting the island from New York City, but her mother was on the mainland when the invasion hit. They may never see each other again because there's no way to know if she's dead or alive.

The details may be different, but the bottom line is the same: We have all lost the familiar base that helped make us who we are. We're adrift. All we can do is move forward and try to understand the biggest question of all: Why? Why has this happened? Why have so many people been killed? Why are the Navy and the Air Force battling each other, and who should we hope will win? That's the most confounding question of all. SYLO held us prisoner, and the Air Force tried to poison us. The Navy murdered anyone on Pemberwick who challenged their authority; the Air Force wiped out thousands on the mainland.

Why? What were they hoping to gain? I can't imagine anything being worth the pain and destruction that this war has already caused. There has to be a reason for it. Someone must be calling the shots. Someone sent SYLO to destroy my home. My life. When I find out who they are, I'm going to do everything I can to cause them the kind of suffering they brought to my friends, to Pemberwick Island, and to me. Maybe then we can start over and establish a new base. A new history. A new home.

If there's any hope of that, we must first search for the truth . . . and hope that what we find won't be worse than what we've already seen.

"We'll take the Saab," Kent said. "It's butt-ugly, but the tank is full."

We had made it safely to a parking lot that was packed with the cars of people who had come to the Old Port for a night of fun and never left. We piled into the ancient burgundy sedan while keeping one eye on the sky. Nobody had to say it, but we all feared that another attack plane would come swooping in. I sat in back with Tori. Olivia rode shotgun.

"Where's the hospital?" Kent asked.

"Head back the way we drove into town," Tori said. "It's near the Western Prom."

"You say that like I know what you're talking about," he said snidely.

Kent started the engine, put the car into gear, and jammed his foot to the floor, launching us out of the parking lot.

"Hey, take it easy!" Olivia cried.

"Easy?" Kent said with a scoff. "Those planes are out hunting. I don't want to get blown up."

"And I don't want to smash into a light pole," Olivia chastised sweetly. "C'mon, Kent, I know you can get us there safely."

Kent backed off the gas.

"Sorry," he said as if he actually meant it.

Olivia had an almost magical hold over Kent. Maybe it was the way she made it seem like he was always making his own decisions, while in reality she got exactly what she wanted. Or maybe it was because she looked incredible in the same short-shorts that she had been wearing since the night before. Or maybe he genuinely cared about her. Didn't matter. Kent was a loose cannon, and if he had to be reined in, Olivia was the one to do it.

"How are you feeling?" I asked Tori.

"Tired, but okay," she said.

I examined the bandage that Olivia had wrapped around her wound while we were on the boat making the run from Pemberwick Island.

"You're not bleeding," I said. "But we have to make sure you don't get infected."

"Yeah," Kent said. "Wouldn't want you to go all gangrene and have to cut your arm off."

Nobody reacted.

"Jeez, I'm kidding!" he complained.

Nobody reacted.

"Fine, I'll shut up and drive."

"Does it hurt much?" I asked Tori.

She didn't answer, which was all the answer I needed. She was hurting.

As we drove through the streets of an empty Portland, I kept glancing to the sky for fear of seeing another dark plane. I rolled down the window to listen for incoming music.

None of us spoke. We were all wound tight, tuned for signs of danger. With each empty street we passed, the enormity of what we were facing grew more real. The idea that thousands of people had been wiped off the face of the earth was beyond horrifying.

Not that the death of any innocent person can be justified, but with a war, there's the grim expectation of casualties. But were we truly at war? If so, the people of Portland hadn't gotten advance notice. They had been attacked without mercy and for seemingly no reason. It's not like a victorious army came in afterward to occupy the city.

It seemed as though the attack was all about death for death's sake.

As bad as it was, there was no way to know if Portland was the only target. What would we find when we left the city? Was the rest of the world safe and watching the grisly events unfold here in Maine? Or were there similar battles raging over New York? And Philadelphia? And Baltimore? And, and, and . . .

Even more sobering, if civil war had broken out in the United States, it would affect the entire planet. We had allies and enemies. The world economy relied on us. A civil war would create chaos everywhere. What we were witnessing would have an impact that stretched far beyond the borders of our little universe.

With those dire thoughts in mind, it was no wonder that none of us could bring ourselves to say much until we reached our destination.

The Maine Medical Center was a sprawling, modern complex of brick buildings.

"Go to the emergency room," I called to Kent.

"Yes, sir!" he replied with mock enthusiasm.

He followed the signs and pulled to a stop in front of the glass ER doors. We all got out and took a quick look around. The parking lot was full, but not a single person was to be seen.

"What's the point?" Kent asked. "We're not going to find any doctors."

"We'll get clean bandages and antiseptic," Tori said. "It's not like I need surgery."

Olivia held Tori by the arm to support her.

I led the group to the front door . . . and nearly walked right into it.

Oops. No power.

Kent pulled open a side door.

"Or we could go this way," he declared smugly.

He held the door while the three of us entered.

The sun was already on its way down. With no power in the building, it was going to be a challenge to find anything—especially since the deeper we walked toward the emergency room, the fewer windows there were.

"We gotta do this fast," I said, "or it'll be pitch dark."

We walked quickly toward the patient-treatment area, more or less guessing at which was the right way to go. Being there brought back memories. Bad memories. The last time I had been in a hospital was the week before, when Quinn and I snuck into his father's office in the Arborville emergency room. We hacked into his parents' computer looking for information about the Pemberwick virus. What we found was the first hint that there actually *was* no Pemberwick virus; the hospital database showed no cases being treated. It confirmed that Captain Granger and his SYLO team weren't telling the people of Pemberwick the truth.

As startling as that was, it was only the tip of the iceberg.

"What's that sound?" Olivia asked.

I stopped short and tensed up, fearing an incoming attack plane. We listened and heard what sounded like a static-filled AM radio.

"Could be a battery-powered radio," I said.

"Yes!" Kent exclaimed. "We can get news out of Boston."

We followed the sound while straining to hear what was being broadcast. There was more static than anything else, but we could occasionally hear the sound of a woman's voice breaking through the clutter. It wasn't clear enough to make out anything specific. The signal was either too weak or the battery was near dead.

"It's coming from in there," Tori said, pointing to a closed door.

I didn't hesitate and went for the door.

Dim light entered the room as I pushed it open. It was enough to see a small office. On the far wall was a desk that was stacked with electronic equipment, some of which had green power lights on. There were several computer monitors lit up and showing colorful data.

"It *is* a radio," Kent said.

"Why do they have power?" Olivia asked with confusion.

"It must be running on batteries," I said. "Or an emergency generator. It looks like the communication room for the ER."

"So what is it picking up?" Tori asked.

The static and voice were coming from speakers mounted near the ceiling. It was a bad signal, but I didn't want to risk monkeying with the touchscreen for fear I would lose it completely. The static continued, along with the ghostly voice of a woman who was broadcasting from . . . somewhere. I only caught every third word.

". . . appeal . . . survivors . . . bloodied . . . attacked . . . join . . . north . . . thirty-six degrees . . . twenty seconds . . . hundred fourteen . . . fifty-seven . . . invaders . . . strength . . . hesitate . . ."

The voice was clipped, and it cut in and out so that whatever she was saying made little sense.

"Maybe we can talk to her," Kent said and went for the radio.

He picked up a microphone on a stand, brought it up to his mouth, and—

"Don't touch that!" barked a male voice from the hallway.

We all jumped in surprise and spun quickly to see a guy standing there who didn't look much older than us. He wore green hospital scrubs and a white lab coat. He had a head of thick, curly black hair and wore large glasses that gave him a wild, bug-eyed look. He pushed past us and went right for the radio.

"I don't want to lose the signal," he said, peeved. "It's tough enough finding it because it's so weak."

He fine-tuned the frequency by moving his fingers over the touchscreen, but rather than bringing the ghostly voice in more clearly, he killed it entirely.

"Damn!" he said, frustrated. "It's over."

The guy touched a few more icons, and the radio went dark.

"Who was that?" Kent asked. "And who are *you*?"

"Jon Purcell," the guy said. "I mean, that's who I am. I don't know who *she* was."

"What was she talking about?" Olivia asked.

"I'm not sure," Jon replied thoughtfully. "She comes on every two hours and says the same thing, I think. It's hard to tell because I only get random words. She talks about survivors and heading west and spews out numbers, but none of it makes sense. I don't even think she's broadcasting live. It might be a recording, like a continuous loop, because it sounds exactly the same each time."

"So you don't know if she's close by or on the other side of the world," I said.

Jon looked at me like I had just asked if fish could sing.

"Obviously she couldn't be on the other side of the world," he said condescendingly. "Radio waves don't follow the curve of the earth. With some repeaters she could be broadcasting from a few thousand miles away, but that's likely the limit."

"Right. Thanks for the physics lesson," I said, not meaning it.

"Do you work here?" Tori asked. "I need some help."

"I'm in transportation," Jon said proudly. "I know every inch of this hospital. What do you need?"

"Not transportation," Ken said sarcastically.

"I was shot," Tori said, gesturing to her shoulder. "I want to clean up the wound."

"Shot?" Jon said in disbelief. "How? Why? What happened?"

"Really?" Kent exclaimed. "The whole city is wiped out by laser beams from the sky, and you get all squirrelly over a bullet wound?"

Jon snapped a look to Kent and walked right up to him. He must have been a foot shorter than tall, blond, preppy Kent, but that didn't stop him from getting in his face. Or rather his Adam's apple.

"That's exactly why I'm 'all squirrelly,' as you put it," Jon said. "There aren't a whole lot of survivors. The last thing we need to do is start shooting one another."

Kent looked as though he wanted to smack the little guy, but he held back.

"Can you please show us where the medical supplies are?" I asked.

"I can do better than that," he replied. "This is your lucky day."

He turned and strode out of the office.

The four of us exchanged confused looks.

"I can think of a lot of words to describe this day," Kent said. "'Lucky' isn't one of them."

"Are we supposed to follow that little nerd?" Olivia asked.

"Yes, you are!" Jon shouted from the hallway.

"Oops," Olivia said, then called out, "No offense!"

She got no reply.

We left the radio room and followed Jon deeper into the ER. The light was nearly gone, but that didn't stop him from walking quickly.

"Hey!" Kent yelled to him. "Transpo-Boy! You may know every inch of this place, but we don't."

"We're not going far," Jon shouted back without stopping.

We followed him through a doorway, and I saw a faint light further ahead. It was enough to recognize that we were in the main treatment area of the ER. Jon led us down a row of treatment stations that were separated by curtains. Each contained a bed for patients. None were occupied.

The light grew brighter as we approached it, and I could see that it was coming from one of the curtained-off sections.

"You've got power?" I asked.

"We've got batteries," Jon replied. "And lanterns."

He stepped past the illuminated curtain and said, "We have company."

Somebody was back there.

"She's been shot," Jon added.

The curtain was pulled back to reveal a tall Asian woman with long, dark hair wearing deep red hospital scrubs.

"Hello," she said with professional distance. "I'm Dr. Kayamori. Please call me Luna."

She was a strikingly pretty Japanese woman with a tanned complexion and long, dark sun-streaked hair.

"A doctor?" Olivia exclaimed. "Thank God."

"I told you it was your lucky day," Jon said, smug.

"Who is injured?" Luna asked.

Tori stepped forward.

"The bullet passed clean through just below my shoulder. There was a lot of blood, but that's stopped now. I just want to make sure it doesn't get infected."

Luna relaxed and broke out in a big, warm smile. I liked her instantly.

"I'll have to take your word that the bullet passed through. It isn't like we can x-ray it. I'll examine you and see what I can do."

She looked to the rest of us and asked, "What are your names?"

"Kent."

"Olivia."

"Tucker."

"I'm Tori."

"When was the last time any of you had something to eat?" she asked.

We all looked to one another dumbly.

"It's been a while," I replied. "Food's been the last thing on our minds."

"Jon, take them to the cafeteria," Luna said. Then to us she added, "Eat the fresh food first."

"Do I have to do this?" Jon whined.

"Yes, please," Luna said firmly. "We are still a hospital, and we will continue to provide care."

"Fine," Jon said, pouty.

He grabbed a small battery-powered lamp and secured the strap around his head so the light shone from his forehead. The bright beam hit us in the eyes. He didn't care.

"Follow me," he said with no enthusiasm.

He shuffled off, keeping the beam on the floor ahead of him. Geek.

"Maybe one of us should stay," I said to Tori.

"I'll be okay," she replied. "Bring me back something to eat. I'm suddenly starving."

"Me too," Kent said, then called out, "Wait up, Chadwick."

"Chadwick?" Luna asked with confusion.

"Don't ask," I said. "He makes up offensive names for everybody."

"Go," Tori ordered. "I'm fine."

I didn't want to leave her with a stranger, but I had the feeling that we were going to have to start doing a lot of things we wouldn't normally do. Olivia and I caught up, and we followed the little guy to the far side of the building.

"Why are you all still alive?" Jon asked with no hint of tact. "We made it because as soon as I saw trouble, I hid in the basement with Dr. Kayamori. The only people who survived were deep underground when the attack happened."

"How did you know to do that?" I asked.

"Because I'm smart," Jon replied. "What's *your* story?"

"We were on Pemberwick Island," Kent replied curtly. "Now we're not. End of story."

He didn't have the energy to relive all the details of what we had been through, and I didn't blame him.

Jon stopped short and turned back to face us. The beam from his headlight burned into our eyes.

"Get that outta my face!" Kent complained.

"You were on Pemberwick?" Jon asked in awe.

"There's no virus, if that's what you're worried about," I assured him.

"I'm not," Jon said. "I never thought there was. It made no sense. How did you get away?"

"Speedboat," was my simple answer.

Jon nodded thoughtfully. "That explains a lot."

"What do you mean?" Kent asked.

Jon turned abruptly and continued to walk.

"About your friend being shot," he answered quickly. "That was a hell of a battle out there on the water."

His reaction to our being from Pemberwick was an odd one, mostly because he didn't press us for more information. You'd think he would have been a little more interested, but Jon was definitely more about Jon than anybody else. He brought us to the cafeteria without another word and led us into the big, institutional kitchen.

"There are fruits and vegetables in the walk-in cooler. Open and close the door quickly. We're trying to keep the cold in for as long as possible."

He tossed me a flashlight, and Kent and Tori followed me into the big cooler. Inside we gathered tomatoes, carrots, lettuce, bananas, and a half dozen apples. All were still fresh, but there was no telling how long that would last. We also grabbed a loaf of bread that didn't look as though any mold had grown on it. Yet. We brought it all outside, spread it on a counter, and made sandwiches.

"Is it okay for us to take this much?" I asked Jon. "How many survivors are in the hospital?"

"Including me and Dr. Kayamori?" he asked.

"Yeah."

"Two."

"You know you're kind of annoying, right?" Kent said.

"That's it?" Olivia asked with surprise. "There are only two survivors in the whole hospital?"

"Why is that a shock?" Jon asked. "People weren't injured in the attack, they were obliterated. Dr. Kayamori wanted to stay here in case people showed up and . . . surprise. Here you are."

"And why are *you* staying here?" Kent asked.

"Why not?" Jon said with a shrug. "There's nowhere else to go."

That was a conversation killer.

We finished making a load of tomato and lettuce sandwiches and stacked them on a bus tray along with the apples and overripe bananas. I grabbed a few bottles of water from next to the silent cash register, and we all headed back to the ER.

When we arrived, the doctor was finishing the tape job on Tori's new, clean bandage.

"She was incredibly lucky," Luna said.

"I was just lucky," Tori said. "If I was *incredibly* lucky, the sniper would have missed completely."

"The entrance and exit wounds are clean. Seems as though the bullet passed through without bouncing around inside. If it had, you'd probably be dead. As it is, you'll be feeling some pain while the muscle heals."

She looked to us and added, "I packed the wound with cotton to allow it to heal from the inside. It'll have to be changed every day or so for a while. I gave her a tetanus shot and some antibiotic tablets. Multiple vitamins too. There isn't anything more I would do even if the hospital were fully functional."

She touched Tori on the shoulder and said, "It will be painful for a few weeks, but you should be feeling better soon after that."

"Thanks, Dr. Kayamori," Tori said.

"Luna, and you are very welcome. I'm just happy I was here to help. It's odd to be the only doctor in a war zone and not have any patients."

We all sat at the nurses' station and chowed on the sandwiches. I would have preferred a big old hamburger, but you can't cook a burger without gas or electricity . . . or meat. Luna placed her battery-powered lantern on the counter, and we sat huddled together in its light, enjoying the simple meal.

"Do you have any idea what happened?" I asked Luna.

"Not a clue. It was about as normal a day as you could imagine. The only interesting news going on was about Pemberwick Island. But after a few weeks even that was no longer big news."

"Unless you were there," Kent groused.

Luna continued, "I was working alone in my office when we heard the first screams. Then the power went out. Jon came running in and ordered me to go to the basement with him. I was too confused to do anything but follow."

"Why her?" Kent asked Jon. "Was she the best doctor here, or just the hottest?"

"Jeez, Kent," Tori scolded.

Kent shrugged. "Just trying to get the picture."

Jon replied, "I'd like to say that I was thinking clearly enough to make those kinds of judgment calls, but the truth is that I had just delivered a load of paper products to the nurses' station next to her office. Dr. Kayamori was the first doctor I saw when the attack began."

"And she's hot," Kent added.

Jon looked embarrassed, and Luna bailed him out.

"It was my good fortune he was there, because he saved my life. We stayed in the basement for a few hours before deciding that whatever had happened was over. It took us quite some time to make our way back up in the dark, and when we finally surfaced, the hospital was empty. Jon and I left to seek help, but, well, you know what we found. We came back and have stayed here ever since."

"It's like they swept the city with that laser weapon," I said. "It even got to people who were indoors."

"Unless they were deep below ground," Jon corrected. "We've met other survivors too. We think that weapon only works at night, but a few planes have been around during the day using other weapons. We've heard explosions. It's like they're trying to finish the job. We don't see them much anymore, though. Maybe they think they got us all."

"The idea that so many people died in such a short time is hard to comprehend," Luna said. "Who could be behind such an evil act?"

"That's what I'd like to know," I said quickly.

We gave Luna and Jon a brief overview of what we had been through on Pemberwick: the Ruby, the bogus quarantine, the SYLO troops from the U.S. Navy who were holding us prisoner, and the discovery that the black attack planes had the logo of the U.S. Air Force.

"No way!" Jon blurted out. He had been fidgeting during the entire story, dying to add his own opinions. He held himself back until I said that Portland had been attacked by the U.S. Air Force. That pushed him over the edge.

"That's just crazy. Why would the Navy be fighting the Air Force?"

"Current theory? Civil War II," Kent said casually while licking tomato pulp from his fingers.

"It's a horrifying thought," Luna said soberly. "If it's true, then it would follow that Portland isn't the only battleground."

"That's what we're afraid of," I agreed. "But if the United States is busy trying to destroy itself, you'd think that other countries would step in to try to stop it."

"Unless they don't want to get attacked themselves," Tori offered.

"Or unless they want us to wipe ourselves out first," Kent said.

Jon suddenly sat bolt upright and looked at his watch.

"It's time!" he said and took off running into the dark.

"Time for what?" Tori asked.

"For the last two days, we've been picking up a radio broad-cast," Luna explained. "It's the voice of a woman, but the signal is very weak, so it's hard to understand."

"We heard it," I said.

"The transmission lasts for two minutes and happens every other hour on the hour. Jon has been trying to decipher it."

"I'd like to hear it again," I said.

Luna grabbed the battery-powered lantern and headed after Jon. We followed her back down the hallway to the small office that held the ER's radio.

Jon was inside, already having powered up the device. He was listening intently to the static while delicately moving his finger across the touchscreen, searching for a signal.

Kent asked, "Who do you think—"

"Shhh!" Jon snapped.

After hearing nothing for several seconds, I was ready to give up and go back to my sandwich . . . when the voice came through.

". . . survivors . . . beaten . . . attacked . . . you safe . . . north . . . thirty-six degrees . . . twenty seconds . . . west one hundred . . . thirty-one minutes . . . repel . . . invaders . . . strength . . . not hesitate . . ."

"It's making me crazy," Jon complained. "I have no idea what she's saying."

"It's the same message every two hours," Luna added. "We think it's a recording."

"Could it be somebody on a ham radio?" Tori asked.

"No," Jon said quickly. "They're broadcasting on an emergency frequency. It's the one used by ambulances to communicate with hospitals."

"So there could be other hospitals hearing this right now?" I asked.

"If they still exist," Jon said. "And they're smart enough to be listening."

"It can't be SYLO, or the Air Force," I said. "Their equipment is, like, high tech."

"We must be listening to other survivors," Tori said. "This could be a call for help."

"Then they're calling the wrong people," Kent said, scoffing.

Tori grabbed a piece of paper and wrote down some of the disjointed words.

"Thirty-six degrees," she said while writing furiously. "That could be a coordinate. But without the whole thing, there's no way of knowing where it is."

The woman's voice abruptly stopped, leaving nothing but static coming from the speakers.

Jon glanced at his watch.

"Two minutes on the dot," he announced. "She'll be back in another two hours."

"Somebody is trying to reach out," Tori declared.

"Reach out to do what?" Olivia asked.

"I don't know," Tori said. "Maybe to find other survivors?"

"So why don't we talk back?" Kent asked.

"I tried," Jon explained. "There's no response. It's another reason why I think it's a recording."

"Well, this is all very interesting," Kent said, sounding bored. "But if we don't know who it is, why they're broadcasting, where they are, or what they want, why are we so interested?"

Tori said, "Because they may know why we're at war."

Jon powered down the radio, and the room went silent.

I grabbed a piece of paper and wrote something quickly. "Luna, don't doctors have to study Latin?"

"A bit," she replied. "I took more courses as an undergraduate, though. I thought it would help in medical school. It didn't."

"Do you have any idea what this says?" I asked. "I'm not sure if I remember the exact spelling."

I handed her the paper. On it I had written down the words that were scrawled like graffiti on the wreckage of the downed Air Force plane we discovered in the Old Port.

Luna held it closer to the lantern and read it aloud. "*Sequentia yconomus libertate te ex inferis obendienter.*"

"SYLO," Tori said.

Luna frowned. "I'm not a Latin scholar by any stretch of the imagination."

"Does it make *any* sense?" I asked.

"*Sequentia* could mean 'sequence.' Or something that follows. I'm not familiar with *yconomus. Obendienter* could be the root of the word 'obedient.'"

"What about *libertate te ex inferis?*" I asked.

Luna gave me a dark look. She asked, "Do you really think this phrase has something to do with SYLO?"

"Either that, or it's an incredible coincidence that it's a perfect acronym," I said.

"Do you know what it means?" Tori asked.

Luna took a breath. She said, "*Libertate* means 'to liberate or free something.'"

"What about *te ex inferis?*"

She handed the paper back to me. "I can only offer a loose

translation, but to the best of my knowledge, *libertate te ex inferis* means 'to liberate, or to save a person, from the gates of hell.'"

Her words echoed through the empty hospital, or maybe they were echoing through my head. I finally got my thoughts together enough to say, "So we could be dealing with a deadly virus, or a powerful and lethal drug, or aliens, or a civil war, and now we've got to add the possibility of something biblical going on?"

Luna shrugged and said, "I don't know. I'm not a religious person. I don't know what happens after death or why we're all here, but after what happened to this city, to these people, I could be convinced that evil truly does exist, because there was definitely a devil at work here, and we have found ourselves standing at the gates of hell."

THREE

I was beyond exhausted.

It was hard to believe that less than twenty-four hours had passed since we had gone to sleep on Pemberwick Island in a tent with a group of rebels led by Tori's father.

So much had changed in a single day.

We decided to spend the night in the hospital and figure out what our next move would be in the morning. Luna gave us hospital scrubs to sleep in. My clothes were rank, but there was no way to wash and dry them. It didn't matter. We could visit a deserted shop in Portland and take our pick of new clothes. Nobody would care.

The best part about the night was that we got to take showers. The hospital's plumbing system still worked, for the time being, and I was looking forward to washing away the grime that had been building up since I took my last shower in the SYLO prison camp. The girls went first, then Kent went with Jon. I thought about bailing and going to sleep, but as tired as I was, I wasn't going to pass up the chance at a shower, so when it was my turn I forced my sorry self to go.

There was a locker room next to the showers, so I dropped my new scrubs there, peeled off my old clothes, and dumped them in the trash. The only thing I didn't toss were my cross-trainers. I didn't want to lose those until I found new ones. I grabbed a towel from the stack near the door and headed for the shower.

The water was still warm. That wouldn't last. Once it ran out, there would be no way to heat it again. There was no electricity and therefore no lights. Or heat. Or refrigeration. We didn't have cell phones or radios or Internet or any of the other things we had always taken for granted. A hot shower was a luxury that wouldn't be repeated until we reconnected with civilization.

As I stood there, enjoying the warmth, I tried to be positive. Our goal was to get to Boston and blow the whistle on those responsible for what was happening on Pemberwick. After that, who knew? One step at a time. Thinking too far ahead made my head hurt.

When I started to fall asleep standing up, I realized I had had enough. I left the shower, went back to the locker room to get dressed, and got as far as pulling on the scrub pants when—

"Oops, sorry," Olivia said with an embarrassed giggle.

I spun to see her standing there with her hand over her eyes.

"Didn't see anything," she said with a chuckle. "Much."

"I thought you went to sleep!" I said as I quickly pulled my scrub top on.

"I couldn't. I want to talk."

Standing there facing her was unnerving. I felt as though I was still naked.

She put her hands on her hips and struck a pose.

"Not exactly a stylish outfit."

It didn't matter that the scrubs were so plain; she looked great. Her short blond hair was still wet. She had it combed straight back, which let her bright blue eyes sparkle in the light from the lantern.

"We'll get new clothes tomorrow," I said.

"And then what?"

"I don't know. We should probably stick to the original plan and—"

"I'm scared, Tucker."

Her voice was shaky. I was afraid she might cry.

"We all are. We'll find your mother and get you home."

She gave me a wistful smile and said, "Not so sure about that. I don't think I'm ever going to see my mother again."

"Don't say that," I chastised. "She probably went back to your home in New York. Or maybe she went to Boston and she's planning on coming back here to find you."

Olivia shrugged. She didn't believe either of those possibilities. Her mother had left Pemberwick to go shopping on the mainland when the attack hit. Odds were that Olivia's fear was justified.

"What about your father?" I asked.

She shrugged and smiled sadly. "He's a long, long way from here."

"So then we'll get you back together with him. And your mother too."

"Do you really believe that?" she asked innocently.

"I do," I said.

I didn't. I had no idea what was possible. I thought my words would comfort her, even if they were lies, but it seemed as though I was only making things worse, for tears grew in Olivia's eyes.

"You're such a good guy," she said. "None of this should have happened."

"You get no argument from me there, but it did. You're not alone here, Olivia. We're going to watch out for each other."

She looked up at me with big, innocent eyes.

"Promise?"

"Cross my heart," I said while crossing my heart.

She walked slowly toward me.

I took a step back and hit the lockers.

She came right up to me and put her arms around my neck.

I looked down into those big blue eyes. It was almost as terrifying as when we faced the black plane in the Old Port.

Almost.

"I really like Kent," she said.

Odd thing to say at that moment, but whatever.

"Me too," I replied, though I didn't like him at all.

"But I can't depend on him. I mean, it's not like we're a couple. Not really."

"Could have fooled me."

"It's true."

"Maybe you should tell him that."

"Why? He wouldn't believe me. Kent only cares about Kent. He thinks every girl is in love with him. You can't rely on somebody like that."

She stared up at me, expecting me to say something.

I had nothing.

"Why are you telling me this?" I finally asked.

"Because I want to know if I can rely on *you*."

I didn't know where this was going. Was Olivia being flirty just to make sure I'd take care of her? Or did she really like me?

"I . . . yeah. Of course you can rely on me. So can Tori. And Kent. We can all rely on each other and—"

She put her finger on my lips to stop the verbal diarrhea.

"I don't mean to make you nervous," she said.

Sure she did.

"I'm not nervous," I said nervously.

Olivia laughed. She was flirting all right.

"You're a good guy, Tucker Pierce. A really good guy. I think you're going to come out of this okay."

That was a weird thing to say. A second earlier she'd been acting all confused and scared, then suddenly she was speaking with total authority, as if she could predict the future.

Like I said, Olivia was an enigma. A dangerous enigma.

She stood up on her toes . . . and kissed me.

I was so surprised that I didn't stop her. Okay, I probably wouldn't have stopped her even if I wasn't so surprised. I wrapped my arms around her back, pulled her close, ignored the horrible mess we were in for a solid four seconds . . . and then snapped out of it and pushed her away.

"You can't do that," I said. "Kent would kill me."

"I told you, we're not a couple," she said petulantly.

"Well, he thinks you are, and that would be enough reason for him to pound me if he knew we were . . . we were . . ."

"We were what? Hot for each other?"

"Yes . . . NO! We're not hot for each other."

I slipped away from her and backed for the door.

"Look, you're great," I said. "You really are. You know I like you. Why else would I have been your tour guide all summer?"

"But you never tried to kiss me."

"Yeah, well, you're out of my league."

"Seriously?" she said, laughing. "After what we've been through? You just got promoted to the majors, Rook."

"Don't call me that! It doesn't matter how I feel about you, or you feel about me, or . . . or . . ."

"Or how you feel about Tori?"

"Don't go there. She and I are really close and—"

"Do you feel about her the way you feel about me?" she asked slyly.

The truth was, I didn't. Tori Sleeper was somebody I had wanted to get to know for years. She may have had issues, but that just made her more interesting and independent. It took a disaster to get us together, but after that we quickly came to rely on each other. It's not an exaggeration to say we owed each other our lives. That's a strong bond that I wouldn't want to break.

Olivia, on the other hand, was funny—and hot. Seriously hot. The idea of being alone with a girl like that, kissing in a shower room, was something I could only fantasize about . . . until now. Did I feel the same way about the two of them? Not even close.

"Look," I said, "we've got to watch out for each other, and complicating things will only make it more . . . complicated. Let's just . . . just . . . pretend this never happened, okay?"

"Okay, except for one thing."

"What's that?"

"You didn't answer my question. Can I rely on you?" she asked. This time she was deadly serious.

"Of course you can."

"Good," she said with finality. "Then you can rely on me too. G'night!"

With that, she turned on her toes and scampered back to the ER.

I was left feeling . . . what? Confused? Nervous? Flattered? I'd liked Olivia since the moment I'd first met her. But messing with her was like messing with Kent, and that could hurt.

Besides, I really did like Tori. I didn't know for sure if she felt the same way about me, but there was definitely something there. It might have been because we were thrown together in scary times and we wouldn't have anything in common once things got back to normal, but I wanted to find out. There would be zero chance of that if she caught me messing with Olivia. And Kent would kill me.

All told, fooling around with Olivia wasn't worth it.

I went back to the ER and slowed down as I passed Kent's bed, fearing he might be lying in wait, ready to pound me. But he was out cold, snoring away.

Everyone was asleep except me.

I got into my own bed, turned off the lantern, and lay there staring up at the ceiling. There were so many thoughts bouncing around in my head that I had trouble nodding off. I needed to focus on one single thought. That's what I did when I couldn't sleep. I forced myself to think of one thing and put up a barricade against all the other annoying worries.

In the past when that didn't work, I would go for a midnight ride.

I decided to do both. I imagined sneaking out of my bedroom

window, climbing down from the porch roof, hopping on my bike, and racing along the deserted, dark roads of Pemberwick Island. I pictured the beam from my headlight on the road ahead, scanning for potholes. I imagined the chilly breeze coming off of the ocean and the smell of sea air.

I also thought about Quinn. We always rode together. Thousands of people had been wiped out in Portland, but I didn't know any of them. Quinn I knew. If he hadn't suggested we take separate boats on our run to the mainland, we might all have been killed. I owed him. The best thing I could do to honor his memory was to survive and to make a difference. Quinn had dreams of leaving Pemberwick and doing something important with his life. In a way, he had done exactly that. Tori and I were living proof.

But that wasn't enough. I wanted to make a difference. For Quinn. And for us.

That was my single thought. That's what I focused on. Strangely, it calmed me. I didn't know what I would find beyond Portland and what I would do once I got there, but I made a promise to myself that I would do whatever I could to make sure that Quinn didn't die in vain. It felt good to have purpose and a goal beyond simply surviving. I was going to make a difference.

Quinn's death would be avenged. Whoever was controlling SYLO would pay for the destruction of our lives and the death of my best friend.

But not right then. I needed sleep.

There was no telling when I'd get the chance to do it again.

FOUR

"Tucker," came a girl's voice from my dream. "C'mon, open your eyes."

It was a good dream. It was Olivia's voice. You can do anything in a dream and not get in trouble for it, so I chose to enjoy the moment.

"I think I'll keep them closed for a while," I said happily. "Why don't you sing a song or something? That would be nice."

I suddenly felt a sharp poke in the arm.

"You're kidding, right?" came the girl's voice, suddenly harsh.

I cracked open an eye to see that she wasn't a dream and she wasn't Olivia.

All I could see was the mass of long black curls that surrounded her face. It was Tori.

I was suddenly very much awake.

"What? Oh? Sorry. I was dreaming."

"You got *that* right. Get up, I want to show you something."

I rubbed my eyes and sat up. The emergency room was slightly less dark than the night before. Daylight must have been creeping in from other parts of the hospital. It was enough to navigate by, but just barely.

"I made breakfast!" Luna called cheerily.

I hopped off the bed and went to the nurses' station hoping to see a stack of pancakes next to a pile of bacon and scrambled eggs. What I saw instead was a tray of sliced fruit and a bowl of bagels. That was okay too.

"Sorry the bagels aren't toasted," Luna said. "But at least there's some butter. We should eat it before it spoils."

I was the last to arrive. Kent, Olivia, and Jon were already eating. Tori seemed more interested in some papers she was reading. With everyone wearing scrubs, it looked like a doctor convention.

"You look a lot better," I said to Tori as I grabbed a bowl of sliced melon.

"I feel better, thanks to Luna."

"But you aren't healed," Luna cautioned. "You have to take it easy."

"Yeah, sure," Tori said unconvincingly. She had no intention of taking it easy; she was just getting back up to speed. "I figured it out," she said, holding up the papers. "It took four tries, but I think I got most of it."

"Most of what?" Kent asked with a mouth full of bagel.

"The message. From the radio. I listened to it four times, and with the notes that Jon took, I—"

"Whoa, wait!" Jon exclaimed. "You were messing with my radio?"

"Yes," was Tori's straightforward reply.

Jon was livid. "That's . . . that's not right. We've got to conserve the batteries. And . . . and . . . do you even know how to use it?"

"Yes."

Tori wasn't one for justifying anything she did. Or explaining herself.

"But . . . but it's not yours! Nobody authorized you to use it."

"The Air Force gave me the authorization to do whatever I damn well please when it killed everyone in Portland."

Tori was definitely back.

Jon looked ready to lose it but couldn't find the words to argue.

"It's all right, Jon," Luna said calmly. "Let's hear what she has to say."

Jon plopped back down in his chair with a huff.

"You listened four times?" I asked. "That means you were up all night."

"I caught sleep in between. Who cares? You have to hear this."

She looked through several sheets of papers that were loaded with scribbles.

"I'm guessing at some of it," she explained. "But between the notes that Jon took and then using a little logic, I think I pretty much know what it's about."

We all stopped eating and gave her our full attention.

Tori took a deep breath as if to calm down. She was actually nervous.

"It starts out with some kind of introduction that I didn't get," she began. "Something about making an *appeal*, or *appealing to all*. I can't tell exactly. But she goes on to say this: *We are the survivors. We have been bloodied, but not beaten. To all of those who have been attacked: Know that we will fight back. Join us. We will take you in and keep you safe.* Then she gives what I think are coordinates, but

I doubt if I got them exactly. *North thirty-six degrees. Twenty-six minutes, twenty seconds. West one hundred fourteen degrees. Thirty-one minutes, fifty-seven seconds.*"

"Might as well be in Greek," Olivia said, scoffing.

"Where is that?" Kent asked.

"No idea, but it would be easy enough to look up," Tori said.

"How?" Kent pressed obnoxiously. "No Internet, remember?"

"We could go to a library," I offered.

"Yeah, but . . ." Kent wanted to shoot me down but realized how stupid he sounded. "Is that it?" he asked Tori.

"No. It finishes with: *We will fight for our home. We will repel the invaders. We will have strength in numbers. The survivors will stand together. Do not hesitate.* She then says the coordinates again, and the message repeats."

Tori lowered the pages and said, "What do you think?"

"I think those are probably the coordinates for the gates of hell," Kent replied.

"Not funny," Olivia chastised.

"Sounds like a call for help from other survivors," I suggested.

"Or a call to arms," Tori shot back. "These could be people like us who got caught in the crossfire and want to fight back."

"Fight back?" Kent scoffed. "Against what? The United States Navy or the United States Air Force? Take your pick. One has their own tactical force that isn't afraid to kill anybody who gets in their way, and the other has weapons of mass destruction like nobody's ever seen before. You think a couple of people using a ham radio can fight that?"

Jon jumped up and ran out of the room.

"Jonathan?" Luna called.

He didn't stop.

"What's up with that?" Olivia asked.

"He doesn't want any part of this bull," Kent said. "Neither do I."

"What if it's not bull?" Tori asked. "What if this is our chance to connect with other people on our side?"

"Whoa, slow down, Lobster-Girl," Kent said. "You're jumping to a whole bunch of conclusions. As far as we know, the only place that got hit is little old Portland, Maine. You're making it sound like the whole world has gone nuts."

"Wake up, Kent," Tori scolded. "The population of an entire city was nearly wiped out. There was a major ocean battle that was bigger than anything since, what? World War II? If this really is a civil war with two branches of the military throwing everything they've got at each other, how can you believe it's only happening in our backyard?"

Kent jumped to his feet and shouted, "Because that's what I want to believe!"

He was breathing hard, and his fists were clenched. His outburst was more about fear than anger. When he spoke I wasn't sure if he was going to scream with rage or burst out crying.

"I don't want to think that the whole world just crumbled. For all we know that broadcast is being sent by somebody holed up right here in the Old Port who wants to rally the troops and board their lobster boats to strike back against Darth Vader. You want to join a revolution? That's what your father did, and look where it got him."

Tori stiffened.

"Ow," Olivia said, wincing.

"You didn't need to say that," I scolded.

"Or maybe I did," Kent argued. "I'm not saying we roll over and hide like scared rabbits, but before I join up with some vigilantes, I need to know a little bit more about what's going on."

"I can help with that," Jon announced.

He ran back into the ER carrying an oversized book.

"It's an almanac from the hospital library," he explained. "We can look up those coordinates."

Olivia said, "Nice. Why are the smart guys always the most obnoxious?"

Jon ignored her and opened the book on the counter. Luna held the lantern for him to see, and Tori gave him her notes. Jon checked the coordinates and thumbed through the oversized almanac, flipping through page after page of maps.

Kent stepped away and took a drink of water while Olivia rubbed his back to calm him down. She leaned forward and kissed him on the cheek while whispering something in his ear.

Seeing that gave me a twinge of . . . what? Jealousy? Not really. It was more about confusion. Olivia was playing both sides. She could still rely on me, but I was definitely going to keep my distance . . . and lock the door whenever I took a shower.

"Got it," Jon announced.

"So where did it come from, Chadwick?" Kent asked.

"There's no way of knowing. But I can tell you the place the message was calling the survivors to."

"Is it the Old Port?" Olivia asked hopefully.

"No, it's the middle of nowhere. I can't be exact because Tori wasn't sure if the numbers were correct, but even if they were a little off, they would still put the spot somewhere near here."

"Where's here?" I asked.

"Nevada."

"Nevada?" Olivia cried. "Like . . . way-out-west Nevada?"

She seemed totally shocked by the idea, as if Jon had said the message came from Neptune.

Jon shrugged. "That's what the coordinates say. Looks like it's in the desert."

I looked to Kent to see his reaction.

He was stunned.

I didn't feel so hot either.

I said, "So there's a call going out for survivors to join up . . . in the desert? In Nevada? Does that mean—"

"Yes," Tori said, cutting me off. "What else could it mean? The attack wasn't just on Portland."

"No!" Kent blurted out. "No way. You're going by a two-minute recording that you could barely understand to decide . . . what? That the entire United States was hit? We have no idea who even made that recording. For all we know it was SYLO! I'm still not buying it."

"I know," Tori said calmly, trying to be less dramatic. "I don't want to believe it either. I hope I'm wrong, obviously. There's only one way to find out."

"How?" I asked.

Tori looked at each one of us in turn and said, "We go to Nevada."

Olivia and Kent erupted.

"What? No! Are you crazy?"

I tried to be a little more reasonable.

"Are you serious, Tori?" I asked.

"We're looking for answers," she replied. "The plan is to go to Boston, but why? Because it's close? Who cares? We have a very real clue here. There are people reaching out. If we're going to drive, what's the difference if we drive for two hours or two days?"

"I'll go," Jon announced enthusiastically. "If the message is real, it could be our best chance of joining up with others like us."

Olivia said, "And what if it isn't real?"

Jon shrugged. "Then we see the country."

Tori added, "And we'll still do what we set out to do, which is to tell the world about what's really happening on Pemberwick Island. What's the difference if we do it in Boston or Cleveland or Nevada? The point is to get back to civilization."

"Unless civilization no longer exists," Jon cautioned.

"That's just crazy," Kent scoffed and stormed away from us.

"What do you think, Luna?" I asked. "Do you want to go to Boston or Nevada?"

"Neither," she replied quickly. "My place is right here."

"Portland is dead," Tori said. "You can't hide here."

"I'm not hiding," Luna said. "And Portland is not dead. You all are proof of that. There are other survivors. Eventually they'll find their way here, and when they do, they may need a doctor. I'm needed right here."

"What about your family?" Tori asked. "Do they live here?"

"In Portland I live alone. My family is in Osaka, Japan, and California. I have not heard from any of them since the attack, but that's no surprise. There is no way to communicate. But when they do make contact, I want to be where I am expected. So for many reasons, I am expected to be here and this is where I will stay. But, Jon, you should go with them."

"To where?" he asked. "Boston or Nevada?"

Luna sighed. "What you're looking for is life, but I can't say which is the better choice. I have no idea. My only concern is that you are all so young. I hate to think of you out on the road. Any road."

"You get no argument from me," Kent said. "I'd rather stay close to home."

"We'll vote," Tori declared. "Do we head west to Nevada? Or waste time by going south all the way to Boston? There are five of us, so there won't be a tie."

"How does *he* get a vote?" Kent said, pointing to Jon. "He hasn't been through what we have."

"This isn't about the past," Jon said with confidence. "You can't change the past. It's about what's going to happen next."

"This is absolutely about the past," Kent snarled. "We're trying to find out what really happened."

"And we'll learn that by going forward," Jon argued, undaunted.

"Forget it," Kent barked. "I'm going to Boston, with or without you guys."

"Okay, that's your vote," Tori said. "What about you, Olivia?"

Olivia looked to Kent and then to me.

"I want to go to Boston," she finally said. "If only because it gets me closer to New York. I want to believe that my mom is there."

Kent put his arm around her and kissed her on top of the head as if he owned her.

"Good girl," he said. "So I guess that means we split up."

"How do you figure that?" Tori asked.

"Obviously the rookie is going to vote with his girlfriend, so let's just call it now."

"All right," Tori said. "I guess that means we split up."

"Wait," I called out.

All eyes went to me.

I chose my words carefully because what I was about to say would set us on a course that would determine our futures and our friendships, for better or worse.

"I don't want to believe that the United States is in ruins," I began. "What we've seen here is bad enough. But the whole point of escaping from Pemberwick was to learn the truth and tell the world about what happened at home. That hasn't changed. We've come a long way, and we're still alive because we stuck together. Like it or not, we're all we've got."

Nobody took their eyes from me. Not even Kent.

"The worst thing we could do is split up."

"I agree," Tori interrupted. "Kent, it would be stupid for you and Olivia not to come with us and—"

"I think we should go to Boston," I declared.

"What?" Tori shouted, snapping a stunned look my way. "You're giving in to him just to keep us together?"

"No, because I think it would be a mistake to go to Nevada. At least right now. The longer we're on the road, out in the open, the better chance there is of being seen by one of those planes. I want to go to Boston because it's closer and I think we'll find out what we need to know there."

"What about fighting back?" Tori asked.

"If Boston is normal, we won't have to go to Nevada. If Boston looks like Portland, we'll rethink. It's not like it's that far out of the way. Let's hope we won't have to rethink."

Tori was angry. She had expected me to side with her.

"So what do you say, Lobster-Girl?" Kent said smugly. "You still going west with Chadwick?"

I took a threatening step toward Kent and said, "Her name is Tori. His name is Jon and my name is Tucker. Not Rook. Tucker."

Tori grabbed me by the shoulder and spun me around to face her.

"I don't need you to fight my battles," she snapped, livid. She turned on Kent and said, "This isn't a contest. You didn't win anything, so stop acting like it."

Kent held up his hands, pretending to show fear.

"Yes, ma'am. Wouldn't want to show you up."

He chuckled and took Olivia's arm to lead her away.

Olivia gave me an embarrassed smile and a shrug as if to say, "I know, he's a jerk."

Tori stuck a finger in my chest.

"This is on you," she said, barely able to control her anger. "If the people broadcasting that message are the only people left who can help us and we don't connect with them because we wasted time in the wrong city, Quinn died for nothing. He's gone, Tucker. So is my father, and I'll do anything to find out why they're dead. Can you say the same thing?"

She stormed off without waiting for an answer, leaving me standing there, rocked. Of all the hurtful things she could have said, that was the most devastating. Quinn's death was never far from my thoughts. I relived the moment again and again. It killed me that Tori would think I had forgotten about him. Though I truly believed it was critical that we stayed together, my decision meant that I was both part of a group . . . and very alone, for I had lost my closest ally.

What I didn't share with Tori, or anybody else, was that something else was driving me. Yes, I wanted to learn the truth about the war and tell the world about Pemberwick. I desperately held on to the hope that life would eventually return to normal so we could go home. But there was something else I needed. Something even more powerful.

I wanted revenge. Revenge for the destruction of my life, for Quinn's death, and for my family being torn apart. I wanted someone to suffer. But who? Who was to blame? Granger? He was dead. The enemy no longer had a face, but that didn't stop me from craving retribution against SYLO and everyone Granger had commanded.

I wanted to tell Tori that she was wrong and that I desperately wanted to know why we had lost our friends and family. I didn't, though, because I knew that wouldn't be enough. I needed someone to pay for what had happened. That was a dangerous road to travel, but it was a road I needed to be on. What I didn't want was for my vendetta to put anybody else at risk, which meant that at some point I would be on my own.

Until that time came, I would stay with the group, and I would do what I could to keep us together and safe, but I also had my own agenda.

I was going to get revenge.

Alone.

FIVE

We were about to step into the unknown.

When we escaped from Pemberwick Island, our destination had been Portland, a town that most of us were familiar with. Now we were faced with the reality of hitting the road to seek out places that would be strange and different even under normal circumstances.

We began with a clear mission but were now flying blind, reacting to events as they happened. I had the disturbing sense of being adrift. It was like our pasts had been erased. I had expected that my future would be spent on Pemberwick Island, working with my dad and one day taking over his landscaping business. That was now somebody else's life, somebody who no longer existed.

With that solemn thought in mind, we did the only thing that made sense to prepare for such a journey.

We went shopping.

Or maybe it should be called looting because we weren't going to pay for anything.

Jon knocked the first item off our list by choosing a car from the doctors' parking garage. Most were expensive and big. More importantly, the keys were in the ignition. There were five of us now, so we needed another row of seating as well as cargo space. Jon picked a big old Ford Explorer.

Once we had wheels, there was no reason to hang around the hospital, so we had to say our goodbyes to Luna. Her last medical treatment was to change Tori's dressing.

"Are you sure you won't come?" Tori asked.

"Positive," Luna replied with confidence. "Besides, I'm thinking you'll eventually be back this way. This is your home."

I didn't point out to her that we no longer had a home.

Luna removed the bandage and the cotton packing, then cleaned the wound and replaced it all with fresh bandages.

"It's healing nicely," Luna said. "Keep it clean, change the bandages as often as you can, and you'll be okay before you know it."

Tori leaned forward and hugged the doctor. For her, that was a dramatic statement. I'd only seen her show that kind of emotion with her father. It reminded me that Tori had now lost both of her parents. Her mother abandoned the family when she was young, and her father was killed by the SYLO attack on the rebel compound on Pemberwick. Tori was now an orphan.

Though my parents were still alive, I felt like an orphan myself. They had betrayed me and the people of Pemberwick by helping the SYLO invaders. I would never wish that they were dead, but in some ways that might have been easier to deal with.

"Keep listening to the broadcasts," Jon said. "You might get some new info."

"I will," Luna assured him. "You're a good friend, Jon. I'll miss you."

Jon wiped his eyes so we wouldn't see that he was tearing up.

"We gotta go," Kent said. "Who knows how long it'll take to get to Boston, and I don't want to roll in after dark."

We all shared hugs and hopeful words that we would meet again, then left Dr. Kayamori to man her lonely outpost.

The Explorer was parked outside of the emergency room. Jon went for the wheel, but Kent clamped a firm hand on his shoulder.

"I'm driving, Chadwick," he declared.

Jon pulled away from him angrily.

"I'm the one who found it," he argued.

"And that matters because . . . ?" Kent asked snottily.

Kent towered over him threateningly. Jon may have been older than Kent, but Kent must have outweighed him by fifty pounds.

"Fine," Jon said with reluctant resignation.

He went for the passenger side, but Olivia was already riding shotgun. He looked into the backseat, but Tori and I were already there. He had no choice but to squeeze past us into the third row.

"I hate riding back here," he complained. "Don't blame me if I puke."

Kent turned around and glared at him. "You do and I'll make you eat it."

"Just drive, Kent," I scolded.

"Sure. Where to?"

"Anywhere I can get some decent clothes," Olivia complained. "We look like we just escaped from prison."

She wasn't far from wrong. We were wearing the dark red scrubs that Luna had given us the night before.

"Target," I said. "We can find everything we need there."

Olivia sat bolt upright. "I will NOT wear clothes from Target!"

Kent squeezed her knee and said, "It won't matter. You'd look good in anything."

Tori rolled her eyes and said, "Okay, Jon, you can puke now."

"Just go with it, Olivia, okay?" I said. "We can't go driving around looking for clothes."

Olivia bit her lip and pouted. "Fine."

With that rocky start, we were under way.

Tori didn't say a word to me. She didn't even look my way. I wanted to think it was because she was as nervous as I was. (I kept looking to the sky in case a dark plane decided to swoop in.) But I knew the real reason. She was pissed. At me. She expected me to back her up in her decision to head straight for Nevada, and it burned her that I didn't. It took a lot to earn Tori's trust. My fear was that with one decision I had lost it and would have to start from scratch to get it back.

The shopping malls were a few miles from downtown. At first there didn't seem to be anything unusual happening there. The parking lots were full of cars, shopping carts were scattered every-where, and colorful flags whipped in the wind, promising big savings on back-to-school supplies. Everything was normal . . .

. . . except there were no people.

"It's just so eerie," Olivia said in awe.

Kent parked directly in front of the big Target store. There was no reason to look for an official space.

"Everybody get something to wear," I said. "Remember, it's warm now but that won't last. Think of it like going camping."

Olivia gave me a stern look. "I have never, not once, gone camping."

"What about food?" Jon asked.

"No room," I said. "We'll pick it up on the road as we go."

"I guess you thought this through," Kent said.

"Just using common sense," I replied and got out of the car.

Tori got out and strode for the store without a word. Olivia was right behind her. She actually had a little skip in her step as if excited about going shopping, even if it had to be at, God forbid, Target. She may not have been a camper, but I'd lay money on the fact that she was a shopper.

"Was Tori serious about going to Nevada?" Kent asked.

"I am," Jon answered.

"I don't care about you," Kent snapped.

"Yeah, she was serious," I said.

"Then she's going on her own," Kent said with a sneer.

"Look," I said, "if Boston looks like Portland, we've got to do whatever we can to find other people."

Kent actually looked as though he was giving that some thought.

"Is it possible?" he asked. "I mean, could other cities really have been hit?"

"Yes," Jon said.

"I'm not asking you!" Kent barked.

"I don't know," I answered. "But it's possible. How could you think it isn't?"

Kent shook his head sadly. "I don't. I just don't want to believe it."

"If we decide to go to Nevada," I added, "you're coming. Olivia too. We have to stay together."

"I told you, you're not in charge," Kent said, looking me square in the eye with defiance.

I held his gaze and said, "If you want to go off on your own, that's your call. But Olivia needs all the friends she can get. Do what you want, but she stays with us."

We sat there staring at one another as if it were a test of wills. Kent may have been two years older than me, but after what we'd been through, that no longer mattered.

"She can do whatever she wants," he said abruptly.

"Good answer," I said and got out of the car to head for the store.

The manual doors were open, and the store was ours. The lights were out, but it was midday and there was enough light coming in through the big windows up front to provide low, gray light throughout the store.

I grabbed a shopping cart and went straight for the men's clothes area, where I grabbed underwear and socks. I also found a pair of jeans and two T-shirts, one short sleeved and one long. There wouldn't be room for a whole bunch of heavy clothes, so I decided to go with thin layers. I also grabbed a zippered hoodie to replace my old dirty model. The first one I picked up was bright blue, but I thought better of it and grabbed a black one. I didn't want to be any more of a target than I already was.

Next stop was the shoe section, where I picked out a pair of light cross-trainers. I started for the changing room to try everything on, but stopped. What was the point? Nobody was around. I took off my scrubs right there in the aisle and put on the new clothes.

From there I went to the luggage area and picked out five identical soft gym bags, one for each of us. I tried to imagine what they would look like full and picked a size that I figured would fit into the back of the Explorer. I took one for myself and put in an extra pair of socks and underwear.

The pharmacy was next. I grabbed Tylenol, a toothbrush, toothpaste, hand sanitizer, disposable shaving razors, and deodorant. In the camping department I grabbed a small flashlight, a camp lantern, and batteries for both. I also picked out a headlamp, a couple of solar blankets, waterproof matches, and a rain poncho. I glanced at all the cooking gear but figured that food would have to be eaten raw or out of a can. I grabbed a pocketknife and made sure that it had a can opener built in. Finally, I picked out a heavy-duty sport watch. Normally I used my cell phone to check the time, but the battery had long since died. It had become a useless piece of junk that I reluctantly had to trash.

I packed all of the gear into one of the gym bags and found that I had plenty of room left over. With my shopping done, I wheeled my cart to the cash registers at the front of the store.

Kent and Jon were already there. Kent had on a red short-sleeved shirt, khakis, and a light green sweater, looking every bit like the preppie that he was with his bleached-blond hair and deep tan.

Jon, on the other hand, still had on his scrubs.

"Don't you want new clothes?" I asked.

"I like these," he replied with a shrug. "Who cares what I look like?"

Certainly not him.

I tossed them each a duffel bag and watched as they filled them with the items from their carts. They had grabbed pretty much the same things that I had, except that Kent also had aftershave and mouthwash. Jon had pads of writing paper and a box of pens. I guess you can tell a lot about somebody by the stuff they think is essential for survival.

Tori arrived next, wheeling a cart with more clothes than I would have liked to see, but I figured they'd fit in the bag. She wore new jeans as well, and an oversized dark green sweater. It looked big on her, but it must have been more comfortable with her injury. I had to smile when I saw that she was wearing a new, clean University of Southern Maine baseball cap. She had pulled back her long, dark, wavy hair and tied it into a ponytail that she put through the back of the cap. It's how I remembered her from home. It made me feel as though we had gotten back to normal, at least in some small way.

"Do you want to go to USM?" I asked.

"No," was her curt reply.

I didn't press.

I gave Tori a bag, and she filled it with her extra clothes, along with various girl-specific items that I didn't examine too closely. She also had some extra gauze pads, cotton, adhesive tape, and alcohol. It was a grim reminder that she wasn't yet whole. Her one unique item was a ten-foot length of flexible rubber hose.

"What's that for?" Kent asked.

"Gas," she replied. "We can use this to syphon it from other cars."

It was probably the most practical thing that any of us had gotten.

Olivia arrived wearing short-shorts, a tank top, and flip-flops. That was the good news. She was also wheeling a shopping cart overflowing with clothes.

"I'm surprised," she said happily. "I had no idea that Target carried such a variety of really nice things!"

The four of us stood there, staring at her blankly.

"What?" she asked, genuinely confused.

I held up the final duffel bag.

"Whatever fits in here comes with us," I said. "Whatever doesn't, stays."

Olivia glared at the bag as if she were a vampire and I was holding a crucifix.

"That does not work for me," she said, shaking her head petulantly.

"Doesn't matter," Jon said with a superior tone. "There's only so much room in the car."

"Then . . . then . . . we'll strap a bag on top!" she declared.

I was going to argue with her but decided it wasn't worth it.

"She's right," I said. "Get a big bag, Olivia. We'll strap it to the roof rack."

"Seriously?" Tori said, peeved.

"Why not?" I said. "You can do the same thing if you want."

"What I want is to get going," she snapped at me. "I'll get some straps for her."

"Thank you," I said.

"Yeah, thanks, Tori!" Olivia said.

Tori ignored her.

Ten minutes later we had Olivia's oversized duffel strapped securely to the roof and four smaller bags stowed in back. It was a strange feeling to have walked out of the store without paying. I felt as though we were doing something wrong, but it wasn't like anybody cared.

"Can we get on the road now?" Kent said while checking the last strap.

"We have to make one more stop," Tori announced.

"Where?" Kent asked, peeved.

"We need guns," was her simple answer.

There was a moment of stunned silence.

"We do?" Olivia finally said in a very small voice.

"We have to defend ourselves," Tori responded quickly.

"You don't really think a gun could shoot down one of those planes," I said, incredulous.

"It's not about the planes," Tori answered without looking at me. "I'm worried about who we'll run into along the way."

"She's right," Kent said. "That dude from the Old Port was ready to blow our heads off."

"But . . . guns?" Olivia said, sounding squeamish. "I've never even picked up a gun."

"I have," was Tori's matter-of-fact answer.

I remembered how she had held Quinn and me back with a shotgun while protecting her house, right after her father had been arrested by SYLO. Between that and the way she took a SYLO soldier out with a Taser, I was confident that Tori knew how to handle a gun.

"I hate to admit it, but I agree with Tori," I said.

"Why?" Tori snapped at me defensively. "Is it so hard to believe that I could be right about something?"

She was still pissed at me.

"No," I said calmly. "Because you may know about guns, but the rest of us don't. I don't want innocent people getting shot . . . like me."

"I'm with her," Kent said. "I'd feel better if I had a weapon."

"You sound a little too enthusiastic," I said to him. "We aren't playing here. Guns kill people."

"Guns don't kill people," Tori said. "People kill people."

"People with guns kill people," I said. "But you're right. We have to be able to protect ourselves."

We drove to the shop where Tori's father bought his guns. Other than her giving directions, it was a quiet drive. I'm not sure if that was because we were on our way to pick up lethal weapons, or because of the tension between Tori and me. She didn't have to like me, or trust me, but I didn't want her to be carrying around so much anger . . . especially if she was also going to be carrying around a loaded gun.

She directed us to a small shop that carried all sorts of sportsman gear. Unlike the other places we had entered, its front door was locked.

"Guess we're out of luck," Kent said.

Tori picked up a rock the size of a bowling ball and heaved it through the glass of the front door. The rest of us watched, dumbfounded.

Jon said, "Somehow this makes it seem more like looting."

Tori reached inside the hole, unlocked the door, and we were in.

It was sportsman heaven. There were displays of every kind of archer's bow you could imagine, camouflage hunting gear, an entire wall of fishing rods and reels, and guns. Lots of guns. One whole wall was taken up by rifles displayed on racks.

Kent ran straight for the weapons. He picked one up and set his sights on a stuffed deer on the far side of the store.

"Say your prayers, Bambi," he declared, laughing.

"Stop!" Tori screamed.

Kent lowered the rifle and looked at her.

"What?" he asked, sounding genuinely clueless.

"These aren't toys," she scolded. "Put it down."

She was dead serious, and Kent knew it. He didn't argue, and sheepishly put the rifle back on its rack.

"I hope this isn't a bad idea," Olivia said nervously.

Tori went for the counter where the handguns were stored. She seemed to know what she was looking for, so I didn't bother asking. Instead, I looked around the store for anything else we might need. I spotted walkie-talkies. If we got separated we would need to stay in contact, so I figured they might come in handy. Better still, I found a solar-powered charger that we could use to keep the batteries at full power.

"Over here," Tori called.

We all joined her.

On the counter were two identical black handguns.

"These are Glock 17s," she said. "Policemen use them."

She picked up one of the guns and expertly pulled the slide back to examine the chamber.

"I'm making sure there are no rounds in there," she explained.

"Bullets," I said. "Calling them 'rounds' makes it seem less . . . lethal."

She ignored me and continued. "It fires a nine-millimeter . . . bullet." She pulled out the clip from the grip and showed it to us. "This holds seventeen . . . bullets."

"The more, the merrier," Kent said.

His eyes were wide as he stared at the gun like a kid who couldn't wait to get his hands on a new Christmas toy.

Tori grabbed several boxes of ammunition from a shelf and placed them on the counter.

"I'll load two magazines but only put one in a gun. We'll keep the loaded weapon in the glove compartment. The other we'll store in the back cargo area, unloaded, with the clip separate. When we get the chance, I'll teach you all how to shoot."

Kent picked up one of the guns and felt its weight.

"What's so hard?" he asked. "You point this end and *bang!*"

He held the gun loosely and pretended to shoot.

Tori grabbed his gun hand and held it firmly.

"If you shoot like that you'll miss, and the recoil would probably kick the gun out of your hand."

"How do you know so much about guns?" Kent asked.

"My father," Tori said as she let Kent loose and started loading bullets into the magazine. "We had to protect our property. Our lobster boats. He wanted me to be totally safe with the weapons in the house, so he taught me well."

I saw the hint of a tear growing in Tori's eye, and her voice cracked. It felt like a couple of lifetimes since her father was gunned down by SYLO, but it was only the day before. She wiped her eye quickly and cleared her throat, as if embarrassed to have shown her emotions.

"You a good shot?" Kent asked.

"That's irrelevant," she replied, back in control. "These guns are only accurate to ten yards, tops. Even then you have to be good to hit anything. These are for our protection. We're not going to be playing James Bond. Hopefully we won't need them, but if we do, we'll have them."

"They still make me nervous," Olivia said.

"Not me," Jon said. "I'm feeling safer already."

"Until I check you out, nobody touches these but me," Tori declared. "Understand?"

She looked at each of us in turn. Everyone nodded, including Kent.

"Now we can go," she said. "Jon, take the ammunition."

She swooped up the guns and headed for the door.

Jon obediently grabbed the boxes of bullets.

I had mixed feelings about having the guns. I could see that we might need them for protection. That made all sorts of sense . . . as long as somebody didn't do something stupid and shoot one of us in the foot. Or worse.

When we got to the car, Tori put the second gun and the ammunition in the rear compartment near the spare tire. She kept one box of ammunition and put it in the glove box up front. She then did a quick check of the gun to make sure there was no bullet in the firing chamber. Satisfied that it was safe, she put it into the glove compartment and slammed it shut.

Tori was now riding shotgun, so to speak.

Olivia opened her mouth, ready to fight for her spot in the car, but thought better of it. With a huff, she got in the backseat next to me.

"I can reach the gun back here if you need it!" Jon announced from the third row.

Nobody responded.

Kent fired up the engine, then turned to face us.

"Are we ready now?" he asked.

"Let's go to Boston," I said.

Kent hit the gas, and we were finally on our way.

SIX

It took two hours to drive from Portland to Boston.

It felt like two days.

We were on edge the whole way because none of us knew what we would find there. Or *not* find. Would the city be surrounded by the military to protect it from attack? Which military would that be? Would SYLO have surrounded Boston like they did Pemberwick Island? Or would the Air Force and their killer planes be in control?

Would Boston even be there?

For the entire trip, we constantly stole quick, nervous glances to the sky for fear that an Air Force plane would come swooping in after us, but none appeared. Was their mission complete? Or had they moved on to another target?

I kept staring at the glove compartment, knowing a gun was inside. I'm not a wuss or anything. We needed to protect ourselves, but the idea of having a weapon so close that could easily take a life was disturbing. I know how dumb that sounds. After all we'd been through, it didn't make sense that I should be so obsessed with a pistol that held seventeen bullets, but I was. I can't honestly say whether I was afraid of the gun or worried that I wouldn't have the guts to use it.

I leaned forward between the two front seats, turned on the radio, and scanned the frequencies. There was nothing to hear but a whole lot of static.

Olivia gave me a weak smile and a shrug.

"It was worth a try," she said sympathetically.

She rubbed my arm as if to console me. I didn't mind, until I saw that Kent was staring at us in the rearview mirror. I quickly twisted away from her without making it seem as though I was twisting away from her.

After we had driven for over an hour, Kent asked, "Should I say it first?"

I knew what he meant. We all did.

The deadly Air Force storm hadn't stopped in Portland.

"It's the exact same," Olivia said, hardly above a whisper.

The entire length of the highway looked like the stretch leading into Portland. Abandoned cars were everywhere, with far more wrecks than we saw in Maine. Vehicles had driven into ditches, slammed into guardrails, flipped into the medians, and crashed into each other. It felt as though we were driving through an auto graveyard.

Or an actual graveyard.

Yet there wasn't a single person to be seen.

"No jet fighter wrecks," Kent pointed out. "Or bomb craters. Maybe there wasn't a battle here."

"Well, something happened," Olivia said. "I mean . . . look."

It was grim enough that the population of Portland had been

wiped out. Boston had ten times more people. When you added in the suburbs that stretched from Maine to Massachusetts, the possibility of what we were headed toward was too much to comprehend.

Olivia said it best without saying a word.

She started to cry.

"There have to be survivors," Tori said, numb. "An entire population can't just be . . . erased."

"There will be," I said hopefully. "Just like in Portland."

"We'll find them," Jon said, doing his best to sound positive.

We were all trying to think practically. It was the only way to keep from going totally out of our minds. I did my best to focus on the present because to think of the big picture was overwhelming. None of us said the obvious, but I knew we were thinking it: If Boston had been attacked by the black Air Force planes and another population center had been obliterated, what did that mean for the rest of the country?

Or the world?

We drove on for several more minutes, moving closer to Boston and deeper into the desolate horror. Kent had to swerve a few times to steer clear of cars that were stopped dead on the interstate. When we passed through the town of South Lynnfield, we were hit with a new grim vision.

"Is that what I think it is?" Kent asked with trepidation.

Ahead of us was a structure that at first appeared to be a partially collapsed building. As we drove closer, the truth became clear in the form of a logo: Delta Airlines.

"Oh no," Tori said with a gasp.

It was the wreckage of a commercial jetliner that had crashed into a strip mall. The tail was kicked up into the air, and the fuselage had been broken in two. The entire wreck was scorched black from a fire that had long since burned out. The only thing missing were bodies.

As we moved closer to the city, we passed no fewer than ten similar burned-out plane wrecks.

"It's like they just dropped out of the sky," I said, hardly believing it could be possible.

"Boston's going to be empty," Olivia said, sounding shakier than Tori. "We're not going to find anybody there to help us."

"I don't understand," Tori said, her voice quivering with emotion. "What kind of war is this? How can you invade a city, wipe out everyone, and then just . . . leave? What's the point? It's insanity!"

"I knew we should have gone to Nevada," Jon said.

Tori shot me a sideways look. I didn't return it.

"Shut up!" Kent shouted. "Just shut up! Everybody. I gotta think."

"Let's keep it together," I said, trying to sound calmer than I felt. "The entire population of Boston can't be wiped out. We'll find people."

"What about the plan to tell the world about Pemberwick?" Tori said.

"I doubt if that matters anymore," I said. "I think the rest of the world knows plenty. Compared to what we're seeing, our little island is irrelevant."

"Not to me it isn't," Kent snapped.

"Yeah, well, change your thinking," I said. "I hate to say this, but we're in survival mode now. I want answers as much as everybody else, but I'm more worried about staying alive. We need to find some other survivors. There's safety in numbers."

"Tell that to the people of Boston," Tori said.

We drove on in silence, skirting abandoned cars and burned-out jetliners. As we approached the city, I scanned the skyline for any buildings that might be missing, but I didn't know Boston well enough to pick any out.

As we drove across the Tobin Bridge that spanned the Charles River and led to downtown, I looked down to see a jetliner floating with its tail barely above water.

"Boston's dead," Olivia said softly and with finality.

Nobody argued.

Kent turned south on Storrow Drive, which took us along the Charles. Looking left to the city, we saw no signs of life. Looking right to the Charles, we spotted two more half-submerged plane wrecks and many small boats drifting free.

"It's beyond a nightmare," Tori whispered.

"I don't think anybody died in those crashes," I said, thinking out loud.

"Impossible," Kent snapped back.

"I'm not saying they're not dead, I just don't think they died in the crashes. None of those empty cars had their doors open. And we haven't seen a single body. Not one."

"Except for the Navy pilot outside of Portland," Kent pointed out.

"He died in the dogfight," I said. "That's different. I don't think there was a battle here. I think people were obliterated by the weapon the Air Force has, just like in Portland. How else could so many people have disappeared without a trace? Same with the airliners."

"Then why didn't the cars disappear along with them?" Tori asked. "Like the buildings in Portland? Or Quinn on the boat or—"

She didn't finish the sentence. The memory was too raw.

"That guy Whittle in the Old Port said it," I offered. "Sometimes the buildings disappeared, other times the light reached inside and took the people without touching the buildings. Who's to say what that weapon can do? Maybe it can target organic life-forms and leave structures intact . . . unless they choose to obliterate them."

"We haven't seen any animals," Jon pointed out. "You'd think there'd be a stray dog or cat lurking around."

"It's horrible," Tori said. "You're talking about a weapon that can sweep across cities and kill thousands of people every second."

"Yeah, I guess I am," I said. "When we saw Portland lighting up that night, it wasn't a battle, it was a mass execution."

"Jeez," Kent said, stunned.

"There wasn't any sound," Tori said, remembering. "No explosions. No crashes. No sirens or alarms. We would have heard that over the ocean."

"It was probably over in minutes," I said solemnly.

Jon added, "Dr. Kayamori and I survived because we were down in the bowels of the hospital where that weapon couldn't reach us."

"Which means there have to be other survivors who were protected the same way," I declared. "We're not going to be totally alone."

"I can't believe this," Tori said, stunned. "We're talking about the United States Air Force systematically wiping out the populations of two major cities."

"Maybe my idea isn't so far-fetched," Kent said. "This really could be an alien invasion."

"Aliens that put Air Force logos on their planes?" I asked, incredulous.

"Who cares what kind of logos they have! Maybe they use the same logo on the planet Nimnac! I've never heard of any weapon that can do this. It makes nukes seem like BB guns."

"I'm sorry. I can't believe that we've been invaded by creatures from another planet," I said adamantly.

"I can't believe *any* of this!" Kent bellowed. "But we're looking at the possible annihilation of the human race. There, I said it. Portland's been wiped out. Boston doesn't look any better. We haven't had communication with the rest of the world in weeks. For all we know, those planes hit every city in the country. In the *world*. What makes more sense? That our own military wiped out the earth's population, or that it's somebody from another world?"

"The entire population hasn't been wiped out," Tori said. "There's SYLO."

"Yeah, until tonight, when those planes show up again and finish off whatever's left of those Navy ships . . . and Pemberwick Island."

"Stop!" Olivia shouted, in tears. "This is horrible!"

"That's one word for it," Kent said. "It's gonna be dark soon. I don't want to be driving around when those planes fire up their ray guns again."

"We should find a place to spend the night," I said.

Kent turned off of Storrow Drive near Fenway Park. Fenway is the greatest ballpark in the majors. At least that's what my father always said, and I had to agree. We'd been to many games there, mostly against the Yankees and mostly to see the Sox get their butts whipped, but that didn't make the park any less special.

It was late September. Playoff time. Fenway should have been rocking. Instead, it was dead quiet and empty, more proof of the horror that had become our new lives. Kent drove us right up to the familiar structure. There were no other cars or vending carts to stop us. Colorful Red Sox banners fluttered in the breeze, a cruel reminder that this was a place where people came for fun. Now it was an empty shell in a city of the dead.

Kent said, "Maybe the Sox were safe deep down in the locker room when—WHOA!"

He jammed on the brakes, and we came to an abrupt stop.

Twenty yards ahead of us, hovering a few feet above the roadway, was a black Air Force plane. It was like we had rounded the bend in a wooded trail and came upon a snake that was coiled and ready to strike.

The moment was frozen in time.

We sat there like two gunslingers, each waiting for the other to twitch. The music of the plane's engines was faint, but I heard it.

"What do I do?" Kent asked with a strained, terrified whisper.

I looked around quickly, hoping to see an escape route, or at least some protection to shield us from the plane. There was nothing.

Tori slowly moved her hand forward and opened the glove compartment.

"You're dreaming," Kent cautioned.

"You have a better idea?" Tori asked.

While looking straight ahead at the plane, Tori eased the gun out and cocked a bullet into the chamber.

"Open the sunroof," she commanded.

"You can't be serious," Olivia cried.

"Open the sunroof," Tori repeated through gritted teeth.

Kent followed orders. He hit the button on the dash and the sunroof slid open while Tori unlocked her seat belt.

"I'm going to stand up and start shooting," Tori said.

"No!" Jon cried. "You'll get us killed!"

"If I'm going to die," Tori said without looking back at him, "I'm going to do some damage first. Kent, when I start firing, get us the hell out of here."

I wanted to stop her but didn't know what else we could do.

Kent tightened his grip on the wheel.

Olivia whimpered with fear.

Jon dropped down to the floor.

Tori slipped out of her seat belt and made a move to stand up . . .

. . . as the music from the black plane grew louder. It was powering up its engines.

Slowly, it began to float toward us.

"Too late!" Kent yelled.

He threw the Explorer into reverse and jammed his foot on the gas.

"No!" Tori screamed and fell back into her seat with a grunt of pain.

I pushed Olivia down to the floor, for whatever good that would do.

Kent was twisted around backward, a wild look in his eyes, as he fought to stay in control of the SUV.

"Is it coming?" he shouted.

"It's rising higher," I replied. "And closing."

"Damn!" Kent bellowed. "Hang on!"

He spun the wheel, and the SUV whipped around so quickly I feared we would flip. We crashed into a couple of garbage cans and narrowly missed hitting a cement light pole, but Kent stayed in control and got us turned in the other direction.

"We can't outrun that thing," I warned.

"We can try," Kent shot back.

I turned to see that the black plane had lifted even higher off the ground and was looming closer. In seconds it would be directly over us.

"Find an alley," I screamed. "Anything to keep it off of us."

"You say that like I'm not already trying!" Kent yelled back.

Tori made a move toward the sunroof again.

"Sit down!" I shouted.

I grabbed her belt and yanked her back into the seat.

She glared at me but stayed put.

"We're reaching the end of the stadium. When I make the turn, hang on," Kent commanded. "I'm going to floor it and—whoa!"

When he turned the corner onto Brookline Avenue, we were faced with a dozen cop cars with flashing lights headed our way.

"What?" Kent screamed.

I thought for sure there would be a head-on collision. Kent

slammed the brakes. The seat belts held us all in our seats, except for Tori. She flew forward and hit the dashboard. I heard her squeal as she hit—and I hoped that the gun wouldn't accidently go off.

The cars all hit their sirens, joining together in a steady, aggressive wail that would have been annoying if it weren't so welcome.

"What's happening?" Olivia asked, stunned.

"I think the cavalry just arrived," I replied.

"They're crazy," Jon shouted. "They'll be blown apart."

The group of screaming cars split apart and passed us on either side.

We all turned quickly to see them chase after the black plane that was now headed in the opposite direction and gaining altitude. It was like seeing a black fox being chased off by a pack of hungry dogs. Only in this case, the fox had lethal teeth that could easily tear the hounds apart.

"I don't get it," Jon said, stunned.

"What is it afraid of?" I added. "It's not like the cops can shoot it out of the sky."

"Or maybe they can," Tori sniffed.

The black plane banked sharply to the left and accelerated, rising into the sky. Seconds later, it was out of sight.

The five of us stared after it, not entirely sure of what we had seen.

"What just happened?" I said, dumbfounded. "I'm not complaining, I just don't get it."

The cop cars had broken off their pursuit and were headed back our way. Their flashing lights were dark, their sirens silent. One car was out in front; the others drove behind in threes. We watched as the lead car came to within ten yards of our rear bumper and stopped.

"Put the gun away," I ordered Tori.

I saw her eyes flare with defiance, but she opened the glove compartment and threw it inside.

I pushed open my door, got out, and walked to the rear of our car. The others followed directly after and stood behind me.

The sun reflected off all of the car windows, so I couldn't see who was inside any of them. We stood that way for a solid ten seconds. I was beginning to wonder if we had found yet another enemy when the driver's door opened on the lead car.

Out stepped a burly guy who looked more like a linebacker than a cop. He was tall with a heavy, dark beard and wore jeans and an "Ortiz" Red Sox jersey. He rounded his car and stood in front of it with his arms folded, watching us.

The other car doors opened, and several more people came out, none of whom looked like cops. There were a few women, but most were men. They were all dressed in street clothes, some in business suits, others in jeans. They all looked to be around my dad's age, or younger.

"You kids are lucky we came along," the lead guy finally said.

"We are," I called back. "I can't believe you scared that plane off. I mean, it could have blown you all away."

"It could have. Those things pack a wallop. But they're fragile. A couple of rifle shots and they drop like a brick. We've tangled before. They know better than to stand up against a posse that's armed for bear."

"Who *are* you?" Tori asked. "You're not cops."

The lead guy looked back to the others. They all laughed as if Tori had just said something very cute, or very stupid.

"We're the closest thing to cops that's left around here," the big guy said. "Who are *you*?"

"We just drove down from Portland," I answered. "But we're from Pemberwick Island."

On hearing the words "Pemberwick Island," they all tensed up.

"There's no virus there, if that's what you're worried about," Tori said.

"No," the guy replied. "We never thought there was. It's just a little surprising to see folks who made it this far. And kids, no less."

"So who are you?" Kent asked.

"You're looking at the last survivors of Boston, Mass.," he answered. "Welcome to Bean Town. Or what's left of it."

SEVEN

"**M**y name's Chris," the big guy said, holding out his hand to shake. "Chris Campbell."

I shook his hand and said, "Tucker Pierce. This is Tori Sleeper, Olivia Kinsey, Kent Berringer, and Jon, uh, what was your last name again, Jon?"

"Purcell. Jon Purcell."

"Welcome," Chris said. "Though I guess that's an odd thing to say. There's nothing welcoming about Boston anymore."

Chris seemed friendly enough, though I wouldn't challenge him to a fight. He had biceps like hams that strained his jersey. He didn't have a trace of a Boston accent—which was strange, considering he was wearing a Sox jersey.

He motioned to the others behind him and added, "You'll meet the rest of my crew soon enough. Where are your parents?"

None of us answered.

"Never mind," Chris said quickly, picking up on the fact that he had touched on a sore subject. "We've all got stories."

"How did you guys survive the attack?" Tori asked.

"Different ways," Chris said. "Bottom line is, we were all deep underground when those bastards hit. I work for Mass Electric. I was working below the Prudential Center when the power went out." He chuckled and added, "I was afraid it was something I did. Thought I was gonna catch hell. Took me two hours to get back to street level, and when I did . . ."

He didn't have to describe what he found.

"Is this it?" Olivia asked. "Are you really the only survivors?"

"Nah, we're just the cowboys."

"Cowboys?" Jon said.

"We got tired of sitting on our butts and boohooing, so we grabbed these cop cars. During the day we sweep the city, looking for other survivors. A lot of people made it, thank God. We round 'em up and bring 'em all together. Like cowboys."

"Yippee ki-yay," Kent said sarcastically.

"Hey," Chris shot back. "It's a good thing. We've all lost family and friends. We gotta take care of each other."

"Sorry," Kent said, chastened.

"Don't worry about it. Gotta keep a sense of humor, right?"

"Do you have any idea why it happened?" I asked.

"No clue," Chris replied. "One minute everything was fine, the next minute the city got swarmed by these flying Darth Vaders."

"'Darth Vader' is right," Kent chimed in. "We think they came from another planet."

"That's just one theory," I said quickly. "We have no idea where they came from, except that they have United States Air Force logos."

Chris was visibly shaken by that. He looked back at his other "cowboys," who looked equally stunned.

"How do you know that?" he asked.

"One crashed in Portland," I replied. "We saw the wreck."

"Seriously?" Chris asked, his excitement growing. "You got a close-up look at one of them bastards?"

"We saw a whole lot that you probably didn't," Tori said.

"Well, then you gotta tell us," Chris replied enthusiastically. "Not knowing what's going on makes it that much worse. Though I guess things can't get much worse than Armageddon."

Armageddon. It was the first time I'd heard that word. Was it possible? Was this the beginning of the end of the world?

We were ready to tell them what had happened on Pemberwick Island, but Chris asked us to wait until we got back to a place he called "the Hall." It was the spot where the Boston survivors were congregating. One of the cowboys went with Kent and Tori in the Explorer. There was no way Tori was going to be separated from her guns. Olivia glued herself to me. There was no way *she* was going to be separated from someone she trusted. Kent started to protest, but Olivia hurried me away before he could say a word.

I really wished she wasn't playing this game, whatever game it was. I didn't need trouble with Kent.

Jon went on his own with one of the other cowboys.

Olivia and I walked toward Chris's police car. Before we got in the back, I glanced at Tori and Kent. As they walked together, Kent put his arm around her like he was being protective. At least I think that's what it was about. Tori didn't shrug him off. I have to admit, I felt a twinge of jealousy, though I had no right to feel that way. We had been thrown together under dire circumstances and had a connection, but that didn't mean we were, like . . . together. She could let anybody put his arm around her while she leaned in close and put her head on his shoulder . . . which is what she did. It was none of my business.

Then again, I thought Kent was all about Olivia. What was *his* deal?

I decided that we had a bigger drama going on and stopped staring at them . . . as he brushed Tori's hair out of her eyes and gently helped her into the back of the Explorer.

Olivia had her arm draped through mine, and the length of her body pressed against my side like wallpaper. She was scared and needed any kind of security she could find. I didn't mind, especially after what I saw between Kent and Tori.

Everyone else loaded up, and as if on cue, the cars took off— but in different directions. In seconds we were moving along the deserted streets of Boston.

"I thought we were all going to the same place?" Olivia said.

"We try not to travel in groups," Chris replied. "You never know when one of them planes will show up. Right after the attack they'd sweep through the city looking for strays, but that's happening less and less. The plane that was after you was the first one I've seen in days. I think they did what they came to do, and now they're done with us."

I thought of the plane that had attacked us in Portland. Was that what it was doing? Searching for strays? With their evil mission complete, would they now leave us alone?

"How many survivors are there?" I asked.

"Hard to tell because they come and go. At any one time there might be about a hundred at the Hall. But there are plenty more out there, scared and hiding. We find 'em every day."

"What exactly is the Hall?" I asked.

"It's like a refugee camp," Chris explained. "There's food and a place to sleep and even some doctors. We pretty much take care of one another."

"If it's so great, why would anybody leave?" Olivia asked.

"Different reasons. Some go looking for loved ones. Others don't want to be in a large group. They're afraid we're sitting ducks. For me, I'd rather be with people. If I'm going to die, I don't want to be alone."

"Do you think the planes hit other cities?" I asked.

Chris gave me a quick sideways look and said, "Don't you? What happened up in Portland?"

"Same thing," I replied.

"There you go. I don't know who those devils are, but they seem to have only one goal, and that's to wipe us out."

That put an end to the conversation.

Every time I tried to imagine the wider implications of what was happening, I was hit with a gut-twisting sense of sadness and dread. How many people had been killed? Hundreds of thousands? Millions? Billions? It was too staggering a concept to comprehend. I found that it was better to focus on the here and now as opposed to letting my mind wander to the big picture. Thinking too far ahead was like looking into a dark hole . . . with a black plane inside, lying in wait.

It had only been a week or so since the attack, but downtown Boston was already showing small signs of disuse. Garbage blew along the sidewalks and collected along the curbs. Broken glass was everywhere, some from smashed windows and some from shattered streetlights. Of course there were plenty of abandoned cars. Many had crashed into buildings or had blown through glass storefront windows. The once busy city was quiet. There was no noise at all, not even from the cooing of pigeons. The only sound came from the wind that blew through the abandoned urban canyons.

I was beginning to accept that this was the new normal. I hate to admit that because it meant I was willing to accept an unfathomable future, but what choice did I have? At least it meant that I could move forward and not crawl up into a ball, wanting to die. That's saying something. I think.

Chris pulled into a parking lot and announced, "We're here."

Olivia and I looked around and had the same thought: "Where's here?"

We were in a nondescript section of the city with no hint of survivors.

"We've still got a short walk," Chris replied. "Like I said, we try to stay spread out. I'm not sure what good it does, but at least it makes us feel like we're taking a little control."

He led us along the sidewalk for a few blocks until we made the turn into an open park, where our question was answered.

"The Hall" turned out to be Faneuil Hall. I'd visited the place with my parents and knew a little bit of its history. The thumbnail description is that there were three three-story brick buildings that dated back to colonial times. Two of them ran parallel to each other and had to be at least a couple of blocks long. Faneuil Hall was originally a meeting place where speeches were given about fighting for independence from England. After that it served as a kind of town hall. It eventually became one of those historic spots that they renovate to look like it did back in the day. At some point the place was turned into a sprawling indoor-outdoor marketplace.

From the outside, the buildings looked as though they were from the 1700s, but inside were aisles of shops where you could buy anything from fried clams to artwork to dog collars. It was mostly a tourist spot. Locals didn't buy refrigerator magnets of the Old North Church. But the restaurants were always busy, which meant it was a spot that drew lots of people.

At least it did before the population was wiped out.

The place wasn't crowded, of course. But I did see a few people walking quickly between buildings, as if they didn't want to be outside any longer than necessary. It was a surprise to see other people, which is further proof that I was getting used to the new reality.

"Here come your friends," Chris said.

From the far side of the public park, I saw a group of the cowboys walking with Tori and Kent. One guy carried our gym bags, though Tori held on tight to her own. Kent had Olivia's huge sack over his shoulder. He really did like Olivia. I don't think he would have carried anybody else's bag. Unless it was Tori's. Okay, stop, Tucker.

From the other side of the building came a few more of Chris's people, along with Jon. We all met up in front of a building with huge white columns over which the name "Quincy Market" was painted in big gold letters.

"This is where you register," Chris explained. "They'll process you through, and then I'll take you to get something to eat. I assume you're hungry."

"Wait, register?" I asked.

"What kind of processing?" said Tori.

"We're trying to be organized," Chris explained. "Lots of people are coming through. Right now, we've got the only record of who survived the massacre."

"Makes total sense," Jon said. "It's like the first census of the new world. It could end up being a historical document."

"New world," I repeated. "I'm not sure how I feel about calling it that."

"It won't take long," Chris assured us. "We'll take your bags and meet you back here."

"I'll hang on to mine," Tori said.

I had no doubt that she had stashed one of the guns in there.

We all exchanged looks and shrugs and headed inside.

Stepping into the old building, we came upon a long counter that was normally a display for historical artifacts but was now being used as a reception desk by three pretty girls who didn't look much older than Olivia. One of them waved for us to come over. I took the lead and went first.

"Hello. My name's Madalyn," the first girl said to me in a welcoming voice that instantly put me at ease. "How are you doing?"

"I'm not sure how to answer that," I replied.

She gave me a sympathetic smile. "I hear you. Welcome to the Hall. Not that anybody really wants to be here, but it's better than being out there alone."

I shrugged.

"We need to get some information before you officially join us."

"Uh, sure, whatever."

"What's your full name?"

"Tucker Brody Pierce."

The girl opened a big, old-fashioned ledger book. Several pages were filled with a long list of names. I guess that's how things had to work in this "new world." We didn't have power to run computers. Madalyn wrote my name down with neat, girl-typical handwriting. She asked me my date of birth, where I was born, and what my parents' names were.

"Great," she said. "Gigi will take your medical history. I'll see you around."

That was my cue to move on, so I slid over to face the next girl in line as Tori stepped up to Madalyn.

"Hello, my name's Madalyn. Welcome to the Hall."

Gigi was an equally pretty girl who asked me all sorts of questions about what kind of diseases I might have or if I had ever had any operations or injuries. She diligently wrote everything down in her own ledger book. I didn't question them as to why they needed the information. Like Chris said, this was the only official record of the survivors. It was all so casual, as if we were checking into the Blackbird Inn for a vacation, not picking up the pieces after an attempt at genocide.

The last girl, Ashley (also cute, for the record), asked me to give her a brief account of where we were when the attack happened and the places we'd been on our way to the Hall. I gave her short answers, which is all she wanted since she was writing it all down. I expected a surprised reaction when I mentioned that we were out on the water when Portland was first hit, and that we had fought our way through the largest air-sea battle in history to get to the mainland, but she didn't even blink. I guess she had heard all sorts of hairy stories. Ours was just another one.

I heard Gigi, the medical girl, ask Tori, "Are you in much pain?"

"I'm fine," Tori replied, tight-lipped.

They were obviously talking about her gunshot wound.

"We'll get you right over to one of the doctors for a look," Gigi said.

She reached for another, smaller book and made a notation.

"You guys are pretty buttoned up," I said to Ashley. "It's like you've been doing this a long time."

Ashley frowned and said, "I know, right? So many people have been coming through. I guess that's a good thing, but . . . it's so sad. At least it helps us focus on something other than the horror of it all."

She had said the exact right thing, but it felt kind of . . . rehearsed. She must have said the same thing a few hundred times. That was good news. It meant there were a lot of survivors.

"That's it," she declared. "You're all set. Head on outside and . . . good luck."

"You too," I said and headed for the door.

The whole process of being questioned, logged, and filed was unsettling. Knowing that our information might be the first census of a new world was humbling, to say the least. But it helped that the girls were friendly and cute. It softened the sting.

I went back outside to wait while the others finished up. Our bags were lined up together, with Olivia's giant duffel on the end.

Tori joined me a few minutes later. We stood together, awkwardly, not sure of what to say or do next.

"Well," she finally said. "That was . . . thorough."

"Seriously," I responded. "I expected them to ask me for a blood sample."

Tori scanned the courtyard, deep in thought.

"What?" I asked.

"I'll go along with the program," she said. "For now."

"Well, yeah. I don't see any better options."

She gave me a hard look. "Are you still trying to ignore that radio message?" she asked.

"I'm not ignoring it, but we found a group of survivors right here. Why would we travel all the way across the country?"

"Because whoever sent that message wants to fight back," Tori replied. "These people seem like they're ready to spend their lives here."

"That's crazy," I said, scoffing. "They're just trying to make the best of it."

"I don't want to make the best of it," Tori said angrily. "My father's dead. I won't forget that."

I didn't bother to tell her that I hadn't forgotten either. I held the grief close to my heart, not letting my true feelings show, because when the time came for me to act, I wanted to do it on my own.

Tori picked up her bag and clutched it under her good arm.

"You do whatever works for you," she said.

The tension between us wasn't just because I hadn't backed her up on going to Nevada. She was regressing back to her old self and closing me out.

"How odd was that?" Kent exclaimed as he strolled from Quincy Market. "I wonder what time they're serving tea?"

"It's wrong," Tori said flatly. "They're taking down useless information while all that matters is that those planes could show up at any time and finish the job."

"They might," Kent said. "So we should make the best of it while we can, right?"

Olivia and Jon joined us soon after. They hadn't spent anywhere near as much time being "processed" as I had. I guess that was because I had already given them the information about where we had come from.

"Now what?" Olivia asked, pouting. "Didn't that big fella say something about food?"

"It's going to be dark soon," Jon pointed out. "I don't want to be outside in case . . ."

He didn't have to finish the thought. None of us wanted to be around if the planes came back at night, when their laser weapons worked. If anything, we needed to be three levels underground.

"See? That wasn't so bad," Chris said as he strode quickly toward us. "Let's get you set up with a place to sleep. Then we'll get you some food and have one of the doctors look at Tori's gunshot wound."

"How did you know about the gunshot wound?" Tori asked.

"News travels fast," Chris said with a shrug.

"Not that fast," Tori countered.

"You'd be surprised. Follow me."

We grabbed our bags—Kent took his *and* Olivia's—and followed Chris across the park to one of the other large buildings.

Inside were lines of stalls that normally offered food and touristy trinkets, but not anymore. That's not to say it was empty. Lots of people were there, but rather than shopping they were busy working on projects. Some were cleaning out spoiled food from the restaurant stalls and sanitizing the place. Without refrigeration, things were going bad fast. Further along, we passed stalls that had already been cleaned out and turned into comfortable places with chairs and couches where people read books or played chess.

Not everyone was keeping busy. We passed a few people who were huddled in chairs, silently crying. Others were curled in corners, their arms wrapped around their legs and their heads buried. Many were alone; some had sympathetic friends with them to offer comfort. It was a sad reminder of how so many lives were destroyed and loved ones murdered.

A few stoic folks gave us a small wave or an acknowledging smile. We may have been strangers, but we all had one thing in common: We were all survivors of the most deadly attack in history.

Chris spoke with many of the people as we walked past, calling out a quick "Hello!" or "How's it going?" Several times he stopped next to a person who was visibly upset just to give them a comforting rub on the back. He was acting like a camp counselor whose main duty was to try to keep everybody happy. But it was more than that. From what we had seen so far, he was taking care of these people when they needed it most.

Since leaving Pemberwick, my friends had looked to me to fill that role. I was never comfortable taking the lead and making decisions, but somebody had to do it. Now it seemed as though we had connected with someone who welcomed that challenge. I'd be lying if I said it wasn't a relief to let somebody else be in charge. It was good to know people like Chris Campbell were around to help keep what was left of the world from spinning into chaos.

Halfway along the building we turned into a doorway to find a flight of stairs leading down. There was a cardboard box full of headlamps inside the door. Chris gave one to each of us. We strapped them on and followed him down below.

"This is where most of us sleep," he explained as we descended. "There's no telling if those planes will come back at night, but since we know it's safer underground, we try to stay down here once the sun sets."

Kent said, "It's like the opposite of being vampires. We've got to hide from the dark."

"You could put it that way," Chris said. "It's kinda creepy, but whatever works for you."

Kent shut up.

We descended to the lowest level of the building. Anything that had been used to run the market had been cleared out of the long basement and replaced by cots along either wall. I could only see as far as the throw of the LED light from my lamp, but I had to guess that there were at least fifty beds on either side. People had definitely made themselves at home. There were makeshift curtains strung up between now useless floor lamps to create small, private living spaces.

Chris led us between the rows of cots where people slept or read books using their headlamps. Chris's cowboys must have pulled them from all over the city. Some people had tacked photos to the walls, but mostly the personal items were suitcases or canvas bags that were kept next to the beds.

Many people were quietly sobbing or staring blankly at the ceiling. I had no doubt that their minds had cast back to the life they had lost. It was gut-wrenching.

Finally, Chris stopped at a few unoccupied cots topped with empty sleeping bags.

"I'm afraid it's coed," Chris pointed out. "I guess that's the least of our problems."

"Speak for yourself," Olivia sniffed, perturbed.

"Fine by me," Kent said and dumped Olivia's giant bag on a cot. He claimed the cot right next to hers.

Tori took the cot on Kent's other side.

"Lucky me!" he declared, beaming happily. "A Kent sandwich."

We all ignored him.

I went to the other side of the aisle, just to be away from Olivia. I dropped my bag on a bed next to one that already had somebody's suitcase at the foot. The cot on the other side of mine was empty, so Jon took it.

"Try not to use the headlamps more than necessary," Chris warned. "We've set up a battery-recharging station, but it gets backed up, and since it's run by solar power, we're at the mercy of the sun."

"Looks like you've got it all figured out," Tori said. It didn't sound like a compliment.

"We're trying," Chris replied. "The food's pretty good too. We've got people scouring the city, and there's still plenty left that's fresh. Can't say how long that'll last. At least when winter sets in, we'll have natural refrigeration."

Hearing that made my heart sink. Winter was on the way, which would add another level of hardship. Days would be short, and there was no heat. More people would surely find their way to the Hall, which meant overcrowding would become an issue. What seemed like a comfortable place to stay and plan our next move might quickly turn into a congested mess.

Once again I had to force myself to deal with the moment and not look too far ahead. The future wasn't a happy place to be.

"Once you get settled, head over to the building across from this one," Chris said. "We've set up a kitchen and mess hall. Help yourself. Tomorrow we'll work you into the system and assign you some duties. Everybody is welcome here, but you're expected to pitch in."

"No problem," Jon said enthusiastically. "Whatever you need."

"Excellent," Chris replied. "As long as we can rely on one another, we'll be okay."

"And live to be old and gray in our little basement commune here in the heart of Boston," Tori said with fake delight.

"We're doing the best we can," Chris said, obviously tweaked by her sarcasm. "Come with me, Tori. You've got to get that shoulder looked at."

"I'm okay," she said curtly.

Chris softened and said, "I'm just trying to help you out."

"Don't be dumb," I said to Tori with no sympathy. "The last thing you need is an infection."

Tori was holding in a lot of anger. She didn't like to be told what to do, especially by someone she didn't trust . . . which was everyone. Including me.

"Fine," she said and stood up, still clutching her bag.

"You can leave that," Chris said. "The honor system works."

"Don't push it," Tori snarled.

"Suit yourself," Chris said with a shrug and headed back the way we came in.

Tori hesitated a moment, then followed. We watched them disappear into the darkness, then looked to each other in the light from our headlamps.

"Well," Olivia said. "This is cozy." She didn't mean it.

"I think it's great," Jon said as he stretched out on his cot with his hands behind his head. "They've thought of everything."

"I don't get you, Jon," I said. "You're acting like this is some big adventure."

"Isn't it?" he replied.

"What's your deal, Chadwick?" Kent asked. "I mean, who were you before the invasion?"

"There isn't much to tell you," Jon answered. "My parents died a while back, and I live alone. Put myself through Bowdoin on scholarships because I'm exceptionally intelligent. Graduated last year. I have degrees in engineering and chemistry. I was working at the hospital to make ends meet until I decided on what to do with my life. But I'm only twenty-one. There's no rush."

"Yeah," Olivia said sarcastically. "The future looks really rosy. We've all got so much to look forward to."

"That's it?" Kent asked. "That's all you have to say about who you are?"

"What do you want to hear?" Jon asked defensively. "You want to know what books I read or what movies I like? You want to know my favorite food? Favorite team? Favorite color? None of that matters anymore, so why even think about it?"

Jon had lashed out so angrily that even Kent backed off. We sat there for a few seconds in silence, while Jon's words ate at me.

"I think you're wrong," I finally said. "I think it does matter. We can't forget who we were."

"Unless you didn't particularly like who you were," Jon said. "Maybe this is a chance to become somebody new."

They were simple but stunning words. It could be that for some people the destruction of the human race might actually offer a new beginning. People who were unhappy with their lives were given a chance to start fresh. To reinvent themselves. There was only one catch . . .

. . . you had to survive.

"I'm hungry," Kent announced. "Who's with me?"

We all were. Olivia, Jon, and I followed him back upstairs, where we deposited our headlamps and headed outside.

Night had fallen. A low, warm glow came from the windows of the long building that ran parallel to the one we had just left. The thought crossed my mind that it might be smart to block off any light coming from the windows that would tip off the Air Force that people had congregated. Apparently Chris and his cowboys hadn't thought of everything.

When we entered, we found ourselves in a large restaurant room. Light came from several battery-powered camp lanterns that rested on many of the tables. It wasn't bright, but it was enough to see by. I guessed there were about thirty people eating. Some sat alone, others huddled in groups. They spoke softly, as if eating in a library.

"Kitchen's that way," one guy said to us, pointing.

I led the others through swinging doors and into a kitchen, where we were instantly hit with a wave of delicious smells.

"They're cooking?" Kent said, surprised.

Other than the fact that the only light came from strategically placed lanterns, the kitchen looked every bit like a fully functioning restaurant kitchen from before the attack. Two chefs were at stoves that held large pots and pans that were bubbling and steaming.

"It's gas," Jon said. "The burners are lit!"

It was a simple yet amazing sight that would have been commonplace only a few weeks before.

"Grab some plates at the end of the line," a friendly chef called out. "Tonight we've got steaks."

"Steaks!" Kent exclaimed. "You mean, like . . . real steaks?"

"Where did all this food come from?" I asked.

"You name it," the chef replied. "We've got people scrounging all over the city. Can't say how long the fresh stuff will last, so get it while you can."

"You don't have to tell me twice," Kent said and hurried toward the food.

We passed through a doorway into a section of the restaurant that was set up to serve the meal. Several people stood behind a long table spread with platters and bowls containing an impossible selection of food. There were salads, mashed potatoes, rice, corn on the cob, apples, baked potatoes, glazed carrots, multiple varieties of soup, and, yes, steaks. Thick steaks. Juicy, cooked-to-perfection, impossible steaks.

"I think I'm dreaming," Olivia said with dismay.

I was too hungry to question it. I grabbed a plate, then thought for a second and grabbed another plate. I filled one with potatoes and fruit, and on the other I picked out the heaviest steak I could find.

The servers behind the counter watched us with bemused smiles. At one point I made eye contact with an older woman chef who had been watching me and suddenly felt self-conscious.

"Am I being a pig?" I asked.

"Absolutely not," she said with a laugh. "If you don't eat it, somebody else will. Just don't make yourself sick if you haven't eaten in a while."

"That's a risk I'm willing to take," I said and continued to load my plate.

The last time I had eaten a hot meal was when we were prisoners in the SYLO camp on Pemberwick Island. How long ago was that? It felt like a lifetime. My stomach thought so too. The smell of food brought on a growl of anticipation.

At the end of the line were juices that actually seemed to be fresh-squeezed. They must have been using up whatever fresh fruit was still around before it went bad. I grabbed a glass of lemonade. This may not have been the greatest meal I had ever eaten, but it sure felt like it.

We claimed a table in the restaurant and ate without a word. Talking would have slowed the input. I had to force myself to eat slowly for fear my stomach would reject the tonnage that I was shoveling down. I also didn't want to look like an animal.

Kent didn't have the same concern. He ate furiously, shoving in whatever he could balance on a fork. Jon wasn't much better. Olivia ate too. I'd never seen a girl gorge the way she did. At one point we made eye contact, and she gave me an embarrassed smile . . . before letting out a deep boomer of a belch.

We both laughed and continued to chow.

At one point the lady server came up and stood over our table.

"I see we have some healthy appetites here," she said warmly. "Don't be shy about going for seconds."

The words were barely out of her mouth before Kent and Jon were on their feet and racing each other back to the kitchen.

"Somebody's going to get sick," Olivia said. "It might be me."

"You wouldn't be alone," the woman said. "Newcomers are always overindulging. It's human nature."

"This is incredible," I said. "I mean, it's a feast."

"Some days are better than others," the woman said. "Everyone has something to offer. It's amazing what can be accomplished when your sole purpose is to take care of one another. Enjoy."

The woman moved on to another table to see how they were enjoying their meal.

"I could get used to this," Olivia said as she bit into a perfectly ripe tomato, the dark red juice running down her chin.

"It's not bad," I had to admit.

"It's all so . . . civilized," Tori said with disdain as she sat down at the table with a plate of food. Her bag was draped over her shoulder.

"What did the doctor say?" I asked.

"Not much. He pulled off the bandage, grunted as if it was exactly what he expected to see, put a few drops of antibiotic or something on the wound, wrapped me back up with fresh gauze, and sent me on my way. He didn't even look me in the eye. Now I know what a dog feels like at the veterinarian. No, I take that back. At least a dog gets a pat on the head."

"He's probably exhausted from treating so many patients," Olivia offered.

"No. He just didn't care. What's with the feast? Are these people living in denial or what?"

"They're making the best of a bad situation," I offered.

"They should spend less time getting comfortable and start worrying a little more about how to stop this from happening again."

She put her head down and ate. A lot.

I said, "You've been doing nothing but criticizing these people, but you sure take advantage of what they've got to offer."

Tori didn't look at me. She said, "Why not? I'm not stupid. But as soon as I'm back up to speed, I'm out of here . . . with or without you people."

That was it. Tori was headed for Nevada. Maybe it was the right thing to do. I didn't know. I needed time to sort out my own thoughts. My only consolation was that she needed some time to heal. Maybe by the time she was ready to leave, I would be too.

After eating, we went back to our subterranean barracks. We were given towels and directed to makeshift showers that were erected in the bathrooms. They were nothing more than hoses stretched across the ceiling with nozzles that dangled overhead. The water was cold but welcome. It wasn't until I was nearly finished that I realized how incredible it was that the water was still running. Just like the gas in the restaurant. The people who had survived to meet up in the Hall were a resourceful group.

When I got back to my bunk, I found that my neighbor had returned and lay on his cot reading. He was a gray-haired guy who looked as though he may have been athletic at one time, but the clock had caught up with him.

"I'm Tucker Pierce," I said, holding out my hand to shake. "Sorry to crowd you like this."

"Jim Hardimon," the guy said as he shook my hand. "You're not bothering me. Plenty of people have come and gone already. You're just the next."

"How long have you been here?" I asked.

"Since the day after the attack. I was in my basement that night, working on the furnace. I complained about having to fix that cranky old thing, but it ended up saving my life."

"How did you find your way here?" I asked.

"I drove into the city from Brookline, figuring I might find some people. I stumbled on this group and helped set the place up, you know, changing it from a tourist trap into a camp of sorts."

"You all did an incredible job," I said.

"Good enough, I suppose. Most of the credit goes to Chris Campbell. He really took the bull by the horns and organized us. Good man."

I glanced over to Tori to see if she was hearing Jim's story. She was pretending not to be listening.

"What happens next for you?" I asked.

He shrugged and said, "That depends on what this is all about. Somebody must have won this war. All I know is that it wasn't the people of Boston. I figure we'll find out sooner or later. Until then,

I'm staying right here. I got no family. Anybody I care about is gone. I can't imagine finding a better place to be living, given the hand we've been dealt. Can you?"

"No," I replied while glancing at Tori. "Considering all that happened, this place is pretty sweet."

"I'm going to milk it until, well, until somebody tells me otherwise. Gotta look out for number one, you know. I suggest you do the same."

With that, Jim rolled over to go to sleep.

I looked at Tori. She glared at me and turned away.

I suddenly felt dead tired. It had been a long, eventful day. I went to sleep with the hope that the next day would break with tradition and be totally boring.

When I woke up, I checked my new watch. Five A.M. At home I could sleep until noon. Those days were long gone. I was wide-awake and knew I couldn't force myself to konk out again, so I got up to do a little exploring.

It was still dark outside, though the sky was beginning to lighten. Dawn was normally alive with the chirping of early birds vying for their daily worms. I did hear the chirrups of a few random birds, but nothing like normal. At least it meant that a few of them had survived. I wondered if any worms had.

I also heard the sound of a running engine. It was the only sign of human life, so I followed it. The noise brought me to the far end of the building that housed the restaurant we had eaten in.

When I rounded the corner, I saw a large delivery truck idling near the back doors. Several people were hard at work unloading it. They carried out boxes of fresh vegetables, bushels of fruit, and at least five sides of beef. These were the scroungers who combed Boston for the food needed to feed our little colony. They probably searched every square inch of the town so that nothing would go to waste. It was good to see that there was still some fresh food around.

I was about to head back to the barracks when I saw another vehicle approach—a bus. It was big, the kind that people used to travel long distances. It pulled up beyond the truck that was being off-loaded and stopped. What was it doing there? Dropping off the next crop of survivors? When the bus door opened, I saw that it was empty. So what was it doing?

My answer came when a door opened at the end of the building and a line of people walked out, single file, headed for the idling vehicle. One of the cute girls who had processed us when we arrived appeared at the door of the bus, holding a clipboard. Was it Gigi? Or Ashley? I couldn't remember. She stood at the vehicle entrance and made a notation on her clipboard as each person boarded.

The passengers were mostly men, but I did see a few women. They didn't seem particularly excited about going wherever it was they were going. They dutifully waited their turn, gave their name to Gigi or Ashley, and boarded the bus. There was no conversation. No pleasantries. No personality to the event at all.

Five minutes later, the door of the bus closed, and the vehicle pulled out. The girl stayed behind and walked to the building, where she was met by . . . Chris Campbell. He checked the clipboard, took her pen, and made a note at the bottom, then handed it back to her. Without a word, they both went on their way.

I don't know why the event bothered me. Maybe it was because I couldn't come up with a logical explanation for what had happened. Or maybe because it looked like the people were being treated like numbers on a list.

It was something I needed to ask Chris about. But not just then. I wanted to have people around me when I brought it up because I had the weird feeling that I had seen something I wasn't supposed to.

EIGHT

Breakfast was just as awesome as dinner. We gorged on bacon and eggs and bagels and fruit and juice.

"This can't last," I said. "Eventually the fresh food will run out, and we'll be eating out of cans."

"Until the cans run out," Tori cautioned.

"We'll have to start growing our own stuff," Jon said. "Didn't you say that you're a gardener, Tucker? You should tell Chris you want to start a farm."

Kent laughed. "Perfect! Farmer Pierce."

I wasn't insulted. Just the opposite. I thought it was a pretty good idea. I knew a lot about plants, though most of my experience was with grass and flowers. How hard could it be to grow corn? Or tomatoes? For a brief moment, I let my mind shoot ahead to what the future might hold for somebody who could provide food for a colony of survivors. I could be a pretty valuable asset.

That image was shattered when I looked at Tori, who stared at me with cold eyes.

"Let me know how that works out for you," she said with disdain and went back to her meal.

I felt my anger grow. Was I pissed at her for being so negative about everything? Or was I disappointed in myself for thinking of a future that involved accepting what had happened? Was I healing? Or giving up?

"I see you've all settled in," Chris Campbell said as he approached our table. "Food isn't bad, right?"

"No complaints," Kent said. "I just hope it lasts."

"That's up to us," Chris replied. "The harder we work, the better we eat."

"We've got to figure out what our assignments are," Jon said enthusiastically. "We want to do our part."

"You will," Chris assured him. "When you're done eating, come over to Quincy Market. We want to hear about your trip here."

"It's a heck of a story," Kent said with a full mouth.

"I've got a question for you, Chris," I said. "I was walking around this morning and saw a bunch of people boarding a bus and taking off. What's up with that?"

Chris shrugged and said, "People come and go all the time. We try to keep a record of it so when people leave, we ask that they do it in groups. It's easier to document it that way."

"People can't just leave whenever they want?" I asked.

"Of course they can," Chris answered quickly. "We just want to make sure we have a record of it. You never know. Somebody might show up looking for a lost kid, and if that kid passed through here, we want to be able to tell them. Olivia, what if your mother came looking for you? We want to be able to tell her you were here and safe."

"If only," Olivia said softly, without lifting her eyes.

"Makes total sense," Kent said.

"Where does the bus take them?" I asked.

"Wherever they want to go, within reason. We've got to conserve gas. Some people want to get to the ocean and find a boat to travel down the coast. Others just want to get away from the city. We don't question. All we try to do is keep track of the survivors who come through here as well as we can." He shrugged and added, "I don't know, maybe it's all a big waste of time, but it makes us feel as though we're doing something positive."

"I think it's really smart," Jon said with enthusiasm.

"Could you drive me to New York City?" Olivia asked.

Chris gave her an apologetic shrug. "I'm afraid that's a little out of our range. Like I said, we have to conserve gas."

"That's okay," Olivia said while staring at her breakfast. "I doubt my mother's there anyway."

Her wistful comment made my heart go out to her. I'd been so wrapped up with my own demons that I kept forgetting I wasn't the only one who had lost family. Though in my case, my parents were still alive—they were just traitors.

"I'm sorry," Chris said to her sincerely, then looked to the rest of us. "Finish up and I'll meet you all over in the market."

He touched Olivia's shoulder in a show of sympathy, then headed out.

I looked at Tori, expecting some critical comment, but instead I saw that she was smiling.

"What?" I asked.

"You're just as skeptical of this place as I am," she said.

"I'm not!" I said defensively. "I just saw something that didn't make sense, that's all."

"There's a whole lot that doesn't make sense here," she said. "I get that you're trying to find some new normal, that's who you are, but I'm not convinced that this is it . . . and neither are you."

"So what do you think we should do?" Kent asked. "They've got a pretty sweet setup going on here; I think we should take advantage." He finished by scooping a forkful of eggs into his mouth.

"Sure," Tori said. "It's great . . . until those planes come back. But, hey, I guess that's okay as long as we're all comfy and well fed until then."

That put an end to the conversation—and my appetite. Tori was right. It wasn't just about survival, it was also about protecting ourselves against whatever force was responsible for putting us on the path to Armageddon.

And getting revenge.

I might have appreciated what Chris and his cowboys had set up, but I wasn't ready to give up. Tori was right about that too.

We finished our meal in silence, then walked to Quincy Market. The same three girls were inside, processing new arrivals. When the first girl spotted us, she put on a welcoming face and said, "Come on in. They're waiting for you right through there."

She pointed to a door on the far side of the room. I led the others through to find a large lecture hall. There were rows of tiered seats where several of Chris's cowboys sat. They faced a low platform where five chairs were set up.

"Come in," Chris called to us. "Have a seat up there."

We each took one of the five chairs and faced the others. A pretty girl, who could easily have been one of the reception girls, sat in front with a notepad and pen.

"Now, start from the top," Chris said. "Tell us everything that happened on Pemberwick Island and bring us right up to when we saw you outside of Fenway."

I did most of the talking, though Kent was quick to add details, usually of his heroics. I told them everything, beginning with Marty Wiggens dying during the football game because he had used the Ruby that was brought to Pemberwick by the villain named Mr. Feit. I told them about Captain Granger and the division of the Navy called SYLO that invaded the island and created a quarantine that was more about keeping us prisoner than rooting out a bogus virus. I explained how they murdered people who tried to escape and about the rebels, led by Tori's father, who planned to retake the island but were ambushed and executed before they could put their plan into motion. Tori spoke about how we tried to escape from Pemberwick on fishing boats and were recaptured, but not before witnessing what turned out to be the attack on Portland. We all talked about the SYLO prison camp and how we escaped by using the Ruby for strength.

We described our ultimate successful escape from Pemberwick, from Feit's death through the desperate speedboat journey that took us directly through the massive air-sea battle between SYLO and the black planes, when Captain Granger was killed. Finally, we described the desolation we found in Portland, the downed black plane that had the Air Force logo, and how we met Jon and decided to travel to Boston.

"From what we saw," I concluded, "there's a civil war going on. Two branches of the United States military are at war. Why? We have no idea. But we know who's suffering, and that's pretty much everybody else."

Chris and the cowboys didn't say much during our story. Every so often they'd ask a question to clarify something, but they mostly listened attentively.

When we finished, we sat there staring at the group, waiting for their reaction.

It was Chris who went first.

"I can't speak for anybody else, but I'm blown away. The idea that this is a civil war is something I never even considered. None of us did."

He looked at the other cowboys, and they all nodded in agreement.

He then added, "Who do you think is giving the orders? I mean, armies don't just fight for the heck of it."

"No clue," Kent answered quickly.

"I don't know about the Air Force," I answered. "But SYLO came to Pemberwick Island under orders from the president of the United States."

"So you think they're the good guys?" Chris asked.

"Not even close," I answered quickly. "Not after what they did to our home. Captain Granger was a monster, and I'm glad he's dead. They're all murderers. As far as I'm concerned, SYLO started this war."

"And you say your parents are working for them?" Chris asked.

I felt all eyes in the room on me, including those of my friends.

I took a deep breath and answered with total sincerity. "They lied to me for years about why we moved to Pemberwick Island. The truth is that we moved there so they could help an invading force turn the place into a prison. They're just as guilty as the soldiers who fired the guns that wiped out the rebel camp and killed Tori's father. As far as I'm concerned, I don't have parents anymore."

Olivia let out a soft gasp.

Everyone waited, expecting me to say more.

I didn't.

Tori reached over and took my hand.

"We'll talk about it another time," Chris said.

"No, we won't," I said.

"So what are we going to do?" Tori asked, changing the subject.

"What do you mean?" Chris said.

"I mean we've got to take charge of our lives. Our futures. We've got to end this."

"How can we end this?" Chris asked skeptically. "We don't even know what this is. You say it's a civil war, but nobody has declared anything. If the president is controlling SYLO, who's controlling the Air Force? Some foreign power? A rebel group of soldiers trying to overthrow the government?"

"Aliens?" Kent threw in.

Nobody acknowledged that comment.

"That's exactly the point," Tori exclaimed. "We need to know why this happened and who's behind it."

Chris took a deep breath and rubbed his face, buying time to think.

"Look," he finally said, "we're all angry and scared. But we're just regular people. What else can we do but focus on survival?"

Tori jumped to her feet. "I know. I get it," she shouted. "We have to eat and we need shelter, and you guys have that covered. Nice job. But we're the lucky ones. We could just as easily be dead. This happened for a reason, and if we just sit around and feed our faces and get comfortable, then eventually our luck is going to run out. Whether you think so or not, we're living on death row, and the executioner is still out there. If I'm going to die, at least I want to know why."

She grabbed her bag and stormed out of the room.

The rest of us sat there in awkward silence for a few long moments.

"She's had a tough time," I finally said. "She saw her father gunned down by SYLO just a few days ago and then took a bullet herself."

"Hey, my father was killed too," Kent said. "But I'm keeping it together."

"Then I guess you're a better person than she is," I snapped. "But if not for her, you wouldn't be here. Don't forget that."

That shut Kent up.

Chris stood. "It's okay," he said. "She's not the only one who feels that way. But we're not here to stage some kind of counter-revolution. All we want to do is get by. If you want to take off and tilt at windmills, that's your choice. But if you stay here, you've got to be cool. We're all on edge, and I can't have somebody stirring things up, or this whole thing will come tumbling down."

"I hear you," I said. "I'll talk to her."

"Great. If you want to leave, just let us know. No harm, no foul."

He went for the door along with the rest of his people.

"We'd like you to stay," Chris said as an afterthought. "We need your energy."

He left, and the others followed.

Kent, Olivia, Jon, and I stayed in our chairs, waiting for somebody to say something.

"She's going to get us kicked out of here," was Kent's first comment.

"What does she want to do?" Jon asked. "Fight back? With two pistols?"

"I don't want to leave," Olivia added quickly. "I feel safe here. Maybe he's right. Maybe my mother will come looking for me. It's possible. I mean, anything's possible, right?"

Kent put his arm around her and said, "Wherever we go, you'll be safe as long as you're with me."

She didn't pull away from him, but she kept her eyes on me. They *all* had their eyes on me, expecting some words of wisdom that I was having trouble finding. I was getting tired of being the one they all looked to for answers. Or explanations. Or assurances that everything was going to be fine when I knew it wasn't.

"I'll try to calm Tori down," I said. "But she's right. Whatever this war is, it's just beginning."

I got up and left the building to search for Tori. I found her sitting alone on a park bench between the two main buildings, clutching her bag.

"I don't trust him," she said as I walked up.

"Who?"

"That Campbell guy. There's something off. With him, with this place. Everything is just too . . . easy."

I glanced around the grounds to see people raking leaves, washing windows, or just strolling along and chatting.

"It does seem strangely normal," I commented.

"Exactly!" she exclaimed. "That's not normal. We all just had our lives wiped out. Millions of people have been killed, and all they care about is that there's bacon for breakfast."

"I hear you," I said. "I think maybe everyone's in denial. It's a lot easier to worry about an empty belly than to stress over the downfall of civilization."

"Then they've given up," Tori said with spite.

"I'll make you a deal," I said. "Let's ride this out for a while. At least until your shoulder gets better. We'll do whatever they ask while you get stronger. Once you're back up to speed, we'll make a decision."

"Would you go to Nevada with me?" she asked.

"I'm not sure," I replied. "I don't know what the right thing to do is."

"And you think you'll know any better after living here in Camp Oblivious?"

"Maybe not, but I wouldn't mind being well fed and safe in their basement while we try to figure it out . . . and heal."

Tori looked at the ground and frowned. She wasn't buying it.

"You have to trust somebody, Tori. It might as well be me."

She kicked at the dirt absently.

"The leaves are starting to turn," she said. "It'll be cold soon. Fall was my dad's favorite time of year."

"He seemed like a great guy."

"He'd want me to fight back," she said.

"I know. But he'd want you to be smart about it."

She nodded thoughtfully.

"All right, Tucker, I'll try it your way. But as soon I'm strong enough to travel, I'm gone."

Tori was true to her word. Over the next several days she didn't rock the boat and did her best to fit in. We all did.

Jon volunteered to help keep the rechargeable batteries topped off. Every day he'd gather lamps from all over Faneuil Hall and bring them to the solar charging station, replacing them with fully charged units.

Olivia did what she did best . . . shop. She got together with the people who scavenged the city for clothes and went out with them every day to pillage the abandoned stores. Her choices tended to be more fashionable than practical, but nobody complained.

Tori was limited by her injury, so there wasn't much she could do that was physical, but she found a perfect job anyway. The cowboys had scrounged up gas-powered generators from around the city, and not all of them were in great shape. Using her knowledge of engines, Tori tuned them up and had them humming. Their main function, now that it was getting colder, was to power the heaters that pumped warm air into the buildings. Thanks to Tori, the people at the Hall would be warm throughout the long winter.

Though she was going along with the program, her gym bag was never far from her side.

I did what I did best: garden. In this case it was a vegetable garden. Winter was coming, so planting anything outside would have been a waste. Instead, I cleared an unused section of one of the buildings that had a skylight and set up rows of planters that we scrounged from a nearby gardening center. In no time I had several rows of tomatoes, carrots, potatoes, and onions growing in the improvised greenhouse. If all went well, there would be enough plants to provide fresh vegetables throughout the winter.

The only one of us who didn't do much to fit in was Kent—no big surprise. At first he was asked to wash windows, but that didn't last more than a minute. Kent didn't do menial chores that were more suited to the lower classes—which in his opinion was everybody but him. Once he blew off that job, he would disappear for hours on end. Nobody knew where he went or what he was doing.

One time I saw him strolling across Faneuil Hall in deep discussion with Chris Campbell. When he saw that I was watching, he walked away from Chris quickly, as if he didn't want me to know that they were talking.

When I would ask him at night what he had done that day, he'd get evasive and say, "Whatever they ask me to do."

He didn't even confide in Olivia—unless she was being secretive about it too.

I didn't press him on it because I didn't want to start a fight. It was obvious that he didn't want to talk about whatever he was doing, and to be honest, I didn't care. As long as he wasn't getting into any kind of trouble that might hurt the rest of us.

We quickly settled into our jobs and the day-to-day routine of making the best of what we had. New people arrived all the time, but our numbers never seemed to grow, which meant that just as many were leaving. Every day I'd hear about somebody who knew somebody who took off. I'd guess that about ten people left every day. For a group that only numbered around two hundred, that seemed like a big chunk of people who didn't want to be there. But everyone had the right to do what they wanted.

It wasn't a horrible way to live, but the real reason for our being there was never far from anybody's mind. The fear of another attack wasn't our only worry. There was real concern over what our lives would be like once the war was over. It was like living in limbo, waiting for the next phase of life to kick in.

The guy in the cot next to mine, Jim, fully believed that we would be living in the Hall for a long time.

"Whoever did this has got to have big plans," he'd tell me. "We could be waiting around for months until we find out what they are, so make yourself comfortable."

Jim gave Chris Campbell all sorts of credit for pulling the Hall together and keeping the people safe and well fed. He got no argument from me. Chris was one of those guys who ran toward problems instead of away from them. I don't know where the people of the Hall would be if he hadn't taken charge.

Besides Kent's secret activities, the only odd part about life at the Hall were the busloads of people who left every morning, like clockwork. Most days I got up early and went to observe the daily bus as it was loaded up with people I'd probably never see again. Many of them I recognized from working around the Hall. None of them had mentioned that they planned to leave, yet there they were, loaded up and headed out.

The marauding planes didn't return, the abundance of food

didn't slack off, and we all had jobs that made us feel as if we were contributing. We had settled into a new normal . . .

. . . until the tenth night we were there.

It started out innocently enough. Better than innocent, in fact, because of Olivia.

She decided that simply surviving wasn't good enough. Her point was that if we were all stuck together in this forced community, then there was no reason that we shouldn't have a little fun every once in a while. To that end, she organized a dance. Yes, a dance. Under her direction, a group of guys arranged strings of outdoor Christmas lights to create a festive atmosphere between the two buildings. Jon scavenged a couple of iPod docks with speakers from somewhere in the city, and Tori's people brought generator power to a makeshift DJ booth. A few people loaned iPods that probably hadn't been used since the day the city was attacked. The stage was set.

At eight o'clock, music returned to Faneuil Hall.

The sound brought people out of the buildings. They gathered slowly and a bit cautiously around the small area where twinkling lights dangled from the trees. I understood their concern. It was night. It was dark. That's when the invading Air Force planes were the most powerful. But nobody had seen a plane for nearly two weeks, and the sound of music was way too tempting to ignore.

Jon played some old-time song I didn't recognize. It was a big-band jazz thing that he must have thought would appeal to all ages. It didn't matter to me. Hearing music for the first time in weeks was like a drink of cold water after having walked a hundred miles through the hot desert.

I couldn't help but smile, and I wasn't alone. The music was magically melting away the tension that had been gripping us all. People circled Jon at the DJ table and stood there swaying, letting their minds go to another place and a better time.

It was all pretty mellow until Kent jumped up onto a bench and shouted, "Enough! Let's have some fun!"

Jon took his cue and changed the laid-back jazz to a thumping, club-mix dance tune.

A few of the older people cringed, but the younger people loved it.

"Whooo!" came an exited cheer from a girl in the crowd. It could have been Ashley. Or Gigi. Or Madalyn.

Kent ran to Olivia and said, "This is your party, let's dance!"

With a coy smile, Olivia went along. Kent pulled her out into the circle of light that was intended to be a dance floor, and the two danced as if they didn't have a care in the world. Most of the people drifted away from Jon to ring the dance floor and watch them while bouncing to the music themselves. The receptionist girls jumped to the center and danced with one another. They were followed by a few guys who danced with them, and soon the place was packed with people, all jumping and bouncing to the music. Even a few older people joined in. They looked awkward, and they couldn't have cared less. After what they'd been through, nothing would ever embarrass them again.

Jon kept the songs coming, switching from one iPod to another. It wasn't the smoothest of mixes, but nobody seemed to care. He kept the energy up and the people jumping as more and more joined in. I caught a glimpse of Chris Campbell dancing with the receptionist girls. Even the boss was letting loose.

I looked across the crowd of dancing bodies to the far side where Tori stood with her arms folded and a disapproving frown on her face. I circled the group and slid my way over to her.

"Man, how bad does this suck?" I said.

Tori gave me a quick glare, then stared back at the dancers as she answered.

"I'm not an a-hole," she said curtly. "I get that people have to blow off steam, but they're living in denial."

"Maybe, but at least they're living. Let's dance."

"I don't dance," she said.

"Me neither. We can just jump around to the music."

Before she could argue, I pulled her into the group of now sweating bodies. Jon changed the tune to another upbeat song that was all over the radio a few weeks and a lifetime ago as I faced Tori . . . and danced. I don't have any moves, but I do have rhythm, so all I did was jump a little and pump my fists into the air, to become part of the pulsating, joyous mass.

Tori didn't move. She was looking for an escape route, but there were too many people crowding her in. She was trapped . . . and getting knocked around.

"Your shoulder," I said seriously and stopped dancing. "I'm sorry, I didn't think."

"My shoulder's fine," she said.

"You always say that."

"This time I mean it," she replied.

As if to prove it, she started to dance. She raised her arms in the air, even on the injured side, and started to spin and sway to the music. Unlike me, Tori could dance, and she proved it.

"Are you serious?" I called over the music. "You're okay?"

She shrugged and spun around. Her long, wavy, dark hair was loose, and it flew around as if it were dancing on its own.

For the first time in a long while, she smiled. Like everyone else, she had gotten lost in the music and the pure joy of letting go.

I was happy to join her and started moving to the beat again.

"Now we're talking!" Kent said and jumped in between us.

He danced with Tori while Olivia settled in front of me. Dancing with her was a whole different experience from dancing with Tori. While Tori spun and bounced and let her arms go like a wild little kid, Olivia had her eyes locked on mine as if she used dancing to share another kind of energy. It made me sweat, and it wasn't because of the jumping around. I turned my back to her, but she grabbed my shoulders, pulled me close, and began moving in rhythm with me.

I really hoped that Kent wasn't watching.

Suddenly, the music downshifted into a slow song.

Uh-oh.

Olivia spun me until we were facing each other.

"Perfect timing," she said.

I didn't agree.

She put her arms around me, pulled me close, and rested her head on my shoulder.

I was trapped, so I loosely put my arms around her, and we started swaying to the music.

Most of the people weren't coupled up, so the dance area thinned out pretty quickly. There would be no hiding. I glanced over Olivia's shoulder to see that Kent and Tori were wrapped up in each other. I wasn't sure if that was good news or bad news.

"I needed this," Olivia said. "I haven't had any fun in forever."

"I know what you mean. Nice job. Seriously."

"Thank you," she said and snuggled in closer to me. "Let's pretend like this is going to last."

I glanced over to Kent and Tori to see that they were dancing just as close. I decided to stop being so nervous and tightened my hold on Olivia.

She responded with a giggle.

"We rely on you, Tucker, you know that? Even Kent. He acts all alpha, but he always waits to see what you think before making any decisions."

"I don't know if that's so smart," I said.

"Maybe not, but you take everything in and make your choices without bringing any of your own baggage."

Olivia had no idea what baggage I was hiding, and that was fine by me.

"You aren't like Tori," she added. "She's trying to prove something."

"She's angry about her father," I said.

"We're all angry," Olivia snapped. "That's no excuse to be dumb. I think we're right where we belong, and we should stay here for as long as we can. If she wants to leave, let her."

I didn't respond. What was the point?

"I like you, Tucker," she said, holding me closer.

That crossed over the danger line, and I loosened my hold on her.

"I like you too, Olivia. You know that. But you and Kent are—"

"Oh, stop," she said petulantly. "Kent doesn't own me."

"But he really cares about you. I'm not going to get in the middle of that."

Olivia looked up at me, and with a flirty smile she said, "You may not have a choice."

"Tucker!"

I felt a hand on my shoulder, pulling me away from Olivia. I expected to turn and see Kent, or Kent's fist. But it was Tori . . . and she looked pissed.

"Dance with me," she commanded.

It wasn't like I had another option. She put her arms around me, not as tightly as Olivia had done, and I followed her lead. Seconds later, we were swaying together as Olivia melted into the crowd.

I felt the tension in Tori's body. There was more going on with her than just dancing.

"What's wrong?" I asked

Her answer was to grow even more rigid.

"Talk to me, Tori," I pressed.

"He tried to kiss me," she said through clenched teeth.

"Oh. Oh? Did you kiss him back?"

"No!"

I let out a short, relieved laugh.

"Why is that funny?" she asked angrily.

"It's not. I'm just relieved. I thought it might be something more, more . . . I don't know. You know?"

If I were being honest, I would tell her that I was relieved because she wouldn't let Kent kiss her. But that might make her even angrier.

"Such a pig," she said. "He hangs all over Olivia, and then tries to kiss me? Seriously?"

"He probably just got caught up in the moment. It's not like we've had a whole lot of chances to act, you know, normal."

Tori pulled back and looked me straight in the eye. "There's nothing normal about Kent Berringer trying to kiss me."

We looked into each other's eyes for a moment and then both started to laugh. Getting bent up about who should be kissing who felt like we were paying a visit to our old lives, where things like that mattered. It felt good. I think it did for Tori too. In spite of her anger.

She pulled me back close as the dance continued. I didn't mind.

"I'm sorry," she said.

"For what?"

"For giving you such a hard time about not going to Nevada. You were right. Being here is good."

"Does that mean you want to stay?" I asked.

She hesitated for a few seconds, then said, "I don't know. I don't want to get comfortable."

"Why not?"

"Because this can't last."

The song changed to another slow tune. Tori and I didn't miss a beat and kept swaying.

"At least being here gave your shoulder a chance to heal," I said.

I felt Tori stiffen again, ever so slightly.

"It is better, right?"

"It is," she said. "But . . . I don't know. It's strange."

"That you healed up?"

"No, that I healed so quickly. Luna said it would take weeks before I felt better. But after I went to see that knob doctor, the wound started to heal incredibly fast. Like . . . impossibly fast. It's nothing more than a small scar now, and I have total movement of my shoulder with no pain. It's like it never happened."

"And you're complaining?" I asked, incredulous.

"No, I'm totally relieved. But how could that be? I mean, he put some kind of antibiotic on it, but that wouldn't make me heal, like . . . instantly. Would it?"

I had no answer for that. It was great news, but another piece in a puzzle that didn't quite fit.

"What do you want to do, Tucker?" she asked.

"Uh, you mean right now?"

"No, I mean about staying here. You've had a chance to think, and I'm better now. Do you want to stay?"

She looked up into my eyes, and for the first time I sensed that Tori Sleeper had doubts. She was always supremely confident in every move she made, whether it was tying a fisherman's knot or running the gauntlet between two burning warships. Now she was conflicted and looking to me for guidance. It was alien territory for both of us.

I opened my mouth to speak, though I wasn't sure of what I was going to say when—

"Stop!" she yelled.

"Uh, what?"

Tori's eyes had gone from questioning to frightened.

"Kill the music!" she shouted for all to hear.

It made everybody jump.

Tori pulled away from me and ran to the table where Jon had the iPods set up.

"Shut it off!" she yelled at him.

Flustered, Jon stopped the music. The marketplace went deathly silent. Nobody moved. All eyes were on the crazy girl who had just pulled the plug on their party.

"What is it?" Chris Campbell asked as he made his way through the crowd.

Tori threw up her hand to stop him.

"Listen," she said.

I'd heard that command before.

Every last person trained their ears to try to hear what Tori was shouting about. They all feared the same thing. Their focus went to the sky.

"I hear it," I said softly.

It was faint but unmistakable.

A rumble went through the crowd as everyone picked up on the sound. It was the last thing they ever wanted to hear again.

"There!" Jon shouted, pointing skyward.

High in the night sky, coming from the west, was the first in a long line of shadows.

The Air Force was back.

NINE

"**E**verybody inside!" Chris commanded. "Move! Now!"

The entire crowd scrambled for the building where we had been safely sleeping below ground. What had been a barracks would now have to serve as a bunker. It wasn't a full-on panicked rush. There were no screams but plenty of pushing and shoving.

I went for the cables that were powering the Christmas lights, but Olivia grabbed my arm.

"Where are you going?" she screamed. "Get inside!"

"I'm coming," I said. "Get out of here!"

She hesitated, as if not wanting to leave me, but Kent yanked her away. The two ran for safety. Jon abandoned his DJ table and was right behind them.

The musical sound of the incoming planes grew louder.

I found the main plug for the lights and yanked it loose, breaking the connection to the generators and plunging the courtyard into darkness. When I turned to head for the building, Tori was there, facing me.

"Does this change your answer?" she asked.

"Can we talk about it later?"

We took off, running for safety.

The courtyard was nearly empty. It had taken only seconds. Tori and I would be the last ones to get inside. We ran to the back of the crowd that was jammed up near the door and had to wait while everyone squeezed through the opening.

I looked skyward, and my knees went weak.

"There they are," I said, barely above a whisper.

It was a cloudless night with no moon. With Boston dark, the sky was alive with stars. Their sparkling light is what allowed us to see the silhouettes of the dark planes.

"My God," Tori said.

There were hundreds of them. This was not a search for stragglers; it was a full-on assault.

Tori and I stood paralyzed, staring up at wave after wave of planes that appeared from the west. They flew in perfect formation, wing-to-wing and row after row.

"They look smaller," Tori observed.

"Not smaller, higher," I replied. "They're way up there."

The doorway was clear. Everyone was safely inside.

Tori and I stood frozen, staring up at the spectacle as the planes kept coming.

"This isn't about us," I finally declared. "They're not here to attack, they're going somewhere else."

"They're headed out over the Atlantic," she said. "They could be going to Greenland, or England, or any one of a thousand other countries."

We continued to gaze up at the massive fleet, no longer afraid for ourselves but thunderstruck by what this show of force might mean.

"Who is commanding them?" Tori wondered aloud, as much to herself as to me. "What is their mission?"

"Hopefully it's to wipe out SYLO," I offered.

She tore her gaze away from the planes and looked at me.

"How can you be so sure that would be a good thing?" she asked.

I wasn't sure of that at all, but I wanted SYLO destroyed and didn't much care who did it. I answered her with a noncommittal shrug and kept my eyes on the sky.

The trailing edge of planes finally passed over us as the entire force continued east, headed for some unknown destination and unthinkable mission.

"We have to tell the others it's safe," I said.

Tori snickered. "Seriously? It isn't even close to safe. But at least they can all get back to their fun."

We entered the building and announced that we weren't under attack. The news traveled quickly, and the tension was soon gone, though nobody felt much like going back out to dance. The party was over.

Tori and I went to our bunks to find Kent, Jon, and Olivia already there. Nobody was in the mood to discuss what had happened, which was fine by me. All I wanted was to fall asleep and get the image of those planes out of my mind. Instead, I saw something that only added to my anxiety.

"Where's Jim?" I asked.

The mattress on his bunk was rolled up, and his suitcase was gone.

"Was he at the dance?" I asked.

"I didn't see him," Jon said. "But I was busy."

"He could have been," Kent said. "It wasn't like I was looking for him."

I lay down on my cot but couldn't relax. Where could Jim have gone? He might have moved to another cot, but that didn't seem likely because most were occupied. I couldn't let it go, so I got up and walked the length of the building, scanning each of the cots with the light from my headlamp.

Jim was definitely gone.

When I got back to my own cot, Tori was awake and waiting for me.

"Maybe he decided to leave," she offered.

"No chance. He was here for the long haul. He told me so every chance he got. I can't believe he'd just take off. He didn't even say goodbye."

"Then he must still be around somewhere," she said. "We'll find him in the morning."

I put my head down on the pillow, but there was no chance I was going to fall asleep quickly. Jim was a fixture at the Hall. He helped to organize it. He had no family left and nowhere else to go. Why would he change his mind and leave?

I eventually drifted off to sleep, and when I woke up the next morning I knew exactly what I had to do, which was the same thing I had done most every day. I was going to see who was leaving on the morning bus.

I tried to get out of my cot without disturbing anyone, but when I stood up, Tori was waiting there, fully dressed.

"I'm going with you," she whispered.

"You don't even know where I'm going."

"You want to see if Jim gets on the bus."

Enough said.

Soon we were walking together in the gray dusk of the chilly Boston morning. I didn't miss the fact that she was clutching her gym bag.

"People leave every day," she said. "Why is this bugging you?"

"Because he didn't want to leave. If he's getting out, something happened to change his mind, and I want to know what it was."

"Glad to hear it," she said.

"Why's that?"

"It means there's hope for you yet."

We didn't say another word until we reached the end of the long building and the spot where I'd watched the bus load up and pull out every morning.

There were no deliveries being made that day. There was only the big bus, empty, with the motor running, waiting for its passengers.

I led Tori to the same spot I'd gone every day, behind a large green dumpster that was tucked up next to the opposite building. From there we had a clear view of the bus and the building it was idling near.

"Why are we hiding?" Tori asked. "If this is all legit, we should go over there and bid the people a fond farewell."

"Yeah," I replied. "But if it's all legit, why do they take off at the crack of dawn? They could just as easily pull out at noon."

"You're even more paranoid than I am," Tori said.

"I'm not," I argued. "I'm just logical, and there's something illogical about this."

The door to the building opened, and the same procedure began that I had been seeing every morning. The pretty cowboy named Ashley came out with a clipboard and stood by the bus. She was soon followed by a line of people who shuffled past, offered whatever information she asked for, then continued onto the bus.

Though it was still fairly dark, I could see everyone. The loading process went normally. One by one the people filed by the girl, she checked something on the clipboard, and they boarded. Nothing was out of the ordinary, until the last guy came out of the building.

Jim.

I grabbed Tori's arm. I'm not sure why.

"I don't believe it," I whispered.

"Guess he didn't love it here so much after all," Tori said.

"Or something changed his mind."

I was about to step out of our hiding place and walk over to confront him, when Jim suddenly bolted from the line and ran off.

We watched in stunned wonder to see two of Chris's cowboys appear from inside the building as if they had been observing the whole time. They were much younger and stronger than Jim and chased him down easily. The two grabbed him by the arms, and there was a brief struggle, but Jim was no match.

I made a move to help him, but Tori held me back. I pulled away from her but stopped when I saw Jim suddenly go limp.

The fight was over. It was like they had given him a tranquilizer, for he instantly stopped resisting and allowed them to lead him back toward the bus. He walked docilely, looking exactly like all of the other people I had seen boarding the buses.

"They were all drugged," I whispered, trying to contain my emotion. "None of them left by choice."

I looked at Tori. Her eyes were wide and frightened.

I started toward the bus again, but she grabbed my arm with the strength that came from hauling lobster traps, forcing me to stay put.

"No," she said with a stern whisper. "Unless you want to end up on that bus too."

I glanced at Tori's gym bag. The bag with the gun.

She saw me and put her foot on it.

"Don't even think about it," she ordered.

I felt incredibly helpless.

The cowboys loaded Jim onto the bus, sat him in a seat, and stepped off. After a quick wave to the driver, the door closed and the bus headed out for . . . who knew where?

Ashley joined the two guy cowboys, and they all casually strolled back toward the mess hall as if nothing out of the ordinary had happened. They were probably looking forward to a hearty breakfast after a job well done. Before they disappeared inside the building, I heard them laugh.

"What the hell is going on?" I said.

"Obviously they're shipping people out who don't want to be shipped out," Tori said. "Maybe it's like a transfer to somewhere else so the Hall doesn't get overcrowded."

"Do you really think it's as innocent as that?" I asked skeptically.

"No."

"They're drugging people, getting rid of them, and lying about it."

"That's only half of it," Tori said. "Where are they taking them?"

I couldn't begin to guess.

"They come out of that same door every day," I said. "I want to see what's in there."

"What if it's one of Campbell's cowboys?" Tori asked.

"We'll play dumb, like we're lost."

"I don't want to be here anymore, Tucker," she said, sounding genuinely frightened.

"Me neither, but I want to know what's going on."

She nodded in agreement.

We came out of our hiding place and walked quickly across the open space between the buildings until we arrived at the door. I grabbed the handle, expecting it to be locked. It wasn't. We exchanged nervous looks, and I pulled it open.

Inside was a small, nearly empty room with one desk on either side of the door. There were bins on both desks that looked similar to the bins I had seen at the reception desk back at Quincy Market, except that they were empty.

"For paperwork," I whispered. "They pass through here on their way to the bus. They must get processed out the same way those girls process people in."

"It's all so . . . efficient," Tori pointed out.

"Yeah, until somebody tries to bolt."

Staying close together, we moved to a door on the far side of the room. I opened it and cautiously peered inside.

What I saw in that next room was far worse than running into somebody who might have caught us snooping around.

"Oh man," was all I managed to say.

Tori pushed the door open the rest of the way. When she looked inside, she had to grab my arm to steady herself.

"This just . . . it can't be," she said numbly.

There were stacks of suitcases piled along one wall that reached nearly to the high ceiling. Hundreds of them. All types, shapes, and colors. Another wall was full of bins that held used clothing. Shirts were separated from pants. Women's clothes from men's clothes. Another set of bins held shoes, underwear, and socks.

I drifted into the room and touched a suitcase that was on the floor in front of the large pile.

"It's Jim's," I said, my voice cracking. I lifted it and added, "Empty. I've been watching people get on those buses for days. Nobody left with their belongings, and nobody came back. This is all their stuff."

"It's like pictures I've seen of the Holocaust," Tori said. "What are they doing to those people?"

I felt nauseated. We'd seen enough. Too much.

"We can't be seen here," I said and headed for the door.

Tori was right behind me. We made it out of that horrible room and back through to the outside door without incident. Once outside, we kept walking and didn't say a word until we were back near the mess hall.

"We've got to tell everyone," Tori cried.

"And say what? 'Hey, everybody! Looks like jolly old Chris and his merry posse of cowboys are sending people off to their deaths.'"

"Yes!"

"No! We don't know who's innocent and who's working with the cowboys or where those people are being taken. If we tell the wrong people, we could end up on the next bus out."

"So what do we do?"

My mind raced through every possible scenario, from breaking into the place where the records were kept to breaking Chris's legs. Nothing seemed like a smart move.

Finally, the right idea hit.

"We have to find out what's going on," I said. "And who's in on it."

"How? It's not like we can ask Chris."

"No, but we can follow the next bus to see where it's taking those people."

"You mean, like, tomorrow?"

"Yes. We'll track the bus to see where it goes. Once we know for sure, we can come back and blow the whistle . . . just before we get the hell out of here for good."

"What about Kent and Olivia and Jon?" she asked.

"I don't think we should tell them anything until we know for sure what we're dealing with. It'll be a lot easier convincing them to go once we have evidence."

"Agreed," Tori said. "It won't be easy keeping quiet about this for a whole day."

"I'm more concerned about how we're going to find a car."

Tori reached into her bag, and for a second I thought she was going to pull out her gun. Instead, she pulled out a set of car keys and shook them at me.

"When Jon first got the Explorer, I found a spare set in the glove compartment. I thought it would be smart to hold on to them in case of an emergency."

"I think this qualifies."

"Yeah, this qualifies."

Tori and I spent the rest of the day trying to act normal. I worked in the garden directly in front of Quincy Market and she did . . . whatever she did. The whole day I spent living inside my head, trying to understand why Chris would be getting rid of the very people he was working so hard to protect . . . or at least pretending to protect. Was he working with SYLO? Or the Air Force? I couldn't imagine who else might want people sent off to their deaths—if that's indeed what was happening. It made sense that he was working for one side or the other. But which? And why?

It was all the more confounding when I worried that we might be jumping to gruesome conclusions. Was there an innocent explanation for what we'd seen? If there was, I couldn't come up with it. Wherever these people ended up, it looked certain that they were being tricked and betrayed.

Betrayal. I knew a thing or two about that, thanks to my parents.

The people in the Hall were being told that this was a safe refuge. They were fed well and protected . . . until they weren't. It struck me as incredibly cold to lure people in with the promise of sanctuary only to send them off to another fate, whatever it was. It was beyond evil. What I couldn't understand was, if the intent of the people running the Hall was mass murder, why were they going through the trouble of pretending it was something else?

The day passed without incident. I avoided Jon, Olivia, and

Kent only because I knew it would be hard not to warn them about what was going on. Olivia would panic and want to bolt instantly. Kent would probably want to take a swing at Chris. And Jon, well, Jon might just come up with a logical explanation for it all, but I didn't want to risk telling him for fear he would tell everyone else, and then Chris would be coming for us.

They would all know soon enough.

When I woke up early the next morning, Tori was already dressed and sitting on her cot with her arms curled around her legs and her gym bag over her shoulder. I gave her a quick wave and got dressed. While trying to make as little noise as possible, the two of us once again climbed out of the basement and stepped out to the predawn morning.

It was cold. Winter was definitely on the way. We walked quickly away from Faneuil Hall, looking around constantly to see if we were being watched. No alarms sounded. Nobody came running. We retraced our steps back to the parking lot where we had left the Explorer several days before.

"You'd better drive," I said. "You've got more experience."

That was an understatement. I wasn't even old enough to have a license. Neither was Tori, but she had been driving her father's pickup truck all over Pemberwick Island to deliver lobsters. I had no doubt that she could navigate the empty streets of Boston. The question was, could she trail a bus without being seen?

"Is the other gun back there?" Tori asked.

I lifted the back hatch to see . . . nothing.

"The cowboys must have found it," I said uneasily.

Tori reached into her gym bag and pulled out the Glock. She

reached in again and took out the fully loaded clip that held seventeen bullets. With one quick movement, she slammed the clip into the handgrip and locked it into place.

"I never shot a person," Tori said. "But I'm willing to try."

We got into the Explorer. Tori fired up the engine, and seconds later we were rolling back toward Faneuil Hall.

"Pull up near the dumpster," I offered. "But keep close to the building."

Tori drove with the headlights off, which made it tricky to see where we were going. The last thing we needed was to slam into a light post. Or a bus. Soon we were gliding close to the building with the dumpster. Tori drove up onto the sidewalk, crossed the brick pedestrian walkway, and pulled to a stop a few feet short of the end of the building.

"I'll kill the engine, and we can watch from outside," she said. "When the bus pulls out, we'll get back in and follow."

"Do you think you can shadow them without being seen?" I asked.

"I have no idea," she said impatiently. "It's not like I've done this before."

She turned off the engine and pulled out the key. When we got out of the SUV, we left the doors open. Getting back in fast was going to be critical.

We crept to the dumpster and took up our familiar position to see that the bus was back and people were already being loaded.

"Jeez, we just made it," I whispered.

"It's going to be full," Tori pointed out.

There were many more people than there had been the day

before. Maybe twice as many. It made me a little nervous to think that Chris might have caught wind that we were on to him and decided to increase his numbers. But there was no way he could have known. Or so I hoped.

Nothing else was out of the ordinary. The girl checked off the names of the victims, they boarded the bus, and the door closed.

"That's it, let's go," Tori said.

We ran for the Explorer and quietly closed the doors after getting in.

"I'll circle around toward the street they took off on yesterday," Tori announced.

She hit the gas and rounded the block that was near the same route the bus had taken the day before. She pulled to the side of the road and waited.

I held my breath.

Seconds later, the bus rolled by in front of us.

"And the chase is on," she declared.

Tori waited a few seconds, then took a quick left onto a street that ran parallel to the route the bus was on.

I rolled down my window in the hope of hearing the bus even when we couldn't see it. It worked well enough; we could hear the steady, low rumble of its engine.

We soon hit an intersection that forced us to turn directly onto the street that the bus was on.

"Don't follow too close," I said. "It's not like we can hide in traffic."

It was still fairly dark. I hoped that would help us blend into the city.

Tori let the bus get several blocks in front of us. It made a few turns, but we saw them all and were able to keep pace.

"It doesn't look like its leaving town," I said. "It's not headed toward the interstate."

The driver didn't obey traffic rules. The bus turned the wrong way onto one-way streets and didn't even slow down for stop signs.

Tori did an awesome job keeping up. There was no way of knowing if the bus driver had seen us, but I felt as though we were doing okay.

"We were here the other day," Tori pointed out. "It's turning onto Storrow Drive."

It was the same route, parallel to the Charles River, that we had taken the day we arrived in Boston. It was also the route we took between Fenway Park and Faneuil Hall.

"Stay on the surface streets," I said. "If we follow it onto Storrow Drive, they'll see us for sure."

I had set an almost impossible task for Tori. We had to drive on the far side of buildings from the bus while trying to keep pace. If there had been traffic, we never would have been able to do it. As it was, all we had to do was swerve past abandoned cars. We traveled like that for several minutes until we saw the bus take the curve that led toward Fenway.

Tori was able to stay focused and shadow the bus from a few blocks away, using the buildings to shield us from sight. When the bus turned onto Yawkey Way, there was no doubt in my mind. Its destination was Fenway Park.

Finally, the bus slowed and stopped in front of an entrance gate to the old ballpark. There were a few abandoned cars a block away, so Tori pulled up behind one. We were a safe distance away but had a clear view of the bus.

"It's safe to say they're not here to catch a game," I said.

Two bulky men stepped out of the gate and approached the bus.

"Oh, that's not good," Tori said.

They were dressed in gray and black, military-like camouflage fatigues and wore black berets. From that distance I couldn't see whether they had any insignias or patches to identify them. From each of their belts hung what looked like a two-foot-long black baton. They didn't appear to have any other weapons. When they stepped up to the bus, the door opened and the victims stepped out. Knowing how Jim had been tranquilized, it now looked obvious that they all had been drugged in some way, for they shuffled along in a line, zombie-like, toward the entrance.

"What the hell is that?" I asked, pointing above the stadium.

There was a giant steel frame peeking up above the stands. Next to it was the top of what looked like a construction crane.

"Did you see that before?" I asked.

"I don't remember," Tori admitted. "But it isn't normal. It's like something is being built inside the stadium."

"That fast?" I said. "I swear that wasn't there a couple of weeks ago."

The last of the victims got off the bus, and the two soldiers, or whatever they were, followed them inside. The bus door closed, and the vehicle pulled out, its mission complete.

"We gotta go inside," I said.

"I knew you were going to say that," Tori replied.

We got out of the Explorer and jogged toward the stadium. We didn't go to the same gate that the victims had entered. Instead, we found a set of stairs leading to a higher level and ran up. Our search for a way in didn't take long. Every last gate was wide open. We slipped inside and found ourselves on the deserted mezzanine. There were no Fenway Franks sizzling or game programs being hawked. There were no peanuts, popcorn, or Cracker Jack to be found. The place was dead.

Tori and I moved cautiously, hugging the walls. There was no telling when one of those soldiers might appear. As we made our way closer to the tunnel that passed under the stands and led to the field, we could hear that the stadium wasn't as dead as we thought. There was activity happening on the diamond, and it wasn't a baseball game.

"It sounds like a construction site," I whispered to Tori.

There was the distinct sound of machinery and hammering and drilling that jumbled together into a storm of white noise. We moved cautiously along the tunnel until we got our first view of the field.

It looked nothing like it did when the Red Sox were playing.

We came out onto the second level of the stadium to look down on what was definitely a construction site. The entire field, including the baseball diamond and the outfield, was gone. In its place was the skeleton of the massive structure that we had seen from outside. It was the frame of a giant dome that covered most of what used to be the field. Metallic, silver skin was being applied to the outside but had only gotten a third of the way to the top, which allowed us to see inside. Looking through the girders showed us that the interior was going to be a vast space, like a circus tent. Or a giant steel igloo. On one side of the dome was the frame of a huge door that had yet to be installed. It looked big enough to drive a truck through.

As incredible a sight as this was, there was something else going on that was even more stunning.

"That's how it went up so fast," Tori said, numb.

Workers were scattered throughout the construction site. Hundreds of them. They were all laboring under the watchful eye of several more soldiers. Many of the workers I recognized from the Hall. One of them was Jim.

The truth became all too clear. People from the Hall weren't being executed; they were being used as slave labor to build this monstrous structure. It suddenly made sense why we were being treated so well. We were being fed and kept healthy so we could build this contraption.

The realization that we were being groomed as slaves wasn't the most disturbing truth we discovered. The workers were moving with impossible speed. Men lifted girders that had to weigh ten times their body weight. Women were hauling material and wielding jackhammers that were almost as big as they were. They swarmed over the structure, dangling from the frame, moving pieces into place with inhuman strength. It was like watching a movie play out in fast motion. It was an impossible sight . . .

. . . that was all too possible.

"It's the Ruby," I said, stunned. "They were all forced to take it."

The purpose of the Ruby had suddenly become clear.

"How great is this?" came an enthusiastic voice from the tunnel behind us.

It was a voice that I recognized but never expected to hear again.

Tori and I froze. She knew the voice too. Neither of us wanted to turn to see if it was true.

"I heard you landed at the Hall, but I'm surprised to see you here at Fenway so soon. You weren't scheduled to start work until next week."

"This is impossible," Tori said in a strained whisper.

I knew it wasn't. Nothing was impossible. Not anymore.

"But that's cool," the guy said. "We can always use a few more hands."

I turned slowly. Though I knew who I would see, it was still a shock, for we had witnessed him being shot dead on a bluff overlooking the ocean and tumbling into the sea.

"Welcome to Fenway," he said with a warm smile.

Mr. Feit had risen from the grave.

TEN

"We saw you die," I said, though I'm not sure how I was able to speak, let alone think.

"That's not exactly true," Feit said, wagging his finger. "I was shot by a SYLO sniper and you saw me fall into the ocean. Very, very big difference."

"No," Tori said, shaking her head as if she could make Feit disappear by force of will and logic. "If the bullet didn't kill you, the fall should have. You dropped a couple of hundred feet, bouncing off rocks all the way down and—"

"Yeah, I was there," Feit said, wincing. "Don't need to relive the details."

"You were dead," I stated flatly.

"Obviously not," he said with a wink. "Unless you believe in ghosts."

I didn't, but at that moment I could have been convinced.

Feit looked no worse for wear. He still acted like a casual, older surfer dude, but he had cleaned up his act. The shaggy hair and beard stubble were gone. His blond hair was now cut short and neat. The earring was gone too. Instead of a hoodie and board shorts, he wore the same gray camouflage fatigues as the soldiers who herded the people from the Hall into Fenway.

Feit was not only alive . . . he was a soldier.

"How?" was all I could say.

Feit flopped down into a stadium seat and put his feet up. He had a paper cup with a straw that he sucked on, looking ready for the start of a game.

"After I fell, did you see a speedboat taking off?" he asked between sips.

"Yes!" Tori said. "People were running ahead of us on the trail down to the water. They got to the hidden boats before we did."

"They pulled me out of the water," Feit said. "I was in sorry shape, I'll give you that. But I was still breathing. Those dudes saved me."

"No way," I exclaimed. "That was only a couple of weeks ago. Nobody heals that fast."

"Really? How's your gunshot wound, Tori?"

Tori's hand immediately went to the spot where the bullet had passed through her shoulder . . . her completely healed shoulder.

"That medicine they gave me at Faneuil Hall," Tori said, thinking back. "What was that stuff?"

"Pretty cool, right?" Feit said with a sly smile as he sipped his drink. "I was back on my feet and ready to go in a couple of days."

"That's impossible," I said with a gasp. "No medicine can do that."

"Yet here I am," Feit said, holding out his arms. "Alive and kicking."

"Who are you?" Tori asked, numb. "Where did you come from?"

She made a move as if to grab him and throttle the truth out, but I held her back.

It was a good thing I did.

Two soldiers in fatigues and black berets stepped out from the shadows of the tunnel. They had been hanging back, watching, ready for trouble.

"Easy now," Feit said with a laugh. "You guys are old friends. I wouldn't want you to get hurt. Or get dead."

Tori backed down, but she twisted the gym bag so it hung in front of her. The zipper was open.

"I'm actually stoked to see you two," he said. "Sounds like you had a gnarly trip to the mainland."

"How do you know that?" Tori demanded.

"It was Chris Campbell," I said. "They're not helping survivors at the Hall, they're prepping them to work here on . . . what is that thing?"

I pointed to the massive construction project taking shape on the field.

Feit stood and walked to the railing, where he surveyed the half-finished steel dome.

"That," he said with pride. "That is salvation."

"Whose salvation?" I asked.

"Mankind's, of course. This is what it's about, Tucker. We're ensuring the survival of the human race. Pretty awesome, right?"

Tori and I exchanged confused looks. I don't know what I expected Feit to say, but that definitely wasn't it.

"Survival?" Tori spat, incredulous. "All we've seen is death."

"True," he replied. "That's a bummer."

"Bummer?" I cried. "Millions of people are just . . . gone."

Feit shrugged. "What can I say? We're at war. War has casualties."

I didn't know what was more stunning: the fact that Feit was alive or his indifference to the massive loss of life.

"What kind of war is this?" I demanded. "There are no sides. No declarations. There's no point to any of it but . . . death."

"Not true," Feit corrected. "This is a war between ideologies. Between visions of what the world is and what it should be. We're talking big-picture stuff here. Bigger than any country or race or religion. This is about righting the ship before it hits the rocks. Isn't that worth fighting over . . . and a few casualties?"

I looked to Tori. She seemed as confused as I was.

"Are you from another planet?" she asked. "I mean, literally?"

Feit let out another laugh. Talking about the deaths of millions didn't hurt his sense of humor any.

"I guess you could say that," he replied.

"So you're an alien?" I asked, incredulous.

"If that's what you want to believe, sure."

"What I want is the truth," I shouted with frustration. "What is SYLO?"

"Ahh, SYLO," Feit repeated. "There are those who choose to soar and those who prefer to crawl in the dirt. The powers that created those mindless storm troopers can't see beyond their own selfish, short-term needs. Those fools are fighting to maintain the status quo while pushing mankind to the brink of extinction."

"But they're part of the Navy," I said. "The president of the United States sent them to Pemberwick and—"

"You're not listening," Feit snapped, no longer the loose surfer dude. "This isn't about countries or borders. We're shaping the future of the entire planet. The United States is irrelevant."

A scream came from the field.

We looked to see a man falling from the highest point of the structure.

"Oh my God," Tori gasped.

I always thought that if you fell from an extreme height, you'd pass out before hitting the ground. I was wrong. The doomed man wailed in terror for the entire four seconds it took him to reach the ground. We were spared seeing the impact, for he dropped out of sight behind the partially constructed outer skin of the dome, but I heard the sickening, dull thud as his body hit and the screaming abruptly ended.

I hoped to God it wasn't Jim. We stared in silence for several seconds, and then . . .

"Oops," Feit said with a dismissive shrug.

"You're using these people," I said, stunned. "That's what the Ruby is for. You're creating superhuman slaves. To do what? Rebuild what you've destroyed?"

"No," Feit said, deadly serious. "They're rebuilding what they've destroyed themselves."

"You're talking in riddles," Tori snarled. "Who are you fighting for? The Air Force?"

"I'm fighting for the future of a doomed planet," he said as if annoyed at having to explain. "This is a finite world. Nothing new is being created. No new water or fossil fuels or space to handle overpopulation. Many choose to ignore that and live in denial. They're wrong. They're dangerous. We're giving the world a gift by taking control. What we're offering is a do-over. A second chance."

"So who are you fighting with?" I demanded.

Feit stood up straight and gave us a mock salute.

"I'm a colonel in the United States Air Force," he replied proudly. "A twenty-year veteran."

"You don't seem like an Air Force colonel," Tori said.

"Really? How many do you know? I used to be a pilot, but now my expertise lies in the field of human behavior. I've been charged with assembling the workforce that will build a better future. It's a huge job. I've been traveling like crazy. Different city every day. I'm kind of beat, to be honest."

"Poor you," Tori said sarcastically.

"What I told you on Pemberwick Island wasn't far from the truth. I *was* testing the Ruby. I wanted to know how much the human body could withstand before, well, before the flame went out. I'm not alone, either. There are plenty of others just like me who have been doing the exact same thing. This isn't some half-baked operation. It's been planned for years."

"By whom?" I demanded. "Who is in charge? Who is controlling the Air Force?"

"Visionaries," Feit said proudly.

"Murderers," Tori said.

"So it really is a civil war," I said soberly.

"You could call it that," Feit replied. "But as wars go, it's pretty much over. We've already weakened SYLO's capabilities and secured most of the population centers."

"What?" I said, stunned.

"Population centers?" Tori repeated, incredulous.

"Oh, come on," Feit said, scoffing. "You didn't think this was only happening in your little corner of the world, did you?"

The weight of his words made my knees buckle. I half fell, half sat in a seat. My entire focus had been on bringing down SYLO. I wanted to destroy the devils that ruined my life. Now it seemed as though the SYLO Navy was defenseless against the might of the far superior Air Force. My enemy was fighting back against an even more powerful and dangerous force. We weren't looking at the mass execution of millions. If Feit was telling us the truth, we were faced with the extermination of billions.

Tori spoke, but barely above a whisper, as if she didn't want to hear her own words.

"You mean you've wiped out the entire population of the world?"

"No!" Feit replied quickly. "That's just crazy."

I felt a short moment of relief. Very short.

"Three-quarters, tops," he continued. "Then again, we're not done. There's some additional cleanup planned, especially in the bigger cities."

It was Tori's turn to sit down.

"Cleanup," she muttered.

Feit went on casually, as if explaining a simple math problem. "We're not planning on total eradication. We need workers to maintain the current infrastructure. At least for a while. Everything will eventually be torn down, re-envisioned, and rebuilt, of course. The project here is just the beginning. The one thing we don't want to do is go back to business as usual. That would defeat the whole purpose."

"And SYLO was trying to stop you?" I asked.

"Sides have been chosen," Feit replied, bristling. "Our methods are extreme, I'll give you that, but they're nothing compared to what would happen if SYLO prevailed. You may think what we've done is barbaric, but if SYLO succeeded, the world as you know it would have ceased to exist. I promise you that. Basically, we're saving the planet. Hooray for us."

"But how can you know that?" I asked, trying to keep my voice from shaking. "You wiped out most of the earth's population on the theory that SYLO would do worse? That's insane."

"It's not insane," Feit said with confidence. "It's absolute fact."

"What proof do you have?"

There was another scream from the field. Another Ruby-fueled worker was falling to his death.

I watched as the horrific scene played out with the same gruesome result. And when I looked back . . .

. . . Tori stood with her legs apart and her hands raised.

Her pistol was aimed directly at Feit.

"Whoa!" he exclaimed and backed off, nearly falling over a stadium seat.

The two soldiers went for the dark batons that hung from their belts.

Tori spun and fired, hitting one of them in the leg. He screamed and fell to the cement floor, clutching his shattered knee. The other soldier held his hands away from his body to show he wasn't going for his weapon.

"Don't worry," Tori said with surprising calm. "A little of that magic potion and you'll be as good as new. Right?"

"Put it down, Tori," Feit pleaded. "I know this is a lot to get your head around, but it's the only way. We're the good guys."

Tori turned the gun on Feit, gripping it with both hands.

"There are no good guys," she snarled. "This is insane."

"But it isn't!" Feit cried. "It's not just about today. We're fighting for future generations. Without us millions more will die. No, billions."

"Then so be it," she said, taking aim. "As long as you're one of them."

Feit held his hands up in a futile attempt to protect himself.

I braced myself for the shot.

Tori squeezed the trigger . . .

. . . as the gun was torn from her hand. It clattered to the floor between the seats.

Tori squealed in pain and grabbed at her hand.

The injured soldier on the ground had his black baton pointed at her. It was a weapon that let loose with a charge of invisible power, much like what the black planes fired in daylight. It was yet another example of impossible technology.

Tori and I stood together, totally exposed. The second soldier had already grabbed his baton and leveled it at us.

"Wow," Feit exclaimed. "You almost had me there."

His casual way of reacting to everything made me hate him even more. The burning in my gut returned. The enemy once again had a face. I didn't think for a second that we could change the course of the war, but I knew whom I wanted to make pay for his crimes.

"I wish you hadn't done that," Feit said. "I was going to give you two a choice. I mean, we go back a long way. I feel bad for you, Tori. Especially since your father got such a raw deal."

His words were like a punch to Tori's gut. I saw her waver as if she might fall back, but she held it together and stood firm.

"What are you talking about?" she asked in a small voice.

"He thought he was staging some major revolt to take back his little island. He had no idea we were using him to get to Granger."

"You . . . what?" Tori asked, stunned.

"Oh yeah. Your father thought he was leading a bunch of local rebels, but half of them were my guys. He was fighting back against SYLO, which is exactly what we wanted."

Tori winced. It suddenly became clear to me why there were so many strange faces in Mr. Sleeper's rebel group. They were Air Force infiltrators working for Feit. There were dozens of strange faces on Pemberwick. I had thought they were tourists who stuck around because of the late summer. Could they all have been Air Force agents?

"It's why we were on Pemberwick Island," Feit continued. "SYLO was there to make a stand. We couldn't allow that. Like I said, we've been planning this for years."

Tori fought back tears and straightened up defiantly.

I realized that I was going to have to get in line to take revenge against Feit.

Assuming we got out of there alive.

"You said something about giving us a choice," I said, desperate to buy some time.

"Right. I was going to let you out of working here. You could have joined my personal team. I don't see that happening now."

"How could you think we would help you?" Tori said with disgust.

"To save your own lives of course," Feit said with a shrug.

He waved to the uninjured soldier and said, "Take them down to the medical unit."

"Medical unit?" I asked.

"Somebody has to replace those two workers who just fell. It's Ruby time!"

Boom!

A huge explosion erupted out on the field. The entire stadium rocked, nearly knocking us off our feet. A plume of fire grew from the center of the steel structure.

The soldiers fell to their knees to brace themselves.

Feit spun around toward the field, looking as stunned as we were. Whatever was happening, it wasn't part of his plan.

Boom!

Another explosion erupted next to the first.

An ear-splitting shriek signaled the arrival of two dark shapes that tore across the sky.

It was an all-too-familiar experience.

They were fighter planes, and not the singing black marauders.

They were U.S. Navy fighters.

SYLO was back.

ELEVEN

Fenway Park was under attack.

We had a short window of confusion to try to get the hell out and away while Feit and his soldiers were focused on something other than us.

The steel structure was doomed. Multiple fighter jets screamed overhead and dropped their explosives before blazing off to make way for others to follow. Dozens of missiles hit the field and exploded, turning the framework into a twisted, melting hulk. The sounds of the explosions and the screaming jets made it impossible to think, let alone hear.

The field was ablaze, its heat turning the mezzanine into an oven. Terrified workers fled for their lives. Ironically, many of them survived because the Ruby gave them the speed and power to escape the inferno.

I pushed Tori to get moving, but instead of running she dropped to her knees to retrieve the gun. I wanted to scream at her to leave it but didn't want to risk turning Feit's attention back to us. It was a frustrating few seconds . . .

. . . that ended when the injured soldier looked our way.

"Stop!" he screamed and lifted his baton gun.

I yanked Tori to her feet and pulled her toward me as the soldier fired. The charge from his gun missed us and blasted the back off one of the stadium seats. It was a far more powerful charge than the one that had knocked the gun from Tori's hands.

They were now shooting to kill.

The shot got the attention of the others. When the second soldier went for his own weapon, I thought we were done.

But Tori had found her gun. She unloaded on them, blasting shot after shot, sending Feit and the soldier down behind the first row of seats.

I grabbed her around the waist and pulled her backward as she continued to shoot, pinning Feit and the soldiers down.

We were nearly at the doors leading outside when I heard a sharp click. Tori had fired her last bullet.

"Move!" I shouted.

I slammed the door open and jumped outside. As soon as we were out, the glass door next to us exploded, sending a spray of glass shards our way.

The soldiers were up and shooting back. The only choice we had was to run.

The bombardment on the field continued. Fenway was rocking, and not in a good way. As each missile hit, the stadium shivered. It felt like we were in a violent earthquake, which made it hard to stay on our feet. We struggled to head back the way we had come, running down the stairs to street level. We were several steps from the ground when a streaking missile tore out of the sky, headed directly for us.

"Jump!" I shouted.

We vaulted over the handrail and fell the last few feet to the side-walk as the missile hit the stairs above us. The force of the explosion threw us forward in a shower of pulverized steel and cement. I hit a light pole with my shoulder and crumpled to the ground. My ears rang, and I had trouble catching my breath, but we weren't dead.

A cloud of dust swirled, making it impossible to see more than a few feet in any direction. A hand grabbed my shoulder, making me jump with surprise. Turning quickly, I saw Tori's tear-streaked face inches from mine. Her long, dark curls were caked with the gray dust of what used to be Fenway Park.

"You okay?" I asked.

She nodded. "We gotta get to the car."

I struggled to my feet and helped her up. We were both shaken, but uninjured . . . and totally disoriented. Tori grabbed my hand, and we ran.

Through the dust cloud I spotted the Explorer right where we had left it . . .

. . . and another fighter in the sky, headed our way. It released its missile and broke off quickly as the rocket shot ahead and ex-ploded into the side of the old ballpark, sending out a wave of brick and mortar that rained down around us.

"I guess SYLO isn't done after all," Tori said breathlessly as we dodged the falling bricks.

When we got to the Explorer, Tori jumped behind the wheel while I got in the passenger side. She fired up the engine while flex-ing her left hand.

"Is it hurt?" I asked.

"Just numb. What are those guns they have?"

"They must be the same kind of thing the black planes have. It shoots a burst of energy."

"That's like science fiction," Tori said. "Since when does the military have stuff like that?"

"That and lasers that evaporate people and disintegrate buildings, and magic medicine that instantly heals injuries, and fighter planes that sing, and red crystals that turn people into super humans before killing them. The Air Force is using some serious technology."

"Why doesn't SYLO have the same stuff?" she asked.

"You're asking me like I might have an answer."

Fenway was tumbling. One whole side had collapsed, making the ballpark look more like the remains of the Roman Colosseum than a modern-day stadium. The Navy fighters continued to scream overhead while launching missiles. The steel structure that Feit called "salvation" was destroyed, yet the punishing attack continued. Terrified people fled from the crumbling stadium. Both soldiers and civilians flooded out from every door, desperate to escape the destruction.

"Drive us back to Faneuil Hall," I said. "The others have to know what's going on."

Tori hit the gas, did a sharp one-eighty, and we sped away from the smoldering wreck that was once Fenway Park.

"Is it possible?" Tori asked, breathless. "Could the Air Force have wiped out most of civilization? How could that help mankind?"

"I don't know. I can't get my mind around any of it."

"What if Feit is right? What if SYLO is plotting something even worse?"

"Worse than genocide?" I asked. "I have trouble believing that."

"Why? Because Feit's a liar?"

"Because my parents are part of SYLO. I don't care what they did to me, there's no way they could buy into something like that."

"And Feit's a liar," she added.

"Yeah, that too."

"Then why did SYLO choose Pemberwick Island to make a stand?"

"I don't know. Maybe they thought they could defend it. They sure sent enough firepower there. What I don't get is how nobody knew a civil war was brewing. You'd think that kind of thing would make the news."

"Maybe the government thought they could stop it," Tori offered.

"What government?" I shot back. "The Air Force is the government too! There's gotta be something else behind this."

"Yeah," Tori said. "If we believe Feit."

The sounds of the attack on Fenway grew fainter as we tore through the empty streets of Boston.

"Does this mean you're with me?" she asked.

It took a second for me to understand what she was asking. "You mean Nevada?"

"That radio broadcast might be the only hope we have of finding people who are ready to fight back."

"Fight back against who?" I shouted in frustration. "SYLO is supposedly trying to destroy the world, and the Air Force has already wiped out most of the population. I'm not seeing a clear choice here."

"If we believe Feit," Tori cautioned.

"The guy's a liar, but everything he just said seems to be true. What we don't know is why it came to this, and who can be trusted."

"Exactly," Tori said with conviction. "The only people we can rely on are survivors like us."

It was the first logical thing I had heard since I woke up that morning.

"Oh man, we've gotta hurry," I said. "Look!"

A squad of twenty soldiers wearing gray camouflage fatigues and black berets was on the street ahead of us, headed in the same direction we were: toward Faneuil Hall. They jogged together, two by two, each holding a black baton gun.

Tori took a sharp right to avoid them.

"Whatever they were building at Fenway is destroyed," she said. "Fenway is rubble. They don't need workers there anymore."

It was a sobering thought. If the survivors at Faneuil Hall were no longer needed, what would happen to them?

"Drive dangerously," I said.

Tori accelerated, flying along a street that ran parallel to the one the soldiers were on.

"Why aren't they on a bus?" Tori asked.

"How should I know? At least it gives us a little time."

"We've gotta be careful," she said. "If we fly in there shouting about how Chris is really with the Air Force, his cowboys could turn on people."

"We won't make a big show," I said. "We've gotta get Olivia and Kent and Jon out. Whoever else we see along the way, we'll tell them quietly. The news will spread fast, and people can slip away without a lot of noise and disappear into the city."

"What if they don't believe us?" Tori asked.

"Then the soldiers will convince them when they show up," I said grimly.

Tori took the gun that was in her lap and tossed it to me.

"The shells are in the glove box," she said. "Load it."

The gun was still warm, the result of having been fired seventeen times. It took me a few seconds to find the lever that released the clip from the handle. I grabbed the box of bullets from the glove compartment and tried feeding them into the clip, but they wouldn't go.

"Other way," Tori pointed out.

I flipped the clip. That made the job much easier. In no time it was reloaded with seventeen more shots.

"I'll carry the gun," Tori said. "No offense. I just don't want you shooting off your foot."

"None taken."

"How do you want to do this?" Tori asked.

We were nearly back to Faneuil Hall, and we needed a plan. We would get there well ahead of the soldiers, but they would catch up quickly.

"Park near the east end of the Hall," I said.

Tori made the last turn off the surface street and pulled to a stop behind an abandoned FedEx truck.

"Are you okay with splitting up?" I asked. "We can cover more ground that way."

"Yeah. Sure. What are you thinking?"

"Find Kent and bring him here."

"How? I have no idea where he goes during the day. He's totally secretive about it."

"I don't know what he does either, but I've seen him eating lunch under the trees on the south end of the complex. If he's not there, forget him and get back here."

"What about you?" she asked.

"Jon's probably at the battery-charging station. I'll tell him to meet you here and then look for Olivia."

"I have no idea where she could be either," Tori said.

"Neither do I, but everybody knows her. Somebody's bound to know where she is."

"Yeah, she's hard to miss."

I thought I caught a note of disdain. Or jealousy. I ignored it.

"Whenever you see somebody, let them know what's going on," I said. "Tell them to spread the word fast, leave their stuff, and get the hell out."

"There isn't much time, Tucker," she said, troubled. "If you can't find Olivia . . ."

She didn't have to finish her sentence.

"I'll find her," I said. "Just try not to attract any attention."

I handed her the gun and the clip. She took it and slammed the clip home.

"I guess shooting Chris Campbell would attract attention."

"Yeah, try to avoid that," I cautioned.

"What if we don't all make it back here?" she asked, looking me dead in the eye.

Tori was the most confident person I had ever met. Back home, when a SYLO soldier had a gun pointed at her head, she had taken him down with a Taser without blinking. She had fearlessly driven a speedboat into a firestorm between burning warships and saved our lives. She had just fired on Feit and his Air Force bodyguards, giving us the cover we needed to escape from Fenway. But in that moment, I saw a hint of fear in her eyes. It wasn't that she was afraid of SYLO or the Air Force or whatever else we might encounter. She was afraid of being alone.

I wished I had something more comforting to say.

"Stay until the soldiers arrive. Once they show up, take off and don't look back."

"Will you do the same?" she asked.

"If it means the difference between getting killed and not getting killed, yes. Pick a meeting place. If we have to take off, we'll go there and wait for as long as it takes for the others to show up."

"Twenty-four hours," she said coldly. "If nobody else shows up by then, they aren't coming."

"Done. Where do we meet?"

"Old Ironsides," Tori replied with no hesitation. "I love that ship."

The USS *Constitution* was a museum-piece warship that was berthed in Boston Harbor. Every schoolkid in New England had been there on a field trip.

"Old Ironsides it is. Wait there for one day and then—"

"Then go to Nevada," she said with conviction.

There was an awkward moment.

I can't say that I loved Tori Sleeper. I wasn't even sure what that kind of love was. Hell, I was only fourteen. I'd had plenty of crushes, but I'd never known what it was like to be truly in love. Frankly, I wasn't in any hurry. Life was just starting. But sitting there in that car, after what we'd been through, it was hard to know whether my life was just starting, or nearing its end.

"I think you're great," I said, fumbling for words.

Tori gave me a small smile.

"I'm still debating about you."

She leaned forward and kissed me. A real kiss. It didn't get all steamy or anything, but it wasn't a quick peck either. It was an all-too-brief vacation from reality.

She pulled away, and we held eye contact.

I think I was breathing, but I can't be sure.

"What was that for?" I asked.

"In case we don't get the chance again," she replied.

She threw her door open, grabbed the pistol, and took off running down the street.

I was left stunned, but I couldn't take the time to dwell on a sweet and confusing moment that was already history.

The Air Force hit squad was on the way.

TWELVE

I had no idea how much time I had before the soldiers descended on Faneuil Hall—or what they would do once they got there. With the project at Fenway Park destroyed, the Air Force no longer needed slaves to build it, whatever *it* was. Would they try to keep up the ruse of the Hall being a refuge for survivors? Maybe they had another project for which they needed some drugged-up workers. Or would they finish the job they began when they attacked Boston and wipe out as many survivors as possible?

Whatever. We had to get out.

The solar battery-charging station was set up on the roof of the north building to maximize the sunlight. I sprinted there, charged up the stairs, and pushed through the door to see Jon walking to a table with an armload of batteries. Yes!

"Thank God you're here," Jon said with a big sigh of relief.

"Why? What happened?" I asked, momentarily thrown.

"I'm way behind," he explained. "Can you grab the batteries from Section D?"

"No! We're leaving. Now. Chris and his cowboys aren't survivors.

They're with the Air Force. They set this place up to collect survivors and put them to work."

Jon gave me a blank look. "What?" was all he managed to say.

"Tori and I saw it. Nobody's leaving here by choice. They're being used as slaves by the Air Force. Did you hear those far-off explosions?"

"I heard something," Jon said, nodding dumbly. "I thought it was thunder."

"It was Fenway Park being destroyed by SYLO missiles."

"SYLO attacked?" Jon asked, incredulous.

"Yes. The Air Force was building something there. It was like a . . . a . . . giant steel igloo, but SYLO took it down, along with the rest of Fenway. Now the Air Force soldiers are headed this way to . . . to . . . I don't know what they're going to do, but I don't want to be here when it happens. Tori's looking for Kent. I came for you and Olivia."

Jon stared at me, still clutching the batteries, with his mouth hanging open.

"Say something," I commanded.

He snapped back to reality and shook his head. "I don't believe you."

"What? Why would I lie?"

"I don't think you're lying, I just think you're mistaken. Chris has taken care of us. Why would he hand us over to the Air Force to be . . . what? Slaves?"

"Because he's one of them!" I shouted with frustration. "They've been fattening us up and letting us build our strength so we could work on their project. But the project is rubble. They don't need us anymore."

"But that's so . . . so . . . implausible."

"Everything that's happening is freaking implausible!" I shouted. "Look, you can do what you want, but I'm outta here. The Explorer is parked behind a FedEx truck near the northeast corner of the building. That's where we're all going to meet. Be smart. Go there and wait for us."

"I'll think about it," he said, though it didn't sound like he meant it.

I wanted to throttle the guy and force him to go, but I didn't have time.

"Do you know where Olivia is?" I asked.

Jon went back to work, placing the batteries in rows on a table as if I hadn't said a word. Or was he just taking time to process the information?

"Jon!"

"When I left the basement, she was still sleeping," he replied curtly. "I think she's prepping lunch today."

I ran back to the stairs.

"Trust me, Jon," I called over my shoulder. "Get outta here. Now."

He didn't even acknowledge that I had said anything. He just picked up a battery and installed it in a lantern. I had the sick feeling that it was the last time I was going to see Jon Purcell.

I half ran, half jumped down the several flights of stairs that led to the ground level of the building and sprinted through the long structure until I got to the stairs leading to the basement. I passed a few people along the way, and I'm ashamed to say that I didn't warn them. It would have taken too long to explain, and based on Jon's reaction, they wouldn't have believed me anyway. If I stopped, even to talk to one person, I wouldn't get to Olivia in time. I promised myself that once I found her and we were on our way back to the Explorer, I'd shout out a warning. There was no way anyone would be more inclined to believe me than Jon was, but it might just put them on alert enough so that when they saw the soldiers arriving, they'd have the presence of mind to protect themselves.

That's how I justified not stopping, but the truth was that I was more worried about saving Olivia than people I didn't know. I hated myself for making that choice . . . but I didn't stop either.

I hit the basement and grabbed a headlamp. People were already up and out, so I found myself running between rows of empty cots. When I finally made it to our section, I flashed my light on Olivia's bunk to find that it was empty.

"Damn!"

I turned back the way I had come, ready to run for the stairs, when I saw the light from another lamp headed my way.

"Olivia? Is that you?"

I would have been totally surprised if it was. How random would that have been? But I was desperate.

The lamp bobbed closer and stopped about ten yards from me.

"Who is that?" I called out.

No answer.

I stood there staring at the light as my skin began to crawl.

"You gonna answer me?" I asked.

"Hello, Tucker," came a calm, familiar voice.

It was the one voice I didn't want to hear.

It was Chris Campbell.

How much did he know about what I knew? I had to force myself to act as though nothing was wrong.

"Have you seen Olivia?" I asked innocently.

"Why?" he asked. "Are you going to ask her to escape with you?"

Uh-oh.

He knew everything.

I felt a surge of energy fly past my head. I ducked as the deadly bolt hit the wall behind me, blowing out a fat chunk of cement.

He knew everything.

My first instinct was to pull off my headlamp. If he was going to shoot me, I wasn't going to make it easy for him. I yanked it off and threw it. Before it hit the ground, the light exploded. Chris was a good shot and had his own headlamp to light me up. All I could do was become a difficult target.

"You think I can't see you?" Chris taunted.

The headlamps were powerful, but cast a narrow beam. I started flipping the steel cots onto their sides to create barriers between us. Each time I flipped one up, I dodged to the other side of the narrow room to grab another one.

Chris had the same kind of energy-shooting baton weapon that Feit's bodyguards had. That eliminated any doubt that he was working with the Air Force—and it confirmed that the soldiers who were on their way weren't going to be paying a friendly visit. He fired and hit one of the cots. The metal springs blew apart, and I felt the shrapnel nick my clothes as it sailed by. He fired again and blew apart a mattress, sending a cloud of stuffing into the air.

The narrow light from his headlamp moved as he did. It gave the dark basement a surreal feel, as if we were trapped inside a strobe light. It was hard to see where I was going, which meant it was hard for Chris to see me as well. That was my one hope.

There was a fire exit on the far end of the building that nobody used. It was my only escape route, so I kept upending beds as I backed toward it.

"You don't have to die here," Chris called out. I sensed the frustration in his voice. "Which is worse: working for us . . . or death?"

My answer was to continue to pick up everything I could find to throw at him. I tossed small tables and suitcases and upended many more beds, all in the desperate attempt to throw him off. He couldn't get a clear shot at me and kept firing wildly. Everything that vicious weapon hit exploded, sending out sharp particles that filled the air.

Finally, my back hit the wall. For a quick moment I panicked, thinking I was trapped in a dead end, until I realized I had reached the far side—and the way out. I quickly slid along the wall until I hit the metal bar on the door. I pushed back, and the door swung open. Once through, I dodged to my right, putting the wall between Chris and me. A second later the door was blown off its hinges.

There was faint, gray light coming from the top of the stairs. It wasn't much, but it was enough for me to see where I was going. I ran for the staircase and climbed, taking three steps at a time. My confidence surged. I was going to make it out . . . and then I had to make a decision. Should I head for the Explorer? Or look for Olivia in the mess hall?

I reached the ground floor and blasted out of the fire door

to find a group of survivors gathered together, looking confused. They had heard the ruckus in the basement.

"This is a setup!" I screamed. "Chris is with the Air Force. Soldiers are headed this way. Get outta here, now!"

I ran off, leaving them dumbfounded. There was no way that any of them would take me at my word and think: "Really? Chris is a bad guy? Thanks for the heads-up, Tucker, old pal, we'll leave right away." But what else could I do? I hoped that the sounds of the fight below would at least get them thinking. If not, maybe seeing Chris chasing me with a weapon would give them a clue.

I ran out of the building and stopped short. Left was the Explorer. Right was the mess hall. And Olivia. Hopefully.

I went right.

As I sprinted for the south building, I passed a few people who were strolling casually, enjoying the cool fall morning.

"Get out!" I shouted. "There's going to be an attack on the Hall!"

I figured the less detail, the better. The people stared at me as if I was crazed because, well, I was crazed. But if my rant saved just one person, it would be worth it.

I blew through the door leading to the mess hall to find . . . nobody.

"Olivia!" I screamed.

It was early for the lunch crew to start work, and Olivia wasn't known for being on time, let alone early. But I had to make sure, so I jammed past the empty dining tables and into the kitchen.

There were two chefs inside, chopping vegetables for the day's batch of soup. They both jumped with surprise.

"Is Olivia Kinsey here?" I demanded.

"In the kitchen?" one chef said sarcastically. "Seriously?"

He knew Olivia.

"Get outta here," I shouted. "The Hall's about to be attacked."

The two chefs looked at each other with confusion.

"How do you know that?" one asked.

The answer he got wasn't what he wanted.

The kitchen door flew open behind me. I dove away in time to miss getting hit by the shot Chris Campbell fired at me.

The chef wasn't as lucky. He took the shot square in the chest. It knocked him back onto the stove, where his jacket caught fire from the burner. The other chef pulled him off the stove and onto the floor to try to smother the flames, but I didn't think it would matter. A direct shot from that weapon probably killed him on impact.

I grabbed a tray and flung it wildly in Chris's direction. It flew like an oversized Frisbee directly for him. It missed, but it made him duck.

That gave me time to dive behind the cooking line. I scrambled on my hands and knees between the tall work counter and the stoves behind it. I had to crawl over the body of the downed chef and his friend, who was still frantically snuffing flames.

"What is happening?" the second chef cried in a panic.

Chris fired again. This time his shot sailed over the counter and hit the giant vat of boiling soup. The steel vessel tore open, spilling the scalding liquid onto the floor. The deluge missed the two chefs entirely, but I was hit on the leg by the boiling liquid. I felt the intense heat through my jeans and had to bite my lip so as not to scream out, but it didn't stop me from moving.

I crawled to the far side of the kitchen, still shielded by the counter, toward a door on the back wall that led to a small room ringed with steel racks loaded with dishes, glasses, and bowls. I scrambled inside as another shot from Chris blasted the tiled wall, sending out an explosion of slivered glass. If any hit me, I didn't know it. I was too charged with adrenaline and fear. I stayed low and pulled over one of the steel shelving units. It was heavy, but again, I was so charged up that it came down as easily as a Jenga tower. The rack hit the doorway, and the plates slid off, crashing to the floor. I jumped deeper into the room and pulled down another shelf, and another. The room was small enough that Chris would have trouble following quickly.

Every second counted. I gave up hope of finding Olivia and now focused on getting out of there. That would be tricky. I didn't want to get shot, but I also didn't want to lead Chris back to Tori and the others.

The small room led to a pantry that emptied out into a common service hallway. I didn't stop to think or strategize; I just ran to daylight, which was through a door on the far end that led outside. I hit the door and blasted out to find myself back in the courtyard between the two buildings. My first thought was to run back to the north building, get inside and out of sight, and make my way east to the far end, where I'd be close to the Explorer.

My second thought was that I wasn't going anywhere.

When I jumped outside, I was faced with a handful of Chris's cowboys . . . surrounding Olivia and Jon.

"Tucker!" Olivia called, scolding. "What exactly are you doing?"

My brain froze. I couldn't calculate another move.

"Jon?" I said. "What the hell?"

"I'm doing this for you, Tucker," Jon replied. "I don't know what it is you saw, but these are our friends. They've done nothing but take care of us. We can't turn on them."

If I hadn't been out of my mind, I would have jumped at Jon and punched him in the head.

"You told Chris I was looking for Olivia?" I asked, hardly believing it myself.

"Yes, he did," Chris said as he walked up behind me, casually tapping the black weapon against his leg. "Jon is far more appreciative of what we've done here than you seem to be."

"Why are you making everybody so crazy, Tucker?" Olivia asked. "They're protecting us."

Other survivors started gathering to see what the ruckus was all about.

Chris and the cowboys stood there with smug smiles on their faces. They knew the truth, and they knew I was done.

I had only one play left: a Hail Mary.

"We've been lied to!" I shouted to the group. "By Chris Campbell and everybody who works with him. The survivors who left here didn't move on. They were taken to Fenway Park to help the murderers build a structure."

There were confused murmurs followed by a guy who called out, "What kind of structure?"

"I . . . I don't know. But it was huge. Right in the middle of the field."

That got a couple of skeptical laughs.

"It's true! But it was destroyed by SYLO. They bombed it. Didn't you hear the explosions? Or see the fighters fly over?"

One of the cowboys shouted, "Maybe it was a monument to the Yankees, and the Red Sox blew it up!"

That got another laugh.

"You don't have to believe me," I yelled to the group. "You're going to find out for yourselves soon enough. There's a group of soldiers headed this way. They'll be here any minute. They don't need us anymore, and I'm afraid they're going to wipe us out the same way they did so much of the rest of the population."

Chris shouted, "Or maybe they just heard how good we have it here and want to stay for lunch!"

That got a cheer from the crowd. They loved Chris. He was their protector. Their benefactor.

He would be their executioner.

"I'm telling the truth!" I screamed. "We've got to get out of here. Now!"

Chris and the cowboys didn't even make a move to shut me up. They knew I had no credibility. I saw them exchange knowing looks and laugh. These guys were ruthless. They knew what was coming, and they were enjoying the warm-up.

Olivia took a step forward and held her hand out for me to take it.

"Let's go, Tucker," she said softly, as if she were trying to calm a raving lunatic.

"No," Chris said. "I think we should all stay right here and welcome these soldiers that Tucker warned us about. What do you think, Tucker?"

That got another laugh.

I wanted to smack the guy. He was keeping everyone together

because it would be so much easier for the soldiers to do their dirty work if we were all in one place.

I suddenly realized that instead of warning these people, I had managed to gather them together like sheep to be slaughtered.

"Come on out, everybody!" Chris commanded. "Looks like we're in for an exciting afternoon!"

People flooded out of the buildings. And why not? Chris was their Santa Claus. He gave them food and shelter and protection from the big bad black planes.

I turned to him and asked, "Why?"

Chris shrugged and answered softly so that nobody else could hear.

"Don't take it personally. You should be proud. You're all making a sacrifice for the greater good."

"Hey!" came a terrified shout. "Look out!"

People suddenly scattered, screaming with surprise and panic.

I figured it was the beginning of the end and that the soldiers had arrived.

"Don't worry," Chris said to me. "It won't be painful."

He was wrong. It was going to be very painful.

The soldiers hadn't arrived . . . it was Tori.

Kent was behind the wheel of the Explorer, headed directly toward us. People dove out of the way of the careening SUV. The group of cowboys stood their ground and pulled out their own baton weapons . . . too late. Kent drove into them, scattering bodies like bowling pins. I heard several sickening thuds as they were hit dead on.

I didn't care.

Olivia screamed.

Chris lifted his weapon and took aim at the car . . . as I took aim at Chris. I threw myself at him and wrapped my arms around his body, driving him to the ground with the best open-field tackle I'd ever made. I landed on top of him and wrestled the black baton out of his hands. I had no idea how to use it, and even if I did I was too close to him to fire, so I did the next best thing: I swung the handle and hit him on the side of the head, knocking his cocky smile into next week.

I shouldn't say that it felt good.

It felt good.

The Explorer screeched to a stop directly in front of us.

"Giddyap, Rook!" Kent shouted.

I looked for Olivia. She stood alone, looking bewildered.

"Get in!" I yelled to her.

She hesitated a moment as if debating what to do.

"Now!" I screamed.

That shook her out of her own head. She focused and ran for the Explorer.

Jon, on the other hand, still looked paralyzed.

"Why are you doing this?" he asked, near tears.

His answer came in the form of another explosion . . . and a scream.

In the center of the courtyard, four people were blown off their feet as the bricks beneath them erupted.

The Air Force had arrived.

On the far end of the courtyard, the soldiers were advancing as if it was a military assault . . . because it was. They walked in a loose formation with one guy at the point and the others fanning out behind him like an arrow, giving each a clear shot at their victims. Every one of them held a black baton gun.

Every one of them opened fire.

"Get in the damn car!" Tori screamed at Olivia.

She ducked down and jumped in the back.

A cowboy took a run at us and fell in his tracks as Tori dropped him with a shot to his legs.

"You coming?" I shouted to Jon.

Jon looked like a deer caught in the headlights. He nodded quickly but didn't move, so I grabbed his arm, pushed him toward the car, yanked the door open, and shoved him inside.

"Go!" I shouted.

Kent jammed on the gas before I could close the door.

All around us, people were being hit. The invisible projectiles of energy peppered the air and blasted people off of their feet. It was exactly as I feared. It was a slaughter. I couldn't help but wonder if any more people would have been saved if I had stopped to warn them earlier.

Kent careened through the courtyard, doing his best to weave through the mass of fleeing people.

I twisted around to look out the back window as the glass shattered, sending a spray of sharp shards into the car.

"Don't stop!" I shouted at Kent.

"Like there's a chance of that," he shouted back.

Another charge hit the ground in front of us, spewing bits of exploded brick into the front grille, which made it sound like we'd been hit by buckshot. It didn't slow us down. We were quickly moving out of range. Kent drove the Explorer out of the courtyard and onto the street, leaving the carnage behind.

Once in the clear, Kent drove even faster. Nobody complained. We wanted to get as far away as quickly as possible. Minutes later we were on the interstate, and Boston was in the rearview mirror.

"We're clear," I said to Kent. "You can go subsonic now."

Kent didn't let up. He was too deep in the zone.

Tori touched his arm gently, making him start as if her touch were electric.

"It's okay," she said softly. "We made it. Don't get us killed now."

Kent's eyes were wild. He looked at Tori as if he didn't even register what she had said.

"Slow down, Kent," she added more firmly.

Kent finally nodded. I could see the tension melt as he eased off the gas.

We drove on without a word. The only sound was our steady, heavy breathing and Olivia's soft whimpering.

"I'm sorry, Tucker," Jon finally said meekly. "I . . . I . . . didn't understand."

Nobody responded. The terror we had just gone through was still too fresh to suddenly start thinking rationally about the fact that Jon had nearly gotten us all killed.

"Where am I going?" Kent finally asked, staring straight ahead.

Tori turned and looked back at me, waiting for an answer.

I looked around at the haggard faces. We may have been kids, but we had also been through more conflict than most adults would see in a lifetime. The fact that we were still alive was nothing short of a miracle.

"We're dealing with two enemies," I said. "There are no good guys to side with or help us out. The only people we can trust are in this car, and others like us."

"What does that mean?" Tori asked.

"It means we're going to Nevada."

THIRTEEN

As we drove south on the interstate, I told Jon, Kent, and Olivia what we had seen at Fenway Park and that Feit was alive. I explained how Feit told us that the battle between the two military forces was about changing the course of the planet. The Air Force believed that the SYLO forces had put us on a path that would mean the end of mankind and that the only way to save the planet was to reset civilization.

Nobody said a word. Nobody questioned. It was just as well. It wasn't like I had any answers. I was only repeating what Feit told us. SYLO and the Air Force were nothing more than tools. There was no way to know who was using them.

I think the reality of what we had just been through and what we had learned had finally settled in and left us all in shock. The fact that Chris and his cowboys turned out to be Air Force villains wasn't the worst of it. The mysterious device being built in Fenway Park was a minor footnote. The attack by SYLO on Fenway was the least surprising of all. It made sense that the Navy was far too huge to have been crippled by one battle. None of those revelations bothered me as much as the most important bit of information we had gotten from Feit.

In their quest to "reset" civilization, the Air Force had wiped out three-quarters of the world's population. It was a reality that was hard enough to accept, let alone understand.

I thought back to the fleet of black planes we saw high over Boston, headed out to sea. Were they on their way to another target city? Were millions more to be killed that night? The possibility was too horrific to believe, but from what we'd seen in Portland and Boston, it could very well be true.

As we traveled along the empty interstate, we saw more of what we had witnessed on our journey to Boston. There were thousands of abandoned cars, though no other signs that we were in the middle of a war. There were no downed fighter planes, no burning buildings. No wounded. No bodies.

No life at all.

The full picture of what had happened was beginning to become clear. The black Air Force planes had passed over like minions sent by the angel of death and vaporized anyone who wasn't lucky enough to have been deep in some basement and safe from their reach. Unlike what had happened to the boat that Quinn had been on, and some of the buildings in Portland and Boston, the sweep left structures intact. The weapon was selective, and it selected people. Animals too. We didn't see any dogs or cats or skunks or most anything else that breathed.

There were still some birds in the sky. It must have been more difficult to target flying objects. For one horrifying second I imagined that the world would soon become a giant aviary. It was like something out of a horror movie.

Everything we were seeing was like something out of a horror movie.

I felt numb. It was impossible to accept such a huge loss of life. I kept searching for other answers. Other possibilities. Other explanations.

I came up empty. The harsh truth was that we were members of a very small club. We were the survivors of the most heinous crime ever committed.

What we couldn't know was what the future held.

"We gotta get gas," Kent said. "We're sucking fumes."

He pulled off the interstate and drove to a gas station.

"What's the point?" Jon said. "It's not like the pumps work."

Tori looked at me and said, "Get a gas can."

She seemed to know what she was doing, so I didn't question. I went into the convenience store that was attached to the station and found a can. I also grabbed a handful of Tootsie Pops. Why not?

Outside, Tori had gotten the hose she took from the Target store in Portland. I'd forgotten all about that. She went to one of the abandoned cars and popped open the gas door. I placed the tank on the pavement below it and unscrewed the cap. Tori fed one end of the tube into the gas tank and sucked on the other. She squinted, waiting for the first taste of gas. When she got it, she quickly spit out the little gas that made it to her mouth and jammed the end into the container. The suction had started the stream, and gas flowed from the car into the red can.

Tori wiped her mouth with her sleeve, and I handed her a Tootsie Pop.

"That's for taking one for the team," I said.

Tori grimaced and tore the wrapping off the candy.

"You're up next," she said and gratefully started in on the pop.

Kent walked up to us with his hands in his pockets. I tossed him a Tootsie Pop. It hit him in the chest and fell to the ground.

"Nice catch."

He picked it up and stared at it as if it was something from an alien world . . . and maybe it was. We hadn't been thinking much about anything that was considered normal in our previous lives. Like candy.

"So?" Kent asked. "Anybody know how to get to Nevada?"

I laughed. Tori did too. Kent finally joined in. It was a brief moment of silliness that we desperately needed.

Tori got it back together first.

"We've got to gear up again," she said. "We'll get a road atlas."

That thought brought us back to our harsh reality. We had to collect supplies again, just as we did in Portland, since we'd left everything we owned at Faneuil Hall. The first time we'd done it, it felt like an adventure. We had high hopes of rejoining civilization in Boston, and it had been a little bit of a rush to take whatever we wanted. Now we were faced with a new normal, and that meant we might have to be raiding stores for a very long time.

This time it felt less like an adventure and more like a curse.

Kent took the gas can and dumped the fuel into the Explorer. He and Tori then moved to siphon another car. While they worked, I went to Olivia and Jon, who were sitting in the Explorer. They were talking about something, maybe even arguing, but I couldn't hear what they were saying, and they immediately stopped when I opened the door.

"Trick or treat," I said and tossed each of them a Tootsie Pop. "Early Halloween."

"Thanks," Jon said and ate his hungrily.

Olivia wasn't as enthused. "I don't eat candy."

Figures.

They both seemed upset, and I had a pretty good idea why.

"It's okay, Jon" I said. "You did what you thought was right."

What I really wanted to say was, "Why the hell didn't you believe me?" but that would have been piling on.

"I'm sorry, Tucker. What you were saying about Chris seemed so . . . incredible. But I'm with you now. I hope you believe that."

I couldn't bring myself say, "Sure! No problem!" Truth was, he was on thin ice with me. He had almost gotten us killed. It's hard to let something like that go.

"Don't worry about it," I said, which meant absolutely nothing.

Olivia was staring straight ahead, as if her mind was miles away.

"You okay?" I asked.

"So many people," she said, sounding dazed. "Gone. It's just . . . impossible to imagine."

"We still don't know what happened to your mom," I said, trying to give her hope but realizing how hollow it sounded.

She gave me a sad smile and said, "You're a glass-half-full kind of guy, huh?"

"I try," I said. "C'mon, be crazy. Eat a lollipop."

I held the candy out to her, and she grabbed my hand. She held me tight and looked right into my eyes.

I felt as if she wanted to tell me something but couldn't bring herself to do it. She was tortured, but we all were. My fear was that she was going to say something like "I love you, Tucker," which I might have welcomed at the beginning of the summer, but not since Kent had admitted he had a thing for her.

And since Tori kissed me.

The last thing we needed was that kind of drama.

"It's okay," I said. "Take it. There's plenty more where that came from."

I gave her a big smile, trying to break the tension.

Olivia returned my smile and took the pop.

"For you, I'll even eat sugar."

The moment had passed, but I was struck by the insanity of our situation. We were alone in a near-dead world. We were all we had. If nothing else, we had to know that we could rely on one another. Without that, we would end up joining the three-quarters who didn't make it.

Kent and Tori finished topping off the gas tank, and we all climbed back into the SUV.

"Now what?" Kent said. "Do I just drive without knowing where we're headed?"

"I'm hungry," Jon declared.

"I need a shower," Olivia added.

Everyone looked to me. Whenever there was a decision to be made, I was expected to be the mediator. It wasn't a comfortable position. If things went bad, I'd get grief, and so far there was very little that had gone right. But we couldn't just sit there staring at one another.

"We have maybe four hours of daylight left," I pointed out. "I say we find a store and gear up again. We'll get a map. Then we should find a place to spend the night. A hotel or something."

"And tomorrow we'll head for Nevada," Tori said.

"Why?" Olivia asked. "Do you seriously think we're going to join up with a merry band of survivors and take back the world?"

Tori opened her mouth to answer, but no words came out. Olivia might not always have the big picture in mind, but those few words had put the plan under the harsh light of reality.

"Seriously," Kent said. "For all we know, the Air Force has already found them and wiped them out. They have radios too. They could have heard that broadcast."

"So what do you want to do?" Tori asked, peeved. "Crawl into a hole and hide?"

"Not me," Jon chimed in. "I want to keep moving."

"But if we're moving, there's a better chance of being spotted by those black planes," Olivia warned. "Hiding out sounds good to me."

"Not to me it doesn't," Tori shot back.

"So then go!" Olivia shouted. "Maybe it would be better if we split up."

"Stop!" I ordered. "Nobody's splitting up, so just . . . relax."

There was a tense quiet in the car.

"We can't do this," I said. "We can't turn on each other. Like it or not, we're all we've got."

Everyone stole looks at one another as if the reality had finally sunk in that our entire universe consisted of . . . us.

"Let's not look too far ahead," I added. "One step at a time. All right?"

There were a few grumbles of reluctant agreement.

"Good. Let's go to the next big town. We'll find a store, gear up, and then find a place to sleep. I don't want to spend the night in this car."

That was one thing that everyone could agree on, so Kent started up the car, and we were off.

The next big town was Springfield, Massachusetts. I'd been there once with my father to visit the Basketball Hall of Fame, but I was nine, so there was very little that I remembered about the city. Kent pulled off the interstate, and within minutes we found a Walmart.

"Seriously?" Olivia complained. "First Target, now . . . *this?*"

Nobody commented.

Walmart was open for business. Or at least it was open. The five of us grabbed carts, split up, and went on another shopping spree through the deserted superstore.

On this trip I was less worried about comfort and more concerned with practical items. I picked up a flashlight, a couple of headlamps, and some camp lanterns. Batteries too. I had always taken electricity and light for granted. Not anymore. I also grabbed some water-purification tablets in the camping area. There was no way to know if we'd always find plumbing with running, filtered water. The last thing we needed was dysentery. There was a big first aid kit in the same area, so I put it into my cart along with a waterproof box of matches and a compass. I took another hoodie, a T-shirt, and extra socks and underwear. In the grocery area I took a bunch of ramen noodle boxes and freeze-dried food packets thinking we could boil water over a fire and have a hot meal.

My last stop was in the book area, where I found Tori thumbing through a large road atlas.

"This is pretty detailed," she said. "Every page is a map of a different state. But it's also got fifty folded satellite maps of each state. "It's not Google Earth, but it'll do."

She dumped it into her cart and moved on. I took note that she had restocked with several boxes of ammunition. Gotta love Walmart. Where else can you buy Fritos and bullets?

We all met at the front of the store, and I was relieved to see that Olivia had chosen much more wisely this time. She only had a pair of jeans, a sweater, socks, and underwear. We all stared at her near-empty cart.

"What?" she asked defensively. "I couldn't find anything I cared to wear."

Everyone had been equally practical, for whatever reason. Jon had thought to grab several walkie-talkies and replacement batteries. Kent had stocked up on bags of trail mix and beef jerky and bottles of Gatorade. Everyone picked up headlamps and lanterns. We were in and out of there in half an hour with our supplies packed into individual canvas bags.

"Okay, Mr. Practical," Kent said. "We took that step. What's next?"

"We gotta find someplace to spend the night."

"I have an idea," Jon said.

Jon hadn't been offering much. He was still the new kid and wasn't all that social anyway. And he had nearly gotten us all killed, so hearing him volunteer an idea was strange.

"Let's find another hospital," he suggested. "There's food and beds, and if they have a radio I can probably figure out how to get it running on the backup batteries."

"You want to hear the broadcast again?" Tori asked.

"I want to make sure there still *is* a broadcast," he replied. "It's been over a week. I don't want to drive a couple of thousand miles for nothing."

"That's really smart, Jon," I said.

Jon beamed proudly, as if he had re-earned my trust.

For the record, he hadn't. But he did have a good idea.

It didn't take us long to find a huge hospital called Bay State Medical Center. We drove around until we found the entrance to the emergency room, the most likely place for a radio. We left the car in front, grabbed our gear, and headed inside.

Jon led the group as if he knew where he was going. I guess when you work in a hospital, you get a feel for how they're set up. Within minutes we were behind the reception desk. Jon scanned the area and headed straight for a closed door. He opened it and . . .

"Gotcha!" he proclaimed.

There was a radio setup very much like the one at Maine Medical Center.

"Give me some time," he said. "As long as they've got emergency power, I can fire this up."

"I'm starving," I said. "Let's hit the kitchen to see what hasn't spoiled."

We left Jon to work and went hunting for the cafeteria. It took a while to find, but it was worth it. There was a pantry loaded with canned food. We also found sealed bags of taco shells and plenty of bottled water. We would eat well that night.

I opened the cold locker and immediately wished I hadn't. The smell of rotting meat and vegetables made me gag. I closed the door quickly, grateful that the seal was tight enough to block the smell.

"Get used to that," Tori said.

We cracked open a few cans and dished out tomatoes, peaches, and some processed meat that I probably would never have eaten in our previous life, but when you're hungry, most everything tastes good. None of us cared about manners. We all just dug in and ate.

"Vitamins," Tori said. "There's probably a pharmacy where we can grab some multivitamins. It's not like we're going to be eating balanced meals."

"Good idea, Mom," Kent said and gave her a friendly hug. Too friendly, if you ask me, but nobody asked.

When we had eaten our fill, Tori loaded up a plate of food and headed out.

"For Jon," she said and walked off.

"You know the great thing about eating like this?" Kent asked. Olivia and I looked at him, waiting.

"No cleanup!" He tossed his plate onto the counter. "Who said Armageddon can't be fun!"

We didn't laugh.

"Jeez, just trying to lighten things up," Kent said, irritated.

"I'm going to find a shower," I said. "Hopefully the water's still running."

"Where should we sleep?" Kent asked.

"The emergency room is probably okay," I said, thinking out loud. "It's below ground."

The sun had set, which meant we were once again in the dark.

I grabbed one of the camp lanterns and went in search of a shower. It didn't take long to find one. There was a locker room near the ER that was probably for nurses. At the far end was a three-stall shower. I put the lantern down outside of one stall, stepped inside, crossed my fingers, and turned the faucet.

A hard spray of water sprang from the showerhead.

"Yes!"

It wasn't heated, but the pressure was good. There were even bottles of body wash and shampoo at each station. After finding a stack of clean white towels, I was good to go. I peeled off my clothes and stood under the cold spray to wash away the grime that had been building over the last few days. It didn't bother me that the water was cold. It felt great. I shampooed my hair and was surprised to feel that a bunch of grit had accumulated on my scalp. It took a second for me to realize I was washing out tiny bits of Fenway Park. I lathered myself entirely to get every last particle of that nightmare off of my body. By the time I rinsed off, the cold water was making me numb, so I shut it off and stood there to drip-dry.

"I'm next," Olivia sang.

I turned quickly to see her standing in the entrance to the shower area wearing only a towel . . . which was a lot more than I was wearing.

"Jeez, Olivia!" I complained. "Again?"

I covered my privates with one hand and reached for a towel with the other. By the time I had it wrapped around my waist, Olivia had stepped into the stall behind me.

"I'll dry your back," she said.

There were too many emotions fighting for control for me to

do anything but stand there like a dummy. I was embarrassed and angry and nervous and, okay, maybe a little bit thrilled that the two of us were standing there together, as good as naked. Olivia gently patted my back with a towel as I stood frozen.

"You shouldn't be doing this," I finally said. "If Kent walks in . . . hell, if *anybody* walks in."

"What?" she said innocently. "We're taking a shower. Like you said, we're all in this together now."

"This isn't what I had in mind," I said, my voice cracking.

"Oh, relax. We're not doing anything wrong. Are we?"

Maybe it was just my imagination or wishful thinking, but the way she said "Are we?" sounded like an invitation. Man, I was tempted. I had followed Olivia around like a dumb puppy all summer just hoping to get a kiss. Now we were standing in a dark shower, alone, nearly naked, and she was rubbing my shoulders even though they had been dry for a while.

"I was thinking," she said. "Maybe we shouldn't go to Nevada."

"Why not? It's as good a place as any."

"Is it? What does Tori think we'll find there? A bunch of survivors we can join up with and fight beside to take back the world from the clutches of the evil Air Force? Or SYLO? Or whoever else may be trying to take over the world? It's a romantic idea, but is it realistic? Or is she just trying to finish what her father started?"

It was a pretty smart observation. Tori loved her dad. It wasn't hard to imagine that she'd want to follow in his footsteps.

"What do *you* think we should do?" I asked.

"Oh, I don't know," she answered dreamily, as if she hadn't really thought about it.

She came around to my front and continued to dry me off, rubbing the towel across my chest. It was making me crazy, but I didn't stop her.

"Maybe the best thing we can do is head south. Somewhere tropical, like the Florida Keys. Somewhere that'll be warm and comfortable, even in winter. We can find a house on the beach and fish for supper and sleep in the sand under a palm tree, and while the rest of the world sorts itself out, we'll be in paradise. Doesn't that sound tempting?"

She stopped rubbing my chest and looked me square in the eye.

I don't think the word "tempting" was strong enough. It sounded great. I imagined lying on the beach with Olivia. Olivia was wearing the red bikini.

"Do you want to go to the beach with me, Tucker?" she asked playfully and took a step closer.

I was a breath away from saying, "Hell yeah!" when—

"Really?" came a stern voice from the door leading into the shower.

Tori.

She stood in the doorway with a towel draped over her arm, ready to take her turn. Instead, she spun around and stormed off.

"Oops!" Olivia said with naughty giggle and a shrug.

I took off after Tori. I felt as though I had been caught cheating, though I wasn't doing anything. Not really. Tori and I weren't even together. Yes, we kissed. Yes, I cared for her. But we never made it official and . . . man, I was in real trouble.

The last thing I wanted to do was hurt Tori. She had become my best friend. Why hadn't I just walked away from Olivia?

Because I'm an idiot, that's why.

"Tori!" I called. "Please, wait."

I caught her before she left the locker room. She spun to face me, and even in the low light I saw that her face was flushed.

"What?" she snapped, obviously peeved.

"We were just talking," I said.

It may have been true, but it was a totally lame excuse. What had been going through my mind was a lot more than conversation.

"I don't care," she shot back, sounding as though she actually *did* care. "You can shower with anybody you want."

"We weren't showering," I argued. "I was finishing up, and she was next."

Tori laughed as if I had just offered the weakest explanation ever.

"And she was in a hurry, so she was helping you dry off so she could get in faster, is that it?"

"No! She was, well, I don't know what she was doing. She wanted to talk. I didn't ask her to dry me off."

"You didn't stop her either."

She had me there.

"Look, Tucker, I don't care. If you and Olivia want to hook up, that's your business. But be careful. You're the one who said we're all in this together. If you piss Kent off, I can't help you."

"I don't want to hook up with Olivia," I said. "It just . . . happened."

Tori scoffed. "Yeah, I saw that."

She turned and walked away, then glanced back and added, "Put your pants on and meet us at the radio. Jon's got it working."

With that, she left.

I was torn between the embarrassment of what had just happened and excitement about the radio. I ran back into the locker room to get my clothes and saw that Olivia was in the shower, casually shampooing her hair as if nothing had happened. I have to admit, I didn't look away at first. I'd never seen a naked girl taking a shower before. Or a naked girl doing anything, for that matter. The sight froze me for an instant. Olivia looked at me and smiled.

That rocked me back to my senses. I turned away and grabbed my clothes.

"The radio is working!" I called to her.

"Be right up!" she called back, but it didn't sound as if she was in any hurry to finish her shower.

I took my clothes out into the hallway and dressed quickly. Whatever had happened, or hadn't happened, between Olivia and me meant nothing. The bottom line was that I had been stupid, and it probably destroyed my friendship with Tori. She had trouble trusting anyone since her mother abandoned her and her father. She had no friends in school and spent most of her time alone. I was the one person she finally put her faith in, and I totally let her down. I kept telling everyone how we had to trust each other, and I ended up being the least trustworthy of all. It was a miserable, lonely feeling.

Olivia turned off the shower. The last thing I wanted was to be alone with her, so I finished dressing fast and took off for the emergency room.

Kent and Tori were standing behind Jon, who sat at a keyboard and a computer screen, just as he had in Portland. The sight of an active screen was jarring because I hadn't seen anything electronic for weeks. I had no idea what any of the numbers or different colored modules meant, but Jon did.

I looked at Tori. She kept her eyes on the screen. Just as well.

"Is it the same voice?" I asked.

"Shhh!" Jon admonished.

I listened and was stunned to hear the same woman's voice coming from the speaker near the ceiling. It was not only the same voice, the radio signal was much stronger, and we were able to hear the entire message.

"We are the survivors. We have been bloodied, but not beaten. To all of those who have been attacked: Know that we will fight back. Join us. We will take you in and keep you safe. Hundreds have already arrived, and more are arriving every day."

The message was slightly different from the one Tori had pieced together. The earlier message hadn't mentioned anything about the number of survivors who had joined them.

Jon was frantically writing as the woman spoke.

"North thirty-six degrees. Twenty-six minutes, twenty seconds. West one hundred fourteen degrees. Thirty-one minutes, fifty-seven seconds."

"Bingo, we got it," Jon exclaimed while writing furiously.

"Please use caution," the voice continued, "for we are being watched. Trust no one. We will fight for our home. We will repel the murderers. We have strength in numbers. The survivors will stand together. Do not hesitate."

That was it. The message repeated one more time and was replaced by static.

Jon waited a few more seconds to make sure it was definitely over, then powered down the radio. The screen went dark, and we were back under lantern light.

"It's pretty much the same message on the same frequency," Jon announced. "Including the coordinates. There were a few additions about how many people they've got and to use caution. The message repeated five times."

"Could it be a trap?" Kent asked. "Like with Faneuil Hall? If we're not supposed to trust anybody, why should we trust them?"

"It could be," Tori said thoughtfully. "Or it could be a lifeline. There's only one way to find out."

A shrieking scream shattered the quiet of the empty hospital.

"Olivia!" Kent shouted and took off running.

I grabbed the lantern and followed, with the others close behind.

Kent sprinted into the emergency room and nearly knocked Olivia down as she came running out. She had on scrubs and a towel wrapped around her wet head. She was in tears as she ran into Kent's arms.

"Somebody's back there!" she cried frantically.

Kent hugged her and looked back to us.

I glanced at Tori, who finally looked back at me. Whatever Olivia had seen, it was more important than the incident in the shower room.

"Do you have the gun?" I asked.

She reached behind her back to pull the Glock from under her sweater.

"Who is it?" I asked Olivia.

She was in a full-on panic and could barely speak through frightened, clutching breaths.

"I don't know," she managed to garble out. "A man."

She pulled away from Kent and ran in the other direction.

Kent said, "I got this," and ran after Olivia.

"Sure," Tori said sarcastically. "You go, Kent. We'll take care of the boogeyman."

I flicked off the lantern and put my headlamp on. The light it threw wasn't as good as the lantern's, but it was focused forward, which meant we weren't blinded by it. I took a few steps deeper into the emergency room, listening for the sounds of any movement.

"Hello?" I called out. "Who's back there?"

There was no answer.

I steeled myself and walked forward, slowly.

Tori raised the gun and stayed with me.

Jon trailed close behind.

The light from my headlamp played over the drapes that separated the treatment areas. Somebody could have been hiding behind any one of them.

"We've got a gun," Tori said loudly. "Come out before somebody gets hurt."

We reached the first drape. I reached out and yanked it aside to see . . . an empty bed.

"Dude, don't be stupid," I called out. "We don't want to shoot you."

We reached the second drape. I wished that the throw of the light were wider. I feared that somebody might be lurking beyond the edges of our sight. I reached out and yanked the second drape aside.

Again, only an empty bed.

Jon said, "Maybe she was wrong. It could have been one of those dummies they practice CPR on."

I liked that explanation. I sure hoped it was true.

We approached the third drape. I reached out to pull it aside . . .

. . . but the drape was yanked back before I could touch it to reveal a deathly pale, skeletal man with wide, haunted eyes. His mouth was open as he let out a pained moan.

Jon screamed.

Tori lifted the gun, but I pushed it aside as the man took a step forward . . . and collapsed at our feet.

FOURTEEN

The three of us jumped back in surprise as the man tumbled to the floor.

Tori was too stunned to even aim her gun at him, and that was a good thing. He wasn't a threat. The guy was skeletal, with bony legs showing beneath his hospital gown. "It's a zombie!" Jon cried.

"No, it's a patient," I shot back. "Turn on the lantern."

I knelt down next to him and killed my headlamp while Tori fired up the camp lantern.

The guy was ancient looking, though I couldn't tell whether that was because he was so old or just really sick. He was nearly bald but had thick, gray beard stubble that looked as though he hadn't shaved in weeks.

"Is he dead?" Jon asked.

I put my hand to his mouth and felt a faint breath.

"No. Help me get him onto a bed."

I grabbed under his arms while Jon took his feet. Lifting him was easy. He couldn't have weighed more than seventy pounds. He moaned when we picked him up. He was definitely alive. We wrestled him onto the bed, and as I started to back away, he reached out and grabbed my arm with a surprisingly strong grip.

"Paul?" he asked with a raspy whisper that felt like a desperate plea.

"Uh, no. My name's Tucker."

He looked confused, as if I had thrown him off by not being Paul.

"I'll get him some water," Tori said and hurried off.

The guy was breathing quickly, as if he was overly excited. Or maybe he couldn't get enough air. Either way, he was hurting. Whatever landed him in the hospital in the first place must have been bad enough, but if he had been lying around in the emergency room since the attack, it meant that he hadn't eaten anything in weeks.

Tori came running back with a paper cup filled with water. I reached behind the guy's neck to help him sit up so he could drink. He felt like a bag of bones.

Tori put the cup to his lips.

"Just take a little," she cautioned.

The guy's eyes were staring off into space, unfocused. But he sensed the cup at his lips and eagerly took a sip. He coughed once, and Tori pulled it away.

"More," he begged.

Tori offered the cup, and he drank it. Most of it, anyway. A lot dribbled down his chin.

"I'll raise the bed," Jon said.

He pressed the button on the side of the bed. It didn't move.

"Oh, right. Duh."

He reached down and cranked the head of the bed up manually.

Jon was hospital savvy. He raised the bed enough so that I was able to ease the old guy back into a sitting position.

"More, please," the guy begged.

Tori took off to get more water.

The man slowly shifted his head toward me, his eyes focusing.

"I'm not Paul," I said.

The guy squinted at me and said, "I know that!"

The cobwebs were definitely clearing out of his head.

"But who are you?" he asked, this time with a slightly less strained whisper.

"I'm Tucker. This is Jon. The girl's name is Tori."

"Screaming girl," he said.

I had no idea what he meant.

"Pretty," he added.

"Oh! That was Olivia. I guess you scared her."

"I guess so," he said and actually chuckled. It made him cough.

Tori came back with another cup of water and a full plastic pitcher.

"Feeling better?" she asked.

He nodded weakly. Tori brought the cup to his lips, and he drank it all down. When he finished, he closed his eyes and let out a satisfied sigh.

"Thank you," he said.

"What's your name?" I asked.

"Doyle."

"When was the last time you ate something?"

"Couldn't tell you. A week? Two weeks? A year? How long have I been in here?"

We all exchanged looks. I couldn't tell if Mr. Doyle was hallucinating or just old and confused.

"I'll get you some food," Tori said and started to walk away.

"No!" Mr. Doyle called out.

Tori stopped and turned back to him. "You have to eat something."

"I'm dying, missy," he said.

"No, you're not," she argued. "You're just weak."

"I'm weak because I'm dying," he insisted. "There's no food that'll change that."

"But you're wrong, if you just—"

"Young lady," Doyle said, his voice suddenly steely. "They brought me here to die. The fact that I'm still breathing is no small miracle. Though it is sort of ironic, considering what's happened."

"You know about the attack?" I asked.

Doyle nodded, then motioned for another sip of water. Tori poured another cupful and handed it to him. This time he drank it himself, though he moved very slowly. I'd never seen an old person in such bad shape. I was surprised that he had the strength to lift the cup of water.

"I was down in the bowels of this place getting another test done. An MRI or x-ray or God knows what. They insist on doing tests to prove that I'm dying. I could tell them the same thing and save everybody a whole lot of trouble."

He started coughing, violently, and clutched at his chest. Tori grabbed the cup, and we watched helplessly as the poor old guy was racked by the painful spell.

Jon looked terrified, as if the guy might die right then and there.

After an agonizing minute, the coughing stopped and he sat back and tried to control his quick breathing.

"You okay?" Jon asked tentatively.

"I'm dying," he said sharply. "What part of that don't you understand?"

"Yeah, but, I mean right now?" Jon asked nervously.

"No idea," the old man said, testy. "If you know any different, please let me know."

"Well, you don't look so good," Jon said.

Tori kicked Jon in the foot.

"Ow!" he complained. "He asked."

Mr. Doyle finally gathered the strength to continue.

"I was in the basement with a technician when the lights went out. Some emergency lights came on so he could see to wheel me out, but when we got up here, they were all gone. Every last person."

"Is that Paul?" I asked.

Doyle looked at me like I was insane and said, "No. Xavier's his name. Paul is my son."

At least that mystery was solved.

"He went outside to see what happened and found a couple of other survivors. I heard all about them black planes and about how they wiped away so many people. Do you have any idea why it happened? Or who's responsible?"

I jumped in before anybody else could answer.

"No," I said.

The others gave me a curious look, but I figured it would be cruel to tell him all that we knew. If he was really nearing the end of his life, he didn't need to know how bad things really were with the world.

"What happened to Xavier?" Tori asked.

"He stuck around for a few days. Good fella. He felt responsible for me. But I convinced him he was wasting his time. He still has a life in front of him, so he set me up with some food and water and took off to find his family."

"And you've been in here alone since then?" Tori asked. "That's horrible."

Doyle shrugged weakly. "I'm not just a cantankerous old coot. I really am dying." He tapped his chest and said, "Congestive heart failure. I've been living with a time bomb for years now. Slowly getting weaker. Nothing anybody can do for it. I don't mean to sound morbid, but given the state of things right now, I'd just as soon the old Reaper came for me sooner rather than later."

I wanted to argue with him and tell him that he should fight until the end because life was worth living and all that, but given the state of things, it would have been a hard sell.

"What's going on?" Kent asked as he hurried up to us.

He got a look at Doyle, and his eyes went wide.

"Whoa!" he exclaimed. "Is he alive?"

"Yes, he's alive," Doyle snarled.

"Oh, sorry, dude," Kent said. "No offense."

"Hello?" Olivia called meekly.

She approached us cautiously. She spotted Doyle over Kent's shoulder and—

"Boo!" Doyle barked.

Olivia gasped in surprise and took a quick step back.

Doyle laughed. He had a sense of humor.

Tori laughed too. I think she liked seeing Olivia look silly.

"Mr. Doyle is a patient here," I explained.

"Oh," Olivia said, embarrassed. "I'm sorry I screamed at you."

"Don't worry about it, missy," Doyle said. "It was the most exciting thing that's happened to me in years."

"That's just sad," Kent said.

It was Kent's turn to get a kick from Tori.

"Ow!"

"What are you kids doing here?" Doyle asked. "Where are your families?"

"That's a very long story," I replied. "We came from Pember-wick Island in Maine."

"Then what'n hell are you doing in Springfield?" he asked.

"Good question," Olivia answered.

"We're going to Nevada," Tori added with authority. "We hear there are a lot of survivors there."

Doyle's eyes suddenly went wide, as if he had sparked to an idea. He smiled, and for an instant I imagined I could see what he looked like when he was a younger man.

"Hey now, you're not seeing a light at the end of the tunnel or anything, are you?" Kent asked nervously.

"I think I can help you," Doyle said, suddenly enthused.

"Doubt it," Kent said with disdain.

"Listen to me," Doyle said. "Paul. My son. Paul Doyle. He's the last family I've got. Just before I ended up here, he called me on the phone and said the strangest thing. He said he wanted me to go somewhere and meet him. Somewhere that was going to be safe.

That's what he said exactly, somewhere that was going to be safe. I had no idea what he was talking about. There wasn't anything dangerous about my neighborhood. I've lived in the same house for sixty years. But he wouldn't explain it any more than that. Said he was taking a big risk just telling me. He wanted me to get on a plane and join him. My son's a practical fella. He's not one for making up stories, so I was inclined to go. But my heart took a turn, and I landed here instead. The next day the attack came."

"So Paul knew it was coming?" I asked.

"He must have!" Doyle said. "He knew it wouldn't be safe here. He knew! I have to tell you, the only thing that's keeping my mind at peace is knowing my son might still be alive and in a safe place."

"Is your son in the Air Force?" Tori asked.

"Air Force?" Doyle scoffed. "Nah. He's an architect. Builds homes. How would an architect know something like this would happen?"

That was a good question. I could ask the same thing about my parents. How did they know the attack was coming? Because they worked for SYLO, that's why.

I asked, "Did he ever mention something called SYLO?"

Doyle frowned. "What kind of question is that? He's not a farmer. I told you, he builds houses!"

"Did he tell you where the safe place was?" Jon asked.

"Kentucky," Doyle replied. "He was going to pick me up at the airport in Louisville."

"But he didn't tell you exactly where it was?" Olivia asked.

"Said he couldn't. It was some big secret. He begged me to

come to him, promised me I'd be safe there . . . and that's what I'm promising you."

"Us?" Kent asked.

"Go to Kentucky," Doyle begged. "Start at that airport and search for anything that might look like a safe haven. You're just kids. If there's any chance of getting somewhere safe, you should take it. Please. Promise me you'll go."

Doyle started breathing hard again as he got carried away with emotion. Tori took his shoulders and eased him back down onto the bed.

"We will," she said. "We'll go there."

"We will?" Kent asked, confused. "I thought you wanted to go to—?"

It was Olivia's turn to kick Kent.

"Ow!" he complained. "Stop that!"

"Good," Doyle said. "Maybe that's the reason I'm still here. Still alive. To give that message to you kids. To tell you about the safe haven."

"Could be," Tori said soothingly, as if she were talking to a child. "You did a really nice thing for us."

"You're good kids," he said. "I want you to be safe. Tell my son that I sent you."

He was starting to sound like a crazy old man again.

"We will," Tori said. "We will. But you should relax now. You're getting a little too excited."

"Yes, yes, you're right. Good idea."

His breath quickened again as if he couldn't get enough air to fill his lungs.

"I'm so tired," he added. "Maybe I can sleep a little."

"That's an excellent idea," Tori said softly. "If you need anything, we'll be close by."

Doyle grabbed Tori's hand and held it to his chest.

"Please, missy, promise me you'll go."

Tori hesitated, then said, "We'll do our best."

Doyle smiled. Her words were a genuine relief to him.

"Thank you," he said.

"No, thank *you*, Mr. Doyle," Tori replied. "You really helped us."

"I did, didn't I?" he said happily.

"Absolutely," Tori assured him.

"That's good. But I think I need a little shut-eye now."

"Okay, we'll see you in the morning," Tori said gently.

She looked up and nodded for us to leave, so we all backed away from the old man to give him his privacy. I pulled the curtain, and we walked quietly to the far side of the emergency room, where we found a small office. No sooner was the door shut than—

"What a loon!" Kent exclaimed. "Was he, like . . . hallucinating?"

"Stop!" Tori said. "He's sick."

"He's sick, all right," Kent said with no compassion. "In the head."

"What if he's right?" Jon asked. "What if there's a safe haven out there?"

"You believe that nutburger?" Kent asked, incredulous.

"Why would he lie?" Jon argued.

"I'm not saying he's lying. I'm saying he's out of his mind. He could have imagined all that."

"And what if he didn't?" I asked.

"No way, Rook," Kent said quickly. "It's a fairy tale."

"Why are you so sure?" Olivia asked. "We believe some mysterious radio voice being broadcast from nowhere. Who's to say what's real and what isn't?"

Kent had no comeback to that. None of us did.

"I'm too tired to think straight anymore," I said. "Let's ask him again in the morning and see if he has the same story."

"So where do we sleep?" Olivia asked.

"There are plenty of beds in the emergency room," I said. "Pick one."

We shuffled out of the exam room slowly. Exhaustion had caught up with all of us.

I found an empty bed and sat down.

Tori stopped at the next bed over, looked at me, and kept moving.

"I'll let Olivia take that one," she said.

"Tori!" I called but didn't have the energy to go after her.

All the guilty feelings came flooding back. It wasn't the kind of drama I needed. None of us did. There were enough challenges ahead.

I lay down on the bed and sank into the mattress. It had been a very long day that started before dawn, when we followed the busload of victims being taken to Fenway Park. That felt like a hundred years ago.

My thoughts turned to the decision we would face the next day. Should we head to Nevada, or investigate this so-called safe haven in Kentucky? To decide, we had to face the future. What were we doing? Were we still on a mission to discover the truth about the war? Or was it now about finding a safe place to hole up until the dust settled?

What exactly was our goal?

I didn't have that answer, but it didn't stop me from wrestling with the question.

It seemed as though we all had different ideas. Olivia wanted to find a warm beach and play it safe. Kent would join her there in a second. I don't know what Jon was thinking. His mind changed with the wind.

Tori was angry, and not just at me. She was all about finding people who were ready to fight back. But against whom? The Air Force or SYLO?

And me? I wanted my life back. But with each passing day, that seemed less likely. Part of me wanted to accept that fact and move on, but I couldn't. My anger was growing too. Someone had to be held responsible. I needed to find out who that was. Would I have a better shot at that in Kentucky? Or Nevada?

My head was spinning with too many thoughts, which made falling asleep impossible, in spite of my exhaustion. I don't know how long I had been lying there, maybe an hour, when I decided to get up and walk around in the hope of clearing my head. No sooner did I get up than I heard whispering coming from the far side of the emergency room. It seemed as though I wasn't the only one who was having trouble nodding off, so I headed that way.

A camp light glowed from behind a drawn curtain where the voices were coming from. They were talking softly so as not to disturb anybody. It wasn't until I was a step away from the barrier that I recognized the voices.

Tori and Olivia.

I froze. Those two never talked to each other. At least not as far as I knew. Olivia had taken care of Tori when she got shot, but since then there had been nothing but tension between the two, and I felt as though I was in the middle of it. Because I was. My instinct was to stop and listen to what they were saying before barging in on them.

"I can't say enough about him," Tori said softly. Her voice hitched with emotion. That wasn't like Tori. She had to have been really upset to let her guard down like that, and in front of Olivia, no less.

"He took care of me when I was hurting and never asked for anything in return. I guess the best word to describe him is 'selfless.' He always thought of others before himself. I can't imagine having anyone else in my life who could fill his shoes."

I couldn't believe it. She was talking about me! To Olivia. She really did have feelings for me. It was a great thing to hear at the end of an incredibly crappy day. My spirits were lifted instantly, though I wondered what Olivia's comeback would be.

"I'm so sorry you lost him," Olivia said with sincere sympathy.

Whoa. Had something been decided between the two? Was Tori professing her love for me as a way to congratulate the victor in the Tucker tug-of-war?

Olivia added, "I try to imagine that my own father was that kind of guy, but I never met him, so I'll never know. I guess I'll just have to pretend."

Crash. Burn. Tori was talking about her father. I felt like an idiot. At least nobody knew I had jumped to such a dumb conclusion. Fool.

"Tell me about your mother," Tori said, sniffing back tears.

Olivia took a sad breath and said, "We're nothing alike. She's always ready for an adventure, but I'd rather just hang out. It was her idea to come on this trip. I fought her. I really did. I didn't want any part of Pemberwick Island, but she insisted. It's the first thing I'm going to remind her of when I see her."

"I like that," Tori said.

"What?"

"You're totally confident your mother is okay."

Olivia chuckled. "I know she is. It'll take more than a little genocide to stop her." She sniffed. Olivia was crying too, but doing her best to hold it back. "I miss her. I wish we'd never come here. I don't want any part of it anymore. I just want to go somewhere and hide until it's all over."

I saw the shadow of Tori leaning over to Olivia and giving her a hug. They were both holding back sobs. These two people couldn't have been any more different from each other, but they were bonded by the loss of their family, their lives, and the danger that lay ahead. Who knew what would happen between them tomorrow, but for a short while at least they were able to give each other some comfort.

It felt wrong to be standing there. Not just because I was eavesdropping on a private moment, but because I had immediately assumed that they were talking about me. It made me feel small to think that that's where my head went. I backed away, hoping they wouldn't discover that I had been there.

I crept back to my bed without anybody knowing I had been up and about. In spite of the fact that I was reeling with too many thoughts, I finally fell asleep and didn't wake up until early the next morning. The emergency room was still pitch-black. A quick look at my watch told me that it was six A.M. I sat up, stretched, and grabbed my headlamp.

Everyone was still asleep, and I wasn't about to wake them. I thought of Mr. Doyle. The poor guy had been living in the dark for too long. Maybe Kent was right. He might have been hallucinating. I decided to check on him and make sure he had enough water.

I picked my way through the dark emergency room, following the beam of my headlamp. Strangely, I was getting used to operating in the dark with only a narrow streak of light to see by. It was probably the way miners lived. I had no problem finding the exam area where we had left the old man.

"Mr. Doyle?" I whispered. "You awake?"

No response. I pulled the curtain aside to find him the way we had left him. Sound asleep. I didn't want to wake him. He could get a drink later. I turned away and started for the exit to see if the sun was up when I realized that something felt off. It was the sound. Or the lack of sound. Mr. Doyle had trouble breathing, as if he was too weak to pull in enough oxygen. It was painful to hear his labored breaths.

But I didn't hear them anymore.

I stepped back to him.

The bed was still up, which meant Mr. Doyle was in a near-sitting position. He lay perfectly still with his hands folded in his lap.

He wasn't breathing.

I started to cry. I couldn't help it. It seems odd to be bothered by the death of one old man when so many millions of people had been wiped out, but this was different. Mr. Doyle's death had nothing to do with the war. He had reached the end of his life and left it naturally. It was a reminder that we were still human. In some odd way it gave me hope. No matter how badly things got messed up, life would continue. Unlike the death of Tori's father and my own parents' betrayal, Mr. Doyle's death was one of the few things that made sense. He was an old man who died because he had a bad heart.

I reached for the blanket to cover his head. As I brought it forward, I saw that he was holding something in his hands. It was a piece of paper. Had he written a note before he died? I took it with two fingers and pulled it away from his lifeless hands to discover it was a small envelope with the hospital's logo. There were two simple words on it, written by the weak hand of a dying man.

For Paul.

The envelope had weight. I opened it to find two rings inside: golden bands. One was large, the other small. Both were inscribed inside with the same date, January 24. I looked at Mr. Doyle's left hand to see that his ring finger held no ring. My guess was that the larger ring was his wedding band. The other, I assumed, had belonged to his wife. The last act of his life was to try to make sure that they would get to his son. It was a very human act in a world that had become incredibly inhuman.

I dropped the rings back inside and put the envelope in my pocket.

"I can't guarantee that your son will get these," I said to him. "But I'll honor your memory by keeping them safe. Thank you for trying to help us."

With that, I lifted the blanket up and draped it over his head.

FIFTEEN

We couldn't leave Mr. Doyle lying in that bed.

After I broke the news to the others, it took some convincing and discussion, but we eventually decided to bring him to the hospital morgue. Olivia didn't want any part of the process, no big surprise. Neither did Kent, but I shamed him into it. Jon found a gurney, and we transferred the already stiffening body onto it. I had to give Jon credit. He took the lead, and why not? He was the only one of us who had experience transporting dead bodies.

It was an eerie procession to the morgue as we moved behind the light of our headlamps. Olivia eventually joined us, but only to hold one of the camp lanterns. She always came through when I least expected her to.

We found the morgue and were all relieved to see that there were no bodies lying on any of the tables. After several weeks and no air conditioning, that would have been gruesome.

"We should put him in there," I said, pointing to the wall of stainless steel refrigerator doors, where the morgue visitors were kept.

"Why?" Kent asked. "There's no power."

"To give him a little dignity," I said. "We can't just leave him out here in the open."

"Hate to break this to you," Kent said. "He doesn't care."

"But I do!" I shouted at him.

"Whoa, easy," he said, holding up his hands. "You'll wake the dead."

"Not funny," Tori admonished.

"Yeah, it is, a little," Kent said with a snicker.

"Look," I said, trying to control my emotions. "I know it won't make any difference to the guy if we leave him in the open or put him in the drawer or bring him to a cemetery and put him in a giant mausoleum. Nobody will know or care either way, but there are some things you have to do because they're right. Every time we take something from a store or drive that Explorer or siphon gas or take food, it makes me feel like we're letting a little bit of civilization slip away."

"So you want to pay for what we take?" Kent said, scoffing.

"No, I'm saying that I'm afraid we're going to forget who we are. Canned food is going to run out. Gas is going to go dry. We may have trouble finding clean water or a warm place to sleep. How are we going to handle that? If we treat Mr. Doyle like he doesn't matter, what's next? Do we start fighting over who gets the biggest piece of fruit? Or ignore somebody who's hurt? Or not give water to a dying man? It scares me to think that we may be headed toward a world run by jungle rules. Survival of the fittest."

Nobody argued. They kept their eyes on the ground.

"I'm sorry," I said. "But I don't want to go there."

I hoped their silence meant they were all imagining what it might be like if the rules of civilization were thrown out. At least Kent didn't crack any more bad jokes.

Tori walked to the wall of freezers, hesitated before choosing one, then reached up and pulled open a door.

I held my breath, fearing that the cooler might already be occupied.

It wasn't.

Tori pulled out the long drawer, and without another word we all worked together to move Mr. Doyle. Even Olivia. We lifted him up to find he was ridiculously light. After gently placing him in the drawer, feet first, Jon slid him inside and closed the door. It locked shut with a loud click that sounded very final.

"Do we say anything?" Jon asked.

We shared looks. What could be said? We didn't even know the guy.

I faced the others and said, "Let's just say we hope he's in a better place and we're glad that he's not suffering anymore. And we thank him for trying to help us out. I guess it says something about somebody when the last thing they do in life is to offer help to complete strangers."

I didn't mention the rings. I'm not sure why. I guess I was afraid that Kent would somehow cheapen it by saying how dumb it was for me to have taken them.

"Amen," Olivia said.

She was crying.

We stood there for a few seconds, offering a moment of silence.

"That's it," Kent declared. "I'm outta here."

It was a disrespectful way to end the moment, but I wanted to get out of there too. We all hurried out of the morgue, up the stairs, and went directly to the outside doors of the emergency room in search of morning light.

I blew through the doors first, stepped into the warmth of the sun, and took a deep breath of fresh air. I needed it. Badly.

It was now full-on autumn. The sky was a brilliant blue, and the trees had become a dazzling rainbow of reds, yellows, and oranges. It was my favorite time of year. It made me think of Halloween and Patriots games and Thanksgiving dinner . . . and school. Would I ever set foot in a school classroom again?

"So what's the verdict?" Tori asked, all business. "Are we going to Nevada or what?"

"I say yes," Kent chimed in quickly. "If there's a chance we can punch back at these bastards, I say we take it."

"Do you really believe there's an army of survivors out there that can stand up to SYLO?" I asked. "Or the Air Force? Or both?"

"I have no idea," Kent replied quickly. "But I hope there is. There are two sides to this war, and I don't want to be on either one of them. Who else can we trust but people like us? At some point, one of those armies is going to win and take over, and I don't want to be at their mercy. We've gotta build some power of our own, and that radio broadcast offers the only hope of doing that."

"Amen," Tori said. "I couldn't have said it better. What about you, Jon?"

Jon was reluctant to answer, but we all stood there staring at him, so he had no choice.

"I'm sorry, Tori," he began. "I know I wanted to go before, but I'm not so sure we can trust that broadcast. Not after what happened at Faneuil Hall. It sounds too similar, like we're being lured in. Even if it's legit, I don't see how a bunch of civilians can fight those armies. Either of them. Like it or not, we're going to be at the mercy of the winning side . . . unless we die fighting them. Now we've got another option. I say we go to Kentucky and see if there really is a safe haven. That's my vote. Kentucky."

Tori skipped Olivia and looked at me.

"What do you say, Tucker?"

"What about me?" Olivia asked. "Don't I get a say?"

"We already know what you want to do," Tori replied. "Florida, right?"

Whoa. Had Olivia told Tori about trying to convince me to go to Florida? Had she painted the idyllic picture of lolling in the warm sand and sleeping under palm trees the way she had with me? I mentally kicked myself for thinking that way. This isn't about you, Tucker. Get over yourself.

"Yes, Florida," Olivia said with confidence. "I agree with Jon. We aren't soldiers. We can't fight these armies. Winter is coming on fast. I say we go to Florida, where it's warm and safe, and wait until it's over . . . but I'm not going by myself."

"Got it," Tori declared. "You all know where I stand. Two say we go to Nevada, one says we go to Kentucky, and one says we go to Disney World. It comes down to you, Tucker."

Once again, the group was looking to me to make a decision. No matter what I said I'd have two people angry at me.

"I agree with all of you," I responded.

"That's not a vote," Kent said quickly.

"Just listen. I'm not so sure about this rebel survivor thing. Maybe it's real, maybe not. Like Kent said, I hope it's true. At least it means we'd have a chance at fighting back and taking control of our own futures."

"Thank you!" Kent exclaimed.

"Good," Tori declared. "We go to Nevada."

"Through Kentucky," I added quickly.

"What?" Tori snapped.

"You're kidding me," Kent complained. "Why?"

"To learn," I said. "If what Mr. Doyle said was true, there are people there who knew this was coming. We might be able to learn something we can bring with us to Nevada. That kind of information could make us valuable to the survivors gathering there . . . assuming they exist."

Tori stared me square in the eye. I was afraid she was going to tee off on me for not supporting her again.

I shrugged and said, "Why not? It's on the way."

She actually gave me a small smile and said, "That's pretty smart."

"I have my moments," I said, totally relieved.

Olivia said, "What if we find this safe place in Kentucky and some of us want to stay?"

"Then stay," I replied. "I hope we stick together, but we've all gotta do what we've gotta do."

I looked to each person in turn, waiting for their response.

The first one to react was Kent. He walked past me, headed for the emergency room door.

"Everybody get your stuff," he said. "We're outta here."

"I still want to go to Florida," Olivia said with a pout.

It was as simple as that. Minutes later we were back on the road and headed south.

We used the atlas to plot a route that would take us south through Connecticut, past New York City, and into northern New Jersey. The route then headed west: We would drive the length of Pennsylvania and on into Ohio. Once through Ohio, we'd head south again and into Kentucky. Our goal was to get to the airport in Louisville, just as Mr. Doyle suggested.

From there it was anybody's guess as to what we would do.

We planned the route to skirt major cities, figuring that if there was any military activity it would more likely be in populated areas. Or areas that *used* to be populated.

We drove very close by the town where I was born and had lived before moving to Pemberwick Island: Greenwich, Connecticut. Part of me wanted to swing by my old house to get one last look, but I knew it would be more painful than heartwarming. I had great memories of living there. I didn't want them spoiled by facing the reality that the kids I had gone to Glenville School with were probably all dead.

We took turns driving. I had zero experience driving on the interstate, but it wasn't like I had to deal with traffic. The challenge was to stay alert and avoid the occasional empty car in the middle of the road.

With each passing mile, we saw more confirmation of the extent of the attack. I had been holding out hope that at some point we would find a town that hadn't been hit and that would mark the outer edge of the Air Force's deadly reach. It never happened.

Allentown, Lebanon, Harrisburg. We passed dozens of towns, large and small. Each one was as desolate and empty as the last.

We stopped several times to siphon gas, usually picking larger SUVs and the occasional Hummer for their monstrous gas tanks. It wasn't worth stopping for smaller cars or hybrids. We made a game out of it to keep things interesting. If you picked a car with more than ten gallons, you could skip your next turn at siphoning. It was dumb, but it helped pass the time. It wasn't like we could listen to the radio, and nobody was in the mood to sing camp songs.

Outside of Pittsburgh we stopped in a small town called Washington to find food. There was a Shop 'n Save grocery store that had everything. We split up and agreed to meet back at the car in twenty minutes.

I went for the produce section. Big mistake. The fruits and vegetables had long since gone bad. The sweet smell of rotting fruit made me gag. I skipped the breads, figuring they'd be stale. I went nowhere near the meat section, or the frozen food.

What it came down to, and where we all ended up, was the cereal aisle. We chowed down on our favorites. Mine was Toasted Chex. I also went through a bunch of cereal bars. After that I swung by the snack section and cracked open a can of mixed nuts. I figured they might be somewhat healthy. I then washed it all down with some warm Gatorade. It wasn't exactly a delicious, balanced meal, but it filled me up.

With every package I opened, I took note of something that usually meant nothing to me: expiration dates. It wasn't that I was worried about the food having gone bad; it was more about the grim reality that in spite of what seemed like an endless food supply, it wasn't going to last forever. The expiration date was a reminder that life, and our survival challenges, would only get more difficult.

Before leaving, I went to the pharmacy, grabbed a toothbrush and toothpaste, and brushed my teeth. I kept the toothbrush and a Speed Stick deodorant that I used for a couple of quick swabs under the arms. On the way out, I picked up a few small bags of nuts for the road.

Kent was waiting at the front door, deep into a bag of Oreos.

"I hope you ate something better than that," I said.

"Yeah," he replied. "I polished off a bag of Cool Ranch Doritos. That's got corn in it, right?"

I didn't feel like getting into a discussion on the importance of eating healthy, so I just smiled and nodded.

Tori arrived with a small basket loaded with vitamins.

"I forgot to get vitamins in Springfield," she said. "We've gotta be good about taking them every day."

"What are you?" Kent asked. "My mother?"

"Do what you want," she said. "But don't blame me if you start feeling like crap because you're eating only sugar and salt."

She stuck a bottle of multivitamins in his jacket and headed for the car.

Kent said, "I think she's got a thing for me. Should I go after that?"

All I could do was laugh and walk away, but the question bothered me. Was he right? Did Tori have a thing for Kent? She was really upset with him when he tried to kiss her at Faneuil Hall, but things had changed since then. She definitely didn't want anything to do with me anymore, not after the shower incident. But I wanted her to trust me again. Did Kent's question bother me because I didn't want drama added to an already difficult situation?

Or was I jealous?

We piled back into the Explorer and drove for another few hours. By five o'clock the sun was sinking low.

"It'll be dark soon," I announced. "We should find a place to sleep."

None of us wanted to be out and about at night. We hadn't seen a single black plane since Boston, but the threat was always there. It wasn't worth taking the chance. Besides, we'd been driving for twelve hours straight.

We found another hospital outside of Columbus, Ohio. After holing up twice in hospitals, we knew the routine. We found a big, modern medical center called Mount Carmel East that was close to the interstate. Without saying a word, we parked in front of the emergency entrance, trudged inside with our bags, and made ourselves at home.

Jon went straight for the radio.

Olivia made Kent search the place to make sure there weren't any patients who might scare her.

Tori went for the kitchen to find dinner.

It was a practiced routine, and one I feared we'd be repeating again and again. The only person who did something a little different was me. I sat down with the atlas to review our planned route to Kentucky and to look for anything that might give us a hint as to where a safe haven might be.

I took out the folded map of the state and spread it out on a counter, looking for . . . I didn't know what. It wasn't like there was going to be a big sign saying: SAFE HAVEN.

"It's not about revenge for me," Tori said as she put a plate piled high with corn and tuna fish in front of me.

I hadn't questioned her, but she obviously wanted me to know where her head was.

"It isn't?" I asked. "You sure sound like you want somebody to pay for your father's death."

She sat down with her own plate of food, and we ate.

"I do," she said. "But that's not why I want to go to Nevada."

"You mean you don't want to fight for all that's right and noble and retake the country?" I said this with a smile, hoping she realized I was overstating things.

She smiled back.

I was happy that we were being civil.

"That would be good too," she said. "But I'm not crazy. The chance that a bunch of ordinary people can stand up to either of those armies is, well . . ."

She didn't have to finish the sentence.

"So then why do you want to go there so badly?" I asked.

Tori sighed. "Because I don't know what else to do. I can't just sit around and wait for someone to tell us where the world is headed."

"I wouldn't worry about finding things to do. We'll be pretty busy just trying to stay alive."

"That's not enough," she argued with passion. "We didn't ask for this. We had no say. Nobody voted on whether SYLO should be allowed to lead us to Armageddon or if the Air Force needed to fight them to save the world. If we just shrug and say, 'Oh well, let's make the best of it,' then we're allowing ourselves to remain victims. We didn't have a say before. Now we do."

We let that sit there for a while as we ate. I was happy that Tori was opening up to me. It wasn't something she did very often. Or ever. Maybe we were becoming friends again.

She said, "I'm telling you this because I want you to know that even if we find some incredible Eden in Kentucky, I'm not staying. I won't blame you if you decide to, and I'd be shocked if Jon and Olivia didn't. Kent says he wants to fight, but he's selfish. If we find a place that's sweet enough, he'll stay. But I won't."

"I'll be honest with you, Tori," I said. "I don't know what I'll do. I hear what you're saying. I don't like being a victim. But I don't want to be stupid either."

"That's why I won't blame you if you stay."

"I'll tell you something else," I said. "It's good to want to fight for control of our lives. I'm all for that. But that's not where my head is."

"I get it. You'd want to stay in Kentucky," she said, obviously disappointed.

"No, I want something else."

"What else is there?"

I hesitated a moment before answering. I didn't want to use the words lightly.

"You may not want revenge," I said. "But I do."

Tori's face dropped. She hadn't expected that.

"I'm angry," I said. "My best friend was murdered, my life was taken from me, and my parents are part of the problem. Oh, and a few billion people were wiped out. Let's not forget that."

"So you want to join the survivors and fight?" she asked.

"Not necessarily. You've seen what we're up against. I'm not suicidal."

"So then what do you want?" she asked, confused.

"I don't know yet. I'm going to keep my options open."

Tori nodded thoughtfully. "I get it, but like you said, we don't want to be stupid. Acting out of anger could be a mistake."

"I'll try to remember that."

"One step at a time, right?" she said with a smile.

"That's my new motto."

"Do me one favor?" she asked.

"What?"

"Before you do anything, tell me?"

"Sure."

She gave me a quick smile and left me alone.

I wondered if she realized that I had just lied to her.

After eating I went looking for Jon. He disappeared soon after we arrived, and I wanted to know if he got the radio working. I went right to the office of the emergency room, figuring that if there were a radio, it would be near there. Sure enough, there was a closed door behind the reception desk, much like in the other hospitals where we stayed. Better still, I heard Jon's voice coming from inside.

My hopes jumped. Not only had he found a working radio, he was talking to somebody! He'd made contact. Was he talking to the survivors? I went right for the door and yanked it open . . .

. . . but the room was dark. Jon sat at a desk that held a radio, but the screens were blank. No power lights were lit. For a second

I thought that I had somehow messed things up by opening the door, but that didn't make sense.

"What's going on?" I asked.

"I couldn't power it up," Jon said. His voice cracked, and he appeared nervous. "Must be the batteries. I've tried everything, but it's no good. I . . . I'm sorry. I did my best."

He was shaken by the fact that he had failed. Jon had a pretty high opinion of himself. Guys like that didn't like to be proven fallible.

"It's okay, not your fault," I assured him. "Wait, who were you talking to?"

"You heard me?" he said, sounding embarrassed.

"Yeah, I thought you had made contact with someone."

"No, I was just talking to myself. I do that when I get frustrated. I have these debates with myself. You know, I take both sides of an issue and hope that one side can shake some ideas loose from the other. Most times I don't even realize that I'm doing it. I know, stupid."

"No, it isn't."

Yes, it was.

"Well, it didn't work this time," he said, sounding defeated. "I'm stumped. Sorry, Tucker, I let you down again."

"No, you didn't. If it weren't for you, we never would have heard the broadcast in the first place. Go get something to eat. We'll try another radio somewhere else."

He jumped up quickly and hurried past me out of the room as if it bothered him to be near the scene of his failure. Jon was an odd guy. He was totally arrogant yet at the same time lacked self-confidence. I don't know why I tried to make him feel better about failing with the radio. That meant less to me than the fact that he had ratted us out to the enemy back at Faneuil Hall. I was glad to have him with us, but at the same time I didn't feel as though I could rely on him if things got hairy.

I didn't really mind that he couldn't get the radio working either. I didn't want to hear that broadcast again. It would just spin the wheels in my head even faster. I had the distinct feeling that tomorrow would be a long day. It was more important to get some sleep, so I closed the door on the useless radio room and found a bed to sack out on.

We all woke early because the emergency room had windows that let in the morning sun. We ate the rest of the canned food that Tori had found, washed up, and headed for the Explorer. It was a brisk morning. I could see my breath. Winter was on the way.

Olivia slid up to me as we walked to the car and whispered, "I'll bet it's about eighty-five degrees in the Florida Keys right now."

I ignored her.

Kent took the wheel, and I rode shotgun. The drive was uneventful. Our gas tank was full, and so were our bellies. There was nothing to do but drive and stare at the empty cars along the way.

We passed south of Cincinnati and crossed a bridge that spanned the Ohio River. When we hit the far side, we were in Kentucky and about a hundred miles from the Louisville airport.

"So here we are," Kent said. "What are we supposed to be looking for?"

I wished I had a good answer to that.

"Let's get to the airport," I said. "Mr. Doyle said that's where he would have flown to meet his son. Hopefully the place is close to there."

"I think we're wasting our time," Kent said. "But whatever."

Driving through Kentucky wasn't any different from driving through Connecticut or Pennsylvania. I don't know what I expected to see. There wasn't going to be some big neon sign reading: SAFE HAVEN—NEXT EXIT. An hour and a half later, we arrived at the Louisville International Airport, not knowing any more than when we had entered the state.

Kent pulled to the side of the interstate, turned off the engine, and looked at me expectantly.

"Well, Rook," he said. "We can't search the entire state. So come up with something or we're on our way to Nevada."

I opened the atlas and gazed at the page that had the full-color map of Kentucky . . . for the five hundredth time. I felt the heat of everybody's eyes on me.

"There's a lot of forested land," I said. "A big camp could have been built most anywhere."

"'Most anywhere' doesn't cut it," Kent pointed out. "It's a big state."

"Whatever this place is, it has to be fairly close to this airport, or else Mr. Doyle would have flown into another airport."

"Where's the next closest big airport?" Jon asked.

I referred to the large-scale Midwest map.

"Looks like we're more or less centered between Saint Louis, Cincinnati, and Nashville. Cincinnati's the closest, maybe a hundred miles north of here. The others look to be a couple of hundred miles away to the east and the south."

Tori said, "So we're looking for a needle in a haystack the size of the Bermuda Triangle."

Our quest to find Mr. Doyle's safe haven was suddenly looking bleak.

"There's another possibility," Kent offered.

"What's that?" I asked hopefully. I was willing to listen to anything at that point.

"The old fart could have been hallucinating."

"Kent!" Olivia scolded. "The man is dead!"

"Yeah, and we're stuck here picking our noses because he sent us on a wild-goose chase. I say we get the hell out of here and—"

"Wait!" Jon exclaimed. "I hear something."

If there was one thing we were getting used to, it was the eerie silence of a world that was no longer functioning. The only sound we had heard for a few days was the chirping of birds and the Explorer's engine.

"I hear it," Tori said. "I've heard that sound before."

We didn't have to wait long to know what it was. They came up on us fast . . . and they were loud. Four gray jet fighters screamed by overhead. They were so low that we could see the numbers under their wings. The sound was deafening. They disappeared as quickly as they appeared, thankfully, and the ear-shattering noise lessened.

"Their gear was down," Jon said. "They're landing."

"Maybe they're looking for the safe place too," Kent said sarcastically.

That gave me an idea. I opened the big foldout map of Kentucky and grabbed the compass from my hoodie.

"They're headed southwest," I announced. "Tori, you're the navigator here. Can you figure out the exact path they're on?"

Tori leaned over the seat, grabbed the map, and spread it out on her lap.

"Get me a pencil," she ordered.

I dug into the glove compartment and came out with a dull number two.

Tori looked around to get her bearings, placed the compass on the map, and twisted the bezel.

"They were headed roughly two hundred forty degrees," she declared.

She drew a straight line, using the edge of the compass's base. She used our position as the center and extended the line to the southwest and the northeast.

"That's where they came from, and that's where they're headed," she said and handed the map back to me.

The map had a lot of detail. It actually looked like a photo taken from a satellite. I followed the line southwest through what looked like a populated area that gave way to densely forested land. I kept following the line, looking for anything that might give us a clue as to where those planes might be going . . .

. . . and saw it.

I held my breath and took a closer look, making sure I wasn't mistaken.

"This is the exact heading they were on?" I asked.

"Unless they made a sudden turn before landing," Tori pointed out.

"What?" Kent asked.

"The line goes right over a military base with a very big airfield," I announced. "I'll bet anything that's our spot."

"How can you be so sure?" Jon asked.

I held up the map and pointed to the base.

"We're looking for a safe place, right? This is probably one of the safest, most secure places in the country."

"Seriously?" Olivia asked. "What is it?"

"One of the biggest bank vaults in the world," I replied. "Fort Knox."

SIXTEEN

"Why is there a big bank vault in middle-of-nowhere Kentucky?" Olivia asked.

"It's not really a bank vault," Jon answered. "It's a structure that was built to hold the gold reserves of the United States government."

"So they've got piles of gold coins lying around like some kind of pirate's lair?" Kent asked.

"Not coins, bars," Jon said. "Tons of them. Literally. The government has used the vault to secure other valuable items as well, like the Constitution and the Declaration of Independence. They were stored there during World War II."

"How do you know so much about it?" Kent asked with skepticism.

Jon shrugged. "History is a passion of mine."

"You are so odd," Kent said.

"I don't know that much about the place," I said. "But look at the map. It's a big freakin' vault in the middle of an Army base near a small town."

Everyone took turns looking at the detailed map.

"The vault itself is a whole building. If I were looking to keep things safe, that would definitely be on my list."

"We're looking for a place that's a safe haven for people," Tori said. "Not gold."

"I know," I said. "But there's plenty of other valuable stuff in the world. The Air Force attack didn't just happen. Even the president of the United States knew it was coming. He's the one who ordered SYLO to set up on Pemberwick Island. If he knew war was coming, don't you think he'd do exactly what Jon just described? Wouldn't he want some things to be protected? Like the Declaration of Independence? Or the Constitution? Or the *Mona Lisa*, for all I know? He could be protecting stuff from the Air Force."

"Or from whoever is controlling the Air Force," Tori pointed out.

"Exactly," I said. "This might be the safest place in the country right now."

"Then let's go!" Jon declared.

Kent and Tori stared at me, waiting for an answer. Again, I was the one who had to make the call.

"What have we got to lose?" I said with a shrug. "Let's go check it out."

I scoped the map and gave Kent directions on how to get there. It looked about thirty miles southwest of the airport on local roads. We followed the course and had traveled for no more than ten minutes when we began to see proof that we were on the right track. It started out as smoke on the horizon. Several fires were burning, spewing huge, black plumes into the air.

"At least there's some life here," Tori said.

"Look," Olivia said, pointing to the side of the road. "Here we go again."

There was a big ditch surrounded by a scattering of rocks. It looked like the deep craters we had seen outside of Portland.

"Those are missile craters," Tori said. "There was a battle here."

"Yeah, and not long ago," Jon added. "The fires are still burning."

None of the fires were near the road, so we couldn't tell what was in flames. We were traveling through a wooded area, and our views were blocked by dense stretches of trees.

"I don't want to see another burning corpse," Olivia said soberly.

We soon approached a scattering of structures that seemed to be the outer edges of the Army base. Even more fires were burning, and we finally saw why as we drove around a bend in the road and—

"Look out!" I yelled.

Kent swerved and barely missed hitting a wreck that was sitting in the center of the road.

It was a black, stingray-shaped Air Force plane.

Kent braked hard and stopped a few yards from it. This plane was in much worse shape than the one we had inspected in Portland. Its outer shell was torn open, probably by the missile that dropped it.

"It's unmanned," I declared.

"How can you tell that?" Tori asked.

"No cockpit. Where would a pilot sit?"

The plane's roof had been peeled off as if a can opener had worked it over.

"Looks more like the inside of a computer than an aircraft," I said. "It's loaded with circuit boards."

Tori said, "So they're definitely being controlled from somewhere else."

I got out of the car to get a closer look. This time the others joined me right away. The first thing I looked for, and saw, was the Air Force logo on the damaged wing.

"Building these must have been some top-secret project," Kent said. "I mean, it looks like a flying MacBook."

"Yeah," I said. "Except for that."

I pointed to a short, silver canister that was fixed inside the wing area.

"Is that the weapon?" Tori asked.

"That's my guess," I replied. "Man, talk about top secret development. When did the Air Force go all Star Wars?"

"They've been pretty good at keeping secrets," Tori said. "This is just another one."

"Guys?" Jon called. His voice was shaking. "You're gonna want to see this."

We joined him on the far side of the plane and looked out onto an expanse of empty farmland.

"I think we're in the right place," he said, his voice cracking.

Spread before us were the remains of dozens of downed black aircraft. Some were relatively intact; others were nothing more than mangled pieces of metal. None were functional. A few had hit buildings on the other side of the road, which is what started the fires. The entire stretch of buildings had been torched. There was nothing left but a half mile of charred, skeletal remains . . . and huge blast craters.

"Looks like some of them blew up when they hit," Tori said. "There's no wreckage whatsoever."

"Yeah," I agreed. "I guess if they get hit just right, the fuel—or whatever it is that powers these things—goes boom. It's like what happened in Portland when you rammed that plane. There was nothing left of it."

"This isn't exactly my idea of a safe haven," Olivia said, stunned.

"We're not there yet," I reminded them. "These planes could have been attacking the base."

Tori said, "Let's go see who won."

We got back into the Explorer, and Kent drove on, rolling slowly past many more wrecks and smoldering craters. Once past the stretch of burning buildings, we found ourselves driving through the woods again.

"I see more wrecks in there," Jon said, pointing.

"You know what I *don't* see?" I said. "Navy fighters. The only planes on the ground are the black Air Force planes."

"Looks like the Air Force got their butts kicked," Tori said. "It's different from what happened out on the ocean when—"

"Whoa, wait," Kent exclaimed. "What the hell is this?"

We rolled past another wreck and came upon a row of abandoned buildings that looked big enough to be airplane hangars. Beyond them was . . . nothing.

"Get closer," I said.

The road went directly between two of the buildings . . . and ended. There was nothing to see beyond it but . . . nothing.

Kent pulled the Explorer up next to one of the structures and killed the engine. We got out of the car and walked forward, moving cautiously past the buildings, tuned for any movement that could mean trouble. Directly ahead of us the road ended at a wide dirt track that spread to the right and left as far as we could see. The road looked to have been cleanly cut off. I took a step off the asphalt onto soft, brown dirt.

An empty expanse stretched ahead of us for roughly two hundred yards. On the far side, there was a swirling white wall that could have been the leading edge of a fog bank or a thick wall of smoke. It was so dense there was no way to see through it.

"Smoke moves, right?" Kent asked, saying exactly what we were all thinking. "How can that just sit there?"

I ran back to the Explorer and grabbed the road map. I unfolded it as I rejoined the others and searched until I found the exact spot where we were standing.

"Tell me this dirt track is on the map," Olivia said.

"No," I said with certainty. "The end of the runway is maybe a half mile ahead of us. According to this map, the only thing between here and there are trees and roads. There's no wide dirt track. This is new. Or at least it's new since this map was made."

Tori said, "It's like something came through and cleared everything out. Buildings, trees, rocks, roads . . . everything."

Olivia said, "Maybe the Air Force didn't lose here after all."

On the map, Fort Knox was more than just an Army base. It was a town. It was supposed to be directly in front of us, but there was nothing out there but a massive white wall. Was this the result of an air bombardment that wiped the whole place out?

"It doesn't make sense," I said. "Why would the Air Force use bombs here and nowhere else? If they wanted to wipe out the base, they could have come at night and used their light weapons."

"I don't think we've got the whole picture," Tori agreed. "Let's drive a little."

We went back to the car and loaded in.

"I don't want to go toward that smoke," Olivia said. "It could be, like, poisonous or something."

"Let's drive along the edge of the dirt," I suggested. "Maybe the smoke will thin out and we can see something."

Kent drove forward and off the end of the road onto the dirt. He made a right turn, and we rolled along on the soft surface. To our right were a few more hangar-like buildings. When we passed the last one, we saw nothing but trees and more crashed black planes. To our left was the fog bank, or whatever it was, on the far side of the dirt track. We traveled parallel to the white wall, unable to see anything beyond it.

"Stop," Tori suddenly ordered.

Kent slammed on the brakes.

"What?" he asked quickly.

"Ahead to the right. Something's coming."

I looked forward to see movement through the trees about a hundred yards ahead.

"Trucks!" Jon announced.

"Let's get out of here!" Olivia cried.

"No, don't move!" I countered. "If we move, they'll see us. Right now we're just another abandoned car."

We crouched low and kept an eye on what turned out to be a

convoy of green military trucks making its way toward the barren patch of dirt.

"Army trucks," Kent said. "Lots of 'em."

I was so used to living in desolation, seeing something as common as a line of trucks now felt like we were witnessing an alien invasion. My heart raced. Who were these people? Where were they coming from, and where were they going?

I couldn't make out much detail until the first truck cleared the trees in front of us and rolled onto the stretch of dirt.

"There's a road up there," Kent said. "It cuts across the dirt."

"Oh my God," Tori said. "Look!"

Painted on the door of the first truck, and the second, and all those that followed was a large white logo that looked like a rising sun. There was no mistaking what it represented.

"SYLO," Kent said in a soft whisper.

The trucks rumbled slowly along the road that crossed the dirt track headed toward . . . what? A white wall of fog? They were definitely military transport trucks, but there was no way to know what they were carrying. People? Weapons? The Ruby?

"Attention!" came an amplified voice. "Stay clear of the convoy."

The hair went up on the back of my neck. I looked at Tori.

Was I hearing right?

She looked as shocked as I felt.

"No way," Kent said, equally stunned.

"Who is that?" Olivia cried. "Where is he? Is he talking to us?"

I went into brain lock. I couldn't accept what was happening or begin to try to understand it.

"Where did that come from?" Jon asked, near panic.

His answer came quickly. A flying plane that didn't look large enough to carry a pilot appeared in the sky beyond the convoy. It skimmed the treetops, headed our way.

"Repeat. Do not approach the convoy," the amplified voice warned.

"What do I do?" Kent asked, looking very much like a deer caught in the headlights.

I couldn't think. I was useless.

"Don't move," Tori demanded. "That thing could be armed."

"So we just sit and wait to be wasted?" Kent whined.

"If that thing wants to waste us," Tori said, "driving away now won't stop it."

The drone plane had a bulbous nose, stubby wings, and twin propellers. Fixed beneath the wings were machine guns.

It was headed straight for us.

"It's got us," Kent whined. "We're going to die right here."

"Don't move!" Tori demanded. "Or we're definitely dead."

The drone cleared the trees and swooped down into the airspace over the dirt track. Its nose was lined up directly with our grill.

"This is your last warning," the voice boomed. "Do not approach the convoy."

"We're not!" Kent screamed.

The drone was nearly on us. Tori leaned forward and grabbed my shoulder. At any second it was going to fire its machine guns.

"I can't believe it," Olivia said with resignation. "We've come so far."

The drone fired. The clatter of its guns was deafening. I tensed up—but it wasn't necessary. The drone wasn't targeting us. It continued firing as it passed overhead. We all spun to see the real target.

A black Air Force plane was hovering a few hundred yards behind us.

It had been flying in total silence, like a silent snake stalking its prey. We hadn't even heard the music of its engines. The plane was no more than three feet off of the ground. Seeing it was a shock that made my stomach fall. Was it headed for the convoy? Or had it been after us?

Either way, its journey was over. The heavy machine gun fire from the drone craft ripped into the black skin of the plane, tearing it apart. The plane must have been crippled quickly, because there was no attempt to fire back.

Olivia covered her ears, and the rest of us followed. It was that loud.

The drone hovered over the doomed black plane, relentlessly pulverizing it with a steady stream of bullets. The black plane shuddered, as if trying its best to stay in the air. Its last gasp of life was to dip one wing to the dirt, then bank as if trying to get away. The drone would have none of that. The attack continued until the black plane dropped to the ground and crashed, kicking up a cloud of brown dirt.

That didn't stop the drone. It continued to fire, shredding the plane. The black predator was long dead, but the drone continued pounding it with a vengeance. As it hovered in place, it drifted into a turn to reveal a SYLO logo on its belly.

Tori said, "If it hits the fuel tank it'll—"

Boom!

The black plane exploded into a massive fireball, just like the plane back in Portland that Kent and Olivia rammed.

"Get down!" I screamed.

We ducked down for whatever protection the seats could provide. The burning cloud of debris spread quickly, and the orange flames licked past us. I winced, hoping that our own fuel tank wouldn't ignite. Though we were inside the Explorer I could feel the wave of heat surge by above us.

It was over as quickly as it began.

I cautiously peeked back over the seat to see the drone circling over its kill, or at least over the crater where the plane had been. Satisfied that its prey had been obliterated, it lifted into the air.

I held my breath, fearing that it would come for us next, but the drone flew skyward and took off after the convoy. The last of the trucks had rolled onto the road that crossed the dirt track as the first in line reached the fog bank and was swallowed up by the smoke. The rest of the convoy followed, each truck disappearing in turn as it entered the mysterious swirling curtain.

Something was definitely in there, beyond the fog.

The echo of the machine guns rang in my ears. We had just witnessed something shocking. Fort Knox was alive. There was no way to know whether it was the kind of safe haven Mr. Doyle's son told him about, but the Army base was definitely occupied . . . and protected.

But that wasn't what shocked us.

It was the voice that came from the drone.

I looked to Tori and asked, "Am I wrong?"

Tori looked pale. "I don't think so."

"Wrong about what?" Jon asked, confused. "What do you think is in there?"

"It can't be," Kent said. He was thinking the same thing we were.

"Can't be what?" Jon demanded to know. "What are you all talking about?"

"The voice," Olivia said, sounding sick. "Either it was a recording . . . or Captain Granger is alive."

SEVENTEEN

The voice.

It was the voice of SYLO.

I'd heard it too many times in my dreams. Or my nightmares. It was precise and emotionless, with a hint of a Southern accent. It was the voice of the man who had invaded my home and trashed our lives. I'd seen the guy coldly gun down unarmed men who tried to escape from his clutches. I watched as he ordered a missile to be fired from a warship that destroyed the town ferry and turned back those who were protesting his occupation of Pemberwick Island.

I listened while he discussed hunting down Tori and me . . . with my parents.

Worst of all, I had been on the wrong end of a vicious helicopter attack on the camp of rebels who were plotting to take back the island from him. It was an attack that killed Tori's father.

But Granger had been killed too. I saw it. He had chased us across the ocean on a Navy gunboat and pounded us with machine gun fire as we skirted our way through the battle between the SYLO

Navy and the Air Force planes. To escape, we had made a suicide run between two burning warships as they collapsed on each other.

We made it out.

Granger didn't.

We'd seen his gunboat explode.

I could accept that Feit was healed by some miracle medicine, but Granger? How could a medicine, no matter how magical, heal a man who had been incinerated?

I felt as though someone had grabbed hold of my gut and was twisting without mercy. Granger was the face of SYLO. He was calling the shots. Literally. His death had been minor payback for the misery he'd caused, but at least it had been payback.

Hearing his voice brutally ripped open old wounds and ignited a rage in me that had been simmering for weeks.

"It was a recording," Kent declared hopefully. "It had to be. The guy has a scary voice. They probably recorded a bunch of warnings like that and use them whenever they want to intimidate somebody."

"It sure as hell intimidated me," Jon said, shaky. "And I never met the guy."

"Could he be alive?" Tori asked the group, though she was looking at me.

They were all looking at me.

"No," I said. "We saw his boat explode."

I said that with far more certainty than I was feeling.

"What could be past that fog?" Olivia asked as she gazed out of the window at the mysterious white wall.

"It's not a place we want to be," I declared. "Not if it's a SYLO base."

Both Olivia and Jon looked glum. They had hoped to find a secure home in Kentucky. What we discovered was something far different.

"I . . . I'm not sure I want to go to Nevada," Olivia said, obviously shaken.

"Let's not decide anything now," I said. "I say we find a place to hole up and rest. We'll spend the night and decide on what we'll do tomorrow."

I got no arguments. I think it was a relief to put off any decisions, at least for a while.

Tori opened the map and did a quick check of the area.

"The closest town is Elizabethtown," she said. "Head west, and then find a way to go south."

Kent didn't have any sarcastic comments about how tricky it was going to be. I think he was too numb to complain.

We rode in silence as he continued along the edge of the dirt stretch. We passed the spot where the SYLO trucks had crossed in front of us to see a paved road that cut across the empty expanse.

"It's like a moat," Jon said. "A dry moat. I'll bet it circles the whole base. They must have leveled everything and cleared it away so that if anybody tries to approach, they'll see them."

"So what's with the smoke?" Kent asked.

"It hides what they've got," Jon said. "They shot down a lot of those black planes. They must have some serious artillery going on in there. If it can't be seen from the air, there's less chance of getting hit."

The sound of incoming fighter jets shattered the silence. They came in low, directly over our heads, on their final approach for landing. Their gear was down as they flew wing-to-wing, dropped closer to the ground, then disappeared into the fog.

I stared after them, straining to see something through the smoke.

"What are you thinking, Tucker?" Tori asked.

"I'm thinking that base is alive," I said.

"And?"

"That's all."

I was actually thinking a whole lot more, but I wasn't about to share it.

Kent found a road the led us west and away from the dry moat. We traveled through more farmland until we found a major road that led south.

"Time to start looking for a hospital," Kent said.

"No," Olivia said quickly. "I can't spend another night in a place like that."

It wasn't exactly a densely populated area. The buildings were few and far between. While Kent navigated past multiple bomb craters and downed planes, Tori continued to scan the map.

"There's a library," she announced. "Would that work for you?"

She asked the question with total sarcasm, but at least she was honoring Olivia's request. It seemed like their moment of mutual emotional support was brief, and over.

"Whatever," Olivia grumbled. "Anything's better than spending another night in a cold, dark hospital."

Tori called out the directions to Kent until we arrived at the Hardin County Public Library. It was a big brick building that rose up in the middle of empty farmland.

"Looks like another hospital," Olivia said with no enthusiasm.

"Tough. We're staying here," Tori declared and got out of the car.

The tension between them had definitely returned.

Inside, we found it was a warm, inviting place. Olivia was right. It was a welcome change from the antiseptic hospitals we'd been staying in.

"Only one problem," Jon said. "No beds."

"Or food," Olivia added.

"How about if Kent and I find a store while you guys figure out how we'll sleep," I suggested.

Olivia glanced at Tori.

Tori stared her down.

"I'll come with you guys," Olivia declared.

"Whatever," Tori said. "I'm starving. Hurry up."

The three of us went back to the Explorer and drove on. It took a while to find anything that resembled a town, but we eventually came upon a big place called the E. W. James Grocery Store. We loaded up a cart with bottled water, powdered drinks, cereals, cans of tuna fish, and various types of crackers. I also found some packages of dried seaweed, figuring it might be our best shot at getting some vegetable-based vitamins. Olivia scowled, but I took it anyway. Kent went for more Doritos and cookies. Whatever.

When we brought our bounty back to the library, we found that Tori and Jon had set up a comfortable place to sleep in the kids' section using pillows and cushions they had gathered from all over the library.

"You going to read us a bedtime story?" Kent asked, while putting his arm around Tori.

Tori gave him a cold look, and he backed off.

We brought the food to a small kitchen that was probably for the staff. We all silently grabbed whatever box, can, or jug we wanted and ate. There was no attempt to make it a civilized meal. When we were done with whatever we were eating, we'd drop it down for somebody else to grab. It was more depressing proof that we were moving further away from civilized behavior.

It gave me the resolve I needed to make a move I had been planning since the moment I'd heard Granger's voice. It was something I had to do alone. If the others found out, they would stop me. I was certain of that.

When we were finished with our uncivilized meal, we left the empty containers where they had fallen and drifted back into the main area of the library.

"I want to show you something," Tori said to me.

She led me to the reference section. It was getting late in the day, and the library was growing dark. We had to put on headlamps in order to read. Tori pulled out a heavy book and opened it on a table. We sat together, staring at the text by the light of our headlamps.

"What is this?" I asked.

"A Latin-to-English dictionary."

I had almost forgotten.

"*Sequentia yconomus libertate te ex inferis obendienter,*" I said. "Does this tell you what it means?"

"Not exactly. I found meanings of individual words, but I have no idea about tenses or conjugations. All I can do is string them together in some rough translation."

She flipped through pages and said, "Most of what Luna told us is correct. *Sequentia* roughly means 'the following.' *Obedienter* can be translated to mean 'obediently' or something."

"What about the 'gates of hell' thing?" I asked.

"*Libertate te ex inferis.* That could mean 'liberated or protected from the gates of hell.'"

"So the wild card is *yconomus.*"

Tori stopped on a page she had dog-eared. "I found a definition but it took a while. I guess it isn't that common."

"As opposed to all the other really common Latin words we use all the time?"

"I mean not common for Latin. I had to look through a couple of dictionaries before I found one that had it."

"So what does it mean?"

She pointed to a spot on the page.

I read, "*Yconomus.* A 'guardian.'"

I looked at her and added, "What the hell does that mean?"

"Put it together like it was English. These guardians obediently protect us from the gates of hell."

I let the concept roll around in my head for a few seconds. "So SYLO thinks they're protecting the world from falling through the gates of hell?"

"Or guarding the gates of hell so they don't open up."

"Bull," I snapped. "You don't protect people by imprisoning them and killing them."

"Unless they were guarding against something even worse," Tori countered.

"Are you serious?" I asked, incredulous. "They chased us down. Granger tried to kill us. He killed your father. How is that justified?"

"I don't know," Tori cried, shaking with emotion. "But there has to be some explanation for what's happening. Feit said SYLO was putting us on a road to destruction. Do we believe that?"

"From what I've seen? Sure."

"Feit's a liar!"

"They're murderers, Tori. Did you forget how they strafed the rebel camp? And then tried to incinerate us with a flamethrower?"

"Feit said half of the rebels were his infiltrators."

"They shot you, Tori. Let me say that again. They . . . shot . . . you. What is it about any of this that makes you think they were trying to protect us?"

"Because *they* didn't wipe out three-quarters of the world's population."

"Okay, so they're less bad than the Air Force. Good for them."

"What if SYLO knew what the Air Force was planning? What if they took over Pemberwick Island to protect it?"

"Protect it?" I shouted. "By cutting us off from the outside world and killing people who tried to leave? That's not exactly heroic."

"But the Navy was shooting the black planes out of the sky."

"Sure they were," I countered. "SYLO set up a base on Pemberwick. They were protecting their own butts. The Air Force wasn't attacking a bunch of lobstermen and rich yacht people, they were going after SYLO. SYLO brought the war to our door."

"Yeah, and the Air Force brought it everywhere else. It was the Air Force that killed Quinn, remember?"

"Because SYLO brought them to the island. Those robot planes might have done the deed, but SYLO was just as guilty. They're all guilty."

We were getting nowhere.

"I'm not sticking up for the Air Force," I said. "Or whoever is commanding them. But I'm not letting SYLO off the hook. Or Granger. You may be able to put all that aside, but I can't."

"Granger's dead," Tori said flatly.

"Yeah. Granger's dead. I hope."

We both backed off to take a breath and cool down.

"I'm going to Nevada tomorrow," Tori declared. "If you want revenge as much as you say, you'll come with me."

"Check with me in the morning."

Tori stared at me for a good long time, as if debating whether or not to say something.

"What?" I asked.

"I need you, Tucker," she finally said. "I've never said that to anybody before. Not even my father."

It was exactly what I wanted to hear . . . and the last thing I needed to know.

"I love you, Tori," I replied.

I don't know why I said that. It just came out. Maybe it was because I wanted to avoid going down the road she had just put us on. It was a road that would mean a commitment for us to stay together. That was a promise I couldn't make. Or maybe it was because I meant it, because I did. I loved Tori, though I didn't know what kind of love it was. She had become my closest friend in the world. I would do anything for her. I guess I wanted her to know that.

She leaned over and gave me a hug. It wasn't all romantic or anything. It was more of a way to show how close we were. It felt good.

"I love you too," she said. "I've never said that to anybody either."

With that, she backed off and left me to wrestle with my own confused feelings. I wished I could say that I wanted nothing more than to be together with Tori. After all we had been through, we had developed a bond that went beyond friendship. Maybe even beyond love. We owed our lives to each other. If not for Tori, I wouldn't have survived. It's as simple as that. She could say the same thing about me. We may have argued and disagreed, and having Olivia as a wild card in the mix didn't make things any easier, but the bottom line was that ever since things started to hit the fan on Pemberwick Island, we took care of each other. In spite of her occasional anger and disappointment in me, I fully believed that she couldn't imagine going on without me.

I felt the same way, except that I *did* have to imagine going on without her. I wanted us to stay together, but there was something I wanted even more, and if I truly loved her, I was going to have to betray her to get it.

I looked back at the dictionary and the entry for *yconomus*. A guardian. I didn't buy that SYLO was guarding anything but their own skins, but Tori's thinking wasn't entirely wrong. SYLO *was* guarding Pemberwick Island. I'd bet they were guarding Fort Knox too, based on the Air Force wrecks outside the base. The question was why? Why did this war happen in the first place? What was truly at stake?

As I sat there in the dark, I felt more certain than ever that I was about to make the right move. I was tired of guessing and speculating and wondering. I wanted answers.

And I wanted revenge.

The one thing I didn't want was to put Tori and the others in danger. I couldn't live with that. I had to hope that they would understand. That Tori would understand.

I joined the others in the children's section of the library. Everyone was lying on the floor, having fixed small nests of pillows. Kent was already snoring. Jon was reading a book. Olivia had her eyes closed, but she was humming a sweet song that I didn't recognize. Tori was lying flat with her face to the wall. I didn't think for a second that she was asleep.

I grabbed a few cushions and found an empty spot near the door that led back to the lobby. I sat down and made myself comfortable . . . but not too comfortable. I didn't want to fall asleep. After about an hour, Jon turned off his headlamp. I waited another fifteen minutes, then I stood and walked quietly through the room, hovering over each of my friends, trying to see if they were asleep.

Kent was sawing wood. Olivia had stopped singing and was lying with her mouth open and drooling. Yes, even hot girls drooled. Jon was breathing heavily. I padded softly to Tori and took a big chance.

"Tori?" I whispered.

She didn't answer. I wasn't sure what I would have said if she'd rolled over and answered me.

"I'm sorry" were my last words to her.

With everyone asleep, I had my chance. I walked quickly back to the area where I had been lying and put on my hoodie and cross-trainers. I thought about grabbing my gear bag but decided I wouldn't need it. There was something else I needed much more.

I padded back to Tori and gently picked up her gym bag. After backing away a few steps, I reached inside and rooted around until I found the gun. I pulled it out and carefully returned the bag.

Quickly, I backed out of the room and into the lobby. There would be no turning back. I was committed. The next minute was crucial. I had to get out of there without the others knowing.

I hurried through the lobby and pushed open the front door of the library as quietly as possible. After slipping outside, I gently eased the door shut until I heard the faint click of the lock. As soon as I heard it, I realized I had made a potentially fatal mistake: I didn't have the keys to the Explorer. How could I have been so stupid? I wasn't even sure where Kent kept them. If they were in his pocket and he was wearing his jeans, I was done.

I ran to the Explorer in the hopes that Kent had left them in the ignition. I grabbed the door handle, took a breath, and pulled it open to see . . . the keys.

I didn't stop to celebrate. The steady chime that rang to signal that the key was in the ignition might be heard from inside. I jumped into the car and quietly pulled the door closed. I sat there in the dark for several long seconds with my eyes on the front door of the library, expecting somebody to come charging out after me.

The door stayed shut. I had made it that far without being discovered, but the next few seconds were the most critical. It was dead silent. The sound of an engine starting up would be heard for miles. I would have to be out of there and on the road before anyone woke up and came to investigate.

My palms were sweating, and my heart raced. I was absolutely confident in my decision, though it meant I was betraying my friends. Especially Tori. She had opened herself up in a way she never had before to admit that she needed me, and my response was to take off on her. Since our escape from Pemberwick Island, I had been trying to convince everyone that unless we could rely on one another, we were doomed. I was about to go against all that I had been preaching. My justification was that I didn't want to put them in danger because of my personal mission. By going alone, I was actually protecting them.

That's what I told myself, but I couldn't shake the feeling that I was abandoning them. Whether it was smart or not, the group looked to me for guidance. It wasn't a job I asked for or wanted, but it was mine anyway. With me gone, there would be nothing to keep them together. Tori would go to Nevada. Olivia and Kent would probably go to Florida. Who knew what Jon would do?

My leaving meant they would be on their own.

I hated that it had come to that, but it didn't stop me from doing what I had to do.

I fired up the engine, jammed the car into gear, and gently stepped on the gas. I didn't want to skid out, slinging gravel. That would have brought people running. Instead, I rolled slowly out of the parking lot with the headlights off.

Before turning onto the main road, I glanced in the rearview mirror.

The library doors remained closed. I had made my escape. It was time to stop looking back, clear my head, and focus on my plan.

After traveling halfway across the country, my driving skills had gotten way better. Still, it was tough to navigate without headlights. I didn't dare turn them on, though. Moving headlights would be seen from miles away—and from the sky.

Once on the road, I realized my second mistake. I had forgotten the map. Idiot! I had to get my head out of my butt and start thinking a few steps ahead or I'd be done before I got started. I drove from memory, retracing the route we had taken from Fort Knox to the library. Luckily there weren't a whole lot of roads or choices to make. I drove north until I hit the intersection we had taken earlier and turned east. This road would take me back to the wide track of dirt that surrounded Fort Knox.

The SYLO base.

When my wheels finally hit the dirt of the dry moat, I drove another few minutes until I arrived at the first of the long hangar-like buildings we had passed earlier. I guessed it would be another half mile or so before I hit the road the convoy of trucks used to cross the dirt moat. I didn't want to drive the final stretch. That would be too risky. The rest of the trip would have to be on foot, so I braked to a stop.

When I opened the car door, I spotted something in the door's storage area. It was one of the walkie-talkies we had taken from the store in Portland. I grabbed it, though I can't say why. I sure didn't need it. Who would I call? Maybe it meant I wasn't ready to admit that I would never see my friends again. It was a comfort. A small comfort, but a comfort nonetheless. I clipped it onto my belt and started walking.

Jon's theory sounded right. SYLO must have cleared the area so that they could detect anything approaching the base. For all I knew the stretch was littered with land mines. I put that gruesome thought out of my head and pressed on.

My heart was racing so fast that I traveled the distance in next to no time. I kept my eyes on the dirt track but tried to be aware of any movement that might mean I'd been spotted. I didn't know what I'd do if I was attacked by SYLO soldiers. Run, I guess. But to where? By the time I'd gone through all the possibilities, I spotted the dark streak that was the road into the fog. I crept up to the closest building and crouched down at the base of its wall. From there I could see both ends of the road. One end stretched back toward the burned-out buildings and field of plane wrecks, the other disappeared into the wall of white smoke.

Up until then everything had gone perfectly, but it was the only part of my plan I had control over. The rest would be left to fate. Or luck. Since the days had grown short, we had turned in early at the library. It was only a few minutes past nine o'clock. That was good. For me to succeed, I needed it dark. If I had to wait until daybreak, I was done. All I could do was wait and be patient . . . and hope that I hadn't made a huge mistake.

Though it was dark, I could still make out the sheer wall of smoke that lay at the end of the road. What would I find in there?

These guardians obediently protect us from the gates of hell.

SYLO.

Murderers.

I wanted the truth. I wanted answers, though I didn't expect them to be comforting. There would be no happy ending to this story. Not after so much tragedy. The most I could hope for was understanding.

And revenge.

I don't know how long I waited there. Maybe an hour. I was huddled down to try to keep warm against the evening chill when I saw light appear and reflect off the road in front of me. I instantly went from drowsy to hyperalert.

Something was coming from the direction of the scorched buildings.

The distant rumble meant it was a truck. I peered around the building to see headlights. It was another convoy—exactly what I'd hoped for. The most dangerous and foolish part of my plan was about to unfold. When the time came, I would have to make a quick decision and hope it wasn't a fatal one.

When the first truck rolled by, my heart jumped. It was a huge garbage truck with the SYLO logo painted on its front door. My luck was holding. The next truck rolled by. It was the exact same type as the first. I looked back to see four more sets of headlights. The sanitation division had arrived to clean up the camp.

Ever since we learned about the possibility of survivors gathering in Nevada to try to fight back, we had wondered if a group of civilians could really make a difference. We were kidding ourselves. We wanted to believe it was possible. It wasn't. As noble as it sounded, I had no doubt that a rebel army, no matter how driven, would be crushed like helpless ants under the heavy boots of two professional armies.

I didn't want to be a crushed ant.

I wanted to be a single bee that nobody saw coming—and that did some damage.

I examined each of the trucks as they rolled by. It was dark so I couldn't be 100 percent sure, but I thought I saw what I needed. If I was wrong, I'd have to crawl back to my hiding spot and wait for another chance. If I was right, the game was on.

The final truck had nearly reached me. I would have a quick second to decide whether to go or not. I looked around to see if there was any security. There wasn't, at least not that I could tell. The last truck was nearly there. After a final glance around for anyone who might be looking my way, I put my head down and sprinted for it.

The garbage parade was moving fast. I had to calculate the angle and hit it on the first try, like chasing down an open-field runner in football. I ran for where the truck would be when I got there.

When I was a few yards away, I reached out for the metal handle that was on the right rear of the massive garbage bin. Below it was a small platform. It was a place for sanitation workers to ride as they made multiple stops.

I dug in and hurtled forward while reaching out. For one brief, terrifying second I thought I'd miss it. There would be no second chance. I leaned forward, willing my fingers to grow longer. With one final burst of speed, I grabbed on and wrapped my fingers around the metal bar. I pulled myself forward and half jumped, half yanked myself up onto the small platform.

My heart was pounding and my lungs ached, but I was on and headed for the fog.

There was no telling what I would find in there. If soldiers were checking the trucks, it would be a short ride. I reached to my lower back and felt Tori's gun. If somebody caught me with that, there'd be no talking my way out of it. I'd be dead.

I knew the risk, but I needed the gun.

We rumbled across the narrow roadway, growing closer to the wall of smoke.

I would soon learn whether we had heard a recorded voice coming from that drone plane, or if Captain Granger had returned from the dead.

If he had, I was about to send him back.

That was my mission.

I would get my revenge.

The truck approached the white wall, and seconds later I was enveloped in the cloud of smoke.

EIGHTEEN

The trucks slowed down and crept through fog that was so dense I couldn't see my hand in front of my face. I listened intently for any sound other than the rumble of the truck engines, but heard nothing. We rolled along for a minute or two before I began to sense shapes through the smoke. My first thought was that I was seeing large statues. The dark objects weren't uniform and didn't seem to have any straight lines. The smallest was the size of a truck; the largest looked like it had solid beams that jutted skyward for thirty feet. I strained to see what they might be and noticed other, smaller shadows moving past them . . . shapes I recognized.

People.

The fog thinned, and visibility grew. I could make out people in groups of two, apparently sauntering along casually with no particular destination in mind. I imagined that they might be couples out for an evening stroll through a sculpture garden.

The smoke cleared further, and I realized I couldn't have been more wrong.

The strolling couples wore red camouflage military fatigues

with dark red berets: the uniform of SYLO. The green-and-yellow rising-sun patches on their berets and their shoulders confirmed it. I was back in the center of a nest of SYLO vipers . . . who had assault weapons slung over their shoulders.

The full realization of what I had found hit hard when the smoke thinned and I saw the sculptures for what they really were: artillery. These were modern antiaircraft weapons aimed at the sky. There were hundreds of them, stretching out on either side of the road.

"Hey, kid!" a soldier shouted.

I tensed up. Should I reach for the gun? No. That would be suicide. These guys were professionals with assault rifles, and all I had was a pistol that I'd never even fired.

I looked over my shoulder to see two SYLO soldiers on the side of the road. Their weapons weren't aimed at me. Yet.

"Bad night to be on garbage duty," the soldier called. He was actually smiling.

"Sucks to be you," the other called.

I gave them a casual shrug as if to say, "What can you do?"

These guys thought I was working, not sneaking in to hunt down their commander.

The convoy moved on, and I soon realized that the smoke was completely gone. I looked back to see that we had emerged from the other side of the fog bank. We had just passed through a wide band of smoke-camouflaged weapons, and now I was inside Fort Knox, where the first thing I heard was . . . calliope music.

I thought I was imagining it. The guttural rumble of the garbage truck masked everything except for the bright, tinny sound of old-fashioned calliope music. I took a chance and swung around the side of the truck to look ahead and confirm that the sound *wasn't* coming from my imagination.

We were passing by a row of jet fighters parked on a runway. Normal jet fighters, not black Air Force marauders. The map had shown us that we were headed toward the runways of the fort when we came upon the wide stretch of cleared earth. The jets made sense.

What I saw beyond the silent row of aircraft didn't.

When I made the decision to penetrate the fog, I expected to find a military base like SYLO had set up on Pemberwick Island. Or maybe the ruins of Fort Knox. Or even an Air Force base full of black fighters that had finally broken through and triumphed. I was not prepared for what was actually there.

It was a carnival. A full-on carnival, complete with rides, tents, strings of colorful lights, and a carousel, which was providing the music.

I jumped off the truck, letting it continue on its way without me. The lure of the carnival was too great. Not that I wanted to ride the rides or try my hand at ring-toss; it was the idea that it existed at all that drew me.

It was about a hundred yards from where I had jumped off the truck to the first row of brightly colored tents. To get there I had to walk across a wide expanse of grass that was far from empty. Every twenty yards or so, there was a metallic, cone-shaped structure that looked like a large teepee. They stood like silent sentries, each rising forty feet toward the sky. I had no idea what they were or what purpose they served. It was yet another mystery, but one that wasn't nearly as strange as the carnival.

As I got closer, I could hear other typical carnival sounds. People laughed and screamed. Adults as well as kids of all ages hurried between the rides. Bells and buzzers signaled a game that was won or lost. The throaty chugging of gas engines powering the rides provided a bed of white noise. There was absolutely nothing out of the ordinary about this carnival, except that it existed.

I reached the row of tents, stepped beyond them, and entered an impossible world of fun and music. The place was jammed with people who were running along the midway, playing the games and lining up for cotton candy and hot dogs. Most wore normal civilian clothes, but many of the adults had on red SYLO fatigues. This was definitely not like the golf course prison on Pemberwick Island. These people wanted to be here. They were having fun.

This was where Mr. Doyle's son wanted to bring his father to be safe.

I wasn't worried about sticking out. There were plenty of people my age who must have been the kids of SYLO soldiers. I doubted that they'd spot a stranger. Or so I hoped. As I walked through the crowd, I saw a mini-golf course; dozens of skill games; a dunk tank where kids threw softballs at a target to knock a SYLO soldier into the drink; and food booths that offered ice cream, sodas, popcorn, hot dogs . . . you name it. There were plenty of rides too. I saw the Scrambler, the Octopus, the Tilt-a-Whirl, flying swings, a carousel, and plenty of kiddie rides. The only thing missing was a Ferris wheel. None of the rides were taller than the steel teepees that were scattered throughout the fairgrounds.

I wasn't used to being around so many people, especially people having fun. It was all so . . . normal, which is what made it so incredibly abnormal. As typical as the scene was, there was something odd about it that I couldn't put my finger on. I stood in the center of the midway and did a slow three-sixty, taking it all in, watching the faces of the happy people, racking my brain to figure out what it was that seemed so off.

The place was magical, yet a little cheesy. Carnivals weren't Disneyland. They were erected quickly and torn down just as fast to be moved to the next location. The tents were faded and patched. The colorful paint on the carousel horses was cracked. Many of the lightbulbs on the rides were burned out. But none of that mattered. Especially at night. Thousands of colorful carnival lights made the place feel like a wonderland . . . just like every other traveling carnival.

That's what was wrong.

"Power," I said to myself.

There was electricity.

I had been so stunned by the sight of the carnival that it hadn't clicked right away. Carnivals were supposed to look exactly like this. They were bright and colorful and cheesy . . . but not in a world without power. SYLO had the means to produce electricity, and by the looks of the carnival, it wasn't from batteries or a couple of generators. This base had juice.

It made me focus on the reality of what I was seeing. This was an oasis. A well-protected oasis. There was a wide expanse of cleared earth that ringed Fort Knox. Inside that ring was a second ring of artillery and plenty of armed soldiers who protected the fort from attack. But what exactly was being protected? A rinky-dink carnival? There had to be more.

I heard the loud clang of a bell followed by a huge cheer. I looked to where the cheering came from to see one of those high-striker games where you try to ring the bell on top of a pole by hitting the base with a heavy mallet, shooting a metal weight up a wire. I'd never actually seen anybody win at that game. I always thought it was rigged.

Clang!

The bell rang again, and another cheer went up.

I wandered closer, not so much because somebody was killing the game, but because the crowd was so enthusiastic about it. It was a show of joy and laughter that filled a void in my soul. The spectators were thrilled, probably more so than the feat deserved. Hearing them laugh and applaud made me understand why this carnival existed.

It was a break from the reality of war. A vacation from the horror. By tomorrow the tents would probably be struck and the rides dismantled, but for the time being these people could forget that they were living inside a ring of artillery and under the constant threat of an aerial attack.

I made my way closer to the action. I wanted to see the guy win again so I could cheer him on like everybody else. I wanted a few seconds of relief. As I wound my way through the loosely gathered group, I could see that the hero of the moment was a SYLO soldier. No big surprise. He was a tall guy, though not particularly muscular. His back was to me, and I could see that he was breathing heavily from the exertion.

"One more time! One more time!" the crowd chanted, urging him on.

The soldier gripped the heavy mallet. The chanting grew louder and faster. The guy took a deep breath, wound up, and slammed the mallet down. He hit the pad, and the metal object shot to the sky, nailing the bell once again.

Clang!

The crowd cheered. I did too. I couldn't help myself. It was silly, but at least it was something positive. There was very little that I had seen over the past few weeks that deserved a simple cheer of congratulations. I felt good for the guy, and for the crowd, and for me. It was nice to cheer for something.

It was a cheer that caught in my throat when the soldier turned around.

He wiped his forehead with his sleeve and handed the mallet to the man in the rainbow-striped jacket who was running the game.

"Show's over," the soldier said. "I'm too old for this."

The crowd shouted "No!" as if to assure the guy he wasn't all that old. He was their hero. He had given them reason to cheer.

He was also their commander.

Not only had he rung the bell, he had done something else that was equally impossible.

He had come back from the dead.

It was Captain Norman Granger.

The man I had come to find . . . and kill.

NINETEEN

The crowd applauded as Granger did his best to look humble.

"Show's over," he said. "As you were."

His people may have been off duty, but he still gave them orders. The crowd dispersed, and I realized I was the only one standing there, still staring at him. I quickly moved away, hovering close to a tent that held a baseball toss game.

I was beyond being surprised by anything. Though I needed to see him to be sure, I'd known in my heart that Granger was alive the moment I heard his voice booming from that drone aircraft. Seeing him brought back so many memories. None of them were good. My hands started shaking. I had to clasp them together to keep from jittering. The last thing I needed was to let my emotions control me.

I needed time to think and plan my next move, but I had to be ready for anything. Half of my mission was already complete. I had seen Granger. The SYLO commander.

His presence on Pemberwick set the wheels in motion for Quinn to die.

He had turned my parents against me.

He was an enemy.

He was a murderer.

I had promised myself that if I found him, I would kill him.

Would killing a soldier in a war zone be murder? I guess that depended on who was doing the killing. Was it justifiable homicide for a civilian to take out a soldier who destroyed his life? I was going to find out. But to succeed, I had to be cold and calculating.

I had to be like Granger.

The SYLO commander strolled away from the high-striker game in no particular hurry. I trailed him, staying far enough behind to go unnoticed. I used other people to shield me from his view, while trying not to look like, well, like I was following him.

Granger walked casually with his hands clasped behind his back and his posture impossibly straight. He surveyed each ride, food cart, and game as he passed, looking them up and down like he was on an inspection tour. At one point he stopped next to one of the tall metal cones. He reached out and touched it, running his hand along the smooth surface as if admiring its workmanship.

His casual inspection tour reminded me of the way he strolled among the bullet-riddled bodies of Tori's father and the other rebels on Chinicook Island, casually examining the victims of his ruthless attack. He showed no remorse or sympathy, and then he ordered his soldiers to torch the woods where we were hiding.

I felt the weight of the gun pressing against my back. Killing Granger would go a long way toward getting revenge for what had happened on Pemberwick. But was I willing to sacrifice myself to do it? This bizarre carnival was in a secure military base loaded with armed soldiers. If I managed to put a bullet into Granger, several more bullets would soon be entering *me*. Not only would it be suicide, there would probably be other casualties. More innocent people would die in the cross fire. Some could be kids. I couldn't let that happen. I had to get Granger alone.

He suddenly stopped walking and pulled a phone from his belt. Apparently SYLO not only had power, they had cell service. Granger listened for a few seconds and then reacted physically to whatever he was hearing over the phone. He tensed up and glanced around as if looking for something. Or someone.

Had he been alerted that he was being stalked? I ducked behind one of the metallic teepees and cautiously peered at him.

Granger turned and hurried away. My guess was that he was looking for a quiet place to talk. With the phone to his ear, he hurried past the furthest tent, away from the carnival and out into the dark beyond.

He was alone. I had my chance.

I followed quickly but not at a dead sprint. I didn't want to attract attention. When I left the lights of the carnival, I had trouble seeing in the dark. I had to follow the sound of Granger's voice as he shouted at the phone.

"Details!" he demanded. "I don't want speculation. I want facts."

He was definitely worked up about something.

"No," he barked with authority. "Not until we have confirmation. Are you in contact with the AWACS?"

He was still moving. Fast. Every so often I'd catch a fleeting glimpse of him as he appeared from behind one of the cones before disappearing behind another. A few seconds went by without me hearing him. Was the conversation over? Where was he going? I had no choice but to keep moving in the same direction and hope I'd spot him again. I rounded one of the cones . . .

. . . and came face-to-face with him.

He had turned around and was headed back toward the carnival.

Granger stopped short. I saw a brief look of confusion cross his eyes. I was familiar to him, but he couldn't place me. Those few seconds of uncertainty gave me the time I needed. I reached behind my back, pulled out the Glock, and held it on him, keeping it steady with two hands.

"Tucker Pierce," he finally said as the puzzle pieces clicked into place.

"Why aren't you dead?" I asked.

Granger was on full alert, though he didn't look as scared as he should have, considering he was facing a gun held by a squirrelly guy with a chip on his shoulder.

He said, "That was quite the stunt you pulled, navigating between those two burning ships. That took guts."

"I saw your boat explode."

"It did. I wasn't on board. The commander was willing to chase you into that inferno, but wouldn't risk my life. He shoved me overboard before turning into that flaming gauntlet. The entire crew was killed."

"Did you order him to follow us?" I asked.

"I did."

"Then you should have been with them," I said with disdain.

"Agreed. But I wasn't, and so here we are. Will you be shooting me?"

"That's the plan."

Granger kept spinning his cell phone in his hand. He seemed far more concerned with the news he had gotten over the phone than with me.

"You're a long way from home," he said calmly, gesturing to his left.

He was pointing to a building that stood a few hundred yards from us. It was a large but squat two-story structure made of light-colored cement. It looked like a fortified bunker with windows.

I had no doubt that it was the famous gold repository.

"Why are you here?" I asked. "Why Fort Knox? Is it about the gold, or the vault?"

Granger lifted an eyebrow.

"You're a smart kid," he said, though it sounded more like an insult than a compliment. "Gold is going to be the foundation for a new monetary system. Or so they tell me. That kind of business is way above my pay grade. I'm just a simple soldier."

"Is that why SYLO has so much firepower here?" I asked. "To protect the gold?"

"To protect the future," he replied. "Are you enjoying the carnival? We're trying to make it as pleasant here as we can."

"Really? Pleasant? SYLO is putting on a carnival while trying to destroy mankind?"

His eyes went wide, and for the first time since I'd met the guy . . . he smiled. It was small, but it was real.

"I see you've been spending time with the Retros," he said.

"The what?"

"The Retros. That's what we call 'em. The black planes. The Ruby. The genocide. They're accusing us of trying to bring about the end of days, so what do they do? They wipe out two-thirds of the planet's population. Does that make any kind of sense to you?"

"They said we needed to start over. To reset."

"And you believe that?" he asked, incredulous.

"I don't know what to believe!" I screamed with frustration.

He thought he had an opening and took a step toward me.

I lifted the gun to his face.

"Stop!" I commanded.

He did.

"I'm scared as hell," I said, "and I hate your guts, so take one more step and I swear to God I'll put a bullet in your head."

It was strong talk . . . that I knew I couldn't back up. Granger knew it too. All I had to do was pull the trigger . . . but I couldn't. I didn't know it for sure until that moment. I wasn't a killer, no matter how badly I wanted him dead. I think the only reason he didn't attack me was to avoid being shot by accident.

"You're backing the wrong horse, son," he said calmly.

"I'm not backing anybody! All I see is the Air Force battling the Navy in a civil war that's killed billions of people. For what? What's the point? Explain it to me."

"No," he said flatly.

"Why not?"

"Because I don't trust you."

"You . . . *what*? You invaded my home, murdered dozens of people, turned my parents against me, tried to shoot me out of the water, and *you* don't trust *me*?"

Granger leaned forward. I lifted the gun until the site was centered between his eyes.

"You should have listened to your mother," he said without flinching.

That threw me.

"My mother?"

"She warned you not to trust anyone, yet here you are, holding a gun on the bad old soldier man you think is the cause of all the problems. How old are you? Fourteen? Fifteen?"

I had to grip the gun tighter to keep my hands from shaking.

"Maybe you're too young to understand, but they're using you, son. Those Retros are like termites. You don't know they're in the walls, eating the wood, until your house falls down."

"Nobody's using me to do anything," I argued lamely.

"Then go give those bastards a message. From me. Tell 'em we're not done. Far from it. Tell 'em to go ahead and try to build another one of their monstrosities. Soon as they do, we'll blow it to dust again, just like in Boston."

His words rocked me.

"Boston," I repeated, numb. "What was that thing? What were they building?"

"A gate to hell," he said with disdain. "They already got one, we won't let 'em get another."

My mind was spinning, desperately trying to make sense of what this guy was telling me.

"Another? They have a gate to hell?"

"For now," Granger said cockily. "They think it's protected, but we'll get that one too. It's only a matter of time. We're going to send those devils back to where they came from."

There was a crazy fire in his eyes that terrified me.

"Where is this gate?" I asked.

"Middle of nowhere," he replied. "Mojave Desert. They think they can protect it out there. They can't. I want you to tell them that."

"No!" I shouted, backing off. "There's nobody to tell. I'm not with them."

Granger laughed. "If you don't want to listen to your mother, listen to me. You gotta be careful about the company you keep."

His hand flashed forward, and he grabbed the muzzle of the Glock. I wasn't fast enough to react as he yanked it out of my hand. He then grabbed the walkie-talkie from my belt.

"You tell 'em," he said. "Let 'em know we're coming."

"Let *who* know?" I asked, pleading. "Feit? He's in Boston. I don't know any other Retros."

Granger looked at the walkie-talkie and laughed.

"We have no beef with you, kid."

"Then why were you trying to kill me on Pemberwick Island?"

"I wasn't," he said with a shrug. "Can't say the same about your friends."

"Wha—what do you mean?"

"I told you," Granger said. "They're like termites. You don't know they're in your house until it's too late."

I was reeling. Of all the things I had seen and heard, this was the most disturbing of all . . . and the most impossible.

"Are you saying my friends are Retros? That's crazy!"

The wailing sound of a siren drowned out the carnival noise.

"What is that?" I asked.

"Damn! I guess they really are coming," Granger snarled.

"Who? Who's coming?"

Granger shoved the walkie-talkie into my chest and tossed the gun away behind him.

"Do the right thing," he said. "Don't make me regret letting you go."

With that he took off running toward the gold repository building.

The siren continued to wail.

"Wait! What's going on?"

The carnival suddenly went dark. So did the floodlights that had been lighting up the vault building. I was left in near pitch dark. The fort had gone still. The calliope was silent. The rides had stopped. Not a single word or shout or hint of laughter came from the carnival grounds.

The siren ended its wail.

It had become deathly quiet.

That's when I heard it.

The music from the sky.

The black planes were back.

TWENTY

I expected to hear the antiaircraft guns start to boom or the scream of jet fighters taking off from the nearby runway. Instead, I heard a sound that meant nothing to me—at first. It sounded as though engines were powering up. The noise surrounded me, seemingly coming from everywhere . . .

. . . because it actually *was* coming from everywhere.

The silver cones had come to life.

I leaned in close to one and heard the sound of an engine running. There were hundreds of them scattered everywhere. Maybe thousands. I had only been through a small section of Fort Knox. For all I knew, the metallic cones were spread throughout the base. But what were they?

The music from the planes grew louder. The planes sent by the Retros.

What did that mean? Retro? I always thought it referred to something that was a reminder of something cool from the past. But the Air Force had nothing to do with the past, not with the kind of technology they were using. And there was definitely nothing cool about the fury they had unleashed on the world.

I heard a metallic *thunk* sound that made me jump. It was followed by another and another. The tops of the silver cones were opening up. The tip of each one separated into four sections that hinged down. The same thing was simultaneously happening with all of them, including the large ones near the vault building. Were these weapons? Were they going to fire on the black planes when they appeared?

Why weren't the jet fighters scrambling? When we drove toward Fort Knox the day before, we had passed the wreckage of hundreds of black planes. They must have tried to attack the fort before. Did the antiaircraft guns pack enough punch to fight them off?

It was nighttime. That meant the destructive light weapons carried by these black planes were operative. If they were allowed to fly overhead, they could wipe out every last person in the fort. They could also disintegrate the gold depository, just like they did with some of the buildings in Portland.

And with Quinn's boat.

I suddenly realized that I was standing at ground zero. If the black planes starting flashing their fire, I'd be done. Granger had given me a free pass out of there. I had to use it. I first picked up the Glock and jammed it into my waistband. Granger hadn't even bothered to take out the clip. He knew I wasn't capable of shooting him. I should have known it myself. If I had been honest with myself and not acted on emotion, I would be sleeping soundly in that library instead of standing in the center of a bull's-eye.

I had no idea of where to go for cover. All I could do was get out of there, and the only route I knew was the way I had come in. I sprinted back toward the carnival and ran straight through the dark midway. Minutes before, it had been packed with hundreds of people. It was now deserted. They must have taken off as soon as the siren sounded. But where did they go? Underground, probably. I wished I knew where. I wanted to be with them.

All around me, the conical engines whined into another gear. Something began to appear at the top of each device: poles that continued to rise until they doubled in height.

Boom!

The ground shook with the firing of an antiaircraft cannon. The planes were getting close. The deep sound shook my gut, literally. It was followed by several fast, sharp whooshing sounds. I looked north, the way I had entered the base, and saw the white streaks of missiles erupting from the wall of fog that camouflaged the launchers. They tore into the sky at a low angle, which meant the planes were still far away. It took several seconds before I heard them explode. I still had time to get out of there.

I sprinted in the general direction of the road that the garbage trucks had carried me in on, keeping one eye on the silver cones and the tall rods that now jutted up from their centers. I wanted to see streaks of laser light shooting from the pinnacles that would obliterate any bad boy that entered the fort's airspace.

What I saw instead was altogether different.

The tall shafts began to break into individual rods that unfolded like an umbrella. Multiple struts that were attached at the top of each spire lifted up, creating a device that looked like a windmill but with blades that were parallel to the ground. The struts continued to lengthen, making the wheel far larger than the height of its base. The machine itself was like nothing I'd ever seen before—and there were hundreds of them, all expanding simultaneously in a coordinated ballet.

By the time the process was complete, the wings of each horizontal windmill nearly touched the outstretched fingers of its neighbor, creating a continuous canopy. Running the length of each strut was a wide "sail" that looked to be made of lightweight, flexible material.

As I watched this evolution, I kept running toward the road that would lead me out of the fort. I wasn't even sure if I was headed in the right direction until my foot landed on asphalt. Yes! I had found the road. I made a left turn and sprinted for the fog.

The antiaircraft barrage increased. Missiles were being fired every few seconds, most heading north—the direction I was headed. The explosions started coming sooner after they were launched. The planes were getting closer.

To get out of the fort, I had to run through the ring of artillery. The black planes would definitely be shooting back at the approaching storm, which meant I had to travel through a dangerous stretch of real estate. Several SYLO soldiers sprinted by me, headed for the massive guns and launchers. They had to know that if the black planes weren't stopped, Fort Knox would cease to exist, along with everyone inside.

The last thing they had to worry about was a terrified kid running for his life.

I had almost reached the inside edge of the fog when the windmill I was under started to spin. I looked back to see that every one of the massive wheels had come to life. The chorus of engines powering up was so loud that it nearly drowned out the sound of the launching missiles.

I had to stop and watch, that's how stunning a sight it was. The fort was under a canopy of giant, whirling fans. Their rotation was just fast enough that the individual blades of each device blurred together. They actually looked pretty, like multiple pinwheels spinning in the breeze.

I could only guess at their purpose. They didn't seem like weapons, so they must have been some sort of defense. Or maybe camouflage. Since the black planes were remote-controlled drones, the multiple spinning wheels might somehow scramble their sensors. The spinning blades seemed light and fragile, which meant they weren't there to absorb the powerful blasts of energy that the planes could fire. It was a hypnotic display that I couldn't take my eyes from . . .

. . . until I was rocked back into the moment by the sound of multiple cannons firing at once. The sudden urgency could only mean thing one thing: The storm had arrived.

Even through the dense fog, I could see the ground erupting as invisible bolts of energy rained down from the incoming planes. Cannons were knocked aside like toys. Soldiers screamed and dove for cover that didn't exist. Through it all, the ground artillery continued to fire.

An explosion erupted in the sky as a black plane was hit. The fireball plummeted to the ground and landed on one of the major cannons, sending soldiers fleeing.

The fog grew even thicker as it mixed with dirt in the air and smoke from burning fuel tanks.

I didn't move. Panic had frozen me in place. It was a surreal scene. Ahead of me was a chaotic battlefield with fire being traded between the ground and the sky. Behind me was a swirling forest of humongous silver pinwheels that looked like something out of a CGI-heavy music video.

Though they were taking massive hits, the cannons continued to fire, and the missiles were still being launched. There were far too many of these weapons for the attackers to take them out completely. The Retros, or whatever they were called, had been repelled before. The multiple wrecks outside of the fort were proof of that. It gave me hope that SYLO might just have the firepower to send them back to whatever gate of hell they came from.

It was a moment of relief . . . that didn't last long.

At the very instant I told myself that none of the planes would get through, one of the planes got through. A black shadow shot by overhead. It was going for the gold—and not in a noble, Olympic kind of way. Another plane shot through, and another. Had the defense completely broken down? Was this the end?

The three black planes hovered in a triangle pattern over the repository building, just as I'd seen them do when they targeted Quinn's boat. Whatever this weapon was, I remembered that it needed the strength of three planes working together to function.

I wondered if Granger was in the repository.

A straight beam of light shot from beneath one of the black, ray-like planes. It was quickly followed by beams from the other two planes. The lights joined together, gained intensity, and shot toward the repository as one combined beam . . .

. . . only to be reflected back into the air!

The purpose of the windmills was suddenly clear. The whirling fans acted like mirrors, reflecting the deadly beam of light. The spinning wheels effectively gave the fort 100 percent protection. The combined, powerful beam of light from the black planes was diffused by the mirrors, sending harmless streaks of light scattering haphazardly. The windmills were not only reflecting the light, they were breaking it up.

It didn't stop the black planes from firing. The unified beam moved away from the vault building, searching for an opening in the defense.

It failed. The spinning wheels continued to deflect the deadly light.

The weapon had been neutralized.

The event didn't last long. When the three planes stopped to hover over the repository, they became easy targets.

With three quick blasts, multiple missiles were launched from the center of the fog toward the interloping planes. Each one found its mark, and all three black jets were obliterated. The explosions were so powerful that the only thing left of the planes was ash that blew away on the breeze. As with the plane that was shot by the drone, when the power cores of these planes were hit, the result was stunning. I couldn't help but wonder what kind of fuel would create such a devastating explosion. Could they be nuclear powered?

Whatever the case, the windmills had done their job. As long as the black planes were kept outside of the perimeter, Fort Knox would be safe. Granger would be safe too.

I guess you can't have everything.

The attack didn't slow down. If anything, the barrage picked up, as if the Retros were encouraged by the fact that some of their planes had gotten through.

I got my senses back and continued to run. I quickly sprinted out from beneath the safety of the spinning windmills and found myself in the middle of the artillery.

A cannon was fired so close to me that I was afraid the sound had ruptured my eardrums. As it was, my ears rang so loudly that I couldn't hear a thing. I staggered a few steps but had the sense to look up in the direction that the cannon had fired.

A flaming plane was falling out of control, headed straight for me.

I had two choices: run or die.

I ran up the road, headed deeper into the fog. A second later the burning plane fell like a dead bird in the center of the road not twenty yards behind me. When it hit it exploded into what must have been a million pieces of flaming junk that flew past me. Unlike the planes that had targeted the vault, its fuel core hadn't exploded. If it had, I would have been incinerated.

I didn't know what else to do but keep running. I knew the general direction I needed to go to get back to the dirt moat, but there was no way I could run in a straight line. I was surrounded by twisted pieces of metal that had once been trucks or missile launchers.

As many wrecks as there were, there were twice as many weapons still firing. The noise was insane. Though the battle was in the sky, I felt as though I was in the middle of it.

I passed a few soldiers who had been injured and were crying out for help. I stopped at one who was bleeding from the eyes.

There was nothing I could do for him but help him to his feet and guide him to one of the trucks where other soldiers were taking cover.

Once he was with them, I ran on and tripped over another soldier. This guy wasn't moving. He was beyond wounded. He didn't need my help.

Seeing the dead body brought the battle into focus. It wasn't just about machines shooting at each other like in some Xbox adventure. This was about people getting killed. But the Retro fighters weren't taking the same risk. They were unmanned. The people controlling them were probably miles away in the comfort of an easy chair as they played what would seem to them like a video game.

For the people on the ground, it was no game.

I couldn't believe I was actually taking SYLO's side. It must have been because I was in the same danger as the soldiers.

I kept running, though I was nearly blind and constantly choking on the smoke. The ground rumbled each time a black plane unloaded its energy cannon. A few times the impact was so intense that it knocked me to the ground. Once I nearly ran into a missile launcher that I didn't see until I was almost on it. Still, I couldn't weave through cautiously. The longer I was in that fog, the better chance there was of not coming out.

Finally, after a lifetime of running and dodging, I sensed that the smoke was clearing. I was almost through! It made me run even faster. I was still on the road, so my footing was good, though I had to be careful not to run into any of the hundreds of pieces of hot shrapnel that lay scattered everywhere. I finally blasted out of the fog . . .

. . . to witness a sight that was even more intense than the one I had just come from.

The night sky was alive with black planes and the bright tracer rockets that targeted them. I thought I would be safe once I had gotten away from the artillery. I couldn't have been more wrong. I was now in the drop zone where the black planes were falling and crashing. The ground was littered with bits and pieces of the downed fighters, with more hitting every few seconds.

This was an all-out assault. There were more planes blown out of the sky in the few minutes since the battle began than we had seen on the ground when we first drove in. They kept coming, too. The planes swooped through the sky like skittering moths trying to reach a tempting flame. There were so many that I was surprised they didn't fly into each other.

All I could do was run and hope that I wouldn't get hit by a falling chunk of flaming metal. I left the road and took a diagonal course across the width of the dirt track, headed toward the Explorer.

It seemed as though the SYLO defenders were doing their job, keeping the Air Force planes from getting close enough to target the fort. I wondered how long they could keep it up. The Retros were throwing everything they had into their assault.

None of the Air Force jets used their light weapons. It must have been because they needed the combined strength of multiple planes for it to work. With all the jets screaming haphazardly through the sky, there was no way they could join forces.

Up ahead I spotted the Explorer and quickly dug into my pocket for the key. I didn't want to be there one second longer than I needed to. I was thirty yards away from escape when I heard a whistling sound. I'd heard that sound often enough to know what it was. I stopped and spun around to see a burning black plane spinning toward the ground.

Toward me.

I had to move, but which way? I was like a deer caught in deadly headlights. At the last possible second, I dove to my right.

The doomed plane soared so close overhead that I felt the heat as it sped by. I hit the ground as it careened the last few yards . . . and crashed directly into the Explorer.

There was a massive explosion as the flames hit the gas tank, which shot a pillar of fire into the air. Rolling away, I heard the zing of speeding bits of shrapnel flying all around me, so I wrapped my arms around my head to avoid getting beaned by a bit of molten metal. I was lucky not to be hit, but I was still in the danger zone . . . with no car to get me out.

I scrambled back to my feet and ran. Soon I was off the dirt track and sprinting toward the road I had taken in from the library. I needed to get away as fast as my legs would carry me, so I ran until my side ached, but that didn't stop me. I can't say how long I ran, but the sounds of the battle eventually grew faint. When I couldn't take the pain any longer, I stopped and put my hands on my knees to try to catch my breath.

As I stood there gasping for air, I gazed back at the battle. There were fewer missiles being fired and far fewer shadows streaking through the sky. The fight looked to be winding down.

SYLO had won. They had repelled the attack. Fort Knox was safe, at least until the next time.

That night I had set out with one thing in mind: revenge. I

had failed miserably. Looking back, it was hard to believe that I had seriously considered assassinating Granger. I was angry with myself—not for failing, but for wanting to do it in the first place. I was lucky to have gotten away in one piece . . .

. . . and with some disturbing knowledge.

Granger was alive, which was bad enough. What he told me about SYLO and the Retros was even worse, yet it did pull the curtain back a little on this confounding war. The Retros were the aggressors. That much seemed to fit. But who were they? Why had they chosen to reset the course of mankind? Why did they think it was necessary? What gave them the right?

SYLO, on the other hand, was playing defense, and though they were outnumbered and outgunned, they were dedicated to stopping the Retros.

The question still remained: Who were the good guys? Had the forces behind SYLO truly put the world on a path to destruction that could only be stopped by the Retros' extreme tactics? Or were the Retros only using that as an excuse to create a new world order that they controlled?

And what exactly was this "gate to hell" that the Retros had and were trying to build more of?

As much as I had learned, I was still very much in the dark . . . and haunted by Granger's warning. It was the same warning my mother had given me.

My friends could not be trusted.

That may have been the most disturbing revelation of all.

TWENTY-ONE

I had never felt so incredibly alone.

In spite of the horror I had seen since the night Marty Wiggins dropped dead during our football game, I had always had someone to lean on. First it was my parents . . . until they turned out to be part of SYLO. I also had my best friend, Quinn . . . until he was killed by the Retros. Or the Air Force. Or whatever they really were. Tori Sleeper and I then forged a friendship that only got stronger as our troubles deepened. Our circle grew, taking in Kent, Olivia, and finally Jon.

We didn't always see eye-to-eye. Okay, we rarely all saw eye-to-eye, but we had each other's backs. Even Kent. He had come through for us at times when I expected him to worry more about his own skin.

Now I was faced with the possibility of one of them being a Retro. A traitor. What other way could I put it? Though the news came from Granger, and I didn't trust that guy at all, some of the things he'd said made me believe that *he* believed it.

As I made the long walk back to the library, I had plenty of time to think. I searched my memory for any clue why Granger thought one of my friends might be a Retro. When I was in the SYLO prison, Granger interrogated me, wanting to know about my relationship with Kent. Did that mean he suspected Kent? Or was he just fishing? Kent had lived on Pemberwick Island his whole life. His family owned property that had been handed down for generations. They didn't exactly fit the profile of someone who wanted to destroy civilization.

The same went for Tori. She grew up on Pemberwick. Her father was a lobsterman, and her mother wasn't even in the picture. She had abandoned them and left her husband to raise Tori on his own. Why would a lobsterman and his daughter want to bring on Armageddon? It didn't make sense.

Then again, Tori's father was the leader of the rebels who were planning to kidnap Granger. That alone marked him as an enemy of SYLO. And many of the people who had joined up with them were Retros, at least according to Mr. Feit. Could Mr. Sleeper have joined up with the Retros and brought Tori along with him? Or was he being used, like Feit said?

Kent's actions might also be questioned. When he and I were prisoners in the SYLO camp, he was hiding a dose of the Ruby that we eventually used to help us make our escape. How exactly did he get that? I never got a full answer. It was implied that Mr. Sleeper's rebels smuggled it in to him, but most of them might have been working with Feit. When we were staying at the Hall, Kent would disappear for hours at a time. Whenever I asked what he was doing, he'd tell me to mind my own business. The Hall was run by Retros. Was he plotting something with them?

Then there was Olivia. There was nothing about her that said "world destroyer." She was more worried about looking good and having fun than about rebooting society. But I had only known her since the beginning of summer. She said she came from New York City, but did I know that for a fact? Was she hiding some dark secret?

Finally there was Jon. None of us knew much about him, other than that he worked as a hospital technician and was a tech geek who tinkered with radios and had a passion for history. He had a know-it-all air about him, but did that mark him as a traitor? It bothered me, though, that he was so quick to put in with Chris Campbell and his cowboys at Faneuil Hall. Was that because he wanted food and a warm place to sleep? Or did he actually send Chris after me once he realized I wanted to escape with the others?

None of these people seemed like they could be playing both sides. Either Granger was totally lying or there was some incredible acting going on.

I wanted to forget the idea entirely, except for one thing Granger said. He admitted that he had no reason to want me dead. Yet he had come after me with all guns blazing. Literally. He torched the forest on Chinicook Island to try to fry me. He sent sharpshooters to blow me away before I could escape the island on a speedboat. Once I was on that speedboat, he personally came after me and tried to blast me out of the water. He was so determined to kill me that he ordered his crew to follow us into that inferno, sending them to their deaths. It sure seemed as though he wanted me gone, even though he knew for certain that I wasn't a Retro. He had to know. He was working with my parents!

It made no sense . . . unless it really wasn't me he was after.

That question tortured me. Was I just an unlucky bystander in this battle with Granger? Was he really after Kent? Or Tori? Or Olivia? He couldn't have been after Jon because we didn't hook up with him until Portland. Did that mean my friends from Pemberwick Island, the people I relied on the most in our struggle to survive, were Retro infiltrators?

The idea seemed impossible, but the pieces of the puzzle fit together well enough for me to consider never rejoining them. But the thought of being on my own was enough to send me back to the library to take my chances.

As I dragged myself along, I made a critical decision. I couldn't stress over which one of my friends might be a traitor. That would be torture.

Instead, I would assume they were all guilty.

It would be easier not to trust any of them than to be constantly worrying about saying the wrong thing while waiting for someone to make a suspicious move. From that simple but depressing assumption, I would work to find which one was a true friend.

Hopefully there would be more than one.

Hopefully it would be all of them.

I was exhausted. My feet were literally dragging, and I still had miles to go. I stopped at the next abandoned car, looked in the window, and realized what an idiot I'd been. Most of these cars still had the key in the ignition.

This car was a small Fiat. It wouldn't replace the Explorer, but it would get me back to the library before I collapsed. The engine turned over smoothly, and in no time I was driving back to face my friends. My hope was that they would all still be asleep and have no idea that I had left.

Yeah, right.

The battle at Fort Knox might have been several miles from the library, but it was still a major fight. Nobody sleeps through something like that. When I pulled into the parking lot, the front doors instantly flew open. Tori was out first, followed by Olivia. Jon and Kent weren't far behind.

"Where have you been?" Olivia cried.

She ran past Tori and threw her arms around me.

"We heard the explosions," she said, nearly in tears. "You were gone, and we didn't know what to think. What happened? Did you see anything?"

I didn't break away from her, but I didn't hug back either. I looked over her shoulder at Tori, Jon, and Kent, who stood together, waiting for an answer.

"Where's the Explorer, Rook?" Kent asked.

"Destroyed."

"What?" Jon exclaimed. "What do you mean, 'destroyed'?"

"An Air Force plane crashed into it," I said with no emotion. "They're called Retros, by the way. That's what Granger calls the Air Force."

Olivia pulled back from me abruptly.

"Granger?" she asked, stunned.

"You talked to him?" Kent asked, equally stunned. "He's alive?"

Tori had yet to say a word.

I decided to tell them the truth and deal with the fallout.

"I went to Fort Knox," I said bluntly. "My plan was to find Granger and kill him."

Olivia gasped and took a step back.

"Oh, Tucker, no."

I pulled the gun from my waistband and handed it to Tori.

"I didn't tell anybody because I wanted to go alone. I didn't expect to be coming back."

"So . . . did you?" Kent asked. "Kill him, I mean."

"No. As much as I wanted him dead, I'm no killer. I had the chance, too. I couldn't pull the trigger. That's when the Air Force attacked."

"Attacked what?" Jon asked. "Where were you?"

"Inside Fort Knox," I replied. "It's a SYLO base that's protecting the gold. When civilization rebuilds, that will be the new currency."

Nobody said anything. They just stared at me in stunned silence.

Jon finally snapped out of it and asked, "So what happened?"

"SYLO defended the base. Hundreds of black planes were knocked out of the sky. One of them landed on the Explorer. Don't worry, Kent, there are plenty more where that came from."

"But you talked to Granger," Kent said, still reeling. "How is he still alive?"

"He was pushed off of the gunboat before they followed us between the burning ships. Simple as that."

Kent let out a long breath.

"Jeez," he said. "Why can't these bad guys stay dead?"

"What else did he say?" Olivia said.

I walked past them, headed into the library. The others followed without question. Once inside, I found a camp lantern and went right for the table with the road atlas. I looked through the index, found what I wanted, and flipped to the map.

When I found what I was looking for, my head went light. I actually had to hold on to the table for support.

"What the hell, Rook?" Kent said impatiently. "What's going on?"

"These guardians obediently protect us from the gates of hell," I said.

"Yeah, SYLO," Kent said. "What about it?"

"Granger called the Air Force 'Retros.' He said the thing they were building in Fenway Park was a gate to hell."

"What!" Olivia exclaimed.

"Seriously?" Jon said. "An actual gate to hell?"

"I don't know. But whatever it was, SYLO wanted it gone, so they bombed it to oblivion."

"What are you looking at?" Jon asked, gesturing to the atlas.

"Granger said there's another one. A finished one. In the desert. He said it was guarded, but SYLO was going after that one too."

"What desert?" Kent said.

"Mojave."

"And where's that?" Kent asked.

I spun the book around for the others to see.

My mouth was so dry I had to swallow before I could speak. "Most of it is in California. Some parts reach into Arizona and Utah. But a very big part of it is in—"

"Nevada," Tori finished.

Kent grabbed the book to take a closer look.

"Jeez, he's right!" He looked at me. "That's what Granger said? There's a gate to hell in Nevada?"

I nodded.

Jon took the atlas and pulled out the separate, more detailed map of Nevada. He reached into his pocket and took out a crumpled piece of paper that he flattened on the table.

"These are the coordinates that the survivors were broadcasting," he explained.

He brought the lamp closer to the map, referred to the coordinates on the page, and made a mark on the map.

"The coordinates are definitely in the Mojave Desert. It looks like a pretty desolate place except . . ."

He bent down closer to the map and said, "It's a park. It's the middle of the desert, but it's a state park called . . ."

Jon didn't finish the sentence. Instead, he looked up at us soberly.

"What's it called?" Kent asked impatiently.

"The Valley of Fire," Jon replied, barely above a whisper.

"Seriously?" Kent exclaimed. "Valley of Fire? There's a gate to hell in the Valley of Fire?"

"No," I replied. "Granger said this so-called gate is somewhere in the Mojave. It's a big place. These coordinates are supposedly leading us to a group of survivors."

"If they really *are* survivors," Olivia cautioned. "We don't know that for sure."

"Kind of a coincidence, don't you think?" Kent said. "Gates of hell, Valley of Fire. Something nasty is definitely going on out there."

We all let that information sink in. Then Olivia said, "So what does it all mean?"

"It means I'm going to Nevada," I said with authority. "I don't know what's out there. Could be survivors. Could be a Retro trap. It could even be a SYLO trap. But whatever's there, it's the center of this whole damn thing."

I looked at Tori, expecting her to be happy about my decision. Instead, she turned and left the room.

I looked at Kent. "What about you?"

He scratched his head nervously and glanced at Olivia.

"Don't look at her," I scolded. "I'm asking *you*. You keep telling us what a hero you are, how about proving it?"

I had hit the exact right nerve.

"All right, Tucker," he said softly. "I'm with you."

"Me too," Jon chimed in. "It's history, right? Can't miss that."

"Wait, what about me?" Olivia cried. "I don't want to stay here alone."

"Then go to Florida, or anywhere else you'd like," I said, hoping it didn't come across as cold as I was feeling.

Olivia was near panic. She looked to Kent for help, but he kept his eyes on the table. She looked back at me with pleading eyes, but I returned a cold stare.

"Why are they called Retros?" Jon asked.

"I don't know," I replied curtly. "I don't care."

"You feeling okay, Rook?" Kent asked, sounding genuinely concerned. "You don't sound like yourself."

"I just spent the night trying to murder somebody and then nearly had my ass blown up about forty times. How do you think I should sound?"

Kent backed off. "About like that."

"In the morning I'll find a car," I declared. "If anybody wants to come with me, meet me outside at nine, ready to go. If you change your mind, sleep in."

I tucked the loose map of Nevada into the atlas and brought it with me into the children's area, where I returned to my spot on the floor. This time I planned to sleep.

I didn't mean to be so cold with the others. It just happened. Without intending to, I'd built a wall to keep myself separated from them. I was flying by the seat of my pants, and staying emotionally detached seemed like the best way to keep from being manipulated . . . if someone was trying to manipulate me.

Tori entered the room and stood over me, dangling the lamp.

"Explain it to me," she said. "Everything you preached about us needing one another and trusting one another and claiming that 'we're all we've got'—what happened to that?"

"We *are* all we've got," I said.

"So that's why you took my gun and snuck out on some mission of personal revenge that could have gotten you killed? How did that help us, exactly?"

"I told you," I said unapologetically. "It was something I had to do on my own."

"But what was the point? To get revenge for Quinn? To make one man pay for disturbing your precious little island? To make you feel a little bit better? How was that supposed to help us all?"

I wished I had a good answer, but I couldn't come up with one. So I told the truth.

"It wouldn't have."

"I told you how much I needed you," she said. "Didn't that count for anything?"

"Of course it did. I'm sorry. I didn't want you to get hurt, Tori—"

"Bull!" she snapped angrily. "You wanted to wage your own little war. It's been like that from the beginning. Everything you've done, every decision you've made, everywhere you've led us was about you feeling sorry for yourself and the life you lost. You may have been traveling with us, but you were always on your own journey."

"You're getting what you want," I argued. "I'm going to Nevada."

"You expected to die tonight," she cried. "You left us. You left me. The only reason you're here now is because you chickened out when it counted. I don't care what you do anymore, Tucker. I'm tired of following you around."

She turned to leave.

"So what are you going to do?" I called. "Are you coming with me?"

She stopped but didn't turn back to me as she said, "I'll be in the car, but from now on we're on our own."

She left the room and I was alone.

Everything she said was true. I had to hear the words to realize it. Anger and loss had driven me to take revenge. It felt like the only way to make the pain go away. Every move I had made, every decision, reflected that.

The others were just along for the ride.

I had convinced myself that I was helping to keep everyone together, but the truth was I was using them to support my own quest. I had been quick to criticize everyone else for not doing what was best for the group, while I was being the most selfish of all.

I wanted to run to Tori and apologize. I wanted to tell her that

I got it. That I was wrong. That I wanted to try again. I wanted to tell them all . . . but I couldn't.

They could be Retros.

Early the next day, I woke before sunrise after not sleeping much. I packed up my gear and brought it outside to the curb. First order of business was to find a new car. I got into the Fiat and only had to drive a few minutes before I found our next vehicle: a Volvo XC90. It had three rows of seats and still enough room for our gear.

I tried not to think about how all of these cars belonged to people who died inside of them.

When I drove it back to the library, Kent was waiting on the steps.

"I was afraid you took off without us again," he said.

He never would have said that before my adventure the night before. Now everything I did was going to be scrutinized and questioned.

"Why would I take off without my gear?" I said, pointing to my bag on the curb.

"Oh. Didn't see that."

"Load up," I ordered. "I want to get going."

As Kent threw his bag in the back, Tori came out of the library.

"Did you have to get such a gas-guzzler?" she asked.

"We can always trade it in," I said. "There are plenty of cars out there to choose from. Is anybody else coming?"

As if in answer, Olivia came out of the library with her bag hanging from her shoulder and her sunglasses on, even though the sun was barely up. She looked as though she was ready for a day at the beach.

"You sure you want to come?" I asked.

She walked right up to me, went up on her tiptoes, and kissed me square on the lips.

"Somebody's got to make sure you eat your greens," she said. She walked to Kent and tossed her bag to him.

"I'm riding up front," she said. "I'm tired of being carsick."

She went right for the passenger door and got in.

Kent shrugged and put her bag in back.

I looked to the library, expecting to see Jon come out. He didn't.

"Do we say goodbye?" Tori asked.

"Goodbye," I said so low that Tori could barely hear it, let alone Jon.

"I'll drive the first leg," I said and headed for the driver's door.

"Wait!" Jon called as he ran from the building with his bag banging around his shoulder. "I was afraid you'd leave without me!"

He loaded up and was given the way backseat. Again.

That was that. We were all going. Even those who didn't really want to. Was that a sign that we had truly become dependent on each other? Or did one—or some—of us go along in order to monitor our movements for the Retros?

With that in mind, I put the car in gear, and we began our journey.

Next stop: the gates of hell.

TWENTY-TWO

It was a tense, quiet, and very long journey.

Jon estimated the trip would cover roughly two thousand miles, which is a very long time to be stuck in the same car with people who were all on edge. We mapped out a route that was the most direct, while carefully skirting major cities. Fortunately most interstates didn't swing too close to downtown areas, and the only time we had to stop was when we needed gas or to pillage a grocery store. Our route took us from Louisville to the southernmost tip of Indiana and on to Illinois. We swung way south of St. Louis, hit Missouri, and headed for Kansas City.

We passed through places I'd always heard of but never expected to visit. I wished I could have appreciated it more. Or even a little. Here we were, traveling across America, but rather than getting a glimpse of all the different cities and places of interest, we saw nothing but abandoned cars, empty skies, and weeds growing up through the roadbed.

Nature was already hard at work, trying to take back control. It would have to get in line behind the Retros, SYLO, and anybody else who wanted to stake a claim on the planet.

We guesstimated that it would take us three days of driving. We could have made it in less, but we didn't dare drive at night. The first night we stayed in a hospital east of Kansas City in a town called Independence. There were plenty of signs all over the empty town that boasted of its being the birthplace of Harry S. Truman. It made me wonder what a former president of the United States would think of the mess his country had become.

We planned to spend the second night near Denver, then push on to Nevada the following day.

Very few words were spoken the entire trip. At least, very few between me and anybody else. I think they were all pissed at me for abandoning them and then acting as if I didn't care. Kent and Olivia cozied up in the third row whenever they got the chance. I heard them whispering and giggling but could never make out what they were saying, not that I wanted to know. A couple of times Jon turned around to look at them, and Kent immediately smacked him and told him to mind his own business.

Tori barely acknowledged my existence and kept her baseball cap down low over her eyes. She had once again become the sullen girl from school who rarely spoke to anyone. I knew by now that it was her way of protecting herself.

I may have been traveling with four other people, but I was alone.

A few times along the way we passed the wrecks of some Retro jets, as well as destroyed Navy fighters and bomb craters. Each time it meant that a battle had taken place nearby, but there was no way to know whether it was a SYLO base or another construction site where the Retros were erecting a gate to hell.

A gate to hell.

What did that mean? I didn't believe for a second that it was literally a gate into the afterlife. That made even less sense than Kent's alien-invasion theory. But if Granger was telling the truth, SYLO would do anything to stop them from building another one. Based on what had happened at Fenway Park, I believed him. That left some questions: What were they? What was their purpose? What power did they give the Retros?

Was the "gate to hell" another monstrous killing machine?

Weighing it all kept my head spinning.

The morning of the second day we got up early, well before dawn, and started on our way to Denver. It was over eight hundred miles away, and we wanted to get there in time to find a place to spend the night. One great thing about driving in an abandoned world was that there were no speed limits. A few times when I was behind the wheel I hit a hundred miles an hour. We all did at one time or another. I don't know if we were in a hurry to get there or to end the torture of being in the car together.

Of course, we had to stop several times to gas up. I usually siphoned the gas while Tori and Kent hit stores for food. Kent loaded up on jerky, which was basically dried meat sealed in plastic that would probably last a hundred years. It was salty and a little too chewy for my taste, but it provided protein. I think.

We had gotten our stops down to a science. Between gassing up, grabbing food, and going to the bathroom, we were never stationary for more than fifteen minutes.

The silence was making me crazy, but I didn't want to make conversation with people I didn't trust. I couldn't discuss plans or strategy for fear that the information would go right to the Retros. For all I knew somebody was using our walkie-talkies to contact them. I decided to hold anything I had to say until we hit the Valley of Fire.

We made incredible time into Colorado and were closing in on Denver before three o'clock in the afternoon—plenty of time to find a place to stay. Kent was behind the wheel, and without any explanation, he took an exit off of the interstate.

"What are you doing?" Tori asked. "We've got plenty of gas."

"Side trip," he said.

That got everybody's attention.

"What are you doing, Kent?" I asked sternly.

"Relax," he replied calmly. "I want to check something out."

"You can't make that call," Jon said nervously. "Tell him, Tucker. That's not how it works!"

"Either tell us what you're doing or get back on the interstate," I said adamantly.

"Look," Kent said. "We've been on the road for hours. My butt is killing me. I just saw a sign back there, and I want to check it out, that's all. No big deal."

"Sign for what?" Olivia asked.

Kent turned around to us and smiled. "It's a surprise."

The rest of us exchanged worried glances that all said the same thing: We'd already had far too many surprises for one lifetime.

I had an added worry: Was Kent leading us into a trap?

"You'll like this," he added. "Trust me."

Unfortunately, trusting him was the one thing I couldn't do. But while we were arguing, Kent was driving us closer to whatever it was he wanted to see.

"Do you have your gun, Tori?" I asked.

"Whoa! Easy there, Rook!" Kent exclaimed. "Don't get all paranoid."

"Then tell us what you're doing," I demanded.

Kent huffed and said, "Fine. This trip has been torture. We all know that. Rook, you're always saying how we have to be careful not to lose our sense of civilization, or something like that. It's not normal to be stealing cars and eating out of cans and living on floors and peeing in pits. I get it, but there's more to it than that. You know: life, liberty, and the pursuit of happiness. Remember that? I don't know about you guys, but I haven't been happy in a long time, and that's about as important to me as anything. So if you'd all just relax, I say we stop worrying about SYLO and Retros and survivors and Armageddon for a couple of minutes and have a little fun."

"What kind of fun?" Tori asked suspiciously.

"This kind," he said and turned the car into a huge, empty parking lot.

There wasn't much to see other than wide-open spaces and a few one-story buildings. As Kent drove us toward the structures, I spotted a sign that actually made me smile.

"The Track at Centennial," I read aloud.

"The what?" Tori asked, confused.

"Go-karts!" Kent exclaimed.

"You've gotta be kidding me," Olivia said sourly. Apparently racing go-karts wasn't on her list of fun things to do.

Tori didn't seem too thrilled either.

But I kind of liked the idea.

"What do you think, Rook?" Kent asked hopefully.

I hadn't seen him this enthusiastic about anything in a very long time.

"I think . . . we ride."

"Yeah!" Kent exclaimed.

"You're *both* crazy," Olivia exclaimed.

Kent parked in front of the low buildings, where there was a snack shop, an arcade, and the track office.

"I'll go find the karts," he said and hurried off.

The rest of us were left in the car.

"What exactly are go-karts?" Olivia asked, perplexed.

"Little cars that you drive around a racecourse," I replied.

"Oh. Like we haven't been driving enough?" she shot back.

"Let's give it a try," I said. "We haven't had fun in a long time."

"Yeah," Tori said sarcastically. "That darn genocide thing really got in the way of my playtime."

"Kent's right," I argued. "We've been going nonstop, so why not take a little break? It won't change anything, except maybe help blow off some steam."

I didn't add that if anybody needed to blow off steam, it was me.

"I'd like to give it a try," Jon said. "We still have a few hours of daylight left."

"All right, let's do it!" I said and got out of the car, headed after Kent.

I was nearly at the building when I heard the sound of a gas-powered engine firing up. I circled the building to see a row of colorful, miniature race cars ready to be taken for a spin. Kent had started the first one and had moved on to another.

"They're easy to start," Kent called over the sound of the engine. "Flip on the red ignition, open the choke, and pull on the handle. Easy peasy."

I chose one of the carts, and after a quick once-over, I saw that it was more or less like starting my father's riding lawn mowers. I powered it on, pulled the cord, and was rewarded by the deep, loud rattle of the gas-burning engine. It was a powerful go-kart. I was looking forward to taking it on the track.

"Everybody take one!" Olivia shouted.

She was holding an armload of helmets that she must have gotten from the office. Olivia was up for fun, but she didn't like taking chances. At least not where there was the potential for injury. Jon followed behind her with several more helmets. We all tried them on until we found one that fit. All but Tori.

She sat alone in the shade of the buildings.

"I'll get her," I said.

I jogged to her and held out a helmet.

"C'mon," I cajoled. "It'll be fun."

"I don't need to have fun," she said flatly.

"I hear you," I said. "It does feel a little . . . disrespectful."

"You could say that."

"Look, this is it. After tomorrow, things are going to change. I don't know what we'll find in Nevada, but I'm pretty sure that whatever it is, we won't be together much longer."

"We're not together now," she corrected.

I held out the helmet and said, "So then why not have a last hurrah?"

Tori looked at it, then stood up and grabbed it. Did I detect a small smile?

"Stay out of my way," she said and strode for the track.

Five karts were powered up and purring. They were so loud that we had to shout to be heard.

Olivia and Jon were already strapped in, ready to go.

"It looks like a Grand Prix–type course," Kent yelled. "Go around clockwise."

I gave him a thumbs-up and put on my helmet.

Tori snapped on her helmet and buckled into a kart, as did Kent.

The first to take off was Olivia. I could hear her screaming with excitement from behind her helmet and over the roar of the engines. She drove out of the pit area, turned left onto the track, and was gone. Jon sped out right behind her. I was next. I settled into the padded seat, secured the safety straps across my chest, buckled up my helmet, and jammed on the gas. The little go-kart lurched forward, and with a roar of the engine, I was off.

I sped out of the pit area and in seconds I was on the wide track. I'd driven go-karts before, but never on a track this big. In a word, it was awesome. After I figured out the nuances of handling the powerful little car, I jammed my foot to the floor and never picked it up. There were long straightaways and sharp turns on the snaking track. The trick was to cut the angles and avoid swinging wide, which would kill your speed.

I easily passed Jon and then Olivia. Both were driving conservatively, slowing down on the curves and not jamming it on the straights. I flew by each with a loud "Wooo!"

"Come back here!" Olivia called playfully. "I'm gonna get you!"

I figured I was the class of the track—until Tori cut me off on the inside in a tight turn and sped past. She even had the presence of mind to throw me a wave as she flew by. I was so busy watching her that I didn't notice Kent coming up on my other side. He blew by almost as fast as Tori, and I got a taste of my own "Wooo!" as he shot past.

I didn't care. I was having too much fun. For those few minutes I felt like a little kid again, because I was. There was nothing to worry about but the next turn, nobody to fear, for they were only trying to pass me, and no mystery about how it all worked. There was no death. No betrayal. No murky future.

It was perfect.

I lost sight of the others and ended up driving on my own for a good long time. That was okay. I was having a blast pushing that little go-kart to its limit, drifting into turns and speeding on the straights. For those few minutes all the dark thoughts and memories were washed away, or at least pushed so far back that I didn't think about them. It was all about the pure joy of a mindless yet thrilling activity.

After four or five laps I realized that I had to pee, so I pulled the car into the pit and killed the engine. No sense in wasting gas. I popped off my helmet and jogged for the building to see if there was a working bathroom.

When I rounded the corner to the far side of the building, I saw something that rocked me and forced me to skid to a stop.

Standing together in the shadow of the awning over the bathrooms were Kent and Tori . . . making out. It was such a stunning sight that I didn't know what to do at first. They were locked together in a full-on, mouth-open, passionate kiss.

I almost shouted something. I'm not even sure what it would have been.

"What's going on?"

"You're kidding?"

"Seriously? Kent?"

"Does Olivia know about this?"

All those words went through my mind, but none came out of my mouth. Instead, I backed away quickly. They didn't even know I had seen them. For some reason, I no longer had to pee.

I walked back to the track, holding the helmet tightly under my arm, not sure of how I should be feeling. Was Tori's anger and disappointment in me what drove her to Kent? It was hard to accept that, because I knew she thought he was a tool. And what about Olivia? As far as she knew, Kent was a puppy dog who would do anything for her. Was this fair to her? And did it matter, since she was coming after me every chance she got? She was an emotional girl. This could really hurt her.

Or me.

Tori and I had a complicated relationship. I had told her that I loved her, and I meant it. But things had changed since then. I had let her down in a big way. She wanted nothing more to do with me, and seeing her with Kent proved it.

I had officially lost everything I cared about.

"Back on the track!" Kent called as he ran past me, headed for his go-kart. "Had to tap the bladder. Admit it, Rook. This was a good idea, right?"

"Yeah," I said. "Excellent idea."

He had no idea that I had seen them.

Kent got back into his go-kart, and I got into mine. He took off a few seconds before me. I rolled out near the finish line, turned left, and punched it. This second go-around was a whole different experience. It wasn't so much fun as it was . . . necessary. I put the pedal to the metal and never let up. I cut corners so tightly that I rumbled over gravel. On one corner I cut inside Kent. It was a dumb, dangerous move, but I didn't care. He had to pull out of the turn to keep from hitting me as I flew by.

I eventually passed Jon and then Olivia. As I rounded the final curve before the finishing straight, I had the fleeting thought of driving the go-kart right off the track, through the parking lot, and out onto the road. Why not? There was nobody to stop me. I could just hit the road and keep on going until I ran out of gas.

But I didn't. I pulled the car into the pit and, breathing hard, killed the engine.

Kent pulled in behind me.

"What was that!" he screamed angrily. "You could have killed us both."

"Just having a little fun," I said. "That's what this was about, right?"

"Yeah, but . . . jeez, Rook. We're all on the same side here."

"Stop calling me Rook," I said with no emotion.

"Aw, lighten up. It's just a dumb word."

I looked him square in the eye. He got the message and backed off.

"Okay, fine, whatever."

He got out of the kart, dropped his helmet in the seat, and

headed for the snack bar. I wondered if he was going to look for Tori, because as far as I knew she hadn't come out on the track again.

Jon and Olivia pulled up, both still flushed and excited.

"That was the most fun I've had in forever!" Olivia exclaimed dramatically. "Kent is a genius!"

I could think of a lot of words to describe Kent. "Genius" wasn't one of them.

I gathered everybody's helmets and put them back in the office. I don't know why. Guess I was still trying to be civilized.

When Olivia, Jon, and I got to the Volvo, Kent and Tori were already inside. *Not* making out. Kent was in the third row, and Tori was riding shotgun. Maybe I imagined it, but the atmosphere seemed icy. Or maybe they were just playing it cool so Olivia wouldn't know what was really going on. Or me.

Olivia jumped in the third row and threw her arms around Kent.

"Thank you, thank you, thank you!" she said. "It's just what I needed."

"That was pretty cool, Kent," Jon said. "I'm glad you talked us into it."

"Yeah, well, I do have good ideas sometimes."

Everything he said had a double meaning for me. I was about to say, "So, Kent, when did you and Tori get together? By the way, are you a traitor?" But I bit my tongue.

We were about to hit the last leg of our journey. The go-karts were a fun diversion but nothing more. It was time to get back to reality. I had to make sure my head was on straight and focus on what lay ahead, not on what could have been.

I drove out of the racetrack and headed toward Denver, where we found yet another hospital. We went through our practiced routines of finding food, washing up, and claiming beds in the ER. Jon didn't even bother trying the radio. What was the point? We would find the truth for ourselves the next day. We went to bed with the agreement that we would get up early to begin the final leg of our journey.

Nevada.

After all the speculation and debate, we were almost there. When we left Colorado, we had to traverse the width of Utah before entering the state of Nevada. The Silver State, as a highway sign proclaimed. Once we crossed the border, it would only be a short leg to the park, and . . . whatever.

The map looked as though we were going to be traveling through some desolate country with nowhere to stop for supplies. There was limited room in the Volvo, so we chose to stock up on bottled water rather than gas. There were plenty of abandoned cars to siphon along the way but no guaranteed spot to find fresh water.

Once again, we hit the road long before dawn. When we loaded up the car, there was a definite pregame feeling. Whatever was in Nevada, we would find it soon. Was it hope? A new life? Would we find a group of tenacious survivors who had banded together to wrestle control back from the two military forces that had decimated the country? Or would we fall into a trap that was set to lure in the stragglers who weren't wiped out the first time?

Or would we find a gate to hell?

I drove first. The camaraderie from the go-kart experience was a thing of the past. We were back to stony silence. I imagined that this was what it was like to be nearing the appointed hour on death row. Up until then, it had all just been theory. What lay ahead was real.

Kent and Olivia were snuggled together in the way back. I wanted to call him out so badly, but if Tori wouldn't do it, I wasn't going to rock the boat.

We drove as fast as the day before, stopping for gas several times. Until then, we had been driving through civilization. Granted, it was an altered civilization, but most of our journey was through developed land. The West proved to be very different. In Colorado, we crossed the Rocky Mountains. I'd never seen anything like them before. It was breathtaking. In Utah, we passed through deserts that were stunning in their natural simplicity, and rugged, unspoiled forests. I'd lived in only two places in my life: Connecticut and Maine. I'd only seen sights like these in the movies or on TV. It was awe inspiring, and depressing.

I would have liked to be seeing them with my mom and dad.

As I took in the amazing vistas, I was struck by yet another disturbing thought. We were used to living in towns with electricity and clean water. We could watch TV and send texts and buy whatever we needed in a store. We had enjoyed all the advantages of living in an advanced, civilized society. And now those luxuries were gone. We had been adjusting to that reality for some time now. What I hadn't considered was what these changes would mean for the ecology of the planet. What plans did SYLO have for the land? Or if the Retros triumphed and were allowed to "reset" civilization, what would that mean for the physical world?

Until then, I'd only thought about the war's impact on people, and cities, and governments. But this was real life. This was our world. What did these military powers have in mind for the most basic aspects of life on earth? Civilization was going to change. Did that mean severe changes for the mountains and deserts and oceans too? The Retros had not only wiped out people, they'd decimated other living things as well. What would that do to the balance of nature? To the food chain? The circle of life had been broken for good.

Once again, I was overwhelmed by the scope of the change that this war had brought.

Kent, on the other hand, was probably thinking about making out with Tori.

He was behind the wheel when we entered Nevada.

"We're here," he announced.

It was as simple as that.

The final leg of our journey was through wide-open desert. The temperature outside rose to 110 degrees. There was nothing to see for miles but sand and rocks and more sand. In the distance were mountain ranges, but they were hundreds of miles away. We were square in the middle of beautiful desolation.

"Look at the temperature," Kent said. "A hundred and ten. Sure seems like we're getting nearer to hell."

"We gotta decide," Jon said. "What are we gonna do when we get there?"

Nobody answered.

"Seriously," he pressed. "We just drove two thousand miles. We've got to have some kind of plan."

"It depends on what we find," I said. "We'll go to where the coordinates say. Who knows? Maybe it's a camp of survivors."

"In the desert?" Olivia asked skeptically.

"What can I tell you?" I said. "This is where we were called to, so this is where we're going. Once we get there, we'll figure out what our next move is."

That seemed to satisfy everyone, though it was a totally unsatisfying answer.

"There!" Jon pointed out.

There was a highway sign for the Valley of Fire State Park.

The tension in the car suddenly amped up.

"It's real," Olivia said with a gasp.

"Here we go," Kent announced and took the exit.

We followed a barely paved dusty road for several miles. Each time we thought we were lost, we'd see another sign that directed us to the park.

Nobody spoke. My mouth was bone dry as we entered the Valley of Fire.

"It's beautiful," Tori said. They were the first words she'd said since we left Denver.

We were surrounded by towering natural sculptures cut from rusty-orange rock. The "valley" was the desert floor. Surrounding us were soaring, jagged peaks of the same amber stone. Looking off into the distance, I saw many other impossible rock formations. It was like a sculpture garden created by nature.

"Are those pueblos?" Jon the historian asked.

He was pointing to several huts that at first seemed like part of the terrain, but when you looked closer, you could see the hand of man. Ancient man, probably. Native Americans.

We had hit the park at the exact right time of day to get the most stunning effect. The sun was sinking toward the horizon behind streaks of clouds that glowed orange and purple. Its fading light spread over the desert floor like warm butterscotch, highlighting the detail of the rock formations and their multiple layers and colors.

Olivia said, "This doesn't look anything like a gate into hell. This is . . . beautiful."

We drove further on, past a section that was scattered with mobile trailers. Abandoned mobile trailers. My mind was already jumping ahead and thinking that we could spend the night in one of them.

We continued until we hit the parking lot and a building that looked like the visitors' center. Kent parked in front, and we all got out.

After traveling in an air-conditioned car, stepping into hundred-degree heat was a brutal shock.

"Okay, maybe this is a gate to hell after all," Olivia commented while dabbing her forehead.

We all glanced around looking for . . . what? We didn't know.

"We're sure this is the place, right?" Kent asked.

"These are the exact coordinates that were being broadcast," Jon replied defensively.

"Maybe the survivors are living in those trailers we passed," Olivia said hopefully.

"If they are, there aren't many of them," Kent said. "I hope we didn't come all the way out here just to hook up with twelve yahoos looking to get even."

"I'll look inside the building," I offered. "Maybe there's a message or instructions or—"

"I hear something," Tori interrupted.

We all listened. The sound was faint at first, but it grew quickly. After spending so much time in silence over the past few weeks, it was easy to hear an alien sound because every sound was alien.

"Engines," I said. "More than one."

"At least it's not music from the sky," Kent said.

The engine sounds grew louder. Whatever it was, it was headed our way.

"What should we do?" Olivia asked nervously.

"Get back in the car," I ordered.

"No!" Tori countered. "This is what we came for. Whatever it is, we're going to face it."

There was a tense silence, then Olivia said meekly, "I wouldn't mind waiting in the car."

"Then go!" Tori snapped at her.

Olivia went right for the Volvo and got in, but she kept her face pressed to the window to keep an eye on what was about to unfold.

A cloud of dust was being kicked up on the road behind us. Something was definitely coming in.

"I'm getting kind of nervous," Jon said. "Should we be prepared to defend ourselves?"

"You have your gun, Tori?" I asked.

"Yeah."

"Don't pull it out unless you think we're done. We have no idea how well they're armed."

"Or who they are," Jon added.

"I'm not an idiot," Tori said.

"Motorcycles," Kent announced. "Harleys."

As soon as he said that, several motorcycles rounded an outcropping of rock and thundered toward us. I counted ten.

"Look!" Jon said, pointing to a ridge behind the visitors' center.

There were four people on horseback looking down on us. They were dressed in jeans and cotton shirts: civilian clothes. It looked like there were four men, but any of them could easily have been a woman. It was hard to tell because they were all wearing cowboy hats.

"Hey!" I called. "Who are you?"

The four didn't answer, or budge. They sat on their horses, silently watching.

The motorcycles roared into the parking lot and turned directly toward us. These people didn't look like military types either. Some wore leathers, like typical bikers. Others had more colorful, out-doorsy jackets and jeans. They all wore full helmets that covered their faces. They definitely weren't wearing uniforms of any sort, which was a relief. They also didn't look to be carrying weapons, which was an even bigger relief.

The bikers rode up and circled us. We huddled closer to the Volvo. It was the only protection we had, and having strangers on motorcycles surrounding us in the middle of the desert was definitely intimidating. They formed a tight circle around us.

"I think we've just been trapped," Jon said.

They continued to circle us until one of the riders raised his hand and they all came to a stop. They didn't kill their engines. All the riders straddled their bikes and looked at us.

"We come in peace!" Kent shouted, holding up his open palm.

"Shut up, Kent," I snapped.

I took a few steps toward the rider who had given the command to stop. I made sure that I held my hands out to show that I wasn't hiding anything.

Unlike Tori.

"We've come a long way," I said. "We heard the radio broadcast. Was that you?"

They continued to stare at us. At least I think they were staring. It was hard to tell because their faces were hidden by the helmet visors.

"We're from Pemberwick Island in Maine," I called out. "Who are you?"

The lead rider's response was to reach into his saddlebag . . . and pull out a pistol.

"Gun!" Kent shouted.

Tori went for hers too late. All the riders pulled out their own guns with practiced precision. It was so quick we didn't have the chance to defend ourselves. Or run.

The bikers aimed and fired.

I had never been shot before, so I didn't know what to expect. I was hit in the chest and knocked back against the Volvo. I thought it would hurt more. That's exactly what went through my mind.

I looked toward Tori to see that she had been hit too. She slid down the door of the Volvo and crumpled onto the asphalt. Her gun was on the ground, out of reach.

The window of the Volvo shattered. Olivia screamed but was abruptly cut off. She'd been hit too. We'd all been hit. The gunmen knew what they were doing. We didn't stand a chance.

The world began to spin. The horizon turned sideways. My knees went weak, and I slumped to the ground. My last thought before losing consciousness was that it was such a beautiful park to be a gate to hell.

TWENTY-THREE

Black.

I couldn't tell if I was awake or asleep or dead.

My head hurt, which was good. As far as I knew, dead people didn't get headaches.

I felt as though I was coming out of a coma, not that I'd ever done that, but I imagined that's what it was like. I was disoriented with nothing to see but . . . nothing.

My senses started coming back online, though there wasn't much input for them to work with. I was lying on something soft. That much I understood. I tried to stand up, but my right leg wouldn't move. I thought maybe I was paralyzed and started to panic. The fear got my heart pounding and my blood pumping, which helped clear my head.

I tried to move my leg again and realized there was nothing wrong with it. I couldn't move because I was shackled. My right leg was chained to the floor.

At least I wasn't dead.

"Tori!" I called. "Kent?"

I was in a big room. That much I could tell from the echo of my voice. As my wits returned, I remembered getting shot and realized I hadn't been hit with a bullet. The bikers must have fired tranquilizer darts. I felt the area of my chest that had been hit, and it was definitely sore.

"Hey!" I shouted. "I'm awake. Why am I chained up?"

A light appeared high in the air. I couldn't tell how big it was or how far away because I had no other frame of reference. The light slowly grew more intense as it warmed up, and I realized that it was a spotlight that had its beam directed somewhere behind me. I rolled over to see what was being lit up and nearly screamed.

I was lying below a giant face.

The thing must have been twenty feet high. It was the face of a woman, based on the puckered, painted lips. The skin was unnaturally white and smooth, which made me realize it wasn't living. The eyes and nose were covered by an ornate silver mask. Attached to the top of the mask and jutting above it were several tall blue and gold triangles that came to points another twenty feet above the face. Each point was topped with a large, golden jingle bell the size of a basketball. Similar blue and gold points circled below the face like a collar. The silver mask itself was intricately decorated with looping detail that looked like waves. There was a half-moon on the forehead and something that looked like an ancient boat. Its eyes were closed, thank God.

Once I caught my breath, I realized it was a carnival mask . . . a very big carnival mask on a very big statue of a face of a very big woman. It appeared to be nestled in a bed of ornate greenery.

"What's your name?" an amplified woman's voice boomed from the general direction of the mask.

If the lips had moved or the eyes opened, I probably would have passed out again. Thankfully it wasn't the big head talking. Somebody was pulling a Wizard of Oz stunt on me.

"Tucker Pierce. Where are my friends?"

"Why are you here?" she asked, ignoring my question.

"We heard the radio broadcast," I replied, and as soon as I said that, a thought hit me. "Wait, the broadcast voice sounded like you. Who are *you*?"

"Where did you come from?" she asked.

I had been through an interrogation like this once before, when I was captured and sent to the SYLO compound on Pemberwick Island. I half expected Captain Granger to come strolling out from behind the big head/mask/statue/Oz/whatever thing.

"We came from Pemberwick Island. We're looking for . . ."

I didn't finish the sentence. I had to be careful. There was no way to know who this woman was or who the bikers were who had drugged and captured us like wild animals.

"Why don't you cut the show and just talk to me?" I asked.

"We need to know exactly who you are and why you came here," she said. "Your friends are safe and are also being questioned. If we are satisfied with your answers, we will join you."

"And what if you aren't satisfied?"

"You will die."

Oh.

I had never been a great test-taker. I hoped I was up to the challenge. The only thing I could do was speak truthfully. If I thought lying would have helped, I would have lied, but without having any idea who my interrogator was, I figured it was best to just tell the truth.

I told her the whole story, beginning with Marty Wiggins's death and ending with the bikers showing up to the Valley of Fire. It took a while. It was a long story.

The mask listened without asking questions. At least I think it was listening. It was hard to tell. It was a mask. My hope was that the others were telling the same story. If somebody (Kent) tried to get clever and head off in another direction, it could doom us all because then none of us would look credible.

I finished the story by saying, "And then I ended up here, chained to the floor, talking to a giant mask. It's been a hell of a couple of weeks."

There was a long silence. I think I was more nervous at that point than at any time before. It was like being a defendant waiting for the jury to come back with a verdict. Only this wouldn't just be a verdict, it would be a sentence: life or death.

The spotlight went out, and I was back in black.

"Whoa!" I called. "I told you the truth. What more do you want from me?"

Another light appeared, only this one was much smaller, and it was moving. It came from behind the big mask, and I realized it was somebody with a headlamp.

One word came to mind: executioner.

I pulled against the chain that held me to the floor in the dumb hope that it would break loose, as opposed to the other dozen times I had tried.

"Look," I said nervously, "there's been way too much killing already."

The person didn't respond. The light moved closer until their shadow loomed over me.

I had a strange reaction. A second before I had been terrified. That terror changed to anger.

"You know what? Go ahead. Kill me. I'm done. You'd be doing me a favor. Use whatever magic weapon you've got and just do it!"

I'm not sure if I meant it. The killing part, that is. But I was definitely tired of being scared and didn't want to deal anymore.

The person stood there for a moment, then reached into a pocket and pulled out a set of keys. The person knelt down and unlocked the shackle around my ankle.

I immediately pulled away and curled into a ball on the far end of the mat.

"How old are you?" the person asked. It was the same woman whose voice had been amplified during the interrogation.

"Fourteen," I replied.

"Jeez," she said and rubbed at her eyes. "You're a baby."

Was she crying?

"I've heard a lot of stories over the last couple of weeks," she said. "But yours takes the cake. You gotta be some kind of special kid to come through all that."

"So you believe me?" I asked.

"It's the exact same story the others told," she said. "So either you've all done a good job of cooking this up or it's the truth."

She had a slight drawl, which made me believe she had come from these parts.

"Who are you?" I asked.

"My name's Charlotte," she replied. "I'm a Clark County sheriff. At least I used to be."

"So you're not with SYLO? Or the Retros?"

"To be honest with you, Tucker, I never heard the term 'Retros' before you all showed up, and all I know about SYLO is that it's the military outfit from the Navy that quarantined Pemberwick Island. We're not part of either."

"So then who *are* you?" I asked. "And would you mind losing the headlight?"

"Oh, sorry," she said as she pulled the lamp off. She placed it on a chair I had no idea was next to me, shining the light back on herself.

Charlotte had short blond hair. Though she was small, she looked wiry and tough, like you'd expect a county sheriff to be. She looked about as old as my mom, but unlike my mom, I wouldn't challenge her to an arm-wrestling contest. She had on her uniform, which was dark pants and a khaki shirt with sleeve patches that said: "Clark County Sheriff." The shirt was wrinkled and worn. She'd been wearing it for a while.

"I'm just like you," she replied. "A survivor of the massacre."

"So the broadcast was real? You're calling out to other survivors?"

"Real as rain, darlin'," she said. "I don't know about you, but I'm not one to take something like this sitting down. No, I take that back. I *do* know about you. You came a long way to be here. You may be young, but you're a fighter."

"What was with the bikers? And knocking us out in the middle of the desert?"

"Security," she replied. "Anybody can hear that broadcast. We meet folks out in the middle of nowhere and bring 'em back here to size 'em up. To figure out if they're with us or against us."

"So there are others?" I asked.

Charlotte chuckled.

"You ain't the only one left in the world with some fight in 'em. They've been coming from all over the country. From Canada and Mexico too. I've been doing plenty of these interrogations. Guess it comes from being a sheriff. I like the whole big-mask thing. Freaks people out. It's good to keep your subject off-balance."

Charlotte liked her job.

"Has anybody failed the test?" I asked.

Her expression turned dark.

"You may think we're a loose bunch of delusional desperados, but make no mistake, young man, we are deadly serious. There have been a couple of bad seeds that the Air Force sent out on a . . . what would you call it? An exploratory mission. They didn't pass the smell test."

"And what happened to them?"

"They were sent back out into the desert," she said with a shrug. "They won't be comin' back."

"Oh man," I said, stunned.

"I didn't give it a second thought," she said. "After what they done, they got off easy."

My head was spinning, and it wasn't because of the tranquilizer. As much as I had hoped that the broadcast was real and we would be meeting up with other survivors, deep down I didn't believe it would happen.

I looked around at the darkened room and said, "So if I passed the test, are you going to tell me where we are?"

Charlotte gave me a mischievous smile.

"Better to show you. The sun's just coming up, thank God. The nights are just too eerie for me. I've lived here my whole life, and there was never a time that the city wasn't lit up at night as bright and sparkly as a Christmas tree. Not anymore. Now every light we've got runs on batteries."

She stood up and offered me her hand. I took it, and when I stood up, my head went weak and I nearly toppled. Charlotte grabbed me and kept me from going over. She had to be a foot shorter than me, but she was strong.

"Easy there, pardner," she said. "You still got some lingering effects. Tell you what. It's tough negotiating through the dark on foot. We'll take a boat."

"A boat?"

"C'mon," she said with a chuckle, and with one arm around my waist to steady me, she led me away from the freakin' giant mask.

I began to get a sense of the room. It was big with a huge sky-light overhead. Once the sun came up, the room would be completely lit. By then we would be gone. By boat. How could a boat be in the desert? Were we still in the desert?

"How long was I out?" I asked as we made our way through the hazy space.

"About twelve hours. Long enough to get you here and settled."

Yeah, settled. Manacled was more like it.

"Where are my friends?"

"I suspect they're headed to the same place we are."

It was still too dark for me to make out any real detail, but it seemed as though we were walking along a narrow city street with shops on either side of a cobblestone sidewalk. But that didn't make sense because we were definitely indoors.

It was about to make even less sense.

"Here we are," Charlotte announced. "Hop in front. I'll paddle us out of here."

"Out of where?" I asked with growing confusion.

"Out of Venice, of course," she said, chuckling.

It sounded like a joke, but we had stopped at a boat that looked very much like a gondola floating in a canal.

"Are we seriously in Venice?" I asked.

"Yup, but not for long."

Charlotte was obviously having fun with me, and I stopped asking questions. When the sun came up, I'd see all I needed to see. I got in the front of the boat, or the gondola, or whatever it was, and sat on a seat that had an ornate cushion. Charlotte picked up a long oar that was yoked toward the stern and pushed us off. In seconds she was churning us along the narrow canal. We passed under elaborately decorated footbridges and slid by open courtyards that had statues in their centers. We also passed dozens of dark shops. We really were in Venice. Was it possible that the survivors flew us across the ocean in the twelve hours that I was out? I suppose anything was possible.

"Is this ever going to make sense to me?" I asked.

"Any second now," she replied with a chuckle.

Up ahead I saw light, which meant the canal would bring us outside. Seconds later we slipped through an archway and into a wide pool. The sun hadn't yet risen, but the sky was bright enough that I could make out detail through the gray haze.

It was like leaving a dream, only to enter a more impossible dream. Venice is one of those cities that you see in movies and in pictures and on TV, so it looks familiar even if you've never been there. There was a tall brick tower near an ornate footbridge that spanned the pool. Gondola docks with red-and-white barber poles ringed the pool.

It really was Venice.

But it wasn't. I also saw huge, modern buildings that loomed over us. I saw what looked like a small volcano nestled amid palm trees, behind which were two pirate ships flying the Jolly Roger. In the distance, I could have sworn I saw the Eiffel Tower.

I was convinced that the tranquilizer was giving me hallucinations.

"Uh . . . what is this?" was all I managed to say.

"Never been here?" Charlotte asked. "Guess you're a little young."

"I don't think you can be too young to be insane," I said.

Charlotte laughed. "You're not insane, though this place has driven plenty of folks off their rocker."

"Where are we?" I asked, with more than a little desperation.

"It's Las Vegas, Tucker. Haven't you ever seen pictures? Or been to the movies?"

Las Vegas. I'd seen it on the map, not far from the Valley of Fire. Things were suddenly clicking into place. Charlotte was right. Las Vegas was the city that never sleeps, or something like that. But it sure looked sleepy to me. Every movie I'd seen of the place showed it with billions of glittering lights. But there was no power for that. Las Vegas was dead.

There were huge billboards advertising shows at places called the Mirage and the MGM Grand. Some had pictures of people who must have been superstars, but I didn't recognize any of them. Men wore tuxedos and women wore shimmering gowns. They were bright and happy and ready to please.

They were probably dead.

It might have been some great destination for people to have fun and see shows and gamble and do whatever else you did in a fantasyland out in the desert, but now it was just another dark, empty city. The word Charlotte used to describe it totally fit: eerie.

Charlotte guided the gondola up to a dock that had ornate columns like you might see in Italy. The real Italy. This was a theme-park copy. She tied up the craft and gave me a hand to get out because my head was still spinning . . . and it had nothing to do with the tranquilizer.

"Let's walk," she said. "Newbies always get a little welcome speech. We'll find your friends in a minute."

We climbed up to street level from the lagoon, where I got a full view of this section of Las Vegas.

"It's called the Strip," Charlotte explained. "It's where most of the big hotels and casinos are all jammed together in a four-mile stretch. Las Vegas is a big city, but this is where most of the action is." She paused and added, "Or was."

We walked out onto the street and took a left, heading toward the Eiffel Tower. As dead as the city was, it wasn't abandoned. Far from it. People wandered out from the buildings to greet the new day. Some stretched. Some jogged. Others just walked quickly, as if working to stay in shape. There were all sorts of people representing most every nationality or ethnic group. All were in civilian clothes. This was not an army. Most of them were older than me, no big surprise, but I didn't see any young kids at all. I guess that made sense. Anybody looking to join up with a band of rebels wouldn't bring their toddler along for the ride.

"Why here?" I asked.

"It's the perfect place to hide out," Charlotte replied. "There's a labyrinth of tunnels that run up and down the Strip and connect all the properties. What better place to stay underground and safe from them damned black planes? You know that drill."

I did.

"It's like a rat warren down there. If those planes ever come looking for us, we can disappear into the depths like cockroaches."

"Have they ever come looking?" I asked.

"Nope, but you'll hear more about that at the briefing. We haven't had a single incident since we started gathering here."

"Is anybody in charge?" I asked.

"There're a couple of guys. Good guys. We call 'em the Chiefs. A few have military backgrounds, so they've kept it all organized. Check this out."

She pointed down a side street, where I saw a group of people jogging in perfect formation, four abreast, with a guy in green camo pants leading the way.

"It's like they're training," I said.

"They are," was her reply.

"How many survivors are here?" I asked.

"Last count was six hundred and fifty-two, including you."

"Exactly?" I asked.

She shrugged and said, "Like I said, we keep it organized. Everybody counts here. We're not playing this loose. There's too much at stake."

"So what's the plan?" I asked. "It's not like six hundred civilians can take on the Retros."

"Don't get ahead of yourself, pardner," she scolded. "You just got here."

We passed more massive buildings that I guess were hotels. I saw one that looked like the Roman Colosseum surrounded by statues right out of ancient Italy. The Eiffel Tower was real, or at least as real as an almost-full-sized replica built in America could be. A gigantic Statue of Liberty stood guard in front of a replica of the New York City skyline . . . that had a roller coaster snaking through it. There was a medieval castle and an Egyptian pyramid guarded by a sphinx. Everything along the Strip was monster-sized: a Coke bottle, a guitar, a golden lion that loomed over the boulevard. I didn't understand what huge replicas of actual places and things had to do with gambling, but I'd never been to Las Vegas, so what did I know?

Charlotte led me into a fancy hotel that didn't look like it was trying to copy any specific country or city. We entered a lobby that had a ceiling covered with thousands of paper flowers of every size, color, and shape you could imagine. It was actually kind of pretty, and less cheesy than anything I'd seen so far.

"This is where we brief the newbies," Charlotte said. "It's a pleasant spot. Puts people at ease."

"You mean as opposed to a giant head that puts them on edge?"

"Exactly," she said with a sly smile.

I liked Charlotte.

She led me through glass doors into a courtyard that looked like something out of a fairy tale. The ceiling was glass with a fancy steel frame that gave the place the feel of a greenhouse. The first thing I saw was a miniature carousel with four brightly painted horses. There was also a twenty-foot-high blue-and-white-striped lighthouse with a small sailboat circling its base. Up toward the high ceiling were miniature hot air balloons that were frozen in flight. Across from them was a floating flock of red and yellow umbrellas that would never stop rain or fall to the ground.

The floor was covered with flower-filled gardens of black-eyed Susans, white daffodils, and pink impatiens. I know my flowers. It was clear that the survivors who had taken over Las Vegas were keeping these gardens in good shape. The entire space was playful and inviting, like somebody's idea of a storybook park. I didn't understand what this had to do with gambling any more than the giant guitar and fake Statue of Liberty, but at least it was a pleasant enough place to hang out.

Others had arrived. There were maybe ten people who were checking out the indoor park, looking as dazed as I felt.

"Tucker!" came a familiar voice.

Olivia ran through the garden toward me with her arms open wide. When she hit me, she wrapped her arms around me and pressed her body square against mine. This time I didn't mind. I was happy and relieved to see her.

"They said everyone would be here, but I didn't believe them," she said, holding back tears.

"You okay?" I asked.

"A little dizzy, but what else is new?"

I laughed and hugged her closer. Olivia may have been distraught, but she still had her sense of humor.

"Easy there, Tucker," Kent said. "Don't get too used to that."

I almost didn't believe it was him. Not because he was there, but because he called me Tucker. Good for him for remembering that I was ready to punch his lights out if he called me Rook again.

"Where's Tori?" I asked.

"Right here," Tori replied as she entered through the door opposite the one I had come through. "Still trying to process."

I wanted to hug her out of pure relief, but I was too busy being hugged by Olivia.

"Is this place wild or what?" Kent asked. "It's like a theme park for vampires. They all hang out in this underground maze and only come out at night."

"I always wanted to see Vegas," Olivia said. "It sounded so exciting. Now it's just creepy."

"What about Jon?" Tori asked.

We looked around, but there was no Jon to be seen.

"Charlotte?" I called. "Our friend Jon Purcell isn't here."

"He will be," she assured me. "They've probably got him coming in with the next group. Don't worry, he's fine. I did his interrogation myself."

"Attention, everybody!" came a booming voice.

A tall, broad-shouldered guy entered the garden quickly. He had a tight crew cut and an open, friendly face.

"Gather round," he called out. "Sorry, we don't have chairs. You can sit or stand. Whatever works."

We exchanged looks, not sure of what to do.

"Go ahead," Charlotte cajoled. "He won't bite."

We walked toward the man, as did the rest of the people. A few men had arrived with the big guy and stood next to him. I flashed back to Chris Campbell and his cowboys, but this group didn't come across as intimidating, like those Retro scum. Body language is everything, and these guys were relaxed and smiling. They must have been the survivors who brought the others here, as Charlotte did with me. Charlotte, on the other hand, stayed with us. We all stood facing the man in the dead center of the garden.

"My name is Matt," the guy announced. "In real life, I'm an EMT who works the Baywatch boat off of Catalina Island near Los Angeles. In this life, I'm one of the Chiefs who organized this little party."

Matt seemed more like a camp counselor than a counter-revolutionary.

"I know you've all got a million questions, and I'll do my best to answer them. But first let me say this: If you're here right now, it means you heard our broadcast and you feel the same as we do. We've all lost our lives. We've lost friends and loved ones. We're victims of a war that we never saw coming. We weren't given a choice or a warning. What happened to us was an unprovoked, unexplained invasion by an unknown enemy. Make no mistake, our situation is grim, to say the least. But if you're here, it means you don't want to roll over and accept what happened. You want to fight back. We do too. It's not just about getting by or survival;

it's about taking our lives back. If you agree with all that, welcome. We're glad you're here. If you don't, then you should be moving on."

He fell silent, giving us each a look and the opportunity to back out. After what Charlotte told me about their security, I didn't think anybody who said, "You know, on second thought, I'd rather not" would live to see another day.

Nobody moved.

"Awesome," Matt said with a satisfied smile. "I didn't think so."

I had a feeling I was going to like Matt too.

"Let me start by telling you what we know. Maybe some of you can add to this, and you'll get the chance. We believe that the United States Air Force was behind the attack. As to why, and who is calling the shots, we don't know. But there's one thing that gives us hope. From what we've seen and what we've put together from the experiences of the survivors who have joined us, the Air Force seems to be heavy on firepower, but light on manpower. Those black drones don't have pilots. They're being controlled from a distance. There are plenty of them, let's not forget that. They are deadly efficient. We've all seen what they can do. What we haven't seen are people. Cities have not been occupied by any kind of invasion force . . . at least none that we've heard of. Nobody has claimed victory or declared that they're in charge. It gives us hope that as powerful as they are, they don't have the bodies to execute a true invasion."

A Hispanic-looking guy called out, "So why did they attack? Just to kill millions of people for the sake of it?"

"Billions," Matt corrected. "And, no, that doesn't make sense. There has to be some other purpose to what they've done, we just don't know it yet."

"What about SYLO?" I called out.

"What about it?" Matt replied. "It's a branch of the Navy."

"Yeah," Kent said. "Another branch that's at war with the Retros."

Matt looked back and forth between his friends who stood next to him as if confused. "What are these kids doing here?" he asked nobody in particular. He didn't sound annoyed; it was more like he genuinely didn't understand.

"We picked them up yesterday evening," one of his friends answered.

"Uh, I'm sorry, guys," Matt said, speaking directly to us. "You're welcome here, but we've set up some parameters. We all agreed that we're not letting kids get involved. Young people are way too valuable to the future of—"

"Whoa, whoa," Charlotte called out and pushed her way to the front of the group to face Matt. "Let's take a beat. First off, these aren't babies. When we talked about protecting kids, we were talking about real youngsters."

"Uh, yeah. Like them."

Charlotte looked back, made direct eye contact with me, and smiled.

"I don't care how old they are," she said. "These young people have been through far more than any of us. They've had contact with the Air Force, or Retros, as they call 'em. They've been in the middle of huge battles between SYLO and these Retros. Turns out, this isn't a one-sided war after all. The Navy is in on it too. It's not just one rogue bunch causing trouble, it's a flat-out civil war."

She had Matt's attention.

Charlotte reached into her pocket and pulled out a plastic baggie full of red crystals. Ruby-red crystals. I heard Olivia gasp with surprise.

"Remember this stuff we took off of that fella who was snooping around here a week or so back? We had no idea what it was . . . but now we do, because of them. The Retros are feeding it to survivors. It gives folks impossible strength and speed and stamina. It's like a steroid on steroids. And you know why they're doing it? They're making slaves out of survivors to help them rebuild. Trouble is, it eventually kills anybody who takes too much. So the way I see it, this confirms what you just said, Matt. These Retros don't have a lot of manpower. They're looking to their victims to do their grunt work. That's good news, and we got it from these young people."

I felt the eyes of the others on us, and it was making me uncomfortable.

"Let me put it to y'all simply," Charlotte said. "They know a hell of a lot more about what's going on than we do, so I'd say we'd be smart to let them do whatever it is they came here to do, because they may end up being the difference between us doing some good or getting slaughtered."

Charlotte smiled at me, then looked back at Matt and added, "Now you go on with your little speech."

Charlotte melted back into the crowd and stood next to me.

"Thank you," I whispered.

"No problem," she replied under her breath. "Just don't screw up."

"I love you, Charlotte," Matt said. "You're a pain in my butt, but I love you."

"I love you too, Matty," Charlotte replied.

A nervous chuckle went through the crowd. It helped take some of the pressure off.

"All right," Matt announced. "We'll see what you guys can offer. If everything Charlotte says is true, you're definitely going to be an asset to this operation."

"What exactly is this operation?" Tori demanded. "We came a long way because you said you were going to fight back. It looks like you've got maybe six hundred survivors here."

"Six hundred and fifty-two," Charlotte called out.

"Sorry. Six hundred and fifty-two," Tori repeated, shaking her head. "You have no idea what you're up against. There are armies battling out there. Powerful, mechanized armies. We've been through an air-to-sea battle that dropped hundreds of planes and sank dozens of warships. These two forces are huge, they're determined, and there's nothing that six hundred and fifty-two people can do to stop them, no matter how angry or dedicated they are. We came here to fight. To make a difference. From what I've seen so far, you're just setting yourself up for a noble suicide."

The room fell deathly quiet.

Matt nodded thoughtfully.

"I hear you," he said without a trace of defensiveness. If anything, his smile was even more sincere. "You're right. There's no way we could go toe-to-toe in the kind of battles you're talking about. But you're assuming we're talking about going to war."

"So then what's the point?" Kent asked.

"Like I said before, the Air Force—the Retros, as you call them—don't have manpower. They have firepower. And we know where that firepower is coming from."

"Where?" I blurted out.

"We know where they're staging their raids from. It's where the black fighter planes gather before taking off on their missions. The thing is, there are incredible numbers of planes, but not a whole lot of people. They may be able to swarm entire cities, but we think they'll have trouble protecting their own backs."

"So you *do* want to attack the Retros?" I asked.

"There are only a few ways to damage an operation like that. It could be bombed from the air. We don't have that ability. It could be invaded by an army. As you pointed out, we don't have an army that's capable of that. But there's a third option."

"Sabotage," Charlotte declared. "We're going to be like silent hunters. Snakes. They'll never see us coming."

"Small groups," Matt said. "Demolition teams. No fanfare. No warning. We'll enter and be gone before they know we were there."

"And take out hundreds of those damn planes at a time," Charlotte said with relish. "By the time the fires are put out, we'll have disappeared back into the desert, invisible until the next time we come calling."

There were positive murmurs throughout the crowd. These people had all lost something, and if they had made this trek into the desert, they were ready for some payback.

Tori said, "Will it be enough to stop them for good?"

Matt shrugged. "Who knows? But it will hurt them, and it's what we can do. That's good enough reason to give it a try."

"I like it," Kent said with glee. "Where is this place?"

"Close enough for us to strike and far enough for us to stay hidden."

Tori asked, "How soon do you plan on—"

"Cover!" came a terrified cry from a woman who ran into the courtyard. "Now!"

Charlotte, Matt, and their friends all tensed up.

"What? Why? We're not doing a drill now," Matt said, confused.

The mood had suddenly changed.

Did I sense true fear in his voice?

"No!" the woman yelled. "It's real. They're minutes away."

She backed out of the courtyard and took off running.

"What's going on?" I demanded.

Matt and the others looked stunned. There was a painfully long moment when it seemed as if they didn't know what to do.

"Talk to me, Matt," Charlotte demanded.

Matt snapped into focus. He had gone from a jovial big brother to a man with a mission.

"Bring them below," he said without a hint of panic. "We'll take cover with the other Chiefs."

"How is this possible?" Charlotte asked, though I don't think she expected an answer.

"Let's hope we get the chance to find out," Matt said. "Go, now!"

Matt and his friends took off running. Most of the others followed.

The rest of us gathered together in confusion. We all looked to Charlotte for answers.

"What's happening, Charlotte?" I asked.

"They've found us," she said soberly. "The Air Force is attacking."

TWENTY-FOUR

The panic was on. Everyone scattered to find shelter.

Tori, Kent, Olivia, and I stayed with Charlotte.

"We've gotta find Jon," I said.

"He's with his escort. He'll be okay," Charlotte said. "We've got to get as deep below ground as possible."

She led us out of the indoor park, through the lobby, and straight into the darkened casino. I'd only seen casinos on TV. They were lively places full of color and light and excitement. Slot machines rang, people gathered around roulette or blackjack tables, and everybody would be having a great time, except for those who were losing, I guess. Bottom line was that they were places loaded with energy.

This casino couldn't have been further from that. It was dark and quiet. There were long rows of dust-covered slot machines that would never again play their electronic tunes, empty tables with no gamers, and restaurants that had the sour smell of putrid food.

Charlotte wove her way through the islands of slot machines as if she knew exactly where she was going. The rest of us followed, trusting that she wasn't just winging it.

"We can access the underground behind the cashier's window," she announced.

There was a far-off rumble that made Charlotte stop and listen.

"They're here," she said, barely above a whisper. "I can't believe they found us."

"Believe it, Sarge," Kent said sarcastically. "This is old news to us."

"It's daytime," I said. "They can't penetrate the buildings with their light weapons."

More rumbles were heard. It sounded like fast-moving thunder, but we knew what it really was. Thunder didn't make the floor shudder.

"Those planes have plenty of firepower during the day," I cautioned. "They can easily—"

The roof over our heads exploded, sending a shower of splintered wood and shattered plaster down on us. We all dove for cover as heavy beams plummeted to the floor.

I ducked under a large roulette table, for whatever good that would do. The massive steel beams crashed to the ground all around me, hitting the metal slot machines and crushing them under their weight. The blast ripped open a hole in the ceiling, allowing sunlight to shine in. The casino was alive again, but not in a good way.

"Keep moving!" Charlotte commanded from somewhere.

I peered out from beneath the table to look for the others. It was nearly impossible to see. The air was filled with dust and debris that reflected the sunlight to create a white haze.

"Tori!" I shouted.

"Right here," she said calmly.

I jumped when I realized she was directly behind me.

"Let's get outta here," I said and grabbed her hand.

We scrambled out from beneath the table and ran in the same direction we had been headed when the bomb hit.

The first bomb.

The second struck the instant we were on our feet. The pulse of energy must have traveled directly through the hole in the roof, for it made a direct hit on a row of slot machines. The heavy metal machines blew into the air like toys. I pulled Tori behind a pillar as two machines tumbled past, banging and clanging as their metal skins tore each time they hit the floor. The machines bounced across the casino floor, spewing coins and bashing others before coming to rest in a pile of twisted steel beams.

"There's Olivia," Tori shouted.

Olivia was sprinting along another row of slot machines. She was headed for a heavy gaming table where I thought she would try to take cover. Instead, she leaned down and reached out her hand.

"You stay here and you die!" she shouted.

I'd never heard her so commanding. I guess fear will do that.

A hand reached up from under the table and grabbed hers. Olivia pulled a dazed Kent to his feet. He nodded and went with her.

A second later another energy surge hit—directly on the table Kent had been hiding beneath. It exploded the table into kindling, sending sharp slivers of wood and a bloom of colorful casino chips flying everywhere. Olivia had just saved Kent's life.

I saw Charlotte take cover behind a bar. As soon as she disappeared behind it, she screamed.

I ran for her, with Tori right behind me. After a pained scream like that, I figured she must have twisted her ankle or slammed into something sharp. I made it to the bar, circled around behind, and saw that she wasn't hurt. At least not physically.

She was kneeling over somebody. A guy. He wasn't moving.

"Is he okay?" I asked.

"No," she said, sounding as though she was trying to hold back her emotions.

"How?" Tori asked. "Did something hit him?"

Charlotte shook her head. She had tears in her eyes. At first I thought they were tears of sorrow, and they were. But they were just as much a show of her building rage.

"He was murdered," she said, gritting her teeth.

"How do you know that?" I asked.

Another bomb flew through the hole in the ceiling, blasting a hole in the floor that sent an avalanche of rubble into the next level down. It was far enough away that we barely paid attention.

"I'm a sheriff," she said. "I've seen plenty of murder scenes. But it doesn't take a crack detective to see what happened here."

She rolled his head to the side, where I saw the telltale gaping red hole that was a bullet wound, square in the middle of his forehead.

"His name was Tom," Charlotte explained. "He was my best friend here, I guess because he was a sheriff too. From LA County. We had plenty of stories to share."

She seemed dazed, in shock from what had happened to her friend.

"I'm sorry, Charlotte," I said. "But we gotta get outta here."

Several more energy bombs hit, turning the once opulent casino into a junkyard.

"This is just . . . wrong," she said, sounding numb. "Why would somebody shoot him? We're all survivors here."

"Find the others," Tori said. "I'll get her to the cashier's window."

I crouched low and ran to the far side of the bar, where I could scan the wreckage of the casino.

"Olivia? Kent?"

No answer.

Through the haze I spotted the word "Cashier" on a wall over a long window with security bars. That was our target. I took off running while looking around for the others. When I hit the wall with the cashier's window, I heard a voice coming from behind it. A familiar voice. I relaxed, knowing that Kent and Olivia had made it. I turned to head back for Tori and Charlotte and heard the voice again.

It wasn't Kent's.

It was Jon's.

"No, end it now," he commanded. "You were supposed to wait for nightfall. Destroying empty buildings is useless. This will only force them to crawl deeper."

What?

I slid closer, listening intently, trying to understand what he was saying.

"It's too late, you idiots, the rats have already gone underground," he said to . . . someone. He sounded angry, which wasn't like Jon at all. There was a sense of authority in his voice that I'd never heard before. It brought me back to the night in Ohio when I heard him talking to somebody from behind the closed door of the radio room. But the radio wasn't working. He told me he was talking to himself.

"Stop the attack," he ordered. "I will not take responsibility for this."

A few seconds later, the bombardment stopped. There was no more distant thunder. Was it a coincidence? The immediate danger seemed to be over, but the reality of a new danger was right in front of me. Part of me wanted to run, but I was tired of running.

I opened the door that led into the cashier's room.

Jon was huddled on the floor under the counter, speaking into a small black device.

He hadn't been talking to himself.

When he saw me, there was a frozen moment when neither of us knew what to do. He then jumped to his feet and jammed the device into his pocket.

"Tucker!" he called out with a more familiar, vulnerable voice. "Are you okay? Where is everybody? I heard this was the way down to safety, but I only got this far when the bombs started falling and—"

"Shut up, Jon," I commanded.

That was all I needed to say. Jon knew I had heard his conversation. He stood up straight. That one small move made him look like a different person. He was always someone who blended into the woodwork. Someone who didn't stand out. A real meek geek. Not anymore.

"I like you, Tucker," he said, once again sounding like the confident guy who had been barking orders into his phone or whatever it was. "I was hoping you guys would make it through this."

"What's the deal, Jon?" I asked. "Were you always with them? Or did somebody get to you and force you to join?"

"It was my mission," he said with a shrug. "I guess you'd call it cleanup duty. We're everywhere, you know."

"Like termites," I said aloud, thinking back to Granger's words.

"Termites?" Jon asked.

"You're a traitor," I said, seething.

"No, I'm actually very loyal. What I am is an infiltrator."

My anger took control. I made a move for him but . . .

Jon pulled out Tori's gun and leveled it at me.

I stopped short.

"You're the one who killed him," I said. "Charlotte's friend."

"He wouldn't leave me alone," Jon explained, as if it was a justifiable excuse for murder. "I had to complete my mission. Besides, what's one more death?"

My anger flared.

"It's not just one more death," I growled. "It's a life. A person with a past and a family and now . . . no future."

"Just as well," Jon said casually. "He probably wouldn't have liked his future anyway."

Without thinking, I grabbed a snow globe that was on the desk and whipped it at him.

It surprised him, and he flinched, giving me enough time to attack. I grabbed his gun hand and wrestled him for the weapon. I'm not a fighter, but I was driven by rage. We had trusted Jon. Taken him in. Taken care of him while he was betraying us at every turn.

It wasn't a contest. I twisted the gun out of his hand and nailed him in the face with my elbow. Jon grunted in pain. I hit him again with my fist, using all of the pent-up frustration and anger that I'd been holding in since day one. So many images flew through my mind. Quinn's death, Granger shooting an unarmed civilian, my mother crying on the far side of the prison-camp fence, the burning skeleton of a pilot in his crashed plane, the dying Mr. Sleeper. So many horrors came flooding back, and they all rushed out through my fists.

"Whoa, easy!" Kent said and pulled me off of Jon.

Kent had entered the cashier's room. Olivia stood in the doorway, watching.

"It's him!" I declared. "He's a traitor!"

Jon scrambled away and got to his feet.

"He's crazy!" he cried, sounding like the old Jon. "He just started going nuts on me! He thinks I shot somebody in the head when all I did was hide in here!"

I spotted Tori's gun on the floor and went for it.

Jon went for it too, but I beat him to it. I backed away, aiming the weapon at him, trying to keep my hands steady.

"Look!" Jon shouted. "He's lost it! Now he wants to shoot me!"

"What's the deal, Tucker?" Kent asked nervously.

Charlotte and Tori entered the room.

"Jon's a Retro," I said with a shaky voice. "He's been playing us from the get-go. He's probably been telling them everything we've been doing. Even back at Faneuil Hall. Remember? He's the one who warned Campbell that we were going to escape."

"That's crazy!" Jon cried. "If somebody got shot, it must have been Tucker who did it. He's the one with the gun."

"Charlotte," I said, trying to keep my voice calm and reasonable. "You want to know how the Retros found us here? It was Jon.

He called in the air strike. But they attacked too early. He tried to warn them off and had to get away from your friend Tom to do it. That's why he shot him."

"Tucker!" Olivia cried. "How can you say something like that?"

"You guys know me," Jon protested. "I've been in just as much trouble as you. Just as much danger. Heck, I'm the one who told you about the radio broadcast! Tucker's just looking for somebody to blame this on."

"Check his pocket," I said. "He's got some kind of communicator."

All eyes went to Jon.

"Empty your pockets, Chadwick," Kent said.

Jon licked his lips nervously. He reached for his pocket.

"I don't know what he's talking about," he said. "If there's something in here, then Tucker planted it, and I'm not gonna—"

Jon rushed me. I was so surprised that I didn't have time to shoot. He knocked me back and went for the door, but it was futile. Kent's instincts took over, and he tackled him as Charlotte pounced. There was a short scuffle before she was able to grab Jon's arm and twist it behind his back. The linebacker and the sheriff had done the job.

While keeping his arm twisted with one hand, Charlotte used her other hand to dig into Jon's pocket. She pulled out a small black device that was no bigger than an iPod shuffle and held it in front of Jon's face.

"What is this?" she demanded to know.

She was being professional, but her anger was bubbling close to the surface.

"I have no idea," Jon replied. "Tucker must have put it there."

"He was talking into that when I found him," I said. "He was telling somebody to call off the attack because everyone had already taken cover. He said they were supposed to wait for nightfall."

Charlotte gave me a worried look.

"That's what he said? They were supposed to wait for night-fall?"

"Yes. They'll be back. Tonight, when those light weapons can wipe out this whole city. There won't be anywhere to hide, not since they know so many people are here. They'll evaporate the buildings until they root us out."

Charlotte nodded gravely. She twisted Jon's arm.

"Where did you get the gun?" she demanded.

"It's mine," Tori said. "I dropped it in the car when we were shot in the Valley of Fire."

"So then where did *you* get it?" Charlotte insisted, twisting Jon's arm further.

He winced but didn't complain.

"Once I passed your silly interrogation, I had your friend take me to our vehicle," Jon said through gritted teeth. "What was his name? Tom? I told him I had to get my medicine. That it was a matter of life and death. I wasn't lying. It *was* a matter of life and death. Tom's."

He gave Charlotte a twisted smile.

Charlotte wrenched his arm so violently I thought it would break.

Jon finally broke down and howled with pain.

"What do we do with him?" I asked.

Charlotte stood and pulled Jon to his feet. She held one of his arms behind his back while Kent held the other.

"There's a holding cell down the hall," she answered. "It's where security puts cheats and drunks until the authorities arrive. We can keep him there and call the Chiefs in."

Olivia stood in front of Jon. She looked at him like a hurt little girl.

"So it's true?" she asked. "You're one of them? Jon, we could have been killed."

Jon started to reply quickly, probably to deny everything. But he stopped himself. Once again, he stood up straight and his personality changed. He gave us all a small, superior smile.

"You're already dead, you just don't know it yet," he said with smug confidence.

Olivia hauled off and slapped him across the face. Jon's head snapped to the side, but he didn't react or whimper.

"Feel better now?" he asked her.

"Yes."

"It won't last."

"Come on," Charlotte said. "Through that door."

I jumped ahead and opened the door so Charlotte and Kent could lead Jon through.

"Flashlights," Charlotte said.

There were a few emergency flashlights fixed to the wall. Olivia and I each grabbed one.

"Here," I said, handing the gun to Tori.

She took it and jammed it into her waistband.

We were in a plain hallway, which was a huge contrast to the extravagant casino we had just left. We had only walked a few yards when Charlotte stopped in front of a door.

"In here," she ordered.

I opened the door to what was probably a security office. There were a few desks still covered with papers, as if whoever worked there had just stepped out for lunch. Charlotte led us down a short hallway and turned into an open door, beyond which was the barred cell used by the casino's security force.

Charlotte and Kent shoved Jon inside, then Charlotte quickly slid the bars closed. She pulled a ring loaded with keys from her pocket and used one to lock the cell door. Old sheriff habits die hard.

"I'm sorry, Charlotte," I said.

"For what?"

"For bringing him here. We had no idea."

"It wasn't your fault," Charlotte said. "We should have smelled him coming. That was my job, and I let him through."

"I can't believe he just . . . turned on us," Olivia said, sounding dazed.

"He didn't turn," I corrected. "He was never with us. Think about it. He turned us in to Chris Campbell when we tried to escape from Faneuil Hall. He was the one who got us to come to Nevada. He told us all about the radio broadcasts and pushed us to find the survivors."

"But he wanted to blow off Nevada and go to Kentucky," Tori said.

"Sure! He wanted to know what that was about too! When we were in Ohio, I heard him talking on the radio, but the radio wasn't working. He was probably using that little communicator to tell the Retros that something was happening in Kentucky. I'll bet he called in the air strike there. No, Jon didn't turn. He was using us from the get-go."

"Got it all figured out, do you?" Jon asked, snickering.

"Shut up, or I'll come in there and shut you up," Kent snarled.

"Sure, come on in, Kent. I'd love for you to try to teach me a lesson."

Jon sounded odd. His breathing was heavy, and his voice was raised.

Kent made a move for the cell.

"Don't," Charlotte warned him.

He stopped.

Jon wrapped his fingers around the bars.

"I'll probably get a medal for this," he said, panting. "We knew there would be pockets of resistance. That's why so many of us are out there."

"I said shut up!" Kent shouted angrily.

"No, let him talk," I said. "How many are out there, Jon?"

"More than you can imagine," he said breathlessly. "We're everywhere. Hiding with you in your wasted cities. Listening in on your pitiful plans. Rooting out nests of pathetic survivors. But this here . . . this was a very big prize. We expected there to be retaliation in Nevada but never like this. Not right under our noses. I'm the one who first heard the broadcast, you know. We sent a few people to investigate, but nobody broke through . . . until me. I may have saved the whole mission."

"Who are you?" I asked. "Why are you fighting SYLO?"

"SYLO," Jon said with disdain. "The guard dogs of a dying society. They're nothing more than a nuisance. The mission will be completed."

Tori and I exchanged worried looks.

"What exactly is the mission?" I asked, trying not to sound too desperate.

Jon wagged his finger at me and smiled slyly.

"You think you want to know, but trust me, you don't."

"But we do," Tori insisted. "Impress us."

She was playing to Jon's ego.

Jon chuckled. "Evolution is about to take a dramatic leap forward. But not just yet. There are still too many of you primates left. Especially in the cities."

He was breathing hard, as if telling the tale was exciting him.

"Primates?" Kent said. "What the hell?"

"Eradication is more complicated with dense population centers. There are too many deep caves to hide in, and we don't want to totally decimate the infrastructure. Before we can begin to re-populate, there needs to be another wave. More pointed this time. More city-specific. We're going back to Moscow and Beijing. London has proved difficult. So has Sydney. New York will feel another bite. Los Angeles is the closest, so it will be the first. Once those cities are cleared, we can begin."

"Cleared?" I said soberly. "That's what you call it? You're talking about wiping out every last living soul."

"Oh no. Not entirely. You primates will serve a purpose. Re-building a society will be labor-intensive."

"You mean you need slaves," Tori said with disdain.

"Call it what you want," he said dismissively.

"You think we're primates?" Kent said, incredulous. "What does that make *you*?"

Jon started yanking on the bars of the cell as if trying to pull it apart. It was a sudden and violent move that surprised us all . . .

. . . and made complete sense.

"Look at me!" I yelled at him.

I flashed the light in his face and saw it. The wild eyes. The heavy breathing. I suddenly knew why he was acting so crazy.

"Where did you get it?" I asked.

"Get what?" Olivia asked, confused.

Jon dug into his back pocket, took out an empty baggie, and tossed it through the bars.

"From the sheriff's pocket while she was twisting my arm," he said. "Aren't I clever?"

Charlotte's hand went to her pocket.

"It's gone," she exclaimed.

I picked up the empty plastic bag.

"There was a ton of the Ruby in here," I said. "Tell me you didn't eat it all."

"I did," Jon said, his voice becoming a high-pitched squeal.

"My God," Tori said with a gasp. "He'll explode."

Jon backed up until he hit the far wall, then charged at the bars. He hit them hard, bounced back, and hit them again.

"You won't make it until tonight," he screamed. "I'm coming for you now."

Tori pulled out her gun.

I put my hand on hers and pushed the weapon down.

"Wait," I said.

The full effect of the Ruby was just kicking in. Jon was like an enraged animal with fire in his veins. He let out a bone-chilling howl, grabbed the bars, and furiously pulled on them. The metal squeaked and groaned, but held.

"You overdosed," I said. "If you don't calm down, you're going to—"

He screamed again. It was primal and filled with anguish and anger. He grabbed the cot, lifted it up, and threw it against the bars.

"Go ahead and shoot me," he screamed. "It'll be like a bee sting."

Olivia backed away, crying.

Charlotte watched in stunned wonder.

Tori, Kent, and I had been through this before. It was nothing new. The three of us watched dispassionately, waiting for the inevitable end.

"Is there anything we can do?" Charlotte asked, horrified.

I shook my head.

"No wonder he wanted me to go in there," Kent said. "He wouldn't have had the guts otherwise."

Jon pulled the cot apart with his bare hands, tearing off a length of metal that he wedged into the door to try to pry it open. His hands bled, but he ignored the pain. He was stronger than the metal tool. So were the cell bars. The metal snapped in his hands.

He screamed in despair, grabbed the bars again, and shook them furiously.

"Let me out," he begged, changing tactics. "I'll convince them to spare your lives. I promise."

Even through the Ruby-fueled insanity, he realized he had made a mistake. The bars were too strong. He turned and ran into the far wall, hitting it square on with a sickening thud. Jon was out of his mind, more so than Marty Wiggins or Kent's father or anybody else who paid the price for taking too much of the Ruby.

"You have to calm down," I said again, though I knew it was no use.

He grabbed one of the cell bars with both hands, and with a primal howl he yanked on it with a frightening fury.

This time the bar broke loose. He fell backward, and with an inhuman cry that showed both triumph and anguish, he landed on the floor.

Tori lifted her gun, though she didn't need to.

Jon lay still.

We all stood there, staring at the now quiet figure on the floor. The beams from the two flashlights played over him.

"Oh, Jon," Olivia whimpered.

"What happened?" Charlotte asked, stunned.

"His body couldn't handle it," I replied. "That's what happens."

"How horrible," Charlotte said with a pained whisper.

"He got what he deserved," Kent said with no sympathy. "And he did it to himself. Idiot."

"Everything is falling apart," Charlotte lamented.

"Not yet it isn't," I said. "But it will. When the sun sets, the storm comes back."

Tori said, "We've got to evacuate."

"What time is sunset?" I asked Charlotte.

"Around six o'clock, give or take."

"So we've got ten hours to put together a plan," I said.

"An evacuation plan?" Kent asked.

"Yes, and a plan to carry out the mission that everyone came here to do. Is that possible, Charlotte?"

Charlotte continued to stare at Jon's lifeless body.

"Charlotte?" I said sharply.

"What?" she replied, as if snapping out of a dream.

"You've been calling for people to come here to fight back against the Retros. Is there a real plan for this sabotage? Are you ready?"

Charlotte looked at Jon's lifeless body. I thought she was going to zone out again, but she said, "We were waiting for more volunteers to show up. There wasn't any time pressure before."

"Well, there is now," Kent said, stating the obvious.

"I get that, junior," Charlotte said curtly. She was beginning to sound like her old self. "Yeah, we're ready. Let's take this to the Chiefs."

She went for the door, and the others followed.

I hung back with Jon's lifeless body.

One suspect down.

Jon was a traitor. Or an infiltrator. Whatever. But his death didn't take the heat off of the others. Jon wasn't from Pemberwick. Granger hadn't been hunting him.

There was still a very good possibility that there was another traitor.

I left the remains of Jon Purcell in the cage where he died. He had given us some valuable information. Disturbing information. But the power and purpose behind the Retros was still a mystery.

We now knew their plan was to wipe out almost every survivor except for those they would use as slaves to prepare for their re-population of the planet. The first big city to be targeted was Los Angeles, but when would that attack happen?

They considered us primates. Lesser forms of life. Animals. We meant nothing to them as human beings, which raised the question: What exactly were *they?*

Whoever or whatever they were, they had destroyed three-quarters of the world's population and were preparing to finish the rest.

Unless we could stop them.

TWENTY-FIVE

Every last survivor in Las Vegas had gathered together in an opulent theater that was supposed to look like the Roman Colosseum. Not that I'd ever been to the real Colosseum, but as far as I could tell, the only thing about this theater that looked like ancient Rome were some huge murals that I guessed were modeled after the originals. Everything else was slick and modern.

We had walked to the meeting along the Strip, past the destruction that the Retro planes had brought to the city. The beautiful indoor park where we had met some of the other survivors had been reduced to a pile of rubble with a few forlorn carousel horses poking their noses out of the debris. The Eiffel Tower had been sheared off halfway to its peak. The upper section and the observation deck lay crumpled across the street. The only thing left of the huge bronze lion were four paws on a pedestal. The giant Coke bottle was smashed. The massive guitar had its neck broken off. Immense holes had been blown through many of the high-rise hotels. The Statue of Liberty was intact, but it lay across the road with its torch hand jammed against a broken palm tree.

As disastrous as it all appeared, Jon was right. The Retros had been shooting at empty buildings. When the final head count was done, there was only one person who had died in the assault. It was Tom, Charlotte's friend. And he hadn't even died because of the attack. Jon had murdered him.

Jon himself didn't count. He wasn't one of us. He was a spy. His body lay alone in the cell that was normally used to hold people who tried to cheat the casino. I guess it was a fitting place for him to die.

The theater was packed, and the people were all nervously chattering.

Tori, Kent, and I took seats in front of the large stage. We had been given that choice position because we had spent the last hour being interrogated by the Chiefs. It turned out that Charlotte was one of them. She hadn't mentioned it before, but it made sense. She knew what she was doing.

We spent the time going over every detail of what we had learned about the Retros. After listening to what we had to say, Charlotte sent us to the Colosseum with another escort so that she and the Chiefs could factor whatever information we had given them into their plans.

The theater was fairly dark since the only lights were battery-powered floodlights that were trained on the stage. Camp lamps were scattered throughout the audience, creating an eerie amosphere in which shadowy people moved through pools of light.

It struck me as risky to have everyone in the same room. If the Retros decided to attack early, a few well-placed bombs would wipe us out entirely.

The crowd hushed when three men and Charlotte walked onto the stage. They were the Chiefs. One of the men was Matt. The second guy went by the name of Harris. No first or last name, just Harris. He had short blond hair and walked like he had a back brace on. Though he had been living in the dark depths of Las Vegas, his white shirt looked as neat and crisp as if he had just ironed it. He definitely looked military. When we were being questioned, he hadn't said much, but he was definitely taking it all in.

The last guy was a beefy character with a shaved head who went by the name of Cutter. Again, no first or last name. He had a thick neck and heavily muscled arms to match. During the interrogation, he was mostly interested to hear anything about how the black planes worked and what they could do. He took particular note of how we described the complete obliteration of so many of the planes when missiles struck their fuel tanks.

These people were professionals. It was easy to see why they were put in charge of planning the attack. All four strode with purpose to the center of the stage and stood in the spotlights.

"Okay, everybody," Matt called out. He didn't have to yell. The acoustics in the theater were perfect.

"We knew something like this would happen eventually," he began. "What can I say? We blew it. The guy slipped through our security. But I want you to know that the kids he came with didn't know what he was up to. They're victims as much as we are."

I felt the heat of a few nasty stares. I don't think everybody agreed that we were totally innocent, and maybe they were right.

Matt continued. "It is what it is. What's more important to

know is that those planes will be back again tonight. Count on it. When it gets dark, Las Vegas will cease to exist."

This prompted nervous murmurs from the crowd.

"Our evacuation plan has us going to Los Angeles," Matt continued. "We can't do that. We learned from the infiltrator that they're planning another wave of mass executions, and the first stop will be LA."

Once again, the crowd broke out with anxious murmurs. Matt had to raise his hands to quiet them down.

"The alternate city for us is San Diego," he announced. "The corridor between LA and San Diego is a busy one. For those who want to go that route, it will be easy enough to disappear. My suggestion is to stay away from the city itself. Any big city. They're going to be targeted again."

A guy stood up in the second row and shouted, "We get it. We gotta get out. But what about the reason we came here?"

Many people shouted their support with "Yeah!" and that got everyone shouting out their opinion.

Matt quieted them down and continued.

"That's what we're here to decide," he said. "We've got to leave here. Today. The question is, do we run? Or do we put the plan in motion that brought us here in the first place?"

Most everyone applauded and cheered the second option. These people were ready for action.

Matt beamed.

"Yeah, that's what I figured. Before we go down that road, you have to understand, it's going to be more dangerous now. We don't believe the infiltrator had any specific knowledge of our plans, so he couldn't pass them along. But the enemy will be on alert now. This mission was never going to be easy, but it just got a hell of a lot more difficult."

The crowd became instantly quiet.

"So I'm putting it out there: If anybody wants to leave, do it now. Nobody will blame you. Take a car and head out. This is your chance. But if you stay, understand that you're in till the end. We can't risk letting any more information get out. If you try to leave after this briefing, you will be shot. I promise you that. I'll give you a minute to think it over."

The normally jovial guy had suddenly turned dark. I believed he meant what he said.

Many in the crowd shared conversations, no doubt rolling around the options.

I knew Tori would want to stay. I couldn't say the same about Kent and Olivia.

"What do you think?" I asked.

"I think I'm scared," Olivia said. "I'm not a guerilla fighter."

She got no argument from me.

"Maybe I should take Olivia out of here," Kent offered. "She won't make it on her own. We'll go to Florida like she wanted in the first place."

Tori said, "So that means you don't want to fight, Kent?"

"No!" Kent said defensively. "I'm just thinking about Olivia. I don't know if she can handle this."

"I can't," she said, obviously shaken. "Look at me. I'm only here because I had nowhere else to go. I don't want any part of a fight. Kent, will you stay with me?"

"You know I will," Kent said reassuringly. "You just saved my life. I owe you, and I won't let anything happen to you. I promise."

I believed he meant it. He really did care about Olivia, and now that she had saved his life he was determined to take care of her. It was out of character for him, which made it all the more noble. Though I respected his feelings, it left me with a huge dilemma. Based on what Captain Granger told me, any one of these three could be Retro infiltrators. I didn't want to believe it, but it was a definite possibility. If Kent and Olivia walked, they could go right to the Retros and tell them we were getting ready to attack, and that would be the end of the survivors. If they wanted to leave, I would have to tell the Chiefs. I had no doubt that they'd assume the worst . . . and that could be the end of Kent and Olivia.

But if they were both innocent, then Olivia was absolutely right. There was no way she could fight, no matter what kind of fight it was.

Neither option was a good one, but if she stayed with us, at least she'd have a chance.

And I could keep an eye on her.

"You can't leave, Olivia," I said. "Neither of you can."

"Why not?" she asked, holding back panic. "Matt said—"

"They're already suspicious of us because we brought Jon in. I don't care what Matt says, if you try to leave they'll assume the worst, and who knows what they'll do. They might just shoot you."

"What?" Olivia cried. "Why?"

"That's what they've done with Retros who tried to infiltrate. I think if you walk out of that door, you're dead."

The two of them looked sick. I was being harsh, but it was the only way I could think of to get them to stay.

Olivia looked to Kent with pleading eyes. "Would they really do that?"

Kent was visibly shaken. "I . . . I don't know. I guess it's possible."

"If you stay, at least you've got a chance," I said. "If you leave . . ."

I let them fill in the rest.

"Now is the time," Matt announced to the crowd. "If you're leaving, go now, and good luck to you."

A handful of people got up and jogged for the exits. Their departure was met with absolute silence. There were no cheers and no insults. There was only stone-cold silence.

I looked at Kent and Olivia. Would they leave? Was I going to have to turn them in as possible traitors?

Olivia fidgeted in her seat.

Kent dropped his head into his hands.

Neither stood up.

It was settled. We would all be in it until the end, together.

When the final door slammed, Matt looked over the crowd.

"Is that it?" he called.

There was no response.

"Fine. I want one person on every door. Nobody comes in, nobody leaves."

A group of men and women scrambled for the exit doors and took up their positions.

"My God," Olivia whispered under her breath. "This can't be happening."

"Are we secure?" Matt called out.

He was answered by the people at the doors, who each called out, "Secure!"

"All right then," Matt bellowed. "We've been preparing for weeks. We've scouted every inch of terrain. We have the plan. We have the will. Today is the day we fight back!"

A roar of approval went up from the crowd.

Kent looked ready to puke.

"Most of you have heard bits and pieces of the plan, but we haven't shared it all for security reasons. It's time you heard it all."

He stepped back, and the Chief with the short blond hair, Harris, stepped into the spotlight. He spoke with the same precision with which he carried himself. His words were clipped and to the point.

"You all know me," he announced. "You also know that I've run many operations for the CIA. There's no sense in keeping that a secret since there no longer is a CIA."

A woman appeared at the end of our aisle with two stacks of paper. She took one from each and passed the stacks to the next person. The same thing happened all over the theater.

"We used gas-powered generators to power the copy machines," Harris explained. "There's nothing classified about the information. We got the images from the city library. One is a road map of the area. The other is a satellite photo. Please take one of each."

When I got mine, I saw that one was a simple road map with Las Vegas near the bottom. There was an *X* designation in the desert that looked to be a hundred miles or so northwest of the city. The other was an aerial photo of what looked like a military air base.

"The map with Las Vegas covers several hundred miles," Harris said. "The *X* marks the location of the airfield you see in the other photo. That base has gone by many names. Groom Lake Test Facility, Paradise Ranch, Watertown, Detachment 3, Air Force Flight Test Center, and several more that refer to the various military detachments that have been based there over the years. It is most commonly known by the simple designation Area 51."

Kent shot me a quick look.

"That's where they keep the aliens!" he whispered.

"It's no secret that this base has been used for decades in the development of advanced military aircraft. Contrary to popular myth, there are no aliens or alien spacecraft hidden there, at least to the best of my knowledge."

I looked at Kent.

He shrugged. "That's what *he* says."

"I know little about the base other than the fact that its primary function was to be an aircraft design and test center. That function has changed. It is now the base from which the Air Force has been launching their attacks."

Matt added, "We've had scouts observing the base for weeks. They see when the fleets take off and when they return. Our guesstimate is that at any given time there are at least seven hundred planes on the ground."

That got gasps of surprise from the crowd.

Seven hundred planes? How could the Air Force have kept that many planes secret from the rest of the world?

Harris continued, "There are no facilities on the base for construction on such a massive scale. Our best guess is that they were assembled at several locations and brought to Nevada. Trust me when I say that the CIA was not aware of it."

Matt said, "From what we learned, they are gearing up for another assault on major cities, starting with Los Angeles. That brings us to our mission."

Matt looked to the bald guy, Cutter. He stepped forward and gazed at the crowd as if sizing them up.

"I have been a proud member of the United States Marine Corps Special Ops for over five years," he began with authority. "I've served in Iran and Afghanistan and a few other places I'd rather not discuss, so I guess I know what I'm talking about, and what I know for certain is that this will be a hazardous undertaking."

The guy sounded a little too proud of himself, but if he knew what he was doing, I wasn't going to criticize.

"Our goal is simple," he said. "We're going to cripple the enemy."

That got a rousing cheer and sustained applause. Cutter stood basking in it.

Matt had to step up and raise his hands to calm everyone down. I think Cutter would have liked the cheering to go on.

"As I said, this will not be easy," Cutter continued. "Small teams will penetrate the base. Each operative will carry ten of these devices."

He held up an object that looked like a silver hockey puck.

"We picked these up on a little shopping trip to Camp Pendleton last week. Each one of these contains enough C-4 to blow a hole through the fuselage and damage the avionics, rendering a drone inoperative. From what we've recently heard, if the charge is anywhere near the plane's power source, it'll do more than just cripple the craft. It'll evaporate it. Either way, if the planes can't fly, people won't die."

That got more cheers.

"Catchy," I whispered to Tori.

She rolled her eyes.

The crowd calmed down, and Cutter continued.

"These devices are completely harmless until the detonator is armed. Observe."

He shook the silver puck. He threw it in the air and caught it. He threw it up and let it bounce off of the stage.

I have to admit, I flinched when it hit the floor.

He stomped on it with his boot. There was no boom.

"You'll go through this again with our group leaders," he explained. "But I will now demonstrate how to make these bad boys dangerous. One: Peel the plastic sheet off of the bottom. That will uncover a layer of adhesive. Two: Slap it onto the fuselage. Trust me, it will not come off. Three: Activate the timer. Each device will be preset to explode exactly thirty minutes after it is made active. The timing is not something you will be able to change. You prime the detonator by entering the four-digit code."

He held the explosive up to show there was a small keypad on the opposite face from the adhesive.

"The code is the same for all the devices. Four-three-two-one. That was my idea. It's easy to remember because there's always a countdown before the boom."

"He's kind of a tool," Tori whispered to me.

Surprisingly, the tool pressed the four buttons.

"Four-three-two-one," he announced.

A green light appeared above the keypad.

"The green light means the clock is ticking. This particular device has been set to detonate in sixty seconds. Six-oh. The only way to disarm it is to input the code in reverse. One-two-three-four. I will not do that."

Even more surprisingly, he didn't.

Cutter moved unhurriedly to the back of the stage and placed the device on the floor.

"Is that thing really going to blow up?" Olivia asked me, incredulous.

From the nervous murmurs in the audience, it was clear that most everyone was wondering the same thing.

"Last thing," Cutter said. "Number four: Get the hell out of there."

He walked quickly to the other Chiefs, herding them protectively to the side of the stage.

The theater had gone deathly quiet. All eyes were on the small silver disk.

"You might want to cover your ears," Cutter announced.

Everyone did as they were told, except Cutter. I guess his ears were too tough.

"This is crazy," Olivia cried. "He wouldn't really—"

The disk exploded with a sharp, short boom that spewed a cloud of smoke from the detonation point.

I jumped, and I'm sure everyone else did too.

It took several seconds for the sound to stop echoing through the huge theater.

Cutter walked calmly back to center stage, waving away the smoke.

"Each one of these devices holds five ounces of C-4," he explained. "This is the result."

A manhole-sized hole had been blasted through the stage floor.

Cutter straddled the damage and said, "These little beauties will tear through the thin hull of a plane like paper. We've got nearly a thousand of these charges. We will put the enemy out of business."

There was a moment of stunned silence, followed by an outburst of emotion. People stood and cheered. They screamed. They whistled. They clapped their hands and patted each other on the back. Cutter stood triumphantly over the hole in the stage and held his arms out as if to embrace the outpouring of emotion.

I have to admit, I got swept up in it too. Before that demonstration I had no idea how a group of untrained civilians could go up against the Retros. Whether it was real or wishful thinking, I now saw the possibility.

We were separated into four groups and sent to smaller rooms to continue the briefing. The four of us went with the group that ended up in a large carpeted meeting room at the Caesars Palace hotel. The room had windows, so we were able to see without headlamps. That was great. But there were no chairs. That wasn't so great. We had to sit on the floor.

The four Chiefs rotated through, each giving us a little more information. With a smaller group we were able to ask questions.

"This all sounds great," one guy said to Harris. "But there's a whole lot of open desert between here and there. What's stopping those Retros from taking us out before we even get there? I mean, we've got some nifty little bombs, but there won't be any armored tanks running cover for us."

"Valid question," Harris answered with cool efficiency. "Our plan is based on one very important bit of information. We do not believe that the base is manned."

Everyone erupted with surprise at hearing that.

Harris sat calmly, waiting for everyone to settle down again.

Kent was the one who stood and put it right to him.

"That's crazy," he said. "It's an Air Force base with hundreds of planes. They've got to be guarding that!"

"You would think," Harris answered. "But we have had eyes on that base for weeks. Mostly the eyes of the Paiute Native American tribe. This is their world."

I remembered the people on horseback in the Valley of Fire who watched as we were being captured by the biker survivors. They must have been tribe members.

"When the base was operative, before the attack, you couldn't get within five miles of the place. The perimeter was under constant surveillance. Now we have scouts who have gotten close enough to see the planes taxiing on the runways. Some have even walked right up to the aircraft parked on the periphery. They've taken note of all the comings and goings. Only on a rare occasion have they seen a living person. So there are people on the base, but not enough of a force to actually defend it."

"How can that be?" someone asked from the back. "Somebody has to be operating the planes."

"They're drones," I said, answering the question for Harris. "We've seen dozens of wrecks. Close up. They aren't large enough for a pilot. They're just flying weapons."

"Exactly," Harris said. "What we don't know is where they are being controlled from. At Area 51 there are very few people. We've seen no deliveries of supplies. No arrivals or departures by plane or car."

"So the base itself could be a drone," Tori said, thinking aloud.

"That's what we think. And because of that, we believe we can send in small teams to get to the planes. Starting two hours before sunset, teams of four will take off in cars, five minutes apart, headed for the base. Each team's map will be marked with the route they should take, where they should leave the main road, and how they should approach the base. All this was provided by the Paiute. Each team member will have ten of the charges you saw Cutter demonstrate. The task is simple: Fix a charge on a plane, activate the timer, repeat the process until all the charges have been set, and get out. You should be at the base for no more than five minutes."

Kent asked, "And where do we go after that?"

"Anywhere you'd like," Harris replied. "Except here or Los Angeles."

"Or any other big city," Kent added.

"This is way riskier than you're thinking," I warned. "There may not be many people there, but these planes have eyes. If one of them catches sight of a caravan of cars headed their way, I don't care if the operator is in the cockpit or sitting at a control console in Russia: They'll come after us."

"Agreed," Harris said. "It's the riskiest aspect of the mission. Our hope is that the enemy will not anticipate us doing anything so audacious and therefore won't be scanning the airfield for intruders. Perhaps there will be an advantage to the fact that they plan to attack Las Vegas tonight. Their attention will be focused here and not on their own base."

Tori said, "So basically we're just hoping they won't be looking."

"Yes, but our confidence is high."

Tori and I exchanged looks. Our confidence wasn't as high.

The briefing continued with Cutter demonstrating how to set the charges again and reminding us that they will detonate thirty minutes after the timer is activated. Matt offered us escape routes and places to disappear after the mission. Charlotte came in to announce that once the mission was complete, the Chiefs would regroup at a yet-to-be-announced location and begin transmitting again to bring the survivors back together.

The whole mission sounded shaky, but the idea of taking out seven hundred of those Retro planes made me want to risk it.

By the time we had finished all of our briefings, it was midafternoon, a few hours before the sabotage teams would start heading toward Area 51. Several people came in with food. They gave us peanut butter and jelly sandwiches, canned fruit, and energy drinks. It wasn't until I had to go to the bathroom and was sent with an escort that I realized nobody was ever left alone. Matt hadn't been kidding. Whoever stayed for the briefing now had vital information that could be sent to the Retros. They weren't taking any chances.

I wondered if my warning to Kent and Olivia had been real. Had the people who took off really been allowed to go? Or were their bodies now lying in the desert?

When I got back from the bathroom, I saw Kent sitting by himself at the far end of the huge room, eating his sandwich. As if the danger of this mission weren't enough, I had the additional stress of knowing that one of my friends might be a Retro infiltrator. My hope was that Granger was wrong about that, but since Jon proved to be a rat, the possibility didn't seem so remote.

In that split second I made a decision to try to find out if I was going to be in even more danger on this already crazy mission, so I took a chance and approached Kent.

"Nervous?" Kent asked as I walked up to him.

He had no idea how appropriate a question that was.

"I gotta ask you something," I said while standing over him. "When we were at Faneuil Hall, where did you disappear to every day?"

Kent stopped chewing. He wasn't expecting that question.

"Whenever I asked, you got all angry and told me to mind my own business," I added.

"Yeah, so?" he said casually. "Now you think it's your business?"

"Yeah, I do," I said boldly.

"Why do you care?" he asked evasively.

"Because after what happened with Jon, I'm not so sure I trust anybody anymore," I said, pretty much spelling out my fear. "We were in a camp run by Retros. What were you doing?"

He *really* didn't expect that from me. Kent sat there and stared me right in the eyes for a good long time. I tensed up, expecting him to leap up and jump me. Kent was a hothead. I knew that from playing football with him.

If he was innocent, he could easily have gotten so pissed at me for questioning him that he might lose it and lash out.

If he was guilty, he was trapped in the middle of a whole bunch of people who just might tear him apart if the truth came out.

Keeping me quiet might be his only play.

He finally took a deep breath and dropped his sandwich on the floor.

"I just lost my appetite," he said ruefully.

I didn't relax.

"I don't owe you any explanation, Pierce," he said. "We're not friends, and I've never liked you much. But we've been through a lot together, and I guess that counts for something, so I'll be honest with you. I didn't tell you what I was doing because I was embarrassed."

It was my turn to be surprised.

"About what?"

"Because I didn't want to work. You and Tori and even Olivia were all pitching in and doing your part and being good little campers, but I didn't want any part of that."

"So what did you do? Nap?"

"Pretty much. I tried to find a place where I could just hang out, but Chris Campbell found me. I thought he was going to be all mad, but he said he had something better I could be doing. He totally busted me, so I had to go along. He didn't take me someplace to work, though; he took me someplace to work out."

"Work out? You mean like at a gym?"

"Exactly. There were a bunch of younger guys working out in an empty health club. Hardcore stuff. Lots of cardio and lifting. Chris said he picked out the most athletic guys to be part of a program to get in top shape in case the time ever came when Faneuil Hall had to be defended. I was psyched. I mean, I like working out, and I was flattered that he thought I was worthy of that responsibility. I was one of the elite who were chosen to protect us all. So here he was giving me a chance to get out of manual labor and do the exact thing I liked so much. I didn't want to tell you guys because I knew you'd say I was slacking."

"You know you weren't getting in shape to defend Faneuil Hall, right?" I asked.

"Yeah, I figured that out. We weren't being trained as commandos; we were being pumped up to be the heavy-lifting slaves at Fenway Park. I thought we were something special, but we were nothing more than trained workhorses. So you can see why I wasn't real proud about letting that out."

"I get it," was all I could say.

"You feel better now, Pierce?" he asked bitterly. "Does that prove I wasn't plotting something evil?"

I almost apologized, but the truth was that while it answered one question, it didn't prove that Kent was innocent.

"I don't care if you like me or not," I said. "But don't keep any more secrets."

Kent chuckled and said, "Don't worry. We'll probably all be dead soon anyway."

"Are you two talking about me?" Olivia asked brightly as she joined us.

"I'm always talking about you," Kent said, being all charming.

He held his hand up to her. She took it and sat down next to him. Close.

"Sit, Tucker," she said.

"Thanks, but my food's over there. I'll talk to you guys later."

I left the two of them feeling only a slight bit better about Kent. At least the biggest suspicion I had about him was put to rest . . .

assuming he was telling the truth. The story sure sounded like typical Kent. He had a very high opinion of himself, and if somebody stroked his ego, he'd go along. Especially if it meant getting out of work. But it still didn't prove that he wasn't a Retro turncoat. And I still had to worry about Tori and Olivia.

I went back to the opposite side of the ballroom to be alone. I wanted time to collect my thoughts and let all of the information sink in. I sat on the floor with my sandwich, ready to eat, but I didn't get the chance.

"We need to talk," Tori said.

"Sure, pull up a piece of carpet."

She sat down and began to eat her sandwich. She didn't jump right in with what she wanted to talk about, which meant something was bothering her. It took a good five minutes of silent eating before she finally opened up.

"I'm not going to be on your team," she announced.

That threw me.

"Uh . . . why?"

"A lot of reasons, but mostly because I don't trust you. There. Done. I'm sorry."

She moved to get up, but I grabbed her arm.

"Wait."

She pulled her arm away but stayed.

"Are you sure?" I asked.

"Yes."

I had to say something. If we left on separate teams, we might never see each other again. I couldn't let it end like that.

"I won't argue," I said. "Do what you gotta do. But I want you to know that I heard everything you told me in Kentucky, and I agree with you. Every move we've made, that I've pushed you guys into making, was about me getting what I wanted. I was wrong. I'm sorry."

Tori nodded. "It wasn't all your fault," she said. "I bought into it. I bought into *you*. I really did believe we needed each other, and for somebody who has taken care of herself for most of her life, that's saying something."

I couldn't have felt any lower.

"That night," she said. "When I begged you to come to Nevada with me . . ."

She had trouble finishing the sentence. The memory stung.

I was wrong—I *could* feel lower.

"I put myself out there," she continued, fighting back tears. "You even told me that you loved me. That moment . . . it seemed as though no matter what happened, we would have each other's backs. Stupid me, huh? You'd already decided to take off on us and go after Granger on your own, didn't you?"

I nodded.

"You should have told me the truth, Tucker," she said, her voice hardening. "The next morning, when I heard what you'd done, that's when it all became clear. I can't tell you how to feel, or what to want, but I deserve to know the truth. We all do."

"I know," I said. "Going after Granger was insane."

"No," Tori said. "Abandoning us was insane."

I couldn't argue with her. Here I had warned Kent about keeping secrets, and I was just as guilty as he was.

"What do you really want, Tucker? What's driving you? Is it

still about getting revenge for Quinn? Do you still think you can go back to Pemberwick Island and mow lawns someday? What is it you think is going to happen?"

She was forcing me to think about things in a way that I had been avoiding for a long time.

"Anger is easy," I said. "It makes sense. So does wanting things to be fixed. It's natural to get all righteous and demand to get back what we lost. It's a lot harder to face the unknown and accept that things can never be the same. So I guess I don't know what I want, and that's the scariest thing of all. Almost as scary as losing your friendship."

I desperately wanted her to look me in the eye, but she wouldn't.

"What is it *you* want, Tori?" I asked. "You've been talking about fighting back, and now you've got your chance. What happens after that?"

Tori stared at the floor for a good long time, giving a lot of thought to her answer.

"What I want isn't about a place," she finally said. "Or going home. Or trying to recapture what I used to have. I'm not so sure I'd want that even if I could have it. What I want is to know what's going to happen tomorrow, and the next day, and to know that somebody will be there with me."

She finally looked at me, and I saw that she had tears in her eyes. That's the moment I fully realized how much I had failed her. She gave me a sad smile and said, "It's the exact same thing I wanted before I ever heard of SYLO."

I wanted to reach out and hold her but didn't dare.

"I wish I could give that to you," I said.

She wiped her eyes and said, "Yeah, well, whatever."

I expected her to leave, but she didn't. It gave me faint hope that maybe we could start over again.

I had been struggling with a decision for a while. It wasn't until that moment that I finally made up my mind. It might prove to be a huge mistake. A fatal one. But I had to take the chance.

"I want to tell you something," I said, lowering my voice to be sure that nobody would overhear. "Back in Fort Knox, before the Retros attacked, Granger told me something that's been torturing me."

"Granger?" Tori said. "Why would you listen to anything he said?"

"Because it made sense."

I had her full attention.

"He told me not to trust anyone. My mother told me the same thing in the SYLO prison."

"So?"

"So he told me that the whole time he was chasing us down, in the rebel camp and through the battle on the ocean, he wasn't after me."

"Of course he was," Tori said, scoffing. "He was after all of us because we were trying to escape from the island."

"No, he wasn't. He was after Retro infiltrators."

"That's bull. There weren't any . . ."

Tori stopped talking, and her eyes went wide. She tried to form words but had trouble putting them together.

"I . . . I'm not a Retro," she finally said.

"I didn't think you were. That's why I'm telling you this."

Tori glanced to the far side of the room, where Olivia and Kent were sitting close to one another, giggling about something.

"I don't believe it," she said, more out of surprise than true disbelief.

"I wish I didn't, but it's hard not to wonder. Especially after what happened with Jon. That's why I put the hardcore press on them to stay."

Tori kept staring at them, as if she were looking for some clue that would tell her they were innocent . . . or not.

"What are you thinking?" I asked.

"What really happened on Pemberwick?" she asked. "Did Granger and SYLO set out to ruin everyone's lives? Or were they trying to protect us?"

"You've said that before. I don't know. It's hard to believe, but it sure makes it easier to accept that my parents were helping him."

"It's time!" Matt announced as he strode into the ballroom.

Everyone slowly got to their feet and stretched.

"Has everyone been assigned to a team?" he asked.

There were general grunts of agreement.

I looked at Tori. This was her chance to bail.

She reached out, took my hand, and gave me a small smile.

I didn't know if she trusted me any more than before, but at least this meant we would be together until the end. I'd take the victories where I could get them.

"Everyone has a starting position?" Matt called out.

Same response.

I looked at the number I was given. Number six. We would be leaving in the sixth wave.

"Good," Matt said. "There's nothing more to say but . . . good luck. I'm proud of you all. Group number one, come with me. I'll come back to fetch the next group shortly."

He strode out of the room as four people hitched up their packs and headed after him. The rest of the room broke out in spontaneous applause. It was a heroes' send-off.

"This is really going to happen," Tori said.

"Sure is!" Kent announced as he joined us.

Olivia was right behind him with wide, nervous eyes.

"I gotta admit," Kent said. "I wasn't sure at first, but now I'm looking forward to this mission. It's gonna feel good to kick those guys where it hurts. Thanks for talking us into this, Tucker."

Olivia winced as if she had been hit in the stomach. She didn't offer me any thanks.

"The main thing we have to do is stay together," I said. "Let's make sure we can always see one another."

"Don't worry," Kent said, as cocky as ever. "I've got your back, whether you think so or not."

"Thanks," I replied. What I didn't say was, "We'd better stay together, because if any of you sneak off, I'll know that you're going to try to warn the Retros."

One by one the teams were called out of the ballroom. Each group got their own round of applause and cheers of encouragement.

During one cheer I leaned in to Tori and whispered, "Did they give you your gun back?"

She nodded.

That was reassuring.

"Team number six!" the escort called.

"That's us!" Kent announced. "Saddle up!"

"Oh God," Olivia blurted out.

As we walked from the room, we got the same applause as the others.

Kent waved to the room like he was some hero who had actually done something to deserve it. Idiot.

The escort led us first to the hotel lobby, where Cutter was waiting with four small backpacks, each holding ten charges.

"You've got your maps?" he asked.

We all nodded.

"Take off at exactly sixteen thirty hours," he said.

"When?" Kent asked, confused.

"Four thirty."

"Oh. Why didn't you just say that?"

Cutter shot him a dirty look and said, "Once you hit the interstate, pick it up to eighty-five miles an hour until you hit the exit point marked on your map. You should have all the charges attached and activated by twenty hundred, uh, eight o'clock. Then get on your horse and out of there, because thirty minutes later . . . boom."

"That's it?" I asked. "That's all the instruction we get?"

"What more do you want?" he asked. "Get out of there *fast*. How's that?"

I didn't like Cutter. He was way too cocky, like he was putting on a show of being a Special Ops guy to impress us.

"Head outside. Charlotte has your ride." He then held out his hand to shake and said, "Good luck, son."

He said it with absolute sincerity and no bluster. That simple gesture made me realize he was just as nervous about what was about to happen as everybody else.

I shook his hand and said, "Thanks. Same to you."

He shook each of our hands. Olivia actually gave him a hug. He wasn't ready for it and was stiff at first, but then loosened up and gave her a reassuring pat on the back.

"I'm sorry you kids have to do this," he said. "But I'm proud that you are. You guys are already heroes. It's an honor to serve with you."

Olivia broke away, and we all headed outside.

Tori whispered to me, "Okay, maybe he's not such a tool after all."

We walked out of the front doors of the hotel, where Charlotte stood in the driveway beside a green Range Rover.

"All gassed up and ready to go," she announced cheerily.

We put our gear in back, and I went right for the driver's side.

"I'll drive, Tori navigates," I announced with authority. I didn't leave any room for discussion.

Charlotte was waiting for me at the driver's door.

"Any questions, pardner?" she asked.

"Only about a million."

"I'm sorry, Tucker. I should have seen through Jon's act."

"That makes all of us," I said. "We spent a lot more time with him."

"But I'm supposedly the expert. It was my job."

She glanced out to the street and the devastation that Jon had brought on. When night fell, it would get far worse.

"I can't believe I'm sending kids off to do something like this," she said wistfully.

"Yeah, well, like you said: We may be young, but we're not kids anymore."

"I know, and it kills me."

She reached out and hugged me.

"You're incredible," she said. "You all are. Please be careful."

"We'll see you afterward," I said. "Somewhere. You realize this is just the beginning."

"Let's hope so," she said.

She walked off to set up the next team, revealing Tori, who had been standing behind her.

"We're really going to do this, aren't we?" she asked.

"Looks like it," I replied. "There's just one thing I gotta know first."

"What's that?"

"Why the hell were you making out with Kent at the racetrack?"

Tori's jaw dropped, and her eyes went wide with shock and embarrassment.

"You saw that?"

I smiled, which broke the tension.

She smiled back and shrugged. "I gave it a shot. What the hell? Big mistake. It was gross."

"Kind of how I felt about being with Olivia in the shower."

"Liar."

"Guilty."

"Hey!" Kent yelled, sticking his head out of the window. "We're on a schedule."

Tori gave me a killer smile and said, "Let's go blow 'em away."

As she hurried around to the passenger side, I gazed out at what was left of Las Vegas. Being part of this operation gave me a jolt of confidence that I hadn't felt in, well, ever. At least not since my old life was destroyed. It was time for payback.

I got in the car, threw it into gear, and hit the gas.

It was a good feeling.

We were finally going on offense.

TWENTY-SIX

The desert is beautiful at sunset.

It was our second journey through the wide-open desolation, and it was just as breathtaking as the first. As the sun dropped toward the distant mountain range, long shadows grew and crept over the desert floor. The colors changed from multiple shades of amber to deep orange to purple and ultimately to black.

Unlike our tense, quiet journey across the country, this trip was full of nervous chatter. The fear of a black Retro jet suddenly appearing over the mountains on its way to blasting us to dust made it difficult to fully appreciate the glories of nature.

"I'm feeling good," Kent declared. "We're gonna get in fast, do what we have to do, and get out even faster. Hit and run. Shock and awe. I'm feelin' it."

He was terrified.

"Where do we go afterward?" Tori asked. "We're pretty much on our own."

"I saw that there's a resort on the California-Nevada border called Primm," I offered. "It's in the middle of nowhere."

"Everywhere out here is the middle of nowhere," Kent said sarcastically.

I ignored him. "I'm thinking we'll find food and a place to sleep. From there we can head west toward the coast."

"Whatever," Kent said. "I'm more focused on the next two hours."

The only person not talking was Olivia.

"You with us, Olivia?" I asked.

"Unfortunately," she replied.

That was about as much of a vote of confidence as we could expect from her. At least she hadn't completely checked out.

I held our speed to eighty-five for the entire time we were on the interstate. We didn't want to catch up to the team ahead of us or lose ground to the team behind. The mission would succeed or fail based on how many of us could get through to the air base. If the Retros smelled trouble, they would have a tough time targeting multiple small targets. At least that was the theory.

"There it goes," Olivia said, sounding wistful.

She was watching the sun disappear behind the distant ridge.

I couldn't help but wonder if we'd ever see it again.

"We should be reaching our turnoff spot soon," I said to Tori.

She checked the map for the four hundredth time.

"It's coming up," she announced.

We reached a fork in the highway and saw the sign that directed us to our next leg.

"Extraterrestrial Highway," Kent read. "Classic."

I made the turn without losing speed. Soon the road began to rise and twist as we crossed over a ridge.

"Won't be long now," I said. "Keep an eye out for a dirt road on our left."

"It's hard to tell where we are," Tori complained. "How are we supposed to see a single-lane dirt road in the middle of—"

"There!" I announced.

If I hadn't been looking hard, we would have missed it. It was an unmarked dirt road that led away from the highway and into the desert . . . toward Area 51. I made the turn and immediately had to slow way down because the road surface was uneven and gravelly.

"I think we've got about twenty miles of this," Tori announced. "Then we look for the contact."

Our contact was a member of the Paiute tribe. The Paiute had escaped with relatively few casualties on the night of the attack. Seems as though the Retros mostly targeted population centers and didn't spend as much time wiping out people who lived in remote villages. It gave me hope that there were many more such survivors scattered all over the country, and the world. Since the attack, the Paiute had been working with the other survivors to scout the air base, help with security, and plan the counterattack.

"It's almost dark," Kent said. "How are we going to see this Injun?"

"Seriously?" I scolded. "Injun?"

Kent shrugged. "Little slack, please. Tasteless comments are allowed when you're putting your life on the line."

I decided to let it go, as did everyone else.

The road was dead flat but led toward another ridge that was covered with scrubby trees and towering rock formations. Somewhere on that rise, our contact would be waiting.

We had traveled for nearly twenty minutes when Tori leaned forward.

"There he is," she announced.

On the side of the road maybe a quarter of a mile ahead was a figure waving a flashlight. I slowed and soon pulled up to an elderly guy who was wearing a cowboy hat, blue work shirt, and jeans.

"Park behind those boulders," the old man instructed.

His face was as deeply lined as the desert. I'd bet that if anybody knew his way around these parts, he and his fellow tribesmen did.

I drove across a stretch of dirt toward a pile of boulders that was fifty yards away. As we drove around to the far side, our headlights set upon our next mode of transportation: a couple of two-seater dune buggies.

"Awesome," Kent said with relish.

"Swell," Olivia moaned with dread.

"Leave your gear here," I said after killing the engine. "Just take the charges. We'll come back for everything afterward."

The old man rounded the boulder pile as we got out of the Range Rover.

"The moon is full tonight," he said. "Travel without headlights. Follow this same road for maybe ten miles. It will take you up through these hills and down to the other side. That's where you'll find it."

"Have you been to the base?" I asked.

The old man looked at the distant hill as if lost in thought. It was an awkward moment. I wasn't sure if he had heard me or understood what I asked.

"It's heap-big trouble out there, right, Tonto?" Kent asked.

I could have hit him.

The old man glared at Kent and said, "Watch your mouth, ass-basket."

"Whoa, sorry, man," Kent said sheepishly. "No offense."

"Yes, I've been there," the man said. "For decades it was closed off. You couldn't get to within a few miles before the military police came out of nowhere to stop you. After the attack, our cell phones went out, so a few of us went to the base looking for answers."

He glared at Kent and added, "Yes, cell phones. We haven't sent smoke signals for a couple of years now."

Kent stared at his shoes.

The old man continued, "We weren't stopped at the outer security perimeter or the main gate. We drove right onto the base. What we found . . ."

His voice caught. It seemed as though he was trying to gather his thoughts. Or come to grips with what he had seen.

"What we found was the angel of death. Only there were hundreds of them, lined up in perfect rows, waiting to fly and spread their poison. The ones we approached were silent. No lights. No hum of engines. But we saw several come to life in the distance and take their turns taxiing to the runway and taking off to . . ."

He couldn't finish the thought. It was too disturbing.

"There weren't any people there at all?" Tori asked. "How is that possible?"

The old man shrugged.

"I don't want to sound like some crazy Indian, but I swear it was like the place was being controlled by an unseen hand. These planes were being moved and manipulated like toys. Giant, deadly toys."

"And nobody tried to stop you?" I asked.

"We never got close to any of the planes that were active. If we had, it might have been different. I know the plan your Chiefs have put together. Chiefs. I love that."

I looked at Kent, who shrugged. "I didn't say anything."

"It can work, so long as you don't come upon a plane that's alive."

"We know that," I assured him. "We've already crossed paths with a few. They can see."

"They cannot see," the old man said sharply. "But they have eyes. They are merely the tools of someone who is not of this earth."

"You mean, like . . . aliens?" Kent asked.

"I mean no one from this earth is capable of committing such wicked crimes against their own kind."

Sobering words, and completely true.

"You must go quickly," the old man said, suddenly all business. "Who will drive?"

"I'll drive Olivia," I said quickly. "Tori, you drive Kent."

"I'm driving," Kent said and sat down in the driver's side of one of the buggies.

It didn't matter to me who drove. I just didn't want Kent and Olivia to suddenly disappear.

"I will wait here until you return," the man said. "If you are not back by midnight, I will assume you will not be coming."

"We'll be back," Kent said cockily. "Once you start hearing the booms, be ready."

He fired up his buggy while Tori slid next to him and strapped on her safety belt. Olivia and I got into our vehicle and strapped in. The old man passed helmets to each of us.

"Once you reach the other side, you might consider leaving the road. It is wide-open space over there."

"Thanks," I said.

The old man reached out his hand and gave me a firm handshake. He tapped Olivia on the shoulder in a grandfatherly gesture.

"Any Indian blessing you can give us?" Kent called out.

"Sure," the old man said. He raised his arms to the heavens and chanted, "O great God of the sky, look over these children and offer them protection so they do not get their asses shot off."

He looked to Kent and added, "How's that, kemosabe?"

Kent gave him a thumbs-up.

With that, I started our engine. It was like being behind the wheel of the go-karts in Denver—times a hundred. These buggies had juice. We were fully encased by a roll bar, though I didn't plan on doing any driving that might end in a roll.

Kent had said it best. Get in fast, get out even faster.

I hit the gas, spun the wheel, and the buggy lurched forward. I led the way, driving back for the dirt road and the hills beyond. The vehicles were so loud that there was no way we could talk without screaming. Just as well. Olivia wasn't in the mood for conversation. She was curled up in her seat in the fetal position, hugging the roll bar. I was worried that when it came time for her to move on her own, she'd freeze. But there was nothing I could do about it, so I kept quiet and focused on driving.

The old man was right. The moon was full, so the desert was lit up like daytime. Good news was that we didn't have to use our headlights. Bad news was that it would be easier for us to be seen from the sky. Or the base.

The road gained elevation quickly as it snaked through the hills. A look back showed me that Kent and Tori weren't following closely. Our tires were kicking up a lot of dust, and they had to hang back or choke on it.

We all had our small packs with the charges between our legs—a vulnerable place to hold explosives, to say the least. I had to keep reminding myself that there was no way they could go off. I envisioned Cutter on that stage dropping the charge and stomping on it. It helped to manage my panic.

We passed a few signs that were difficult to read because of our speed, but the bold headlines were clear enough. I caught the words "Restricted Area" and "No Trespassing." That meant we were inside the first security boundary that had kept curious alien-seeking tourists away for decades. All it did was amp up my adrenaline.

After ten minutes of twisting, bouncing, and coughing through kicked-up dirt, we crested the ridge and got our first view of the desert floor beyond. I skidded to a stop and killed the engine. Kent drove up right next to us and stopped as well. It was going to take a few minutes to process what we were seeing.

I could understand why the military had chosen this place to test their planes. The desert floor stretched out in front of us for what looked like hundreds of miles in every direction. It was a dead-flat natural airfield surrounded by protective mountains.

Straight ahead, maybe thirty miles away, was the air base known as Area 51. It was nestled at the base of a small ridge of mountains that loomed up behind it.

The base was lit. It had power.

The buildings were dark, but the lights on the ground outlined the runways. It looked like a medium-sized airport, complete with large hangars and many smaller buildings that could have been for maintenance, or manufacturing, or offices, or vaults to hide aliens, for all I knew. There was nothing about the physical base itself that seemed out of the ordinary.

The stunner was what we saw on the runways.

They were there. The black planes. Hundreds of them. Many hundreds. They were lined up, curved wing to curved wing, looking like a massive school of dark stingrays waiting to wipe out what was left of mankind.

"If we're primates," Tori said, stunned, "what are they?"

Olivia was whimpering. I didn't blame her. The sight of these murderous planes was beyond disturbing. Knowing that they were preparing to set out on another killing spree to wipe out those they missed the first time around was almost too much to comprehend.

Almost.

Seeing these planes may have been sobering, but it also forced me to focus on the job at hand.

"We came here to fight back," I said. "I never thought we'd make it this far, but here we are. We've got the chance to shut this place down, and I believe we're going to do it."

"Now you're talking, commander," Kent said and clapped me on the back.

"But for how long?" Tori asked. "Are these all the planes they have? Or can they just build more?"

"We aren't the only survivors," I said. "There are millions of others. Taking out these planes might buy time for a real counterattack. Who knows? Maybe it'll come from SYLO. If we knock the Retros off-balance, it might give SYLO a chance to finish them off."

"SYLO?" Kent said, surprised. "Since when did you start rooting for those jack wagons?"

"We think they were trying to protect Pemberwick Island, Kent," Tori said.

"By trying to kill us?" Kent asked, incredulous.

I wasn't about to tell them what Granger had said about one of my friends being an infiltrator.

I said, "All I know is that the planes from this base wiped out three-quarters of the world's population. Who would you rather side with? Monsters who consider us to be worthless animals? Or the people trying to stop them?"

"I'll side with the winner," Olivia said sadly.

"All right," I declared. "Then let's win."

"No!" Tori cried.

"No?" Kent echoed.

"Shut up!" Tori shouted. "Something's in the air."

We heard it before we saw it. It was a helicopter. The sound of the engine was unmistakable, and it was getting louder.

"Let's go!" I shouted and ran for the dune buggy.

Kent and Tori jumped into theirs, and we all strapped in quickly.

"It has to be SYLO," Tori called out. "The Retros don't fly choppers."

"Let's hope they really are trying to protect us," Kent shouted.

"Let's hope they don't lure out any Retros," I called back.

"There!" Tori called out and pointed to the sky.

All we could see was a black shadow moving across the star

field, for the chopper had no lights. It was flying high—too high to spot us. I hoped. It drifted in from the direction we had come from and hovered directly over us.

I held my breath, for whatever good that would do.

All of our eyes were on the black shape. Even Olivia looked skyward.

The chopper hovered there for several seconds, then peeled off and flew back the way it had come.

"What if it saw us?" Kent asked nervously. "It could be going back to get more choppers."

"Why?" Tori asked. "Why would they be worrying about us?"

"Seriously?" Kent said incredulously. "Did you forget how Granger tried to gun us down? I don't care why he was doing it, he did it."

I knew why he was doing it, but I kept quiet.

"If Kent's right, we don't want to be here," I declared. "If not, we still don't want to be here. We've got a job to do."

"Then let's roll," Tori declared and popped on her helmet.

"When we hit the desert floor, we'll go off-road," I called to Kent. "We can travel next to each other to avoid the dust storm and then stop a few hundred yards from the closest plane. Make sense?"

"Yippee ki-yay!" Kent called.

We fired up our engines, and the sound of powerful motors once again filled the desert night. I hit the gas and launched forward, careening down the road that snaked its way from the ridge. It took only a few minutes before the road leveled out and we were back on the desert floor. Another huge sign was displayed next to the road that said, not too subtly, that we were in a restricted area and were subject to arrest. There was also a sign that said: NO PHOTOGRAPHY.

I yelled to Olivia, "Good thing we don't have a camera or we'd *really* be in trouble!"

She didn't find that funny.

Kent and Tori caught up, and Kent gave me a thumbs-up.

I motioned that I was headed off-road, and he nodded in understanding. I jammed my foot to the floor, turned the wheel, and rolled onto the dry, flat lake bed that would lead us to the infamous Area 51.

There was no way to know if we'd have success, or what that success would mean in the larger war. There was every reason to believe that we would never make it out of this place. Only one thing was certain: We were on the last leg of a journey that began on Pemberwick Island, brought us through the nightmare that our country had become, and found us knocking on the gates of hell.

What we would find once we got inside was anybody's guess.

TWENTY-SEVEN

Driving across the desert floor was exciting . . . and terrifying.

It was a breakneck dash across wide-open terrain that left us totally exposed as we moved closer to the death machines that had changed our lives and forever altered the natural course of human events.

I was glad to be behind the wheel. It helped me stay focused. There were too many conflicting thoughts racing through my head. For the longest time, I had put a face on the enemy. Captain Granger. He had held us prisoner on Pemberwick Island and coldly murdered those who crossed him, including Tori's father. But as the scope of the conflict revealed itself, it seemed possible that Captain Granger and SYLO might have been using their extreme tactics to battle an even greater enemy: the Retros.

I had come close to murdering Granger. That's how deep my rage went. It was confusing to try to refocus that anger onto a fleet of faceless machines. I needed to hold someone responsible. But who? Was it Feit? I didn't think so. He was just a cog in the machine, like Chris Campbell or Jon Purcell. I wanted to know who was behind the heinous plan. Was it an individual? A rogue group of Air Force officers? An extremist arm of the government that took control of the Air Force and its most advanced, lethal technology? It might even be a foreign government that was intent on bringing down the United States.

Or was Kent's theory the truth? Were we battling an invasion from another planet? As strange as it sounds, that would be the easiest explanation to accept, based on the impossible technology they had. It went back to what the old Paiute man said. He couldn't believe that anyone of this earth could commit such horrible crimes against their own people. We might be battling an advanced civilization from another world that considered the people of earth to be primitive and expendable.

I wanted to hate somebody. I wanted a villain. I wanted somebody to suffer for what was happening. I would have to settle for putting the villains out of business and hope that someday, somehow, the guilty would be brought to justice.

I scanned the desert to both sides, looking for signs of the other teams that were doing the same thing we were. The Chiefs' plan called for the base to be surrounded by dozens of teams that would converge on Area 51 like a tightening noose. I thought I saw a couple of kicked-up dust clouds in the distance, which would mean that other teams were racing for the planes. We would need every one of the teams to get through, because after seeing all those black planes, I worried that we wouldn't have enough charges to damage them all.

As we drew dangerously close to the base, I realized that there wasn't a fence surrounding it. I guess it wasn't needed. Nobody got this far when it was officially in operation.

I wanted to get close enough to our targets to avoid a long

walk but didn't want to get so close that we might alert someone. It was a strange game of chicken. I finally couldn't take it anymore and waved to Kent that we were stopping. I gradually slowed as Kent pulled up next to me. We both killed our engines, and the silence of the desert returned.

I pulled off my helmet and listened for any signs of life from the base. There was nothing. I did hear what could have been the engines of other dune buggies off in the distance. Or was it the mysterious helicopter that had checked us out? I couldn't tell, but it made me realize that as much as we hadn't seen a single soul since the Paiute man and were in the middle of nowhere, we definitely weren't alone. But there were no alarms. No counterattack. No defensive move from the base whatsoever.

It was looking as though the base was truly unmanned.

I got out of the buggy, tossed off my helmet, and grabbed the pack with the charges.

"Rest of the way on foot," I announced.

Kent and Tori joined me, ready to go.

Olivia didn't move.

Uh-oh.

"We gotta go, Olivia," I commanded.

She took off her helmet but stayed curled in the fetal position.

"I can't," she replied in a small voice.

"We can't leave you here," Tori scolded.

"Yes, you can," she whined. "One less person won't make any difference. Take my stupid bombs. You can still use them."

Tori gave me a concerned look. "We're not leaving you alone," she said more forcefully. "It's too dangerous."

"More dangerous than going into that place?" she cried. "I don't think so."

She could have been telling the truth and was too scared to move—or she could have been stubbornly pretending to be scared so we'd leave her alone so she could warn the Retros. Either way, I didn't know how to force her to come.

"Jeez, enough, Tucker," Kent said. "You already bullied her into coming this far. What's the difference if she stays here or not? I'll take her charges and set them."

"Thank you, Kent," Olivia said.

I looked to Tori for help.

She had an idea, but it was a drastic one.

She had taken out her pistol.

If Olivia was an infiltrator, she could jeopardize the entire mission. If she refused to come with us, there was one thing we could do to make sure she wouldn't give us up.

Tori raised the gun.

"No," I commanded sharply.

It was meant for both Kent and Tori.

I grabbed Olivia's pack of charges.

"I'll set her charges." I then looked right at Tori and said, "Olivia will be here when we get back." I looked at Olivia and added, "Right?"

"Where else would I be?" she asked innocently.

Tori gave me a grave look and returned her pistol to her belt.

I could only hope that I wasn't making a horrible mistake. I wanted to believe that Olivia was exactly who she said she was, but I had to accept the fact that she could have been lying. But so what?

What could I do about it? If I couldn't pull the trigger on Granger, I sure as hell couldn't pull it on Olivia. Or let Tori do it.

But what if I was wrong? No, I had to go with my gut and let her stay behind. I told myself that the operation was already too far along. Even if Olivia was an infiltrator, there wasn't much she could do to stop it.

That's what I told myself, anyway.

Kent knelt down next to Olivia and smoothed her hair.

"We won't be long," he said soothingly. "You'll be fine here."

He really did care about her, in spite of the fact that he kept trying to hook up with Tori. Kent may have been a dog, but he had genuine affection for the girl who had saved his life.

"Thank you," Olivia said. "I'm sorry. I just can't."

"Olivia," I said and waited until she looked at me before continuing. "You're a good person. I know you are. We don't have to leave you here, but we will because you're our friend and we care about you. Please remember that."

She closed her eyes, as if trying to keep from crying.

"I'll be here," she said softly.

I believed her. I didn't think she would do anything to hurt us.

Either that or I was an incredibly bad judge of character.

"Let's go," I said while hoisting the second pack of charges onto my shoulder.

Kent kissed her on the cheek. "Be right back." He joined Tori and me and declared, "Now or never."

The three of us strode toward the base.

"You sure about this?" Tori asked me.

"No," was my honest reply.

"I am," Kent said. "We are taking this place down."

We had stopped driving a few hundred yards from the edge of the first taxiway where several black planes were lined up, nose-to-tail and wing-to-wing. Until then, we had only seen them in flight, or crashed. Now they were sitting on landing gear. Each had a tripod base that kept the craft a few feet off the ground. They didn't need wheels since they were able to take off and land vertically.

"I feel like we're entering a den of sleeping lions," Tori said with an uncharacteristic quiver in her voice.

I raised my hand, and we stopped fifty yards from the first plane.

"They're in perfect rows," I said. "We'll each take one row and work our way in. Kent, you take the middle row. We'll be to either side of you."

I wanted Kent between us so that Tori and I could keep an eye on him to make sure he was doing what he was supposed to be doing. Unlike with Olivia, I didn't trust Kent.

"What about the extra charges?" Tori asked.

"You two wait for me at the last plane Kent sets. I'll keep going and meet you back there."

"Fine," Kent said. His voice was shaky too. "Let's just get this done."

We moved quickly, covering the last empty stretch in silence. We went directly to one plane and stopped.

Being so close to the sleeping beast made my stomach twist—and there were hundreds of them. The plane was a machine designed for killing. There was no other way to put it. Moonlight reflected off of the slick, dark logo of the United States Air Force.

All the questions as to why our own military would try to over-throw and control the world came roaring back.

But it wasn't time to theorize.

It was time to fight back.

I pointed to the first plane, then to Kent. He nodded. That was his row. I pointed to the plane to its right, then to Tori. She got it. I pointed to myself and then to the plane that began the row to the left. That was mine. I clapped Kent on the back to get him moving. He hesitated a second, took a deep breath, and sprinted for the plane. I looked at Tori, pointed to my eyes, and then to Kent.

She knew what I meant. We had to watch him.

I then leaned over . . . and kissed her.

She touched my cheek, gave me a small smile, and took off running for her plane.

The faster we could get this done, the faster we could get out of there. In the back of my mind I felt that even if Olivia surprised me and betrayed us, we could get in and out before any Retros showed up . . . assuming there were any Retros around. This seemed like a fully automated operation that was controlled from somewhere else.

I sprinted for my plane while pulling the first pack of charges from my shoulder. I tried not to think of the destructive power each of these little bombs contained. If one went off in my hand, I'd be dead. I had to have faith in Cutter and his lethal toys.

I reached the first plane, knelt down, and quickly pulled out one of the charges. Without stopping to think about anything that might go wrong, I peeled back the protective plastic sheet on the bottom and pressed the disk against the underbelly of the plane as close to the center as I could get. Having the planes up on their tripods made it easier to place the charges in what I hoped was a vulnerable spot. Once the charge was secure, I entered the code, 4-3-2-1, and the green light flashed on.

I clicked my watch into stopwatch mode and hit start.

We had thirty minutes to get out of there.

I looked over to the next row of planes, which was twenty yards away. Kent was under the plane on his back, setting his own charge. He finished, then crawled and headed for the next plane in line. So far, so good.

I did the same.

Cutter was right. It was simple. I moved to the next plane and repeated the process. I imagined the same thing happening all over the base. Hundreds of survivors were crawling on their bellies, dropping off little packages of revenge . . . and hope. The action meant we weren't powerless after all. Did it mean we could win our old lives back? That might have been too optimistic. But at least it offered some hope that we had a shot.

I kept looking over at Kent and caught glimpses of him repeating the same process. It gave me confidence that Kent was legit . . . and even more concern about Olivia.

I soon planted the last of my ten charges. Once I had set the timer, I looked to see Kent and Tori waiting for me beneath Kent's last plane. I hurried over to join them.

"I'll make this quick," I said.

"Give me half of them," Kent demanded.

"No," I shot back, maybe too quickly. "Wait here. I'll be right back."

I didn't give him a chance to argue and took off for the next plane in the row where he had been working. I dug into Olivia's bag and found the first charge. Setting the next set was as easy as the first. However, when I set the eighth charge, I found myself at the edge of an empty stretch of taxiway. At the far end, maybe a hundred yards away, sat an enormous hangar . . . that was coming to life.

I stayed under the eighth plane for whatever cover it would give me and watched with growing fear as bright light seeped from the edges of the gigantic single door. It was the first sign of activity at the base.

My hope was that whatever was inside was being controlled from somewhere far away and whoever was at the console would have no idea that hundreds of saboteurs were silently swarming the place.

But my fear was that Olivia had sounded the alarm. I was about to scramble to the next planes to set the final charges when I saw movement near the hangar. A soldier wearing black-and-gray camouflage fatigues and a black beret walked around from the far side and crossed in front of the door.

Hanging from his belt was a black baton weapon.

The base wasn't empty after all. There were Retro soldiers here.

Still, there was only one, and if he knew the base was infested with enemies, he didn't show it. He was far enough away that I felt I could still set the last two charges and get out of there, but I had to be careful. I didn't want to draw his attention to my movement. I lay flat on my belly and crawled toward the next line of planes, trying my best to be invisible. I slipped under the plane and got up on my knees to set the next charge . . . when I heard a sharp *crack* sound and was suddenly thrown back onto my butt by a powerful blast from . . . I didn't know what.

Had the charge gone off? That wasn't likely, because there was no bang, and I was still in one piece.

"Get out from there!" a man yelled.

Guess I hadn't tried hard enough to be invisible.

I saw a hole in the side of the plane that could easily have been in my head. The shot had barely missed me, but its charge was still powerful enough to knock me down as it flew by. This guy was shooting to kill. I looked up to see the soldier from the hangar charging my way.

I ducked underneath the plane, scrambled to the far side, got back to my feet, and started to run . . .

. . . as I heard the low crack of another weapon being fired. I felt the surge of energy blow past my head, making my hair stand up. It missed me by inches and nailed another plane. This guy was way more concerned about stopping me than avoiding damage to the aircraft. I took a sharp turn around the plane, away from where I knew Tori and Kent were hiding . . . only to come face-to-face with the pursuer.

It wasn't the guy from the hangar. It was a second soldier, and he was only a few yards away from me, with his black weapon up and leveled at me.

I froze.

"Who the hell are you?" he called.

I had the brief thought that he had no idea that anybody else was on the base. Maybe the alarm hadn't been sounded after all. I was just stupid enough to have been spotted.

"Uh . . . ," I stammered. "I wanted to see what was going on here."

"Now you see," he called back. "And now you're dead."

He tightened up, ready to fire. My brain locked. All I could do was brace myself for the end. I wondered how badly it would hurt.

There was a gunshot—but I wasn't hit.

Can't say the same for the soldier. He fell to the deck, dropping his weapon.

"Come on!" Tori shouted.

She and Kent had come running as soon as the shooting started. Tori held her pistol.

"Come *on*!" Kent whisper-yelled.

I was still too stunned to think quickly. I turned their way, ready to run, when—

"Stop right there!"

The soldier from the hangar had arrived, and he wasn't waiting for an introduction. Tori lifted her pistol and fired, but he was too far away for her to be accurate.

The soldier didn't have the same challenge. He stood only a few yards from me. Point-blank range. I had nowhere to go. No place to take cover.

He took aim at me.

It was all going to end right there.

The soldier fired . . .

. . . as someone jumped out in front of me.

Olivia.

"What?" I screamed in stunned wonder.

She took the lethal charge square in the chest and, with an anguished cry, fell to the ground.

The soldier stood there as stunned as I was, but not for long. He raised the baton again . . .

. . . too late. Tori had closed the distance and unloaded her clip, firing wildly at the soldier. He turned to fire at her but was thrown back from the impact of more than one bullet.

I knelt down over Olivia and was yanked away forcefully . . . by Kent. As I fell back, he huddled down next to her and lifted her head into his lap.

"You're okay," he cried in panic. "We'll get you back. They'll fix you."

There was no obvious wound or blood. Whatever weapons these guys used acted differently on living beings, much like their light weapons. Still, even without any obvious wound, it was clear that Olivia was hurt. Badly.

She looked up at Kent with surprisingly focused eyes and said, "It's okay."

Kent was in tears. He tried to lift her, but Olivia cried out in pain, so he eased her back to the tarmac.

"No, no, you are not going to die," he wept. "I'm not going to let you die."

Tori and I knelt over her, opposite Kent.

Olivia grasped Kent's hand and squeezed weakly.

She looked up at me and said, "I'm sorry. For everything."

"You saved my life," I said, choking back my own tears. "There's nothing to be sorry for. I don't know what to say to thank you."

She smiled. For a brief moment I saw the beautiful, flirty girl in the red bikini who I had an instant crush on the moment she arrived on Pemberwick Island.

"Just say you'll forgive me," she said.

"I forgive you," I said, though I wasn't sure for what.

She gave me a weak smile and said, "You're right, Tucker. I really am a good person."

"Hang on, Olivia," Kent cried. "We'll carry you to—"

Olivia's eyes closed.

"No . . . no . . . ," Kent cried.

He caressed her hair, willing her to come back.

Tori put a hand on Kent's arm to quiet him.

He looked at Tori with an expression of stunned anguish like I had never seen before and hope I never will again.

Tori put a finger on Olivia's neck to check her pulse. Those few seconds felt like a lifetime.

"She's gone," Tori whispered.

The girl in the red bikini, the girl I had spent my last normal summer with before fleeing together from untold dangers, was dead.

I was numb.

Kent wasn't. I felt his rage grow like heat that pulsed from his body. He gently eased Olivia's head to the ground, then lashed out and pushed me to the ground.

"You killed her," he growled through gritted teeth. "You forced her to come here, and she died to save you."

He wound up, ready to hit me, but Tori tackled him, knocking him to the ground.

"Stop!" she commanded.

Tori was strong. Maybe stronger than Kent. She wrestled with him and wrapped him up with a bear hug.

"I told her I'd protect her," Kent wailed as he fought to get to me, "and he killed her."

I jumped to my feet and pinned Kent to the ground. Between the two of us, he couldn't move.

"Get a grip!" I commanded with a stern whisper. "Or we're all dead. There have to be more soldiers around."

"I'll kill you," he growled. "I swear I'll kill you."

Tori stuck her nose right in Kent's face and spoke in an intense whisper. "If we don't get out of here right now, we'll *all* die."

"I want to die," he said, crying. He pointed at me and added, "And I'm taking him with me."

A loud horn sounded that echoed across the desert floor. Was it an alarm? Would more soldiers come running?

The huge hangar door began to open. The intermittent horn was an alert, like the beeping of a truck backing up.

Kent stopped struggling as we all focused on the event.

What was in that hangar? We should have run, but none of us made a move. We wanted to know.

Bright light blasted out from within, making me squint. I released Kent and shaded my eyes from the intense blast.

Kent didn't run or attack me. He was as mesmerized by the sight as Tori and I were.

"There's something in there," I said. "Something big."

The door continued to open, revealing what at first appeared to be a black shadow. As my eyes adjusted to the light, I realized the truth.

"Oh my God," Tori said, breathless.

"Is that what I think it is?" Kent asked, stunned.

It was.

It was a black Retro plane.

A giant one.

It had to be ten times the size of the others. It was the exact same design, looking like a giant stingray, but the tips of its curved wings stretched out so wide that I wasn't sure if it would fit through the huge hangar door.

"That's how they're going to do it," I said, my head swimming.

"Do what?" Tori asked.

"Wipe out Las Vegas," I said. "It took three of those smaller planes working together to create the beams of light that destroyed buildings. That thing has got to have the power to do it alone."

"And it won't stop there," Tori said, dazed.

"No," I added. "Los Angeles."

"So all this was for nothing?" she asked with more than a touch of desperation.

"No," I replied. "We're not done yet."

I stood up and started running for the hangar.

TWENTY-EIGHT

It was my turn to get tackled.

Tori grabbed me from behind and, with incredible strength for someone so small, held me in place.

"No," she barked. "It's suicide."

"So what?" I said. "We're all going to die anyway."

"What do you think you're going to do?"

I held up the pack with the last two charges.

"It may not be enough to bring down something that big, but they'll definitely do some damage. Maybe enough to keep it from taking off."

"No, not again. You're not going alone!"

She was scared, and I didn't blame her. Tori was tough. Heck, she'd just gunned down two soldiers. But when it came to losing someone close to her, she broke down.

"It'll be okay," I said softly, trying to sound as though I was in control enough to be making smart decisions. "I'll set the charges and be right back."

"This isn't your show, Tucker," she scolded. "You think you

can do everything on your own, but you can't. If there's anything I learned about myself, it's that. I told you how much we needed you. How much *I* needed you. Well, you need me too."

"I don't want you to get hurt," was all I could think of saying, because it was the absolute truth.

Tori smiled and said, "I think we're way beyond that. Give me one of the charges. With two of us planting them, there's a better chance of one of them having some meaning."

Her moment of weakness was over. I knew her well enough to know that it was impossible to talk her out of something once her mind was set.

Besides, she was right. I needed her.

A loud hum came from the hangar. The giant craft stood eight feet off the ground on the same kind of tripod as the smaller fighters. Light appeared beneath the plane as a section of its belly dropped down to create a ramp. A guy wearing a gray Air Force flight suit appeared from inside and walked down.

"This one's not a drone," Tori declared.

The pilot, or whatever he was, left the plane and casually walked deeper into the hangar. He had no idea that a gun battle had taken place outside and three people lay dead on the tarmac.

"Give me one of the charges, Tucker," Tori demanded.

I reached into the bag, pulled out the remaining two disks, and gave her one. I stuck the other into my back pocket and tossed the pack. However this was going to play out, we were going to be in it together.

Kent had gone back to Olivia. He sat on the tarmac with her head in his lap.

In spite of Olivia's quirkiness and dangerous games, I really had liked her. We'd only known each other since the beginning of summer, but her sense of humor and constant quest for fun made it one of the best summers ever. Once the trouble began, in spite of her constant complaints, when put to the test she always rose to the occasion. She cared for Tori when she was shot. She ran down a Retro plane that was about to blow us away. She saved Kent from being killed in the casino. And in the end she gave up her life to save mine. When all was said and done, Olivia may have been the strongest one of us all.

Not that it mattered anymore, but her sacrifice proved she wasn't a Retro.

"I'm sorry, Kent," I said. "I cared about Olivia too."

As badly as I felt for Kent, I was angry with him for not letting me process my own feelings about Olivia's death and her sacrifice. But it wasn't the time to fight that fight.

"Go," he said while keeping his eyes on Olivia's serene face. "Set the charges and run. But don't come back here. If I see you again, I'll kill you myself."

I knew Kent was speaking from a dark, raw place, but his words still rocked me.

"Then Olivia will have died for nothing," Tori scolded.

Kent reacted as if stung.

"She shouldn't have been here at all," he said with anger. "If he hadn't bullied her into it, she'd still be alive. I won't forget that."

"Neither will I," I said. "Try to save your anger for the Retros."

"I will," he declared. "And when they're done, I'm coming for you."

"Take Olivia back to the dune buggies," Tori said. "We'll meet you there."

"Don't," Kent said and turned his back. "I mean it."

His anger aside, there was a good possibility that we would never see Kent Berringer again. I'm sorry to say that I didn't like the guy. His family's wealth made him act as though he was better than everyone else, especially those who worked for them, like my father and me. He never missed a chance to put somebody down or show off. We had been thrust together because of the quarantine and then the war. We never would have been friends otherwise. But still, we had been through more together than most close friends.

All of that made it hard to believe that he was a Retro infiltrator. It was beginning to look as though Granger was dead wrong.

I felt horrible that Olivia was dead, and I felt bad for Kent. I truly believed that he loved her. I understood his anger toward me. I wished we could have made peace before going our own ways.

It had come to this: Quinn was dead. Jon was a dead traitor. Olivia died to save my life. And Kent had checked out.

Tori and I were the last ones still fighting.

Maybe that's the way it was supposed to be.

An explosion rocked the tarmac. It was far away but unmistakable. It was followed by another, and another.

"The first team," Tori said. "Their charges are going off."

The sound came from the far side of the base. It was the spot where the initial teams were told to infiltrate. The explosions kept coming, roughly a minute apart as the detonators wound down to zero. Small clouds of smoke drifted up in the distance. It was satisfying to know that each explosion meant another plane wouldn't fly. Things were going exactly as planned—except with us.

The giant plane in the hangar made destroying the small planes seem like a waste of time.

Another pilot ran down the ramp of the massive plane and joined the first. The two hurried out of the hangar toward the sound of the explosions.

This was our chance.

We took off on a dead run for the hangar.

Explosions continued to erupt in the distance as the destruction spread. The Chiefs' plan was working perfectly. The noose had tightened around Area 51.

A fire alarm sounded, and the roar of emergency trucks racing toward trouble could be heard in the distance. That meant there actually were some people manning the base. They must have been maintenance people because they sure weren't concerned with security.

Until then.

As we ran for the brightly lit hangar, I scanned back and forth, looking for an armed soldier, or another pilot, or a firefighter, or anybody who might try to stop us.

"We should put these on opposite sides of the underbelly," Tori said, breathless.

"No," I countered. "I don't want to take any chances."

"What does that mean?"

"I'm going on board."

Tori didn't argue. We were past debating anything.

We entered the hangar and stopped only a few feet from the beast. The giant plane loomed over us, looking far bigger than it did from outside. We stood together gazing up at the behemoth in wonder and fear.

"It really is the angel of death," Tori whispered.

"So let's kill it."

We headed for the ramp. Before stepping up, I looked back at Tori to suggest she take out her gun. I needn't have bothered. She already had it out. She gave me a nod of confidence that I sorely needed. I took a deep, nervous breath and climbed up.

The ramp brought us into the belly of the plane. It was a cavernous cargo bay, which meant the plane was used to transport large items . . . when it wasn't wiping out civilizations. The skeleton of the plane was visible, along with the supports and joints. This was a practical vehicle. It wasn't built for comfort. The entire structure looked like it was made of the same black composite material as the outside skin.

Ahead, toward the nose of the plane, was a closed hatch that looked as if it would lead to the cockpit. Since the two pilots were gone, I didn't worry about anybody being there. Just the same, I put my finger to my lips as a warning for Tori to be quiet.

There were a couple of jump seats along the bulkhead, but this plane wasn't designed for transporting people. On one side of the enormous bay was a large silver canister the size of a hot-water tank. I'd seen the miniature version before. It looked exactly like the devices we had seen in the wreckage of the fallen planes.

It was the laser weapon.

"This isn't good," I said.

Tori shook her head with awe.

My fear about what this plane could do was justified. This weapon was far bigger and probably way more powerful than the ones carried in the fighters. When the smaller planes fired on Tori's father's boat and killed Quinn, it took the combined light beams from three different planes to create a single, intense ray of energy that was strong enough to disintegrate the boat. And Quinn.

I had to believe that the bad boy on this giant craft didn't need any help.

I pulled out the explosive disk and nudged Tori to do the same.

"Put yours in the middle of that thing," I said, pointing to the weapon. "Fix it low so it won't be obvious."

"What about yours?" she asked.

"I'll find someplace where it will do the most damage."

Tori went to the weapon to lay her charge while I scanned the craft for something that looked like an engine. I skirted the hatch opening at the top of the ramp and went for the tail. These weren't ordinary planes with traditional jet engines. Instead of the roar that comes from fuel-burning turbines, these planes emitted oddly pleasant musical notes. What kind of engine did that? What did it look like?

The hold was as wide as it was long. This was no sleek, stream-lined aircraft. It was shaped more like a sci-fi flying saucer than an aerodynamically efficient jet. But these things could move and maneuver way better than any conventional jet. They could take off and land vertically, hover in place, and launch in an instant, all while firing their weapons.

I walked to the rear to see a silver-metallic cabinet that ran the width of the craft. It came up to my waist and was four feet deep with a flat surface. It was sealed. There was no way to see what was inside. I tentatively reached out, put my palm on the top—and quickly pulled it back.

The surface was warm. My hand tingled. Whatever was inside was active. It may have been the engine, or the fuel supply, or the powerful weapon that worked during the day firing bursts of destructive energy for all I knew. Whatever it was, it was an integral part of the plane. It was as good a place as any to set my charge.

I pulled the disk out of my pocket, peeled off the protective layer to reveal the glue side, and fixed it to the dead center of the cabinet near the deck.

"What is that thing?" Tori asked as she joined me.

"I'm hoping it's the engine."

I programmed in the code and entered it, then reset my stopwatch to zero.

In thirty minutes the plane would be crippled.

"Let's get out of here," Tori said.

She got no argument from me. We started for the front of the plane . . .

. . . as one of the pilots charged up the ramp.

We froze. If he turned around, he'd see us and we'd be done.

The guy was in too big of a hurry to do anything but sprint to the hatch at the front of the plane. When he opened it, I caught a quick glimpse of a high-tech console with multiple computer screens. It had to be the cockpit. The pilot jumped inside and slammed the hatch behind him.

"We gotta go, now," I said and pulled Tori toward the ramp.

A high-pitched whine filled the cargo area as the ramp began to lift back into the plane.

"No!" Tori cried.

We dove for the rapidly shrinking exit . . . too late. The ramp had become a hatch that sealed the plane with a solid, sucking sound.

We were trapped on board.

"Look around for a release lever," I urged.

We began a frantic search for an emergency release that would blow open the hatch.

We came up empty.

Tori whispered, "It's okay. Relax. We've got half an hour. By then we'll find a way to get—"

The plane lurched.

We were moving.

I heard the musical notes. They were coming from the sealed locker at the rear of the plane. At least I was right about one thing: That was the engine. There was a slight tremor that told us we were under power. There was another bump and the unmistakable sway that meant we were airborne. A mechanical humming followed, which must have been the landing tripod retracting. The plane lurched again. We were moving, which made it difficult to stand upright. Without windows, we had no visual reference to tell us which way we were going or how fast.

"The cockpit," I said. "Get your gun."

She gave me a quick, nervous look but shook it off and pulled out the Glock. We managed to stumble our way toward the hatch. Tori stood with her feet planted and the gun stabilized with both hands while I went for the small handle. She gave me a quick "ready" nod. I reached for the handle . . .

. . . and we were both thrown to the deck.

The plane had accelerated so quickly that we had no time to brace ourselves. We were climbing, fast. Tori and I were thrown to the deck and had trouble sitting up under the g-force caused by the acceleration.

"The seats!" I called out.

We struggled against the pressure of acceleration to crawl to the jump seats that were lined up against the fuselage on the opposite side of the craft from the laser weapon. We had almost gotten there . . . when the floor disappeared.

Tori squealed with terror, and I think I shouted too.

It took a second for me to realize that the floor hadn't actually vanished but had become transparent. It was horrifying to see the ground fall away as we quickly rose into the night sky. The deck was just as solid as before. It was just . . . invisible.

I tried not to look down as we pulled ourselves up and onto the jump seats. As soon as I planted my butt in the seat, a soft plastic strap automatically appeared and lashed me in. Same thing happened to Tori. It was yet another example of the advanced technology that these planes possessed.

Tori and I held hands for strength and gazed down between our feet to witness the sea of black planes on the ground as we rose above the airfield. Many of them had billows of smoke spewing from their damaged fuselages, the handiwork of the saboteurs.

"It's not enough," I said.

"What isn't?"

"The Chiefs guessed that there were seven hundred planes. There have to be three times that number. Even if every charge cripples a plane, the Retros will still have a massive fleet."

Tori stared at the ground far below and shook her head. "And one monster plane that can do more damage than any of them."

The runways grew small very quickly as we moved not only higher, but also away from Area 51.

"Are we going into space?" Tori asked numbly.

It sure seemed like it. This plane was definitely something out of science fiction. We sailed high over the desert with nothing but the faint sound of the musical notes to tell us we were under power. It was about as comfortable a flight as could be, other than the disturbing sensation of looking down at a floor that wasn't there . . .

. . . and knowing we'd been shanghaied by the enemy.

"We've got to do something," Tori said. "You know they're not just taking this monster out for a joyride."

That's when it hit me.

"I was right," I announced. "Look."

I pointed to the ground to see that we had already left the desert. Though it was dark, I could make out buildings and homes. I saw a dark racetrack and many industrial buildings.

"About what?" Tori asked.

"We're headed for Las Vegas," I said solemnly.

Sure enough, the darkened buildings of the Las Vegas Strip came into view. I could make out the sprawling hotels, the Stratosphere Tower, and even the Statue of Liberty lying on its side.

A loud hum came from the silver canister across from us. The nefarious weapon had come to life. A bright beam of light shot from underneath the plane. It looked very much like the multiple beams of light that had joined together to kill my friend, only far more intense. It was a sight I hoped I'd never have to witness again. It made my heart ache . . . and my blood boil.

The powerful beam hit the Venetian hotel, with its canals and gondolas. The entire structure lit up—and disappeared. All that was left was a deep, empty sand pit. The lagoon, the bridges, the tower, the *buildings* were all gone in seconds.

"Like Portland," Tori said with a quivering voice.

The beam focused on the hotels across the street with the same result. The huge hotels lit up and were gone. The pirate ships in the fake lagoon disappeared. The fake volcano vanished. Every last man-made structure evaporated.

There was no escaping this purge.

I hoped that Charlotte had evacuated in time.

I hoped that *everyone* had evacuated in time.

The plane hovered over the hotel with the fake Roman Colosseum theater where the survivors had met to prepare for the raid. Seconds later it was gone, along with every last statue, fountain, and building. In seconds the terrain was returned to the way it had looked hundreds of years before.

"They're sweeping it all away," Tori said. "They knew exactly where the survivors were hiding, thanks to Jon."

I fumbled around the jump seat, looking for a way to release the safety strap.

"What are you doing?" Tori asked.

"Trying to get out of here."

"To do what?"

"Las Vegas is done," I said. "I'm more worried about the next stop."

"Los Angeles," she said, breathless.

"This is how they're going to finish the job. They could easily fly this monster over every major city and do exactly what they're doing to Las Vegas. Hell, they could probably do it all in one night."

She let that horror sink in, then said, "The bombs. Could we detonate them faster?"

"I don't know how," I said.

I fumbled with my hand under the seat until I found a lever. I pressed it and the safety straps instantly retracted. I found Tori's lever and released her too.

"What do we do, Tucker?" Tori asked.

I looked to the hatch up front. There seemed to be only one choice.

"We hijack the plane," I replied.

TWENTY-NINE

The ground sped by far below.

The massive Retro plane was finished with Las Vegas and was moving on, probably to Los Angeles, where it would complete its murderous sweep of that city. From there, who knew?

According to my stopwatch, only five minutes had gone by since I had set the charge to try to damage the big plane. That's all the time it took to delete Las Vegas, and at the speed we were traveling, it would only be a few minutes before Los Angeles was in range.

"The pilot has no idea we're here," I whispered to Tori. "We'll surprise him and force him to land at gunpoint."

"What if he won't?"

"Shoot him," I replied. "Hit his leg or his arm or anything that'll tell him we're serious. You okay with that?"

"Absolutely."

It was hard to believe we had been hardened to the point of calmly talking about shooting people, but if the choice was between winging somebody in the leg or watching as thousands of people were obliterated, it was a no-brainer.

"Ready?" I asked.

Tori took a nervous breath and nodded.

I hurried forward toward the hatch door. It was an unnerving sensation to walk across the transparent floor as the ground flew by beneath us. Once I was there, I turned back to Tori.

She raised the gun.

I reached for the handle, gave her a small nod, and yanked the door open.

I hadn't planned on doing what I did. I was acting totally out of instinct. I started screaming wildly, hoping it would add to the shock of our arrival.

There were two pilots sitting at the wide console, not one. The cockpit was huge, with plenty of room for me to run in and target one of them. I went for the guy on the right, the copilot. With my adrenaline pumping, I was ready to grab him, yank him out of the chair, and throw him to the floor so Tori could hold the gun to his head.

I took one step inside. The copilot spun around, and I froze.

"Wha—?" he gasped with surprise.

The guy in the copilot's seat . . . was Mr. Feit.

He was as stunned to see me as I was to see him, and I took advantage.

I leaped forward, grabbed his shirt, and pulled him out of his seat. Feit was bigger than me, but I had surprise on my side . . . and anger. I finally had my chance for revenge. Seeing him gave me the added boost of adrenaline I needed to take the guy apart.

I whipped him around and slammed his back against the rear wall of the cockpit. The force must have knocked the air out of his lungs because I heard him grunt with pain and gasp for breath. I kicked his legs out, and he went down to the deck. Hard. I quickly twisted one of his arms behind his back and pulled his hand up to his shoulder, making him squeal.

I'm ashamed to admit that I enjoyed hurting him.

No, I'm not.

Tori jumped behind me, sat on his legs, and jammed the muzzle of the Glock into his lower spine.

"One shot and you're a cripple," she snarled.

"Land the plane!" I ordered the pilot.

The cockpit looked more like an elaborate computer workstation than the controls of a plane. There were no mechanical toggles or switches. Instead, the console was made up of multiple touchscreens. There was a narrow windshield in front, but the line of video monitors beneath it was what gave the pilot the information he needed. There were several live views of the ground, along with multiple indicators of various functions.

There was no wheel or joystick. The pilot seemed to be guiding the plane by sliding his fingertips across a touchpad.

If there was ever a moment when I bought into Kent's theory about the Retros being from another planet, it was then.

The pilot was the same guy we had seen running up the ramp. He didn't look much older than me, with short military-cut hair. Both he and Feit wore gray flight suits.

His eyes were wide and frightened. He had no idea what to do.

"Sir?" he asked, near panic.

"Stay the course!" Feit bellowed.

Tori jammed the gun barrel into Feit's back, making him grunt.

"I swear I'll do it," she warned.

"What the hell?" Feit bellowed. "I can't get rid of you people!"

I had my knee on Feit's cheek, squeezing his head into the deck.

"Land the plane, Feit," I demanded. "If you think we won't shoot you, you are dead wrong."

The pilot bolted out of his seat and dove at Tori.

Neither of us expected that.

Tori didn't react in time, and it cost her. The pilot knocked her off of Feit and went for the gun. The move threw me off-balance, and that was all Feit needed to twist free and shove me back against the control console. I hit my head and saw stars but fought through it and launched myself at Feit, driving my head into his chest.

We hit the hatch, and it flew open, sending us tumbling into the cargo bay. The hinges must have been on springs because as soon as we cleared it, it slammed back shut.

A shot went off inside the cockpit. Then another.

I heard Tori yelp.

I tried to go back for the hatch, but Feit kneed me in the gut.

I doubled over as he pulled away from me and scrambled to get back to the cockpit.

Though I was hurting, I couldn't let him get back in there. Not if Tori was hurt.

I struggled to my feet and went after him. I wrapped my arms around him and kept driving my legs forward, using his momentum and mine to drive his head into the hatch, making a sickening thud.

He was just as amped as I was and pushed off the bulkhead with his foot, sending us both backward and down to the invisible deck.

I caught a brief glimpse of the ground flashing by below. We were no longer in the desert. There were buildings down there. Many buildings. We were over civilization and headed for Los Angeles.

Feit shot an elbow backward and caught me in the temple, snapping my head back. It was all he needed to pull away from me.

But he was dazed. He couldn't think fast, let alone move quickly. He struggled to get to his feet.

I wasn't much better off. My ears rang, and colors swirled around me. I had to force myself to focus. If I didn't end the fight soon, he would crush me. Any advantage I had was gone. He was an adult. A soldier. He knew how to fight. All I was was angry. If he was able to get himself together, I was done.

I spotted the jump seats. Feit was gathering himself up a few yards in front of them.

I pushed off the deck and charged him again.

This time, Feit knew I was coming and whirled around to face me. He stood up straight. Big mistake.

It was like a tackling drill I had done hundreds of times before. I got down low and led with my shoulder. I hit him square in the chest and pumped my legs, forcing him backward. Feit staggered back and landed in the jump seat.

Instantly the safety straps wrapped him up and locked him in. But he could still use his arms and legs. I couldn't back off. I drove my forearm into his neck and held it there, jamming it against his windpipe.

My face was now inches from his. Feit's nose was bleeding. It was probably broken. His hard breathing sent disgusting bits of blood and spit into my eyes, but I didn't back off.

"Land this plane," I demanded, seething. "You are not going to hit Los Angeles."

"You can't stop this, Tucker," he hissed. "We've already won."

"Who *are* you?"

Feit's labored breathing turned into a gruesome laugh as he said, "Don't you get it?"

"No. Explain it to me."

"We're *you*!"

His strange answer made my brain clutch for a brief instant. It was all the opening he needed to hit the release latch with his free hand to retract the straps. He shoved me, and I careened backward, fighting to keep from falling.

Feit launched out of the chair.

I got my balance and ran forward, cutting the angle to beat him to the hatch.

But he wasn't going for the hatch.

He dropped to his knees and reached underneath the jump seats to grab something.

Whatever it was, I couldn't let him get it, so I put on the brakes and headed his way . . .

. . . as he pulled out a black baton weapon.

He quickly turned it my way.

I froze. He had me.

Feit's face was a mess, thanks to me. He was covered in blood from a smashed nose that was still spewing.

Through the gore, he shrugged and laughed. He always laughed.

"You know something? I don't like you that much anymore," he said and raised the weapon.

Boom!

The plane rocked so violently that we both fell to the deck.

Boom!

We were jolted again as I saw a white flash of light through the transparent floor.

Two gray fighter jets screamed by below us.

We were under attack.

SYLO had joined the party.

Feit was disoriented. I had my chance and dove at him, grabbing the black weapon. We both had two hands on it, struggling to twist it out of the other's control. Whoever lost would be dead.

It wasn't going to be me.

Instead of pulling back, I pushed forward. Feit hadn't expected that and fell onto his back. I did a somersault over his head while still clutching the baton. The weight of my body and the force from the move gave me the power to wrench the weapon from his grasp. I kept rolling, got to my feet, and spun back to face him.

Feit was still flat on his back. He was done.

I glanced quickly at the weapon, trying to figure out how to fire it. There was a button that was flush to the grip handle right where my thumb rested. I aimed the baton toward the silver canister on the far side of the cargo bay and pressed it.

There was a slight jolt as the weapon chugged in my grip, but not enough to make me lose control. The charge of energy hit the silver canister but only caused a slight dent. Whatever that thing was made of, it was strong.

More important, I knew how to use the gun.

"Get up," I demanded as I took aim at him.

Feit slowly got to his feet.

"In there," I said, nodding toward the cockpit. "If you so much as fart, you're done."

The guy was beaten. He nodded and shuffled toward the hatch with no argument.

I stole a quick glance at my watch.

In eighteen minutes the charges would explode.

I stayed close behind Feit, but not close enough for him to attack me. He pulled the hatch open, and I saw that the pilot was back in his seat. In one hand he held Tori's pistol, aimed at something I couldn't see. I had to believe it was Tori, and if he was aiming the gun, she was still alive.

"Put it down!" Feit ordered.

The pilot gave him a confused look. The guy was terrified. Can't say that I blamed him. We were being attacked. I wondered if the massive plane could maneuver like the smaller fighters. If not, we'd be shot out of the sky . . . and maybe that would be a good thing.

My question became irrelevant when two black Retro jets flashed by beneath us. The attack had become a dogfight. More black jets arrived to protect the mother ship as even more SYLO fighters arrived. The two sets of planes screamed past and around each other in a confused aerial ballet.

The SYLO fighters fired their missiles, but the Retro planes blew them out of the air before they could reach their target.

Us.

"Sit down," I ordered Feit.

I wanted him in his seat, where I could see him.

"Drop the gun," Feit said to the pilot again.

The pilot gave me a panicked look, then dropped the gun to the deck and turned his entire attention to the controls.

"I'm okay," Tori called out.

I stepped into the cockpit and saw that she was sitting on the deck on the far side. She was alive, but she wasn't okay. She clutched her thigh, where she had been shot. I kicked the gun across the deck to her. She gladly picked it up with her right hand while clutching her injured leg with her left.

"Seriously," she said. "I'm okay. But I'm sick of getting shot."

She lifted her hand from her leg to reveal a blossom of blood growing on her jeans.

The control screens were alive with the frantic sights of the dogfight. About six different cameras, as well as the long windshield in front, gave a full-circle view of the activity outside.

A SYLO jet was headed directly for us. It launched a missile and then broke off. Seconds later the missile exploded in the air. It rocked us, but that was all.

"Where did they come from?" the pilot asked, frantically glancing at Feit. He was all squirrelly, as if he didn't have much combat experience. "How could they know we're headed for Los Angeles?"

"I doubt if they do," Feit said. "The fools probably think we're going to attack Catalina Island. Relax, the fighters will keep them off of us."

"Why would they think you'd attack Catalina Island?" I said.

Feit shrugged as if it was no big deal. "It's a SYLO base, like Pemberwick Island."

I looked down through the deck to see that we were over the ocean. Below us was a fleet of warships. I flashed back to the air-and-sea battle we had gone through to escape from Pemberwick.

Tori's theory was true. SYLO *had* been protecting Pemberwick Island from the Retros, just like they were now protecting Catalina.

But Feit wasn't going after Catalina. He was headed for Los Angeles and what were probably thousands of survivors. Maybe hundreds of thousands.

I glanced at my watch. Sixteen minutes.

"Turn around," I demanded.

Feit looked over his shoulder and gave me a hideous grin.

"We're not landing," he declared.

"Not here you're not. You're going back to Area 51. Now. Right now."

The pilot gave a questioning glance to Feit.

"Let me see," Feit said. "That would be . . . no."

I fired the weapon at the plane's console, blasting out two of the video monitors.

Feit and the pilot threw themselves out of their chairs for protection.

"Those jets may protect you from SYLO," I said. "But they can't get to me. You've got a choice. Turn this thing around and fly back to Area 51, or I'll take it down right here. One way you lose this plane and die. The other way you give yourself a chance."

"Take this down and you die too," Feit said, though with a hint of genuine concern.

I answered by firing two more shots into the console, hoping I wasn't hitting anything vital.

"A Retro said we primates were already dead, we just didn't know it yet. I guess that means we have nothing to lose. If we go down, so be it, but we are *not* going to Los Angeles."

I raised the baton, aiming it directly at Feit's head.

I saw terror in his eyes.

I loved it.

"Bring us around," Feit ordered the pilot.

"But, sir," the pilot protested. "We'll face a court-martial—"

"We'll deal," Feit shot back. "Bring us around."

"Yes, sir," the pilot said and crawled back into his seat.

After a few swipes of his finger on a screen, the plane banked hard. We were constantly being buffeted by the force of missiles that were exploding all around us. I had to have faith that the Retro fighters would continue to protect us . . . even though the mission had been aborted.

"I'm getting questions," the pilot said as he touched his ear. He was being contacted by someone. "They want to know why we're coming about."

Feit said, "Tell them we're having technical difficulties." He gave me a snide smile and added, "I'd call this a technical difficulty."

"Step on it," I said.

"Isn't there somewhere else you'd like to go?" Feit asked sarcastically. "The Bahamas? Paris? Sydney? You've got the most advanced aircraft ever created. Let's take it for a spin."

"Area 51 will do just fine," I said. "Not that I don't trust you, but you've got ten minutes to get us there. If we don't make it by then . . ."

I raised the baton threateningly.

I felt a slight surge of power as the pilot accelerated. The ground sped by in a blur. There were fewer explosions and no jets in sight. SYLO must have thought that they had repelled the dark invader.

"Why are you here, Feit?" Tori asked. "I thought you were all about slave labor and rebuilding. Does this mean you get your hands dirty with the killing too?"

Feit didn't answer. It was the first time that he wasn't quick to run off at the mouth.

"I'll take a guess," I said. "I think you're a bigger part of this deranged mission than you've let on. If you're on the deck of this new plane, you're not just some officer who's carrying out orders."

"I'm flattered," Feit said. "Is that why you keep following me?"

"I guess it is," I said.

"How do you feel, Tucker?" he asked, regaining some of his confidence. "Did it feel good to shatter my nose? And shoot at me? Which is better? Causing physical pain, or knowing that you outmaneuvered me this time? Does revenge feel as good as you imagined it would?"

I didn't answer right away. Feit really was an expert on human behavior. He knew what was driving me. I wanted to give him an honest answer, but first I had to decide for myself how I actually felt.

"What do you say?" Feit pressed. "Doesn't revenge feel great?"

"No," I said. "But it will."

The smile fell from Feit's face. For a change, he wasn't laughing. Time was running out.

I glanced down to see that we were back in the desert and flying over the desolate landscape. I noticed a few shadows streak by below us and looked to the remaining video monitors.

We were being escorted by Retro fighters.

"One minute out," the pilot announced.

I glanced at my watch. Five minutes till the boom.

"What happens when we land?" Feit asked.

"Nothing," I replied. "Set down in the middle of the base, and we'll all get off."

"And then?"

"Then Tori and I leave."

Tori stood up and limped over to me.

"Can you walk?" I asked.

"It hurts," she said. "But I can move."

"You're a lousy shot," she said to the pilot.

The pilot ignored her.

The base appeared below us. The plane slowed and hovered above the runway, then began its descent.

"What are you going to do, Tucker?" Feit asked. "You realize there's nowhere to hide."

"Who said anything about hiding?" I said. "Maybe you're the one who should be looking for cover."

Feit laughed, but his heart wasn't in it. He knew something was going on but had no idea what it was.

The landing tripod extended, and with a thump, the plane set down. I heard the whine of the engines as the ramp was lowered to the ground.

"Everybody out," I said.

My heart was racing. I stole a quick look at my watch.

Three minutes left.

Feit and the pilot walked ahead of us down the ramp.

I held the black weapon in one hand and had my other arm around Tori's waist to help her walk. She was in pain, but she wouldn't admit it. We walked down the ramp and didn't stop, moving past Feit and the pilot.

"That's it?" Feit asked, genuinely surprised. "You're just going to walk off into the desert?"

"That's it," I said and picked up the pace. "See ya!"

"How big is this going to be?" Tori whispered to me.

"No idea."

The pilot had set us down in the middle of a nest of idle planes. The survivors may have disabled hundreds of them, but that had barely dented the fleet.

I picked up the pace, but it was hard for Tori to move any faster.

Retro fighters hovered over the giant plane like vultures.

"How much time?" she asked.

"One minute."

I glanced back at Feit.

He stared after us, looking confused. He sensed that something was wrong, that he had missed something, but he didn't dare come after us. He knew we'd both shoot him without a second thought.

We hurried past an endless row of Retro fighters.

"If the explosion tears into the power plant," I said, "there's not going to be much left of that plane."

"Or us," Tori said nervously.

Headlights appeared in front of us, headed our way. I feared it was a Retro plane coming to life but realized it was too small . . . and too loud.

Tori lifted the pistol, but I put my hand on hers to push it away.

"Don't bother," I cautioned.

"We can't let them recapture us," Tori cried.

"I don't think we have to worry about that," I said. "Retros don't drive dune buggies."

Tori squinted ahead, trying to make out detail as the headlights grew closer.

"Survivors?" she asked.

The buggy sped up to us, and for a second I thought it was going to run us down, but the driver flew by and skidded to a stop, spinning the buggy until it faced back the other way.

"Kent!" Tori exclaimed.

"Need a lift?" Kent asked.

I jumped into the seat next to him and pulled Tori down on top of me.

"Drive!" I demanded.

"What?"

"Go!" Tori shouted. "Punch it! Get us out of here!"

Kent didn't get it, but he obeyed. He jammed his foot down on the gas and launched us on our way.

I looked back to see that Feit was watching. He took a dazed step toward us. I could sense the wheels turning in his head, calculating the facts. He knew something was wrong. Suddenly, he spun around and ran back up the ramp. The pilot was right behind him.

I heard Feit scream at the pilot, "Get us out of here!"

"What's going on?" Kent yelled above the whine of the engine.

"Shut up and drive," Tori yelled.

Twenty seconds.

The giant plane's ramp retracted. Fifteen seconds.

The craft shuddered and rose a few feet into the air as the tripod retracted.

Ten seconds.

We reached the end of the line of Retro fighters and charged on into the desert.

"This better be good," Tori said.

Five . . .

The first charge blew out the side of the plane. It was the charge that Tori had placed on the silver weapon.

Kent looked back. "What the—"

"Don't stop!" I shouted.

The massive plane listed to the side. Its wing dipped and hit the tarmac.

The hovering Retro jets backed off.

The plane was about to crash. That's when the second charge went off. The charge that I had attached to the engine. The impossible, singing engine that could generate so much power.

The explosion was far greater than what the C-4 was capable of. Whatever fueled that incredible engine, it was volatile. The C-4 was nothing more than a detonator. The result was as close to a nuclear explosion as I ever wanted to experience.

The plane erupted in a massive fireball of white light.

"Jeez!" Kent screamed.

The burning light was charged with its own power. As it spread, it engulfed the Retro planes that had been hovering above, causing them to explode, list, and fall to the ground. As each hit, it created its own violent eruption.

More explosions followed, joining together into a massive cloud of burning material that spread across the tarmac toward the idle fighters.

It was a domino effect. The expanding incendiary cloud engulfed each plane in turn, igniting their individual power sources along the way. It caused the destructive fireball to grow even larger and move faster. It tore across the ground, eating up the planes like a molten tsunami . . .

. . . that was headed our way.

A single fireball blasted into the sky from the center of the inferno. But rather than explode, it continued on into the air until its flame was extinguished. Or it disappeared. I couldn't tell which. For a fleeting moment, I thought I saw a dark shadow emerge from the flame and fly off. It didn't look like shrapnel.

"It's getting hot," Kent yelled.

The heat at our back was becoming unbearable. We couldn't outrun the monstrous fireball. If it continued to expand, we'd be incinerated.

Kent gripped the wheel and kept the pedal to the floor.

The burning cloud had reached the outer ring of planes. Multiple explosions erupted, expanding the cloud into the desert.

Tori hugged me close and gripped Kent's leg.

"We did it," I said calmly.

I wanted that to be our last thought. We did it. We had destroyed the Retro fleet. The entire fleet.

We had our revenge.

The wall of fire ate up the ground behind us, looking for more fuel to feed on. But there was no more to be had. The flames rose into the sky in one last gasp and burned out.

"Whooo!" Kent screamed—but he didn't let up on the gas.

Tori laughed. There was nothing funny; it was all about relief. She pulled me close and planted a solid kiss on my cheek.

"We sure as hell did," she said in triumph.

Kent finally slowed down and turned the buggy around so we could look back on the base, or what was left of it. The powerful fireball was gone, but in its wake it left a base that was ablaze. All of the hangar buildings were burning, lighting up the desert night. The fires silhouetted the thousands of burning wrecks of Retro fighters. I would have been surprised if any of them had been spared.

It was total annihilation.

"What the hell did you do?" Kent asked, stunned.

"I guess we put the charge in the exact right spot. Yikes."

I looked at Tori and laughed.

"'Yikes' is a good word," she said.

We watched as the multiple fires wiped out whatever was left of Area 51 and the Retro fleet.

I gave Tori a squeeze and said, "*Now* it feels great."

Tori turned to look at Kent. "You came back."

Kent didn't respond at first. I couldn't tell whether he was searching for a snide comeback or fighting back the urge to kill me. It turned out that he was trying to find the right words . . . to tell the truth.

"I saw you guys get on that plane, and then when the ramp

closed—" His voice cracked as he fought to keep from crying. "And then it took off. Jeez. You were both . . . gone. Just like that. I didn't know what to do. I guess it made me realize that I was on my own. It wasn't a good feeling, you know?"

"Oh, I know," Tori said.

Kent forced a smile and said, "But then the plane came back. It came back! I had to see if you were on it. If you were okay. What else could I do? Like you said, Tucker: We're all we've got."

That was the first time I actually liked Kent Berringer.

"Thank you," I said.

Tori gave him a kiss on the cheek.

"Where's Olivia?" she asked.

I was glad she asked. I wasn't going to risk it.

"A few other survivors showed up once the shooting started. They took her." He looked right at me and added, "She shouldn't have come here."

I didn't want to tell him I suspected Olivia of being a Retro in-filtrator. What was the point? She was dead. We would never know one way or the other. The time would come when we could talk about it, but it wasn't then.

"I know," was all I said.

We sat in silence for a few moments.

"I'll tell you one thing," Kent said as he gazed at the smolder-ing ruins of Area 51. "We are seriously badass."

I couldn't help but laugh. Tori laughed too. It was a moment of pure joy and relief.

Victory had never been sweeter.

But the celebration ended quickly.

Kent's eyes caught something and went wide. "Uh-oh," he exclaimed.

"What?" Tori asked with surprise.

"We're not alone."

He pointed to the dark sky above the rise that surrounded the dry lake bed. There was a light. A moving light. Something was in the air and headed our way.

THIRTY

"**W**hat do we do?" Kent asked nervously.

We all watched with worry as the light flew closer. The telltale sound of the Retro planes wasn't there. Instead, we heard the sound of a conventional engine.

"It's the helicopter," Tori declared.

"With its lights on," Kent added. "Now that we did all the dirty work, they're not afraid to show themselves."

"What do we do?" Tori asked.

"I'm tired of running," I said. "If you guys want to take off, go."

Nobody moved. They were as tired and as curious as I was.

Soon the dark silhouette of the helicopter sailed over us. It looked to be a military chopper like the kind SYLO used to drop commandos on Pemberwick Island. It circled around and touched down thirty yards from us, kicking up dust. As soon as it landed, the engines were killed, and the rotors slowed.

"Now what?" Kent asked.

"Whoever it is, I want to face them," I declared.

"Then let's go," Tori said.

I helped her out of the buggy.

"What?" Kent exclaimed. "You got shot again?"

"It's what I do," Tori replied with a shrug.

Kent came around to her other side, and she draped her arms over both of our shoulders to keep weight off of her injured leg. Without another word, we approached the craft. The only sound coming from it was the ticking of its cooling engine. The three of us walked to within a few yards of the slowing rotor and stopped.

The helicopter had the markings of the United States Navy.

"SYLO," I said.

A light shone from within, and the side door slid open. A soldier wearing red fatigues stepped out carrying a powerful flashlight. He was in silhouette, so it was hard to see who he was.

"If it ends here," I said to the others, "we have to know we did everything we could."

We all tightened our hold on each other, for whatever support it would offer.

The soldier strode toward us. He was a tall guy who had the bearing of a disciplined military man. I knew who it was. I didn't need to see his face.

"Granger," I muttered.

"No way," Kent gasped.

Captain Granger marched up and stood facing us.

"Is anyone injured?" he asked, all business.

"I took a bullet in the leg," Tori replied.

She lifted her leg to show how blood had soaked the entire upper portion of her jeans.

"We'll take care of you," he said. "What exactly happened here?"

"We destroyed the Retro fleet," I said matter-of-factly. "What does it look like?"

Granger looked toward the burning rubble . . . and chuckled. He actually chuckled.

None of us knew how to react to that.

"Incredible," he finally said. "Absolutely incredible."

"What do you want?" I asked.

"We've got an ark on Catalina Island," he replied. "We'll take you there."

"Aren't you worried that we might be Retros?" I asked.

"Not after this," he answered.

"He thinks we're Retros?" Kent asked, incredulous. "That's nuts."

"I'm not going with you," I said to Granger.

"Whoa, you're not?" Kent asked, surprised. "I don't like these guys any more than you do, but what else can we do?"

"You go, Kent," I said. "Tori, you should too. I don't want any part of them."

"I'm not going without you," Tori declared. "We're not splitting up now."

Kent was torn. He looked at Tori and me, hunting for a clue to help him decide what to do.

"If we don't go," he asked Granger, "will you shoot us?"

"No," was Granger's simple answer.

"Then I'll stay with my friends. Jeez, I can't believe I'm doing this."

"I appreciate your reluctance," Granger said. "There's so much you don't understand."

"Then why don't you explain it to us?" I said. "Start by telling us what you're doing here."

"We were observing your operation from the air," he said. "The Retros aren't the only ones with infiltration capabilities. We've been inside the group in Las Vegas from day one."

Another soldier jumped from the plane. He was a stocky guy who was as wide as Granger was tall. I knew who he was too.

"Cutter," Tori declared.

The Special Ops marine approached and stood next to Granger. It suddenly became clear how Cutter was able to come up with all of those explosive charges.

"I stand by what I said," Cutter announced. "It's an honor to serve with you guys."

"You used those people," I said to Cutter. "You had them do your dirty work."

"This is war, son," Cutter replied. "We don't have the same firepower as the Retros. We've had some success with large-scale operations, like the one at Fenway, but eventually they'll wear us down. It's inevitable. Our only hope has been to incorporate less conventional methods. The survivors who gathered in Las Vegas weren't coerced. They did exactly what they wanted to do. We just gave them some help."

"Just one question," Kent said. "Are you the good guys?"

Cutter chuckled. Granger didn't.

"Yeah," Cutter said. "I'd like to think we are."

"That wasn't a solid yes," I pointed out.

Granger said, "Then maybe someone else can convince you."

He turned to the chopper and made a motion for someone to join us.

Another person stepped out of the helicopter, a smaller person who didn't appear to be a soldier. It looked like a woman. She approached tentatively.

"If you don't want to take my advice," Granger said, "you should really start taking hers."

"Tucker?" the woman called.

My knees buckled.

It was my mother.

She ran to me and threw her arms around me. She was crying. Once I got over the shock, I cried too. The last time I had seen her was from the opposite side of a prison fence on Pemberwick Island. So many conflicting emotions were hammering at me, but the bottom line was that I suddenly felt like myself again: a fourteen-year-old kid. We hugged for a good long time as I did my best to pretend that everything was going to be okay.

"What are you doing here?" I asked.

"I thought I'd lost you," she cried. "Then I got word you all were out here and . . . I had to come. I'm so sorry, Tucker. It wasn't supposed to happen like this."

That brought me back to reality.

"Really?" I asked, pulling away. "How was it supposed to happen?"

"We wanted to protect you," she said, wiping her eyes. "That's all it was ever about."

"Yeah, well, it didn't work out that way, did it?"

She shook her head.

"Where's Dad?" I asked.

"Still on Pemberwick. He's fine. Your mother is too, Kent. They're safe."

She looked at Tori but had no comforting words for her.

"I'm so sorry about your father."

Tori shot a steely look at Granger.

"How do *you* feel about that, Captain?" she asked coldly.

Granger stiffened. "It's a tragedy when innocent civilians become victims of war. Make no mistake: We are at war, and I am deeply sorry for your father's death and for whatever role I played in that."

"What about all the other innocent civilians you killed?" she asked. "Are you sorry about them too?"

"No, because they weren't innocent," Granger replied. "My mission was to root out the Retro infiltrators on Pemberwick Island in order to protect the remaining population. I have no regrets about that. Your father was being used by them, Miss Sleeper, as were several of his friends. I'm sorry to have to say that, because he was fighting for what he thought was a noble cause. You should be proud of him."

"You don't have to tell me that," Tori said bitterly.

"You sorry for trying to kill us too?" Kent asked accusingly. "If we hadn't gotten away from you, the Retros would still be in business."

"They are still very much in business, young man," Granger said coldly.

"They are?" Kent said, sounding less cocky.

"Please come with us," Mom said. "I know you have trouble believing me after all you've been through, and I don't know how else to say it, but we really are the good guys."

I glanced at Tori and Kent. They looked as confused as I felt.

"You told me not to trust anybody," I said to my mom. "Turned out to be good advice. But you haven't been telling me the truth for a long time. Why should I put my trust in you?"

My mother winced, as if the words stung her. I didn't mean to hurt her, but it was how I felt.

"Because your father and I have been working with SYLO for a very long time, and we know that they are our only hope for the future. And because I'm your mother."

I wanted to believe her, maybe more than anything I've ever wanted in my life.

"You kids have seen a lot," Granger added. "More than most. You know what we're up against."

"But we just blew away the entire Air Force," Kent argued with a hint of desperation. "It's over, right?"

"This was an impressive operation," Cutter said. "There's no denying that. But wars aren't determined by a single battle. The Retros aren't done. Not even close."

"Please, Tucker," Mom said, pleading. "Come with me. All of you. Please."

I looked at Kent and Tori and said, "I'll do whatever you want. I just don't want us to split up."

"I say we go with them," Kent said quickly. "It can't be any worse than being lost in the desert."

I turned to Tori. "What do you think?"

Tori looked at Granger. I saw the hatred she held for him. But I also saw that she was torn. And injured. There was so much that still didn't make sense. So much we didn't know. We had already decided that despite his cruel tactics, Granger and SYLO had been protecting Pemberwick Island from the Retros. Was that enough to trust him, in spite of his deadly tactics?

"I guess we have to play the odds," Tori said. "If you're willing to go with them, Tucker, I'll go too."

"Oh, thank God," Mom said with total relief.

"Good. Let's not waste any more time," Cutter commanded. "Load up."

Granger made a move to help Tori, but she pulled away. She wanted nothing to do with him.

Kent and I took her arms and helped her toward the helicopter.

"Find a seat and buckle in," Granger ordered as he took his place up front next to Cutter, who strapped himself into the pilot's seat. "Put on headsets," Cutter called to us. "It'll be about an hour to Catalina."

We helped Tori climb aboard and saw that seats lined both sides of the chopper, facing the center. Mom sat on one side. I chose the opposite side. Tori sat next to me, and Kent sat next to my mom. We all buckled in and put on headphones.

"Everybody set?" Cutter asked through the intercom.

We all gave him a thumbs-up. The engines whined, and the rotor began to turn. The blades quickly picked up speed, and in minutes we were airborne. The chopper gained altitude quickly, and we got our first good view of the ruins of Area 51.

The destruction was complete. Every last building was either on fire or a charred wreck. There wasn't a single fighter plane left intact.

I had to agree with Kent. We were seriously badass.

Only one thing disturbed me. It was the shadow I saw launch from the monstrous plane. What exactly was that?

"I don't care what anybody says," Kent said through his headset. "It sure looks over to me. They're done."

"You need to see something," Granger said.

I didn't like the tone of his voice.

We flew north for maybe five minutes, traveling over barren wasteland.

"Bring us a little lower," Granger ordered Cutter. "Once around quickly. Keep your wits about you."

The helicopter dropped fast and banked to the right.

"Take a good look," Granger said.

We all strained to look out of the small windows.

Once my eyes adjusted, I was able to make out detail on the ground.

"Oh my God," Tori exclaimed.

The desert was littered with the wreckage of a battle. A huge battle. There were downed jet fighters as well as wrecked Retro jets. Hundreds of them. We had seen the aftermath of battles before, but nothing like this. Not only were there untold numbers of downed planes, but also the burned-out remains of tanks and assault vehicles. The ground itself was torn apart from the impact of multiple explosions. The carnage seemed to stretch out for miles in every direction.

We were flying over the physical remains of a nightmare.

"What happened?" were the only words I managed to croak out.

"I've seen a lot in my time," Granger said. "But nothing remotely like this. It was the greatest battle of all time . . . if you could use a word like 'great' to describe something this horrible. It's the night it all began. Hard to believe it was only a few weeks ago."

I thought I actually detected a hint of emotion in his voice. The steely soldier had a conscience.

"Who won?" Kent asked, cutting right to the chase.

Granger turned around to look at us and said, "That's yet to be decided. Like Cutter said, wars aren't determined by a single battle."

"Look!" Tori shouted. "Is that what I think it is?"

Tucked near the foot of a mountain was another air base. It wasn't as large as Area 51, and there were no fighter planes on the runways. What was there instead was a massive steel structure that looked like a colossal igloo.

"It is," I exclaimed. "It's the same thing they were building in Fenway Park."

To me it looked like a giant beehive: innocent looking from the outside but hiding danger.

"Look at the base of that thing!" Kent declared frantically. "The big door! Oh man."

Like the structure being built in Fenway, there was an immense door built into the dome. It was open, and bright light shone from within. A shadow moved through the light. Something was coming out from the depths of the dome.

It was a black fighter plane.

"What is that thing?" I asked.

"That," Granger replied, "is the gate to hell."

"Incoming!" Cutter yelled.

The chopper was hit. It shuddered and began to spin. The rotor whined as the craft counter-rotated, desperately clawing at the air to try to maintain altitude. I glanced out of the window to see the ground approaching quickly. We wouldn't be in the air much longer.

Kent screamed in panic. Tori grabbed my arm.

The SYLO commander was right.

The Retros weren't done.

Not even close.

TO BE CONTINUED . . .